Terri was surprised with the way her mind had come to grips with this situation. Although having an armed maniac chase her through the woods was the most dangerous, the most terrifying thing that had happened so far, it was real. She understood what was happening, knew the face of her enemy. Having her husband murdered, her life ruined, her friends killed—all at the hands of an unidentified someone who might have been named Connie—had left her confused, numb, miserable, barely able to cope. It had seemed impossible, too awful to be real. But what was happening now was very real indeed. And for the first time, Terri had some control over the situation.

She could fight back.

Fawcett Gold Medal Books
by B. W. Battin:

ANGEL OF THE NIGHT

THE ATTRACTION

THE BOOGEYMAN

THE CREEP

PROGRAMMED FOR TERROR

SMITHEREENS

SMITHEREENS

B. W. Battin

A Fawcett Gold Medal Book
Published by Ballantine Books
Copyright © 1987 by B. W. Battin

All rights reserved under International and Pan-American Copyright Conventions. Published in the United States by Ballantine Books, a division of Random House, Inc., New York, and simultaneously in Canada by Random House of Canada Limited, Toronto.

Library of Congress Catalog Card Number: 87-90878

ISBN 0-449-13222-5

All the characters in this book are fictitious, and any resemblance to actual persons, living or dead, is purely coincidental.

Manufactured in the United States of America

FAWCETT GOLD MEDAL • NEW YORK

A Fawcett Gold Medal Book
Published by Ballantine Books
Copyright © 1987 by B. W. Battin

Library of Congress Catalog Card Number: 87-90839

ISBN 0-449-13222-6

Manufactured in the United States of America

First Edition: September 1987

To Dominick Abel,
for his efforts and counsel

PROLOGUE

Getting out of her car she stood in the dirt driveway, staring at the place. The small white frame house sat on a weed-choked lot about three miles from town. Although the roof didn't leak, the shingles were old and grubby and worn. Above them on a bent mast stood the remains of a TV antenna, most of whose parts had been stripped away by storms. The paint on the house was beginning to blister and peel. A beer can lay in the weeds at the edge of the driveway. She'd lived here for two years. With Jack. She hated Jack.

He was a crass, mean-spirited man who slapped her around when he was drunk or when things had gone badly for him at work. But then all her relationships with men had been unhappy. That Jack was the most physically brutal of her men made him no worse than the others. She wasn't afraid of him. Physical bruises often healed more rapidly than the other kind. And what was the worst he could do, kill her? The night he'd held a knife to her throat, she'd calmly told him to go ahead, she didn't care. It was her ultimate weapon against him, that she didn't care.

Gloom seemed to hang over the house, defying the brightness of a sunny Alabama afternoon. This was an

1

unhappy house, a place where those who had received little that was good from life passed their miseries on to others. Screw you, Jack, she thought. I don't need you anymore.

She hadn't realized that she hated Jack until today. Until she saw the picture in *Southeastern States Business Review*. Stunned, she'd stared at it. And after a while— she was uncertain how long—she'd gotten up from her desk, walked from the office, driven here. She hadn't told Mr. Tillotson she was going; she'd simply left. The job no longer mattered. The caption under the photo had read: *Georgia's Businessman of the Year, Stanley Ferguson*.

Glancing at her watch, she walked to the front door. It was about four o'clock, and she wanted to be packed and gone by the time Jack got home, about an hour and a half from now. Unlocking the door and stepping inside, she removed the house key from her ring and laid it on the stained arm of a green living room chair.

All the furnishings in the house were shabby. Jack spent his money on things like his shiny new black pickup that stood high off the ground and had a CB radio and rifle rack in the rear window and a row of extra headlights mounted on the roof. Jack loved the truck. He could give a damn about things like furniture.

The floorboards squeaked as she hurried along the short hall. In the bedroom, she quickly got her suitcase from the closet, opened it on the bed, and began packing. The double bed was unmade. It sagged slightly in the middle.

The stuff from her dresser and the closet all fit into one suitcase. She didn't care much about clothes, so she didn't have many. Just a few things to wear to work and some blue jeans. Hurrying into the bathroom, she grabbed her comb and makeup and other toiletries. She wanted to be gone, out of here, on the highway. On her way to a new beginning.

And if it didn't work out the way she hoped it would,

2

what then? But she didn't want to think about that. If it happened, she would have to deal with it. For now she was going to hope. How many years had it been since she'd dared to hope?

When everything was packed, she sat down on the edge of the bed, taking a moment to figure out whether she'd forgotten anything. Her eyes darted around the room, coming to rest on the nightstand. Opening its drawer, she removed Jack's gun and a box of ammunition. He had other guns, rifles, and expensive handguns that he kept locked away in the spare bedroom, in a heavy gun cabinet he'd bought and to which he had the only key. The weapon in her hand was a .25 automatic. She knew a little about guns, enough to load and fire the pistol. She would take this one with her. For protection, she told herself.

And as she thought that, she realized that the term had two meanings: for the defense of a woman traveling alone and another, deeper meaning. The gun might also have to be used to protect her inner self, that part of her that for the first time in years was going to be open, vulnerable. She shook her head. For now she was going to hope. She checked the gun to make sure it was properly loaded. As she pushed the clip back into the handle, she heard a door close.

For a moment she froze, her mind trying desperately to analyze the situation, to sort through the possibilities, and then she rushed to the window. Jack's black truck was outside, parked next to her rusty old Chevy. The front door of the house opened.

"Babe, where are you?" Jack called from the living room. It was all he ever called her, Babe. She was unable to recall his ever using her true name. The house seemed completely silent for a few moments; then his footfalls were coming toward the bedroom.

Quickly grabbing her suitcase, she shoved it beneath the bed, then slipped the gun under a pillow. When she turned around, Jack was standing in the doorway, watching her.

3

Had he seen what she'd done? An invisible hand gripped her insides, squeezed.

"You going somewhere?" Jack asked. Dressed in jeans and a western shirt, he was a tall man with thinning brown hair and brown eyes that were staring at her icily. And suddenly she knew that, for the first time, she was afraid of him. Because she had hope now, a purpose, a chance. And Jack could take the hope away from her.

"What are you doing home so early?" she asked, hoping her voice didn't reveal how fearful and vulnerable she felt.

"Teamsters are on strike against the cement companies," he replied. "Can't do much if we can't pour foundations, so everybody got laid off." Jack worked construction. For the past few months he'd been employed by an outfit building a subdivision about fifteen miles from here.

"How long do you think the strike'll last?" she asked.

Jack shrugged. "Till it's settled." His blue eyes studied her. "I asked you if you were going somewhere."

Had he seen the suitcase? Was he trying to trap her in a lie? "What makes you think that I'm going somewhere?"

"Why are *you* home so early?" he asked, ignoring her question.

"I . . . well, I was laid off, too."

"Laid off?" He smirked, as if he knew she was lying, as if he was enjoying himself.

"Well, not exactly laid off."

"What then?"

"I was fired."

"Why?"

"Mr. Tillotson made a pass, and I told him no." She had to be careful. One lie always led to more, and after a while you had a whole system of them. You lost track of them all. If Jack kept questioning her, she'd trip up, contradict herself. What would he do to her for lying to him?

4

"You never did answer my question," he said.

"Which . . . which question?"

"I asked you if you thought you were going anywhere."

She caught his use of the word *thought*. Clearly he had no intention of letting her go anywhere. "I don't understand," she said weakly.

"You don't, huh."

She shook her head.

He held up her house key. "I found this on the arm of the chair. Lying there like you weren't going to need it anymore, like you were leaving it for me."

"My key ring broke. I—"

"Stop lying," he said, flipping the key and catching it like a coin.

She started to protest, to say she was telling the truth, but there was no point. He knew she was lying. She stared at him, waiting to see what would happen next.

Slipping the key into his pocket, he stepped toward her, and before she knew what was happening, his open hand hit her face, the force of the slap knocking her backward onto the bed. Instantly he was straddling her. He slapped her again. And again.

"Teach you to lie to me," he said.

She smelled the booze on his breath. He'd stopped off somewhere and had a few. If he was drunk enough, he might beat her bad. It had happened before.

"Jack," she cried. "Stop it. Oh, God, please stop it."

He hit her again, with his fist this time, and her vision blurred. The blow had broken her lip. She could taste the warm coppery flavor of blood. Looking up at his face, she saw that he had a distant, distracted look, as if he wasn't even really aware of what he was doing. He was upset because he'd been laid off, because she was about to walk out on him. It wasn't really personal with him. He was just taking out his frustrations. Later he'd apologize.

His fist slammed into her face again, and she realized that he might not apologize this time, that he might be

5

planning to really hurt her, worse than he ever had before. She'd been on the verge of sneaking away, without even telling him. Maybe it *was* personal this time. Maybe he wanted to kill her.

"Ja—" Her cry was interrupted by his fist.

Her arms were pinned to the bed by his knees. She tried to reach back to the pillow under which she'd placed the gun, but she was unable to do so. Suddenly Jack climbed off her, yanking her from the bed. For a moment she was standing, and then she sank woozily to the floor because her legs were unable to support her. Jack kicked her in the side. She was certain now that he was going to kill her.

Grabbing her blouse, he ripped it open. Then he tried to do the same with her bra. When it refused to tear, he yanked furiously at it, the straps digging into her flesh. Suddenly something snapped and the brassiere was ripped from her body. Tossing it aside, he advanced on her.

She tried to crawl under the bed. She had her head and shoulder beneath it when he grabbed her legs and pulled her away from it. She braced herself for another kick, but instead he picked her up and threw her on the bed. He pulled her skirt and panties off, then began unbuckling his jeans. She told herself to just lie still and submit. Maybe if she didn't resist, it wouldn't be so bad. His pants were off. He began taking off his shirt. Then she saw the feverish look in his eyes, and she knew that submitting wouldn't make any difference. He was going to rape her and beat her no matter what she did.

Her hand slid upward, finding the pillow, searching for the gun. It wasn't under the first pillow she tried, so she slipped her hand under the other one. Still no gun. Jack was down to his undershorts now. He pushed them down, revealing his erection. Suddenly the only thing that mattered to her was finding some way to prevent Jack from raping her. Where was the gun?

Forcing her brain to function, she tried to figure out what

could have happened to the automatic. If it wasn't under the pillow, where was it? And then she knew. It must have slipped off the end of the bed when Jack threw her onto it—or when he was hitting her. Jack was naked now. He'd even removed his socks. He moved toward the bed.

Using all the strength she had left, she pulled herself to the edge of the bed and slipped over the side. Pain shot through her left side when she hit the floor.

"Shit," Jack said. "Where the hell do you think you can go?" Although she couldn't see him, she could hear the floor squeak as he came around the bed. She crawled under it.

The suitcase was there, along with a lot of accumulated dust. Still she didn't see the gun. Jack's face appeared between the bottom of the bed and the floor. He grinned.

"You think you can hide from me under there?" he asked.

His face disappeared, and then the bed lurched to the side. He'd kicked it, she realized. It moved again, and she moved with it. She had at most a few seconds. He would tire of this and either fling the bed aside or drag her out from under it. Where the hell was the gun? She saw it, just as Jack reached under the bed and grabbed her ankle. It was behind the suitcase. She reached for it, her fingers touching the handle, and then she was being dragged away from it. When she was completely out from under the bed, Jack stared down at her, smirking.

"So you were going to walk out on me, huh."

She shook her head, pleaded with her eyes. Jack reached for her. She tried to get back under the bed again, but he had her leg. With the other one, she kicked at him, getting him in the stomach. Although the blow hadn't been solid, it was enough to make him relax his grip on her leg, and she pulled away from him, slithering back under the bed, pushing the suitcase aside, grabbing the gun.

The bed rose and was flung away. Jack stared down at

7

her, angry now, wanting to hurt her some more. He kicked the suitcase out of the way. Finally, he saw the gun. She aimed it at him.

"Shit, Babe, you ain't gonna shoot me."

She switched off the safety.

He grinned. "No way, Babe. You ain't got what it takes to blow someone away."

The bullet hit him squarely in the center of his chest, a small hole appearing among the curly brown hairs. As he staggered backward, a stunned expression on his face, she shot him again.

Later, after she'd cleaned herself up and felt a little better, she was in her old Chevy, heading northeast, toward Atlanta. She's used makeup to hide the bruises on her face. Some of her injuries couldn't be hidden, like her split lip and black eye. But her external wounds would heal. And when she got to Georgia, so might her internal ones.

Ahead was a sign informing her that she was twenty miles from Montgomery. With daylight savings time, it wouldn't be dark for a couple of hours yet. She'd wait for dusk to start looking for a motel.

She tensed as an Alabama highway patrol car came up behind her. The cruiser lingered there a moment, then sped up and passed her. Don't panic, she told herself. Jack's body probably won't be discovered for days. No one ever goes there.

She didn't feel any remorse about having killed him. He was just another in a whole series of jerks, and he deserved what he got. She'd never loved him, not even at first. She hadn't loved anyone for a long, long time. She wondered if she still knew how, if she could still give herself, risk the pain. But then it was silly to worry about that, for pain was an old friend, something she could count on.

She hadn't decided what to do in Atlanta; she needed to make some plans. She couldn't just barge right in and say,

Hello, here I am. It was going to be more complicated than that.

Things will be all right, she told herself. After twenty years of hell, I've paid my dues. I'm entitled to get back what I lost.

"Yes," she said out loud. "I sure as hell am."

ONE

Terri Ferguson put milk and a box of cold cereal on the table in front of her husband. He eyed the breakfast cereal disdainfully.

"It was your idea to give up eggs, Stanley."

He sighed. "If I'd known it meant eating cardboard chips in milk, I wouldn't have done it."

Reluctantly Stanley poured some of the cereal into his bowl and added milk. For years the centerpieces of his breakfast had been eggs—boiled, scrambled, or poached. Then, after reading a magazine article about eating for a healthy heart, he'd abruptly changed his eating habits. Skim milk, less red meat, more chicken and fish, no more than two eggs a week. To Terri's surprise, cutting back on steak, prime rib, and roast beef had been fairly easy for him. Giving up eggs and bacon and sausage in the mornings had been hell.

Pouring herself a cup of coffee, Terri joined her husband at the breakfast table. She watched him as he glumly consumed his cereal.

Terri enjoyed looking at him as much now as she had when they first met and she'd fallen madly in love with him. They'd been in college then. She was an ordinary-looking girl with reddish-brown hair and freckles. He was a tall young man with curly hair that was thick and dark, a face that was a combination of strength and kindness, and a smile that was all warmth and good humor. In short he was a hunk, and to this day she was amazed that she'd been the one who'd landed him.

"You're still a hunk," she said.

Caught by surprise, he looked up and their eyes met. "You, too," he said.

"*I'm* a hunk?"

"Well, the female variation of the term."

"Which is?"

"Well, I think I once told my roommate in college that you were built like an old brick shithouse."

"*That* was supposed to be a compliment?"

"The highest."

They stared at each other for a moment, and then they simultaneously broke into laughter.

They had both turned forty this year. Although Stanley had taken the event in stride, she'd found it a little unnerving. You began to notice the little changes in your aging body, things like needing glasses to read, how quickly your muscles got sore from exercising. And you began to realize things, like you wouldn't live forever. Sure, you always *knew* it, the way you knew the people in nursing homes had once been babies and children and adolescents, but the knowledge was an abstraction, nothing that applied to you, except as a dimly sensed future too far away to worry about. And then you turned forty.

God, she thought, what will turning fifty be like?

Stanley hadn't changed much over the years. His curly hair was still full and thick, and the only gray that had creeped in was just a hint above his ears. Terri wasn't sure how much she'd changed. Although her hair was still reddish-brown, the lack of gray might be natural and it might be due to the rinse she'd begun using at the insistence of her hairdresser a few years ago. She had no intention of abandoning the rinse so she could find out.

Like Stanley she was still fairly trim. The first hint that

she had officially become middle-aged was the thin lines on her forehead. Mother's worry lines, Stanley called them, the natural result of raising a daughter through high school and sending her off to college. Each one, he said, represented a segment of their life together, and because their lives were rich and full each line was something to be cherished. But then Stanley, who owned one of the biggest furniture stores in the Southeast, had begun as a salesman. He had a way with words.

"What you going to do today?" he asked.

"This morning I've got tennis with Marlene. This afternoon I've got a ceramics lesson, which I may have to cut short because the council's got a board meeting at two-thirty." She was the treasurer of the Meadowview Council for the Elimination of Hunger, which raised money to help feed needy children—not just in Meadowview but throughout metropolitan Atlanta. Actually, there weren't any malnourished children in Meadowview—except maybe teenage girls with anorexia nervosa. Meadowview was one of Atlanta's most affluent suburbs.

"I've got to go," Stanley said, getting up from the table.

Terri rose, too, moving to him and slipping her arms around him. He gave her a quick peck, then hesitated and gave her a better kiss, a slow, passionate one.

"Oh, boy," Terri said, suddenly aroused.

Stanley smiled. "Wish I didn't have to go to work right now."

"You're the boss. Who's going to reprimand you for being late?"

He took a moment to think it over, then said, "Almost any other day I'd take you up on it, but today I've got a meeting with the department heads first thing. What am I going to tell them if I don't show up?"

"How about that you were making it with a horny forty-year-old?"

"You think you can hold on to that feeling until I get home?" he asked, giving her a squeeze.

Terri shrugged. "Maybe. But it'll ruin my tennis game."

He grinned. "Well, never mind holding on to it. This evening we'll build it back from scratch."

He gave her a quick kiss, then hurried out the door leading to the garage. A moment later, looking through the window above the sink, Terri saw his brown BMW going down the street. She watched as it passed a beat-up Chevrolet that looked out of place in this neighborhood where some homes were selling for a million dollars, and then the BMW turned the corner at the end of the block, and disappeared.

An hour later, dressed for tennis, she hurried into the garage and slipped behind the wheel of her Mercury station wagon. As she backed out into the street, Terri watched to make sure the automatic garage door closed; then she drove away.

The street was lined with expensive houses, beautifully landscaped. Her only complaint about the area was that it lacked trees. Oh, it had some, but they were young, not like the grand trees in some of Atlanta's older neighborhoods, trees with trunks several feet thick, trees that turned streets into tunnels of shade in the summertime. Meadowview, like many areas in suburban Atlanta, was new, the result of the city's rapid growth; the community had been mostly woods and farmlands a few years ago. It took time to grow big old shade trees.

At the end of the block Terri turned left. Glancing in the rearview mirror, she noticed that the old Chevrolet she'd seen earlier was now behind her, and she wondered absently who owned it. Terri was sure she hadn't seen it around the neighborhood before. Perhaps it was driven by a teenager hired by one of the neighbors to do some yard work or something like that. It crossed her mind that it might belong to a burglar, but she dismissed the notion. Surely a thief would have more sense than to drive something so out of place.

The next time she glanced into the rearview mirror, the car was gone.

* * *

Captain Eugene Cantrell of the Chickasaw County, Alabama, Sheriff's Department held a handkerchief over his nose, trying not to breathe any more than absolutely necessary. Detective Sam Johnson, also pressing a handkerchief to his nose, stood beside him. They were looking at the body of a white male, about forty. Naked, he lay on his back, two bullet holes in his chest. The clothes he'd apparently been wearing were scattered around the room. The bed was askew, as if it had been shoved aside.

"Ripe as he is, I'd say he's been dead the best part of a week," Johnson said.

Cantrell nodded. The mail carrier had reported that something might be wrong here. The box had been filling up with letters, and when she'd come to the door to deliver a package, she'd noticed the smell seeping from the place. A uniformed deputy had checked it out, discovered the door unlocked, found the body.

"Let's get out of here," Cantrell said through his handkerchief. When they were outside, breathing clean air again, he said, "We need to take pictures before the coroner gets here."

"I'll do it," Johnson said. "No point both of us going back in there."

Cantrell used his car radio to call for the lab man. When Johnson emerged from the house, camera in hand, the detective looked as though he might lose his breakfast, but after a few moments in the fresh air he seemed to recover. Cantrell had emptied the mailbox into a cardboard carton, which he'd set on the hood of their unmarked blue car so he could look through the victim's mail. Johnson put the camera in the car, then joined him.

"Anything?" he asked.

"It's all addressed to Jack Martin."

The box contained bills, a sporting magazine, lots of junk mail, and one personal letter. The return address indicated that it was from A. Martin in Little Rock, Arkansas.

"I'm going to get a warrant to open this," Cantrell said, showing Johnson the letter. "Also that package."

"Return address on the package is Roberts and Smith in Charlotte, North Carolina. Ever hear of it?"

Cantrell shook his head. "Sounds like a place that would sell hats to English gentlemen or something like that."

"Not the right size to hold a hat. Too long and thin."

Cantrell grunted. He was a tall, thin man with sandy hair streaked with gray. Nearly as tall, Johnson was fifty pounds heavier. The black detective was one of those guys who worked out and exercised to stay in shape, so his weight was all muscle. Johnson was real handy to have around when things got physical.

"So, what do you think happened in there?" the captain asked.

"Family fight of some kind. Or a lovers' quarrel."

"Sounds about right, him being naked and all, the bed pushed out of position the way it is. As soon as the coroner and the lab are through, I guess we'd better check with the neighbors, see if he had a wife or girlfriend."

"Or boyfriend."

"Homosexuality in Chickasaw County?" Cantrell said. "You've got to be kidding."

"Yeah, the Baptists would never permit it."

The coroner arrived. He was a chubby doctor named Knox who wore rumpled clothes and was usually half plastered. He didn't seem to notice the odor, leading Cantrell to wonder whether alcohol could deaden the sense of smell. After his examination, Knox informed them that the victim had been dead about five days, and that the cause of death was apparently the result of the damage caused by the two bullets that had been pumped into him. He'd know more after the autopsy.

Perkins, the lab guy, arrived as Knox was leaving. A young man with red hair, he was a civilian, an employee of the county health department, but he was as good at lifting prints and gathering evidence as anyone Cantrell had seen. Perkins got his equipment case and accompanied

Cantrell and Johnson into the house. Up to this point, the detectives hadn't disturbed anything, but now that the photos had been taken, the coroner had come and gone, and the lab guy was here, it was time to give the scene a thorough going-over.

"Eeeeeyuk!" Perkins said as they entered the room in which the body had been discovered.

"What's the matter?" Johnson asked.

"What do you mean, what's the matter? The smell."

"Smell? What smell?"

Wrinkling his nose, Perkins ignored him. Putting down his equipment case, he got out a small vacuum cleaner, located an outlet, and plugged it in. "I'm going to give the place a general going-over; then if there's anything specific you want me to do, just holler."

Cantrell said okay, and Perkins switched on his vacuum. Beginning in one corner, he would divide the room into sections, using a separate bag for vacuuming each one, labeling each bag as he changed it. Johnson turned to the dresser, examined the things on its surface for a moment, then pulled open the top drawer. Cantrell picked up the blue jeans the dead man had apparently been wearing. Neither he nor Johnson were using handkerchiefs now. They were getting used to the odor—to the extent one ever got used to it.

In the pockets of the jeans, he found some keys on a ring, one loose key, a pocket knife, forty-one cents in change, and a wallet. Dropping the other things into a plastic evidence bag, he opened the wallet. The name on the driver's license, as on the letters in the mailbox, was Jack Martin. Comparing the photo on the license to the face of the dead man, Cantrell decided the victim was indeed Jack Martin. The wallet also contained a Social Security card in the name of Jack Martin, business cards from a gunsmith and a place that sold tires, cash totaling fifty-two dollars, an American Rifle Association membership card, and a photo of a group of people standing in front of a frame house. Written on the back of the photo were the words, "Ma, Pa, and the gang, Xmas '75."

"Wasn't robbed," Cantrell said, dropping the wallet into the plastic bag.

Johnson glanced at him without saying anything. Neither of them had seriously considered robbery as a possibility. Johnson closed the drawer he'd been looking into and opened the one below it. A moment later, he held up two hair rollers.

"There was a woman here once," he said. "Blond hair." He dropped the rollers into an evidence bag.

Cantrell moved to the closet. The clothes were all men's, and all casual, inexpensive things, nothing fancy. Leaving Johnson and the lab man to check out the bedroom, Cantrell went into the bathroom. It needed cleaning. The mirror was spattered and the toilet bowl was stained brown. He found one toothbrush. The medicine cabinet contained a man's razor, shaving cream, Band-Aids, aspirin, cotton swabs, and a half-empty bottle of Pepto-Bismol. Then, in the wastebasket, he found facial tissues on which lipstick had been blotted. He put them in a plastic bag.

Giving the sink's metal stopper a twist, he lifted it out. Clinging to it were numerous hairs, most of which were long and blond. He put the entire stopper into an evidence bag. Returning to the bedroom, he found Johnson on his knees, peering under the bed.

"Looks to me like there was a woman living here, and she split very recently," the captain said.

"Could of split before he was killed," Johnson said.

"Yeah," Cantrell said, "could have." But they both thought it unlikely.

In another room, Cantrell found a gun cabinet, which he unlocked using the keys he'd discovered in Martin's jeans. Although it contained an assortment of firearms, none seemed likely to have been the murder weapon. Martin had been shot with a small caliber gun. The cabinet contained a .357 magnum, shotguns, high-powered rifles.

Two hours later, after they'd finished checking the house

and the property and the pickup outside, they hadn't found the murder weapon. Perkins went back to the lab. Cantrell and Johnson began checking the neighbors.

The nearest of them lived two-hundred yards down the road in a large farm house with a nicely maintained square of grass out front. The place was set back from the road a couple of hundred feet. As Cantrell drove up the dirt drive, a large yellow dog came out to bark at them. It kept its distance as the detectives got out of the car and headed for the front door. Cantrell noted the satellite dish sitting on the ground near a corner of the house.

The area was a mixture of woods and meadows and a few farms. Once, Cantrell recalled, this part of the county had been truly rural, populated by people who scratched their living from the soil. Now it was semirural. The people worked in town, shopped at the mall. They planted a few vegetables, maybe had a chicken or two, and told themselves they were living in the country.

The door was opened by an attractive woman in her mid-thirties who wore designer jeans and a checked shirt. Her silvery-blonde hair couldn't possibly have been that color originally. Cantrell and Johnson showed their badges, and she invited them in. Her name was Jenny Nealy. When they were all seated in the neat and nicely furnished living room, Cantrell told her why they were there.

"Oh, my goodness," she said, looking a little pale.

"Did you know him?" Cantrell asked.

"No, not really. I . . . well, I didn't like him very much. He shot at our dog once, threatened to kill her if she got on his property again."

"Do you know where he worked?" They'd found pay-check stubs from a construction company at the house. Cantrell was just double checking.

"No. Like I said, I really didn't have much to do with him."

"Did he live there alone?" Cantrell asked.

"No. There was a woman. I don't know her name."

"His wife?"

"I don't know. A couple of years ago he was living there alone. One day she just showed up, and she's been there ever since."

"What did she look like?"

"She was middle-aged, blond, kinda plain looking, I guess. And she was real trim. I always wondered if she was one of those people who could eat anything and never gain an ounce."

"Could you be more specific about her age?"

She frowned, thinking. "Well, I'd always thought she was my age or maybe even younger, but I'd only seen her from a distance. One day I was driving by with Tom—that's my husband—and she was at the mailbox. I got a good look at her face for the first time, and I realized that she must be at least forty."

He asked her to be more specific about things like the blond woman's height, weight, and hair style; then he asked, "Did she have a car?"

"Yes. It's an older car, green I think, all rusty and battered looking. I don't know what kind it is."

"We'd also like to talk to your husband. Is there a number where we can reach him?"

"Sure. He's got an office in town, on Choctaw Avenue. He's the agent for Southeastern National Insurance." She gave them the phone number.

The detectives spent the next couple of hours checking with other people in the neighborhood, none of whom knew any more about Jack Martin and the blond woman living with him than Jenny Nealy did. One of them, a teenage boy, said the blond woman's car was a twelve-year-old green Chevy Malibu that looked as if it burned more oil than gas.

The watcher observed the tennis match through the tall chain-link fence that enclosed the courts. The contest was between a dark-haired woman in a blue tennis outfit and a woman with reddish-brown hair who wore white. Both were trim; they moved nimbly and tirelessly in pursuit of the ball. Even so, they missed it a lot. They seemed to be every-so-often players, not well-practiced ones.

The watcher was only interested in the woman in white. Her name was Terri Ferguson, although the watcher hadn't known that when she followed her here.

Terri Ferguson had checked in at the counter at the tennis club entrance; then she'd gone into the lounge, presumably to wait for her playing partner. The watcher had gone to the counter, reading the entry in the clerk's notebook upside down: Ferguson, ten A.M., court six.

She'd already known the woman's name was Ferguson. She wanted to know her first name. To the well-tanned athletic-looking blond woman behind the counter, she said, "Excuse me. Was that Stacey Ferguson I saw a moment ago?"

The clerk studied her a moment, then replied, "There was a Mrs. Ferguson just checked in, but her name's Terri."

"Oh. I guess I got the wrong person."

The blond woman smiled politely.

Terri Ferguson hustled across the court, backhanding the ball just hard enough to drop in on her opponent's side of the net. The other woman, who'd been playing at the baseline, rushed the net, but she never had a chance.

"Fifteen-love," Terri Ferguson called out.

The other woman tossed the ball to her, and Terri retreated behind the baseline to serve.

The watcher had played tennis at one time. It was long, long ago. In another life. Before a whole string of men, two unsuccessful marriages, three suicide attempts, a stint in a mental hospital. Oh, yeah, the watcher thought, my list of accomplishments just goes on and on.

Terri's opponent won the next point. The women were fairly evenly matched. The watcher studied Terri Ferguson, noted her nice figure, her exuberance, the way her hair seemed to bounce as she darted around the court, her expensive outfit, her top-of-the-line tennis racquet. And she realized that she loathed this woman, for in a large part,

Terri Ferguson was responsible for everything that had happened.

Terri Ferguson would have to pay the price for that.

The price could be a simple lesson in humility, a chance to learn what it was like. Or it could be much worse. The next few days would tell.

TWO

"I never did make it to my ceramics class today," Terri said.

She and Stanley were sitting at a cloth-covered table for two at Mont's, one of their favorite restaurants. They often ate dinner out, since their schedules didn't allow much time for cooking. Terri was usually out of the house all day, doing something, and Stanley often worked long hours at the store, sometimes staying until long after it closed at nine. Tonight he'd gotten home about seven, looking tired. It seemed to Terri he'd been looking tired a lot lately.

"Stanley."

"Hmmm." He was studying the menu and didn't look up.

"I think you might be working too hard."

He put down the menu, his eyes finding hers. "What makes you say that?"

"Lately you just seem so"—she searched for the right words—"so drained when you get home."

He smiled. "The business keeps getting bigger, more involved. When you grow, there's more work. It's the price of success."

There was something in his eyes, something Terri was unable to identify. It was more than just fatigue. You could

22

work hard, feel tired and good at the same time. What she saw in her husband's eyes was that something was worrying him, wearing him down. His gaze abruptly shifted to the menu, as if he'd suddenly become aware that he was revealing things he didn't want to.

"Why didn't you make it to your ceramics class?" he asked, changing the subject.

"My tennis match with Marlene ran longer than I'd planned. It would have been a real rush to get to the class, and then I'd have had to leave early so I could make it to the committee meeting. Anyway, I called Richard, and he said I could come in on Saturday."

Stanley nodded. Terri was wondering whether she'd seen anything at all in his eyes now, except maybe just the tiredness of a man who works a lot and has a lot of responsibilities. He'd become a salesman in an Atlanta furniture store when he graduated from college. By saving his money and getting a Small Business loan, he'd started a furniture store of his own in one of the most rapidly expanding parts of the city. He'd sold the business, making a nice profit, and opened the store in Meadowview, which had grown until it was huge, almost the size of a shopping center all by itself. He had hundreds of employees. Ads for Ferguson's Furniture City ran constantly on the Atlanta TV stations.

Terri had never worked. She'd become pregnant right after they were married, and after Michelle was born she had been a full-time mother. Her only contribution to Stanley's success had been the money left to her when her father died. She'd put the whole fifty thousand into the furniture store.

Terri had never really known her mother, who had died when she was a year old. Although her dad had passed away nearly fifteen years ago, it still hurt to think about it. They'd been extremely close, maybe because he'd never remarried, each of them having only the other.

Terri turned her attention to the menu. The restaurant specialized in seafood. It was on the outskirts of Meadowview, which meant it was at the extreme outer edge of metropolitan Atlanta. The place had once been a barn, and it still had a rustic look about it. The floor was made of highly polished wide planks; the rough wood ceiling was supported by massive beams. There were no antique animal yokes or farm tools on the walls. The place had more class than that.

Terri ordered blackened Louisiana redfish. Stanley, who didn't share her love of things that were hot and spicy, had grilled swordfish.

"You think Michelle's doing okay in college?" Stanley asked.

The question surprised her. "Sure. She had a two point eight her first semester. What's wrong with that?"

"It's below a B average."

"By two-tenths of a point."

He frowned. "It's still below it."

"That's pretty close to the grade point averages we had, and as I recall, we made it through without any difficulty."

"Was my grade point that low? I thought it was three point something."

"I think you graduated with a two seven."

He frowned again. "Really?"

"Really."

"What was yours?"

"You don't want to know."

"Come on. Tell me."

"Three point one."

The waitress arrived with their orders before Stanley could respond.

When they walked to the restaurant parking area about forty-five minutes later, they held hands. And at that moment, she felt completely content, without a single problem, confident that the future held no unpleasant surprises.

Stanley drove the BMW out of the parking lot and turned toward Meadowview. They passed a drive-in theatre, a few hundred yards of undeveloped land, and then a fast food place. Ahead was a cluster of neon signs belonging to gas stations and more fast food places. Street lamps appeared at the edge of the road, and a sign that read Meadowview City Limits.

Terri saw a familiar-looking car going in the opposite direction. "Was that Marlene?" she asked.

"Where?"

"In the white Cadillac."

She turned around to get another look. The white car was too far away now for her to be able to see who was driving it. And then she noticed the car behind her. An old one, beat-up, rusty. It looked like the car that she'd seen this morning as she left the house. And again as she left the tennis club.

"Well?" Stanley said.

"Well what?"

"Is it Marlene?"

"I don't know. I never got a look at the driver."

"Then what are you staring at?"

Terri didn't answer. She was sure it was the same car. Was it following her? And if it was, why? There was no reason why anyone would want to tail her. Then she thought of one. And she didn't like it. The driver of the car could be a psychopath, someone who wanted to rape her or— She refused to continue with this line of thought.

"Turn right at that gas station," she said.

"What?"

"Turn right."

"Why?"

"Just do it, Stanley. Please."

He complied, and they were on a paved street that had brick homes on one side, a golf course on the other. The houses appeared to be four-bedroom models with two-car garages. Moderately priced housing by Meadowview standards. Terri looked through the rear window. The old car was still behind them.

"Now then," Stanley said, "would you mind telling me—"

She cut him off. "Stanley, I think someone's following me."

"Who? That car behind us? What are you talking about?"

She told him about seeing the car this morning as she left the house and again as she left the tennis club. "It's the same car, Stanley. I'm sure it is. It's green, and a piece of the grille is missing."

"Let's find out," Stanley said. He turned a corner. They were on a road that ran along another side of the golf course. There were no houses here, though. Only empty space where houses would be built someday. The battered car still followed them.

"Okay," Stanley said. "I'm going to find out what this is all about." He pulled to the side of the road and stopped. The other car stopped, too, a hundred feet or so behind him.

"What are you doing?"

He opened the door and got out.

"No," Terri said. "Don't do that. There's no one around. Whoever's in that car might have a gun. Or maybe it's a gang or something."

"I'm just going to find out what they want."

Dammit! she thought. Why are men always so impossible when it comes to things like this?

"Stanley, please . . ." But he was already out of the BMW, walking toward the battered car.

He was about halfway to it when it started moving again. For a second Terri thought it was going to run Stanley down, but it roared past him, then past her, and disappeared, leaving behind a cloud of smelly exhaust smoke.

"Did you see who was in it?" Stanley asked as he got back into the BMW.

"No, I couldn't see into the car at all."

"Neither could I. And I didn't think to try to get the license number. Wish I had."

The license number. Terri hadn't thought about it either.

When they were on the way home again, Stanley said,

"If you see that car again I think you should call the police."

The thought that this could be serious enough to involve the police chilled her. "Do you think . . ." Her words trailed off. She wasn't certain what she wanted to say.

"I think that now that he knows we're on to him, he'll leave us alone. If you should see him again though, I think it would be a good idea to get his license number and give it to the police."

They rode the rest of the way home in silence, and by the time they got there, Terri had pushed the person in the rusty car from her thoughts. If he showed up again, she would do as Stanley had said. Until then, she wasn't going to worry about it.

When they were inside the house, Stanley sat down on the den couch and switched on the TV set, using the remote control. He began changing channels. Terri made two dry martinis at the bar, gave one to Stanley, and sat down beside him.

"Thanks, " he said. "You know, with the cable, there must be a zillion channels on this thing, and there's absolutely nothing worth watching on any of them."

Sipping her drink, Terri slid her free arm around him. "You remember what we were talking about as you left this morning?"

He switched off the TV. "I remember."

"Are you sure that's the color you want?" the salesclerk said doubtfully. Slightly overweight, she was a middle-aged woman with shoulder-length blond hair. "With your fair complexion, I think I'd recommend something similar to your regular hair color."

"It has to be this color," the customer said.

"To use this color, you'll have to color your eyebrows to match."

"I understand. Is there something I can use that wouldn't be permanent, that I could wash out afterward?"

The salesclerk nodded. "Oh, yes. There are a lot of different products that you could use."

"Do you carry any of them?"

"No, we don't handle cosmetics, but any drugstore ought to have what you need."

The customer looked around the shop, her eyes taking in the faceless plastic heads bedecked with long hair, short hair, hair that was curly or straight, hair that was platinum or brown or red or almost any other color one could wish for. Spotting what she wanted, she strode across the room, leaving the salesclerk behind.

"This one," the customer said, holding up a blond wig. "But in the other color."

Joining her, the salesclerk eyed the wig skeptically. "With your rounded face, you might want to consider something a little longer and without the curls."

The customer shook her head. "No, I want this one in the other color."

"Let me see if I have it," the salesclerk said, keeping any further thoughts on the matter to herself. She headed for the back of the shop, disappeared through a doorway. Reappearing a moment later with a box in her hands, she said, "I've only got one. Let's see how it fits."

The wig fit perfectly, and a few moments later, the customer was in her battered Chevy, the wig in a box beside her on the seat. It was a pretty spring morning, sunny and pleasant, the oppressive heat of summer still a couple of months away.

There was only one more thing to be taken care of before she was ready to do what she came here to do. If things went right, it would be the beginning of a new life. All the things that had happened to her wouldn't matter anymore. They'd be forgotten, no longer relevant. Her life would be as it was always meant to be.

That was how she hoped things would go. It was what she wanted more than she'd ever desired anything else. And yet she knew things might not go as she wished them to. If life had taught her anything, it had taught her that. Things often didn't go as you wished them to.

Which was why she'd bought the wig.

And although she hadn't fully realized it when she left Alabama, it was also the reason she'd brought the gun with her.

Captain Eugene Cantrell sat at his desk in the portion of the Chickasaw County Courthouse that was used by the sheriff's department. His office was small and shabby looking, a dingy cubicle with a worn wood floor, yellow paint that had been bleached nearly white on one wall by years of summer sunlight shining in through the window. Made of stone, the building was old, much too small to house the various departments of county government. Its antiquated electric system often blew fuses. Even in the mild Alabama winters, the courthouse was drafty and cold. Three times a bond issue had been placed on the ballot to build a new courthouse; each time the measure had been resoundingly defeated.

This was the Heart of Dixie, as it used to say on the state's license plates. This was law-and-order country, George Wallace country, fry-'em-in-the-chair, support-your-local-police country. Until it came time to pay for it. Until the good God-fearing, criminal-hating folks of Chickasaw County had to shell out a few more dollars in taxes.

Cantrell had considered quitting. But, like the bond issues, the decision to resign just never quite got off the ground. Chickasaw County was home. He'd been born here, raised here; he loved it here. And he liked his job. Being a cop made you part of an exclusive club. Your life depended on the people you worked with, and that made you closer to those people than to anyone else. It was a relationship that even wives had a hard time competing with, which was why so many cops got divorced, Cantrell supposed.

At least he'd escaped that problem. His relationship with

Marie hadn't been without an argument here and there, but they'd never fallen out of love. And they'd been together for twenty-five years.

In front of him on the scarred wooden desk was the folder on the Jack Martin case. He opened it, sighed, flipped it closed. He already knew what it said. Nothing had been added to it in days.

Forty-eight hours. Somebody somewhere had figured out that if there weren't any good leads in a homicide investigation within forty-eight hours, the odds of the killer's being caught started getting real long real fast. Well, Jack Martin had been dead for five days before they'd even found him. And that had been a week ago. It added up to twelve days, enough time for the killer to go to Hong Kong or Argentina or the North Pole.

The prime suspect was Martin's girlfriend, but Cantrell still didn't even know her name. Apparently, no one knew her name. None of the neighbors knew it, nor did any of the men Martin had worked with on the job. Martin's mother, father, and some other members of his family lived in Little Rock. Cantrell had talked to all of them on the phone. None had even known he had a girlfriend.

The house and utilities were all in Martin's name. They'd found letters and paycheck stubs in the house, all of them Martin's. They'd been collecting the mail sent to the dead man's address, all of which had been addressed to Martin. No one had reported a woman missing who fit the description of Martin's girlfriend.

The package being delivered by the letter carrier who discovered Martin's body contained a telescopic sight for a rifle. The picture in his wallet turned out to be an old snapshot of his parents, two brothers, and one sister. The coroner said Martin apparently hadn't had sex before he was killed.

The woman living with Martin had left many things behind. Makeup, threads and fibers and buttons from her clothing, hairs that were naturally blond, hundreds of fingerprints. To make use of this evidence you had to have a suspect you knew, someone whose prints and hair and clothes and makeup could be compared with the samples taken from the crime scene. Cantrell had sent the prints that weren't Martin's to the FBI, which had put them into its computer. The machine hadn't recognized them.

Which meant Martin's girlfriend had never been arrested. Or maybe she had, and her prints never got forwarded to the Bureau. Or maybe the computer screwed up. Oh, hell, he thought. If anyone's screwing up here, it's me. I'm the one's supposed to find her. The guy was whacked in my county.

And then an idea hit him. If you thought about something long enough, you realized that there was something else you could do, something you'd overlooked. He phoned the motor vehicle department in Montgomery and asked a guy he knew there to run Jack Martin's address through the computer to see whether anyone else had used that address on a driver's license or car registration. The guy said he'd call back.

"Why you want to junk it if it runs?" the man asked. A plump fellow with a ruddy complexion, he wore oil-stained blue jeans and a red plaid shirt, one of whose sleeves had been repaired with a green patch. On his greasy cap was a yellow and black logo that said CAT.

"I can't afford to keep fixing it, and it's against the law to just leave it somewhere," she said.

"Car that old, that rusty, I can't get much off it in the way of parts. I can only use it for scrap." He nodded in the direction of the yard. A grease-stained road wound its way between mounds of old cars and refrigerators and stoves. In the background a crane was picking up cars, dropping them into a machine that squeezed them into metal cubes.

"How much?" she asked.

"Twenty-five dollars."

She tried to think of something good she could say about the car to get his price up, but she was unable to do so.

The radio didn't work. Nor did the heater. The wipers only operated on one speed, and the rubber blades were frayed. The tires were bald or nearly so.

"I'll take the twenty-five," she said.

"Come on into the office," he said, turning toward a shack made of unpainted, splintered boards. "I'll give you a receipt."

She followed him. There were only two signs on the structure. One said USED AUTO PARTS and the other said BEWARE OF THE DOG. She didn't see a dog.

Twenty minutes later, a teenager came in, looking for a carburetor manifold for an old Dodge V-8 he was trying to fix up. The junkyard man said he didn't have one. She got a ride back into town with the boy, who let her off at the Dixie Darling Motel, where she was staying. The boy hinted that it would be okay if she invited him in. She didn't.

She was all set now. All she needed was another car, and then it would just be a matter of waiting for the right opportunity.

THREE

Connie Jane Stewart.

Not Constance, but Connie. The motor vehicle department had also supplied her Social Security number, her date of birth, and the license number of her vintage Chevrolet. Captain Cantrell smiled, thinking, My, how quickly things can change.

He dialed an in-house number on the phone. To the woman who answered, he said: "Betty Lou, this is Cantrell. I need an NCIC check and local warrants on Connie Jane Stewart." He gave the woman's date of birth and Social Security number. Betty Lou said she'd get right back.

The captain leaned back in his chair, his eyes finding the old ceiling fan above him. It hadn't worked in years. The motor housing was greasy, the blades streaked with dirt. He studied it for a few moments; then his phone rang.

"Negative on Stewart, Captain," Betty Lou said.

"Okay, put her into NCIC, and put a locate out on her. Wanted for questioning in connection with a Signal One. Put her car in, too." He gave her the make, model, year, and license number. Then he dialed another in-house number. The phone clicked, buzzed, became silent. "Shit," he muttered.

The county had purchased the cheapest phone system it could find, which used equipment made in Korea or Sri Lanka or some such place. One moment it worked fine; the next it didn't work at all.

"Johnson!" he yelled.

The detective appeared in the doorway to Cantrell's office. "You hollered?"

Cantrell nodded. "Damned phone's fucked up again." He scribbled the information about Connie Stewart on a piece of paper, which he handed to the detective. "Martin's girlfriend."

Johnson examined the paper, looked up. "How'd you identify her?"

"Something I should have thought of sooner. I had the motor vehicle department put the address into their computer and see if any names other than Jack Martin came out."

Johnson nodded approvingly. "I'll remember that. You run an NCIC and warrants check on her yet?"

"Both negative. Check and see if she's got a sheet."

Johnson nodded, disappeared. He'd have to go through the files by hand. Although the department had a computer for running NCIC and warrants checks, everything else was done the old-fashioned way. The job of keeping track of the county's lawbreakers was probably within the capabilities of a decent home computer. But the cost of an Apple II was more than the county was willing to shell out for law enforcement.

When Johnson returned, he said, "Nothing on her, not even a traffic citation."

Cantrell grunted. Both he and Johnson knew that it was equally possible that the department's overworked, underpaid clerks had simply failed to record what Connie Stewart had done. Cantrell opened the phone book, found the name Stewart. There were about twenty-five of them.

"Let's call all the Stewarts in the book," the captain

said. "I'll go down to Michael on South River Road. You take them from there to the end."

An hour and a half later, they'd talked to all the Stewarts who were home, and none of them admitted knowing anything about a Connie Jane Stewart, age thirty-eight, who'd been living with a man named Jack Martin.

Alone in his office, Cantrell again leaned back in his chair, studied the inoperative ceiling fan. Connie Stewart was thirty-eight, living with a guy who worked construction, driving a twelve-year-old car. What did that say about her? All sorts of stereotypical images came to mind. A working-class woman, divorced, someone who worked as a waitress or barmaid. But he knew these things were idle speculation; he knew almost nothing about Connie Stewart. And he wouldn't until he located someone who could tell him about her.

Or until he located her.

Where are you, Connie Stewart? he wondered. What are you up to right now?

Connie Stewart sat bolt upright in bed, perspiring, trembling. She was unable to figure out where she was. The small dark room in which she'd found herself seemed completely unfamiliar. Through the lone window came a red glow that seemed to flicker at regular intervals, as if it were responding to a slow but steady drumbeat.

Going to the window, she looked out. The red glow was coming from the tall neon sign that said DIXIE DARLING MOTEL. A neon girl leaned slightly from the waist, then straightened, leaned, straightened, her movements accounting for the flicker coming through the window. Presumably the neon girl was the Dixie Darling.

Connie knew where she was now. She'd been awakened by a nightmare she was unable to remember. It happened to her from time to time, waking up terrified, but not knowing of what. Turning on the light, she found her wristwatch on the dresser and discovered it was only nine-fifty-five. She was still dressed, which meant she must

35

have lain on the bed, unintentionally slipped off to sleep. Connie switched on the cheap black-and-white TV set that sat on a small table beside the dresser. Some commercials came on, then the news. Connie sat down on the bed.

The room, standard cheap motel, could have been in Oregon or Kansas or Maine. The bed wasn't firm, but unforgivingly hard. The ceramic tiles in the shower had been covered with white paint that was flaking off. The fake wood veneer on the furniture had begun to peel in places.

The newscaster was talking about bloodshed in the Middle East. Connie tuned the woman out. There was always bloodshed in the Middle East. It wasn't her problem; she didn't want to hear about it.

She recalled having watched Terri Ferguson play tennis. The image triggered memories of her own childhood. Dressed in a new white outfit, she was on the court, playing against Jesse, the brother of one of her girlfriends. Connie was about thirteen, still struggling with all the changes occurring to her body. Jesse was a year older. He was a bad tennis player.

No one kept score at that age, since the kids were rarely evenly matched and there usually wasn't much doubt about who was the better player. In this case it was Connie. The boy had difficulty returning her serve, and after missing one that almost anyone should have been able to handle, he threw down his racquet, glared at her with sweat running down his face, then stalked off the court.

Confused, Connie watched him walk away. She'd been beaten by better players often enough. It happened. It wasn't anything to get upset about. She didn't understand.

She tried to figure out what had so upset the boy as she walked home. The tennis court was only two blocks from their big white house. The place was set well back from the street. Their driveway curved through the huge lawn that George, their black gardener, kept immaculate. They played croquet on the lawn sometimes. Connie loved croquet.

Finding her mother, Connie told her about the incident with Jesse.

"You did it all wrong," her mother said, smiling. She was a slender woman with blond hair like Connie's. She always wore beautiful clothes, usually pastels that seemed to float around her as she moved.

"All I did was play. Jesse was the one who did it wrong. He really is a bad tennis player."

"But he was beaten by a girl. That shamed him."

"Then he should have learned to play better."

Her mother shook her head. "No, Connie. Now, listen. You're almost a woman, and it's time you learned something. A woman never beats a man at anything. You see—"

"But it's not my fault he's no good."

Her mother smiled indulgently. "You still shouldn't beat him."

"You mean I should *let* him win?"

"Why not, if it makes him happy?"

"I don't care if he's happy. If he wants to win, he should play better. He's just a bad sport when he loses."

"But you made him angry, Connie. And it wasn't necessary. Listen to me now. You're a very pretty girl, and when you get older, you're going to marry someone with a good future. His job will be to support you. Your job will be to make him happy."

Connie stared, said nothing.

"Even for a pretty girl, it's not always easy to get a good man. So you've got to be very careful to never be pushy or demanding, to never show him up."

"Like by beating him at tennis?" Connie asked hesitantly.

"Yes. Like that."

The memory faded away. Connie had no feelings about

it. It was just something that had happened. Back then. When she was someone else.

Pictures of a traffic accident were on the TV screen now. Smashed cars, the injured on stretchers, flashing lights. There were more commercials, then a story about a demonstration against abortion. STOP KILLING BABIES, one sign said. ABORTION IS MURDER, proclaimed another.

Connie recalled her first abortion. She had been in Gainesville, Florida, where she'd stayed after dropping out of college rather than returning home. She'd called her father, asked him for money.

"Why do you need it?" he'd said.

"I haven't found a job yet, Daddy. I need it to buy some food and pay the rent."

He was silent a moment. "How much do you need?" he asked finally.

"About five hundred dollars."

"That's a lot of money, Connie."

"I know, but I need some clothes. My rent's a hundred and—"

"You dropped out of college over our objections, and then you refused to come home. You won't do anything for us, and yet you think you can call up just any time and ask for money."

"I'm sorry, Daddy. It's just—"

"As our daughter, you have certain responsibilities. You're supposed to meet those obligations. You're supposed to behave like a Stewart. That means you work hard to do what's expected of you, even if it isn't always what you happen to want to do. At all times you're supposed to act like a lady, and I'm not sure that's what you're doing there. Who are your friends? What kind of people do you associate with there?"

"Other people my own age. Young adults."

"College dropouts, Connie? Like you?"

What was she supposed to say? That the only people she knew were the men she'd slept with? That one had been a graduate student in philosophy, another a bartender, another an unemployed mechanic? That she needed the money for an abortion and that she'd slept with so many men she had no idea who the father was? She considered telling him these things, but she didn't do it, for if she did he would never give her the money.

"I'm just trying to find myself, Daddy. That's all. I just need a little freedom so I can figure out where I'm going."

He sighed. "All right, Connie. I'll give you the money under one condition. You have to promise to go back to college."

Connie hesitated, as if she were thinking it over. "All right, Daddy, I promise."

"I don't mean that you'll go back sometime. I mean when the next semester begins. Do you understand?"

"Yes, sir. I understand."

"Okay, Connie," he said, sounding relieved. "I'll send you the money."

Abortions weren't legal in the United States then, so she'd gone to Puerto Rico, where illegal abortions were easier to come by. The fetus had been removed from her body in a dingy building with a sign out front that said Clinica Medica. It had cost two hundred and fifty dollars plus her airfare. She'd flown back to Florida immediately afterward. The next day she'd had cramps so bad that she had to stay in bed. But after that it was as if nothing had happened.

As she'd known she would, Connie broke her promise to her father. Although furious, he didn't completely disown her. That came later.

The next morning, Connie went through her large straw purse, removing everything that had her name on it. There really wasn't that much, her driver's license, the card that said she was enrolled in the health insurance plan at the place she used to work, a couple of other things. She had no credit cards or library cards or membership cards. Putting the things that could identify her in a glass ashtray, she burned them. If she got caught doing what she was about to do, at least the police wouldn't be able to find out she was Connie Stewart, who was wanted for murder in Alabama, simply by looking in her handbag.

Next Connie got a pair of pliers from her purse. The pliers were the only tool she'd carried in the old Chevy, and she'd retrieved them before sending her car to the machine that turned autos into cubes of metal. Going to the closet, she got a coat hanger, untwisted and straightened it so that it became nothing but a length of heavy wire. With the pliers, she made a small hook on one end, then bent the wire into a loosely coiled circle, and slipped it into her purse beside the gun.

Taking the box containing the wig, Connie walked the six blocks to the nearest bus stop, waited for a bus headed into Atlanta. One arrived in twenty minutes. Connie stayed on the bus until it stopped at a large shopping mall. There she bought some insulated wire, alligator clips, and a small pocket knife. Sitting at a public bench at the mall, Connie made two short loops of wire with clips on both ends. Then she caught another bus, asked the driver how to get to the airport, and accepted a transfer slip.

At the airport, she went to the parking area where passengers left their cars while they were away. As jets whined overhead, Connie looked for a car that was old enough not to have a steering wheel lock. She knew how to remove the lock, but the job required tools she didn't have. A man she'd known briefly had showed her how it was done, along with how to get inside a locked car, how to hot-wire the ignition. His job had been repossessing cars from people who were reluctant to give them up. Connie couldn't recall the man's name, only that he had treated her a lot like Jack Martin had.

She spotted what she was looking for, an old green pickup. Glancing around to make sure no one was watching, Connie pulled the coat hanger from her purse, straightened it, and slipped it between the window and the rubber seal. A second later, she had the small hook around the locking button. Gently but firmly she pulled up on the wire, lifting the button.

Quickly she climbed into the truck. Its interior was stifling, a solar oven on a clear day like this. Lying on the floor, she looked under the dash. When she'd spotted the wires she was looking for, Connie scraped the insulation off three of them, connected the short wires with the alligator clips to them. One of the clips hung down below the dash, connected to nothing. Sitting up, she pumped the gas a couple of times, then touched the clip to what appeared to be a grounded spot near the steering column. Sparks jumped from the clip, and the starter came to life. A moment later, she was driving out of the parking lot.

The truck's owner had left the airport parking ticket in the visor. She paid the bill for two days' parking. There was no way of telling how long the owner would be away, but there was reasonably good chance that the truck wouldn't be reported stolen for a couple of days. Which was why she'd come to the airport. She didn't want to risk taking a car that almost surely would be reported stolen an hour or two after she'd taken it.

When she reached Meadowview, Connie drove to a neighborhood of expensive homes and parked. She was across the street and three houses down from the Ferguson house. Today was Saturday. She'd watch the house over the weekend, wait for an opportunity. If none presented itself, maybe she'd go to the furniture store on Monday. She could decide that later.

On the seat beside her was a newspaper. Connie picked it up; the paper was three days old. Flipping through it, she came to the page with the crossword and other games on it. At the top of the page was an anagram. Connie got a pen from her purse. She loved to work anagrams.

Terri examined herself in the big bathroom mirror, making sure her hair and makeup were satisfactory; then she hurried downstairs. She found Stanley in the den, watching a basketball game on TV.

"I'm off to my ceramics lesson," she said.

He nodded, his eyes remaining on the TV set. "If I'm not here when you get back, I'll be at the store."

"Why don't you take the day off? You don't need to go to the store seven days a week. That's what you've got all those high-priced assistant managers for, so you don't have to do everything yourself."

"Saturday's our busiest day."

"The store won't go belly-up if you're not there for a day or two. It survived while we were on vacation."

Which had been three years ago, two weeks in the Bahamas. Since then, she hadn't been able to pry Stanley away from the store for more than a few hours at a time. His idea of a day off was to put in a little less time than usual on Saturdays and Sundays. He did take the whole day off on Christmas, but he seemed about as happy about the idea as Ebenezer Scrooge had been before the three ghostly visitors caused his change of heart.

Stanley was looking at her peculiarly, she realized suddenly, as if he was on the verge of telling her something. A few silent moments passed; then he said, "Well, I guess you'd better get going, or you'll be late."

"Stanley," she said slowly, "is everything okay?"

"What could be wrong?" he asked, giving her a warm smile.

That wasn't exactly a firm reassurance that everything was fine, but Terri let it go. If Stanley had something on his mind, he'd get around to telling her about it in his own good time. Prodding him would accomplish nothing. She kissed him on the forehead.

"I should be back about five," she said.

"Make us an enormous ceramic something or other—you know, something that will drive guests crazy trying to figure out what it is."

"Stanley, I can barely make an ordinary pot." She

laughed. "Of course, if I brought one home, chances are people would have trouble figuring out what it is."

"They'd all think it was art. We could sell them for outrageous prices."

Responding with a wave, Terri rushed out of the den. A moment later she was in her car, driving away from the house. She barely noticed the old pickup parked across the street.

Connie had solved the anagram and started on the cross-word when the Ferguson's garage door began going up. There were two cars inside, a brown expensive-looking one and a white station wagon. The station wagon backed out, then came toward her. Terri was driving.

The situation couldn't be better. Connie started the truck, drove around the corner, and pulled to the curb. Reaching under the dash, she disconnected one of the alligator clips, and the engine died. Then, carrying the box that contained the wig, Connie walked toward the alley that ran behind the Ferguson house.

The alley was clean, graveled, without any weeds or spilled garbage cans. In this neighborhood, even alleys were pretty. Even so, tall fences and walls and bushes con-cealed this place of trash cans and garbage trucks from the eyes of the people in the expensive houses. For Connie this was perfect; no one would see her enter the Fergusons' property.

Their backyard was surrounded by a high wood fence with a gate. Connie tried the gate. It was unlocked. Step-ping through it, she found a yard that had apparently been professionally landscaped. It had brick walkways, a fountain. There were flower beds that had yet to be planted, rose bushes that were beginning to bud, every-thing neatly arranged, set off by timbers that had been set in the ground.

As she headed for the large covered patio, Connie slipped her hand into her purse, felt the gun. She hoped she wouldn't need it. Or the wig. They were just a precaution.

Because things didn't always work the way you wanted them to.

Her heart was pounding madly. This, Connie realized, could be the most important moment of her life. She stepped onto the patio.

FOUR

"Sure made a mess of things, didn't they?" Captain Cantrell said, surveying the smashed console TV set, the overturned chair, the couch with its upholstery slashed.

"We was over to Tuscaloosa when it happened," Ben Weaver said.

He was a stocky man with sandy hair cut in a flattop. He always reminded Cantrell of a Marine drill sergeant. The detective had no idea whether Weaver had ever been in the service. He knew him the way he knew a lot of people in Chickasaw County, by name, by sight, by occupation, by what he heard, but he didn't really know the man.

"We were there for the funeral of May's mother, so both her and the kids were already pretty upset, and when they saw this . . ." He completed the sentence with a wave of his hand. "I sent them over to my brother's house so they wouldn't have to look at it."

"Anything taken?"

"Electronic stuff mostly. A little TV set, Sally's stereo stuff, things like that."

The house was unpretentious but nice, with new blue carpeting, decent furniture. Before being vandalized, the three-bedroom frame home had apparently been clean and well cared for. Cantrell felt sorry for Weaver and his family. But then a house that had been trashed could be put back in order. As a cop he'd seen a lot worse things, things that were far less easily fixed.

Cantrell supposed that in bigger police departments captains didn't handle residential break-ins. They probably didn't work Saturdays either. What could you do? The Chickasaw County Sheriff's Department had neither enough officers nor enough money to allow for cops who sat behind a desk all day and didn't do any real police work. And here a gas skip was real police work. A burglary was a big case. Unsolved murders were extremely rare.

Not that the sheriff's department was exceptionally good at catching killers. The few homicides that occurred in the county were usually the result of family fights, murder-suicides, or barroom brawls. Cases in which the murderer was known and usually apprehended immediately. Cases like the Jack Martin murder were unusual. Maybe that's why the case bothered him, kept tugging at his thoughts.

"Why do people do things like this?" Weaver asked with tears in his eyes. "I can understand somebody breaking in here to take stuff, but why do all this?"

"There's no explaining it," Cantrell said gently. "There's a lot of bad people in the world, crazy people, sick people. You hope not to ever run into any of them, but every now and then you do."

"In the kitchen, they pulled everything out of the refrigerator and stomped on it," Weaver said. "Just to ruin it. I can't see any other reason."

Cantrell took a report on the burglary. While he was getting Weaver's statement, the man said, "I'll bet it was someone from out of town. Maybe somebody from Birmingham, came in on the freeway. Nobody from around here would do a thing like this."

Cantrell didn't bother to tell him that there were indeed people right here in good old Chickasaw County who'd gleefully do a thing like this. A couple of guys in particular

46

he planned to look up and see if just maybe they had some of the things that had been taken from Weaver's house.

The phone rang. Weaver spent a few moments looking for it, finally finding it beneath an overturned reclining chair. He answered it, then looked at the captain. "For you," he said.

"Cantrell."

"Captain, it's Johnson. I've got something you're going to like. A letter addressed to Connie Stewart showed up in today's mail at the Jack Martin place. It's from her employer—former employer, I guess you'd say now."

"Would there be anyone there on a Saturday?"

"At this place I can guarantee it, Captain. She worked at Tillotson Ford."

"I'll meet you there."

Ray Tillotson was a chubby balding man with a cigar jammed in the corner of his mouth. On the walls of his office were numerous awards from the Ford Motor Company commending him for his accomplishments as a car dealer. He leaned forward in his desk chair and blew out cigar smoke.

"She just walked out one afternoon and never came back. Didn't say she was leaving, didn't quit, just left. She had a few days pay coming, so we mailed it to her. I guess that's what was in the letter you found, her paycheck."

Tillotson's office was nothing fancy. It was fairly small, with moderately priced furniture, a place to work in, not to impress people. Cantrell and Johnson sat in vinyl chairs.

"Can you give me the exact date she left?" the captain asked.

"Hang on." Tillotson picked up the phone, dialed two digits. "Patty, this is Ray. When did Connie Stewart leave?" He listened a moment, then said, "No, I mean what day exactly." He waited. "Okay, Patty, thanks." He hung up. "It was the tenth."

According to the coroner, that was the day Jack Martin died. Cantrell said, "What exactly did she do?"

"Secretary, clerk, that sort of thing. We have three of them. There's an unbelievable amount of paperwork involved in the car business."

"She do a good job?"

"Far as I know. Probably you ought to talk to Patty Eckert about that. She's in charge in that department, and she knew Connie Stewart a lot better than I did."

"Would she have filled out an employment application?" Cantrell asked.

"I'm sure she would have."

"Can we see it?"

"I'll tell Patty it's okay to show it to you." He picked up the phone.

Patty Eckert turned out to be a prime example of why it never paid to assume what people looked like. Without really realizing he was doing it, Cantrell had pictured her as twenty-eight or so, attractive, most likely with curly blond hair. The real Patty Eckert was a prim-looking Southern lady with her gray hair in a bun. She was about sixty.

Her desk was in a room with three others, but apparently she was the only secretary working today. Cantrell and Johnson pulled over chairs, sat down.

"Is Connie wanted for something?" she asked.

Cantrell told her what had happened, that they needed to talk to Connie Stewart about it.

"You mean she was associating with that man who was killed?" She seemed shocked. "I mean, I knew about the murder, but I had no idea that Connie may have been involved."

"What can you tell us about her?"

"About her personal life, not much I'm afraid. She didn't talk about it. I knew that she was divorced, and I suspected that . . ." She hesitated, searching for the right term. "Well, that she might be living with someone." Her distasteful expression made it clear what she thought of such behavior.

"Do you know where she was from?"

"Tennessee, I think, bless her heart. I really do hate to see anyone get in trouble. I think maybe trouble followed Connie. It's too bad. I think inside she was a pretty nice person. I tried to get her to go to church with me once, but she wouldn't do it. I wish she had. I think it would have helped her a lot if she'd been able to take the Lord into her heart."

"Yes, ma'am. Did she have any friends that you know of?"

"Bobbi Sue—that's the other girl that works here in this department—Bobbi Sue and me, we never saw her away from work. Like I told you, I had my suspicions, but I really didn't know what she did when she wasn't here."

"Was she friendly with Bobbi Sue?"

"Bobbi Sue's just out of high school. I think she was a little afraid of Connie. Not that Connie did anything to Bobbi Sue. It's just that Connie was divorced and all and that we suspected she was living with somebody. I guess you'd have to say Bobbi Sue's a little shy, bless her heart. She's a nice little girl though. She really is."

"Do you have her address? We'll have to talk to her."

"I'll get it for you," Patty Eckert said, getting up and moving to the file cabinets behind her.

"While you're there, would you mind pulling Connie Stewart's file. I'd like to see her application."

Johnson copied Bobbi Sue Turner's address and phone number as Patty Eckert read them off standing at the open file cabinet. She returned to her desk with a file folder, which she handed to Cantrell. It was all there. Connie Stewart had been born in Nashville and graduated from high school there. She attended college at the University of Florida, but didn't graduate. Past work experience ran from secretarial to waitressing. Parents: Jonathan and Rebecca Stewart of Nashville. Person to notify in case of an emergency: Jack Martin. The space for personal references had been left blank. The captain passed it to Johnson.

As they left the administrative section of the dealership and stepped into the showroom, Ray Tillotson hurried over n, saying, "I've got a real good deal on a Tempo w Thousand trade on anything you bring in, even ha ve to tow it." Moving closer, he lowered his "For police officers, it's fifteen hundred." He ...ked.

Saying they weren't in the market right now, the officers left. When they were outside, Cantrell said, "I'm going to go to Nashville and talk to Connie Stewart's parents."

"You'll never get it approved."

"Johnson, I'm not going to *ask*. I'm going to do it, then submit a request for reimbursement when I get back. This is Saturday. The comptroller's office is closed till Monday. This is an emergency." He smiled.

"One of the benefits of being a captain," Johnson said. "You can get away with shit like that."

"And while I'm off spending money the county doesn't know I'm spending, why don't you go see Bobbi Sue."

"I'll bet she's cute."

"What makes you think so?"

"Fresh out of high school, with a name like Bobbi Sue, she's gotta be cute."

Cantrell didn't tell him how he'd pictured Patty Eckert.

Terri was wondering why she'd ever taken up ceramics as she drove away from the frame house in which Richard Altman lived and conducted his ceramics classes. The earthenware pot she'd been making had developed numerous cracks when she'd fired it, and she'd had to throw it away. Despite Richard's assurances that these things happened and that the next pot would probably come out just fine, Terri was dejected.

She'd called to see whether Stanley was home, getting no answer, which meant he had to be at the store. It was about five o'clock; the store closed at five-thirty on Saturdays. Even so, Stanley could be there for hours if he got involved in something. Just him and one of the assistant managers, going over the inventory or something like that. Terri sighed.

She didn't want to go home to an empty house. Stopping at a red light, she considered going by Marlene's place. She needed to talk to Marlene about some fund-raising ideas for the Meadowview Council for the Elimination of Hunger. They were both on the board of directors of the organization, which was continually falling short of its fund-raising goals. Marlene's house was only a few blocks away, to her left. When the light turned green, Terri hesitated, then continued straight ahead, toward her own home. It was too close to dinner time to drop by Marlene's unexpected.

She was driving through a neighborhood of three-bedroom middle-class homes now, houses that might belong to plumbers or electricians or police officers. Houses that cost half again as much as they should, just because they were sandwiched between two of Meadowview's more expensive neighborhoods. One of them was the neighborhood where she lived.

As she approached Fulton Street, which would take her home, Terri put on her turn signal and began to slow the station wagon. Then, abruptly changing her mind, she stepped on the gas, turned off the turn signal. She simply didn't want to go home to an empty house, sit around, watch television, wait for Stanley.

I'll go for a drive, she decided. There's still some daylight left. I'll take a short drive in the country.

When she reached a through street that was also a state highway, she turned left, heading away from metropolitan Atlanta.

Mary Ann McCabe drove slowly, studying the house numbers. She was looking for 4213 Lyndale, where Edna Baker lived. Mary Ann's one-year-old son Nathan was strapped into the special child's restraining seat beside her.

To make some extra money she had put up a notice on the church bulletin board saying she'd do typing for a dollar a page. Edna Baker was writing a book about her cats. It didn't sound like much of a book, but Mary Ann's job was to type it, not evaluate it. And she could make a couple of hundred dollars, maybe more, depending on how long the book was.

It was easy money really. In typing class at high school she'd timed out at eighty-five words a minute with no mistakes. If she was willing to risk an error or two, she could do around a hundred. Only thing she was ever really good at. She'd made Cs in nearly everything else.

"Ta-ta-ta-ta," Nathan said in his high-pitched baby's voice.

"Ta-ta-ta-ta, to you, too," she said, reaching over and giving him a gentle tickle with her finger. The baby giggled.

Her plans had been to get a job as a secretary after she got out of high school, but it hadn't worked out that way. She'd gotten married, gotten pregnant with Nathan, and although it didn't show yet, there was another one on the way. One in the oven as Gil liked to put it.

He said he wanted four in all. All Mary Ann could say to that was that he'd either better give her a break between so she could earn some money or hope Beecher Chevrolet would start paying its mechanics better.

The houses in this neighborhood were absolutely gorgeous. Mary Ann had no idea what they cost, but she suspected the numbers were so big they'd frighten her. For her it was silly to even dream of living in Meadowview. Mr. Beecher of Beecher Chevy might live here, not the people who worked for him.

Suddenly a woman dashed in front of her car, and Mary Ann jammed on the brakes. Nathan squealed excitedly. Mary Ann saw a flash of white and blue clothing, reddish-brown hair, and then she saw the gun in the woman's hand. Abruptly the woman turned and ran back in the direction from which she'd appeared.

"Gibble," Nathan said, but this time Mary Ann ignored him. My heavens, she thought. What was that woman doing with a gun?

Mary Ann wondered whether she should find a phone,

call the police. Did she want to be involved in this, what-ever it was? She'd have to wait for the police to arrive, show them the house, get her name in their report, maybe even testify in court. She would be causing trouble; she would be making people mad at her. Besides, she hadn't heard any shots. And as far as she knew carrying a gun was okay as long as you had it out in the open where everybody could see it.

"Eeeeee!" Nathan said.

"Let's get out of here," she said to the baby. "This is none of our business."

Mary Ann didn't mention the incident when she finally located Edna Baker.

It was about five-thirty when Cantrell's flight landed at Nashville Metropolitan Airport. Even though he'd called at the last minute, he'd had no trouble getting a seat on the short flight from Alabama. The plane had been half-empty. He took a cab to the Stewarts' house. He'd phoned them from Alabama; they were expecting him.

The Stewarts' house was right out of *Gone With the Wind*. Although as an Alabamian, Cantrell had seen all sorts of Southern architecture, no one in Chickasaw County had a place like this. It was huge and white, with tall col-umns in the front, and it was surrounded by giant shade trees, flower gardens, grass that looked flawless. It was hard for Cantrell to believe that anyone who'd worked as a waitress and a secretary and had lived with Jack Martin could have come from a place like this. A maid answered the door. The policeman identified himself, said he was expected.

"This way, please," the young black woman said.

Cantrell stepped into a wide hallway whose walls were made of massive hardwood panels. On the right was a big mahogany table with an enormous display of cut flowers. It made Cantrell think of a funeral home. The maid led him past a broad stairway with a carved wood balustrade, showed him into a room on the right.

"You wait here in the library," she said. "I'll tell Mr. Stewart you're here."

The term *library* seemed a misnomer to Cantrell. It had only one bookcase, and that was filled with leatherbound volumes. Books, the detective suspected, that were strictly decorative, not for reading. The thinking had probably gone something like this: Well, if we're going to call it a library, it should have books; and if it's going to have books, they should look nice. Cantrell wondered if they knew what the titles were.

He walked over to the bookcase. The volumes were by Thomas Hardy, Dickens, Twain, even Plato. Cantrell noticed that the brown covers seemed to be color coordinated with the design on the wallpaper.

Clearly more used than the bookcase was the big wooden bar at one end of the room. It had a sink and most likely a built-in refrigerator. Cut glass goblets were lined up at one end. The detective wondered what kind of expensive booze he'd find if he looked, but he didn't look. He was about to examine the portrait of some guy dressed in riding clothes when the Stewarts came in.

"Captain Cantrell, I'm Jonathan Stewart."

He looked to be in his early sixties, with gray hair that was still thick. Cantrell figured it was professionally styled because it was full and sort of fluffy-looking and yet clearly conservative at the same time. Stewart's blue eyes appraised the Alabama police officer coolly.

Although Stewart hadn't bothered to introduce the woman, Cantrell assumed she was Rebecca Stewart. Close to her husband's age, she was tall and thin, with shoulder-length wavy blond hair. Cantrell thought she had probably been beautiful when she was younger. Even now she had a smoothness, an elegance about her. The only thing detracting from her appearance was her eyes, which looked tired, defeated. The three of them sat down, the Stewarts on a couch with shiny upholstery, Cantrell in a matching chair.

"Is Connie all right, Lieutenant?" Mrs. Stewart asked. "Do you think anything's—"

"Captain," Jonathan Stewart corrected. "He's a captain."

"Yes, I'm sorry. I mean captain. Do you think anything's happened to her, Captain?"

"I don't have any reason to think so," Cantrell said. "I'm just trying to locate her."

He had told Jonathan Stewart over the phone that Connie had been living with someone who'd been found shot to death and that she was now missing.

"Is she a suspect in this man's death, Captain?" Rebecca Stewart asked.

"I don't have any proof against her, Mrs. Stewart. Right now I just need to talk to her, find out what she knows about what happened. Do you have any idea where she is?"

"No," she said softly. She studied her hands, which were folded in her lap.

"Captain," Jonathan Stewart said, "there's something you should know. We haven't seen or heard from Connie in more than fifteen years." He fixed his cold blue eyes on Cantrell. "I had two daughters, Captain. One of them is happily married and living in Louisiana, the mother of two kids of her own. The other girl chose to lead a different sort of life. She decided that she no longer wanted to be part of this family, that she no longer wanted to be our daughter."

"What happened?" Cantrell asked.

Stewart hesitated, apparently trying to decide whether he should discuss such things with a stranger; then he said, "If I answer your questions, can I count on you to be discreet?"

"I'll be on a plane back to Chickasaw County this evening, Mr. Stewart. No one there has ever heard of you."

Stewart sighed. "That's not the case here in Tennessee. I own a construction company, some broadcasting stations, and a record company, to mention just a few of my holdings. I'm also involved—at least behind the scenes—in politics. Anyway, you get the idea. The last thing I need is a scandal involving my family.'' He sighed. ''People here don't know about Connie. If anyone asks, we say she's happily married and living in Florida. That's where she was when she decided she didn't need her family anymore.''

Rebecca Stewart had continued staring at her hands while her husband talked. Cantrell couldn't read her. Did she see things the same way her husband did? Or did she have different feelings about Connie?

''Would you mind telling me the whole story, Mr. Stewart,'' the Alabama lawman said. ''I need to know it.''

Rebecca Stewart looked up. ''Connie was a wonderful girl all the time she was growing up,'' she said. ''She was very active. She loved to play tennis and volleyball and things like that. She was better in sports than a lot of the boys, I'm afraid.'' Connie Stewart's mother paused, remembering. ''She was a pretty girl, with lovely blond hair. Still, she was very shy around boys.''

''Not after she went to college, she wasn't,'' said Jonathan Stewart bitterly.

Rebecca gave him a look that was pure grief. Cantrell was opening a lot of old wounds here.

''When she was in high school,'' Rebecca continued, ''she used to get tremendous crushes on different boys. If the boy didn't notice her, she'd be heartbroken. Connie was just the opposite of her sister, Cindy.'' She shook her head. ''Cindy was a year younger, but she had everybody in school asking her out. It was the difference in their personalities. Cindy just naturally attracted boys, while Connie was always awkward around them.''

''I don't really think that's what the captain needs to know,'' Jonathan said patiently. His wife glanced at him, went back to staring at her hands.

''The problem with Connie,'' Jonathan said, ''began when she was attending the University of Florida. We'd planned to send her to Vanderbilt, but we changed our

56

minds because she was so insecure in so many ways. She needed to get away from home, meet some new people, see something besides Nashville. It seemed like a good idea at the time, but it didn't work out very well.

"She dropped out in her second semester. She never discussed it with us, never even told us about it. We learned that she was no longer in school when the university notified us. Needless to say, we were quite upset. When we called her, she said that she didn't want to be in school, she wanted to . . . to find herself or something like that. It didn't make any sense. I told her to come home, we'd talk about it. She said no, she wanted to stay in Florida. I should have insisted right then, but I gave in, still thinking that if I left her alone she might grow up, get her act together. I never would have done it if I'd known what was going on."

He glanced at his wife, but she was still staring at her hands, not meeting anyone's eyes.

"For the next year or so, we only heard from Connie when she needed money," he continued. "She'd promise to go back to school or to come home if we'd send money; then she'd break the promise. Finally I went to Florida to talk to her. I found her apartment, but not her. I spent two days there, but she never showed up. I had business to tend to, and I couldn't stay any longer. When I got back home, I arranged to have a private detective find out what she'd been doing. What I learned was shocking."

He started to speak, then hesitated, as if he was trying to decide how much to tell. Finally he said, "She was shaming herself." He shook his head. "But that's just a euphemism, isn't it, Captain? Hell, she was screwing every guy she could get her hands on. One-night stands, shacking up with a different guy every night. The ROTC guys at the university had her number on the bulletin board. You know what they called her? The Duty Punchboard. That was their little nickname for her.

"You know what she was doing the weekend I was there looking for her? She was in Tampa with some Air Force guys. They'd sneaked her into the barracks, and they were all taking turns in the sack with her. You know what she did with the money I gave her? She used it to go to Puerto Rico and get an abortion."

Cantrell had met women like that when he was in the service. Nymphomaniacs. They always seemed to gravitate to the military. Because there were so many swinging dicks available, he supposed. He'd always been curious about women like Connie Stewart. Although they seemed constantly anxious to have sex, he wondered whether it was really sex they wanted or something else. Most of them, he figured, needed help. And he wondered whether anyone had really tried to help Connie Stewart.

"After I got the detective's report, I phoned Connie and told her that I knew what she'd been doing. I ordered her to come home immediately. She screamed at me, swore at me for checking up on her. I told her that she could not behave the way she was and remain a member of this family. I may not have handled it too well, but I was furious. I called her a slut and a whore—and probably some other things as well. I told her she had to come home immediately, or she would no longer be my daughter."

He fell silent, remembering, his thoughts turned inward.

"I take it she refused," Cantrell said.

"She used words no lady should ever use, Captain, words even I'd never heard before. Then she hung up. We haven't seen or heard from her since."

Now Cantrell knew how much help Connie Stewart had received. She'd been given an ultimatum, backed into a corner; and like most people put into such positions, she'd reacted emotionally, made the wrong decision.

"Does she have any friends here in town," Cantrell asked, "someone she may have kept in touch with?"

Jonathan Stewart shook his head. "There's no one."

"How about her sister, Cindy?"

"Cindy hasn't heard from her either. She wouldn't want to. She felt shamed by her sister, the way we all felt."

Cantrell glanced at the silent Mrs. Stewart, wondering if

that was how she felt too. He said, "Do you have a picture of Connie?"

"No. There was no reason to keep them," Jonathan Stewart answered.

"I have some," Rebecca Stewart said softly. "The most recent was taken when she was eighteen, just before she left for college. I have the negative, too, so you can have the print if it will help, Captain."

"I'd appreciate that," Cantrell said.

Jonathan Stewart looked at his wife appraisingly. He didn't seem surprised that she'd kept pictures of their disowned daughter. Cantrell decided he didn't like rich people very much. Chickasaw County was full of rednecks and bigots and the like, but they were simple people who believed what they'd been taught, didn't question it much. What was the Stewarts' excuse for being the way they were?

"Do you happen to recall the name of the private detective who did the work for you in Florida?" Cantrell asked.

"No," Jonathan Stewart said. "It was too long ago."

"Greenfield," his wife said. "I remember it because of the song."

When somebody remembered a name after so many years, there was probably more to it than just the title of a song, but Mrs. Stewart's private anguish was not Cantrell's concern. His job was to find whoever murdered Jack Martin.

"Can I get that photo from you?" the detective said.

Mrs. Stewart left the room, returning a few moments later with a five-by-seven photograph that she handed to Cantrell. The face in the photo was that of a rather ordinary American girl. Blond hair with a slight wave. A somewhat awkward smile revealing even teeth. Pretty in a youthful sort of way, but not beautiful. She looked somewhat like her mother must have looked at that age, except that Rebecca Stewart had a sleek kind of beauty that was missing in Connie. Connie the shy tennis and volleyball player. Maybe Connie the murderer.

Cantrell stood up. "Thank you for your trouble," he said.

Two hours later he was on a plane back to Alabama.

FIVE

It was nearly dark when Terri got home. Pulling into her driveway, she pressed the button on the door opener control, which was clipped to the visor. She was surprised to see Stanley's BMW in the garage. He had actually managed to tear himself away from the store after only a few hours.

Her drive in the country had been pleasant. She'd driven slowly, passing barns and livestock pens and fields that were being readied for planting. The clean sweet smell of freshly turned earth had filled the air. A native of Miami, Terri had lived her whole life in an urban environment, and there was a part of her that had always wanted to live in the country, maybe run a small farm or something like that. She'd never get Stanley to agree to it, not now anyway, but maybe he'd be willing to retire somewhere rural. She hoped so.

Getting out of the car, the garage door automatically closing behind her, Terri felt relaxed, at peace. She realized a silly smile had crawled onto her face.

"Stanley, I'm home," she called, stepping into the kitchen.

No lights were on in this part of the darkening house. She presumed Stanley was in the den, reading or watching television. Putting her purse on the island that separated the kitchen eating and cooking areas, she moved through the large living room and into the hallway. At the end of it was the den, which was dark. Had he fallen asleep in his chair? She walked to the den doorway and looked in. The room was deserted.

Returning to the other end of the hall, she headed up the stairs, turning on the lights when she reached the top, as the house was getting quite dark now. Their bedroom was empty; the relaxed glow she'd been feeling a few moments ago had been replaced by uneasiness. Where the hell was Stanley?

On impulse, she checked the other three bedrooms. Two just served as guest rooms. The other belonged to Michelle. Terri stood in the doorway of her daughter's room for a moment, taking in the neatly made bed with the big teddy bear sitting at its head as if awaiting breakfast in bed, the posters on the walls of rock and roll singers Terri had probably never heard of. It was still a little girl's room, even though its occupant was away at college, growing up.

Terri hurried back downstairs to check the rest of the house. The dining room, laundry room, and pantry were empty. She checked the den again, the living room, the kitchen, the garage. Calm down, she told herself. Stanley's just over talking to one of the neighbors.

Hurrying into the kitchen again, she grabbed the phone book from the small table beneath the wall-mounted phone and looked up the number of the Jenkinses, who lived next door. She made a mistake dialing it and had to start again. A woman answered.

"Sarah, this is Terri Ferguson next door. Uh, by any chance is Stanley over there?"

"Over here? No, I haven't seen him in a couple of weeks at least."

"Oh. Well, thanks. I just got home, and Stanley's car is here, and he isn't. I'm just trying to locate him."

"I'm sure he's around somewhere."

"Yes, I'm sure he is."

Terri called the next-door neighbors on the other side and the people across the street. No one had seen Stanley. Then she realized that there was still one place she hadn't looked. Rushing to the back door, she opened it and peered into the dark backyard.

"Stanley!" she called. "Are you out there?"

She switched on the outside lights, but they only illuminated the patio, beyond which was nothing but blackness. She thought, five-hundred-thousand-dollar house, and the only outside lights are pitiful low-watt bulbs on the patio.

"Stanley!" she yelled again. But the night was silent. During the summer, she would have heard the fountain flowing, but Stanley hadn't turned it on yet. Nothing stirred in the shadows.

It was ridiculous to think Stanley was out there. Why would he be in the backyard when it was too dark to see anything? And he would have answered her when she called his name. Unless something had happened to him. Unless he'd fallen and hurt himself, and was lying unconscious out there in the darkness. She hurried into the kitchen and got a flashlight. Then she moved through the yard, shining the light into the corners, behind the bushes and trees, finding nothing.

Inside the house, the phone started ringing. Certain it had to be Stanley, Terri dashed toward the door. She was about halfway to the house when her toe caught on something. Suddenly there was only air beneath Terri's feet, and then she thudded to the ground, sliding on a hard, unforgiving surface, scraping her hands and knees. Looking up, she saw the fountain, a birdbath-looking thing that dribbled water into a pond below when it was operating. She had landed on the cement walk that circled the pond. Remarkably the flashlight was still working. It lay in the grass about ten feet in front of her. The phone had stopped ringing.

Sitting up to assess the damage, Terri discovered that she was okay except for some abrasions and bruises. She tasted blood, which meant she must have bitten her lip when she fell. Terri got to her feet. Although shaky, she could walk. She picked up the flashlight.

Back in the safety of the kitchen, she sat down at the table. Her heart was still beating rapidly; she was still shaken. Then she remembered the telephone. Had it been Stanley—calling to tell her where he was? Maybe he was at the store. Maybe his car hadn't started, and he'd called a cab or had one of his employees pick him up. Going to the phone, she dialed the store number, let it ring. No one answered.

Should she call the police?

What would she tell them, that she didn't know where her husband was, that she hadn't seen him since early this afternoon? They'd laugh. They'd think Stanley slipped out to have a few beers with his buddies or something like that, forgetting to inform his worrywart of a wife. And when Stanley turned up with a perfectly reasonable explanation for where he'd been, she'd feel foolish. Maybe he was on the way home right now, being driven by someone from the furniture store.

He'd have left a note.

No, not necessarily. Stanley could be forgetful at times, especially when his mind was on the store. Possibilities circled in her head. He could be cheering on the company bowling team. He could have decided at the last moment to go to some sort of Chamber of Commerce meeting.

He could be having an affair.

But that was ridiculous. When your husband was cheating, you were only unaware of it if you chose to be unaware, chose not to see the all-so-apparent indications of it, chose to believe the lies. Stanley had never been unfaithful. She was sure of that.

Examining her scraped hands, Terri noticed some grains of sand embedded in one particularly bad spot on her left palm. She went to the sink and thoroughly washed her hands. She was drying them when she heard a thump.

Standing perfectly still, Terri listened, hearing a car door slam somewhere down the block, a dog bark, the normal sounds of night. Her eyes had automatically been drawn to the ceiling. Had the sound come from upstairs? The master bedroom was directly above her. Was someone there?

Had Stanley come home while she was out back and gone upstairs to change? Terri called his name, getting no answer. She headed for the stairs.

Terri was on the landing when it occurred to her that if somebody was in the house, it could be a burglar, someone who might assault her, maybe even kill her. She stopped, considering that. She'd noticed the chain on the front door earlier. The door was locked. The automatic door had closed behind her after she'd driven her car into the garage. It couldn't be opened without the control. Certainly no one could have sneaked in the back door while she was outside. No one was here unless it was her husband.

"Stanley."

No one answered.

She started up the stairs again. Even if no one was here, the thump had not been her imagination. If something had fallen, she would find out what.

The master bedroom looked as it had. No one was here; nothing had been disturbed. The lamp beside the bed was still upright and on its table. There were no open windows that could allow a breeze to move the curtains, causing them to knock something from a dresser or table top. But the noise had come from this room. Terri was sure of it.

And then she noticed that the door to the bathroom was open an inch or two, just enough for Terri to see a narrow vertical strip of the blue-and-white wallpaper. There was no reason for the door to be in that position. It was kept open unless the room was in use. And it wasn't in use now, for no lights were on. Terri was unable to recall whether she'd checked the bathroom when she was here earlier. She didn't think she had.

Terri took a tentative step toward the bathroom, and then she nearly screamed, because the door swung open and Stanley was on his hands and knees, trying to crawl toward her. Behind him on the blue ceramic tile was a long red smear. His eyes found hers, and they were full of pain and confusion, and they were pleading for help.

She rushed to him, hearing her voice say his name, babble things that were incomprehensible. She didn't know what had happened, what to do. She was trembling.

"Stanley . . . what . . . what . . ." Words wouldn't come.

Stanley wasn't crawling now. He was on his back, although Terri was uncertain how he'd gotten that way. Blood covered the front of his shirt. His eyes once more finding hers, he said, "Connie."

"W-what?" she said, still too confused to comprehend what was happening.

"Connie," he repeated, and there was a look of disbelief mixed with the pain on his face. His eyes closed.

Suddenly Terri's confusion vanished. Stanley was seriously injured. She had to get help. Scrambling to the bedside table, she snatched the phone from its cradle, dialed 911, gave her name and address, and said she needed rescue and an ambulance. "Hurry," she sobbed. "Oh, please hurry."

Rushing back to Stanley, she pushed the hair off his forehead, looked at his closed eyes. He seemed so still, so . . . no, she thought desperately. It's going to be all right. The rescue people and the ambulance people will be here soon, and everything will be all right. Hearing a distant siren, Terri rushed downstairs to unlock the front door.

A red rescue truck pulled into the driveway, its red lights flashing, its siren dying. A man and a woman leaped out, got their equipment, and hurried toward the house.

"What's the nature of the injury?" the woman asked.

Terri realized she'd hung up without telling them anything except that a man was badly hurt and to hurry. "He's all bloody," she said. "I . . . I don't know what happened."

"Where is he?" the woman asked.

"Upstairs. Follow me."

Terri ran up the stairway and into the bedroom. Stanley lay as he had when she left him. The paramedics rushed past her, bent over Stanley.

"He's . . . he's . . ." Terri didn't know what she'd intended to say. The paramedics ignored her.

The woman was giving Stanley mouth-to-mouth resuscitation. The man was straddling Stanley, rhythmically pressing with both hands on his chest. Terri stared, transfixed, her brain refusing to accept what a part of her mind already knew. The paramedics looked at each other, a silent communication passing between them. Then there were more sirens outside, and a voice called out from downstairs.

"Up here," the male paramedic yelled.

A moment later two ambulance attendants with a collapsible gurney hurried into the room. They set it down beside Stanley, eased him onto it, and carried him out of the room. For a moment, Terri just stared at the spot where Stanley had lain; then she ran after him. She rushed out the front door in time to see the gurney being pushed into the ambulance. The attendants were saying something to a police officer.

"I'm going with you," she said.

Suddenly a policeman was blocking her way. "I'm going to have to ask you some questions," he said.

Terri shook her head. "Not now. I've got to go with Stanley."

"I'm afraid that won't be possible," the officer said.

"That's my husband there!" she screamed, trying to push the cop aside. He held her as easily as she could hold a doll.

"You have to stay here."

"No! I've got to be with Stanley! I've got to make sure he'll be all right!" Tears were streaming down her cheeks.

The officer held her, forced her to meet his gaze. "You can't help him, ma'am."

Her mind refused to accept the implication. She began beating on the cop with her fists. He grabbed her wrists.

"No," she said in a voice that sounded like a frightened child's. "I can't stay. I can't. Can't."

"Ma'am," the police officer said gently, "your husband's dead."

Noooooooooooooo! Uncertain whether she had actually screamed the word or whether it had just been in her mind, Terri felt her knees buckle, and then everything went black.

SIX

Terri heard voices, unfamiliar voices. And then her surroundings came into focus. She was on her living room couch. Two men in suits were conferring on the other side of the room. Stanley was—she tried to force the knowledge from her mind, as if refusing to accept what had happened could make it not so.

"You okay?" One of the men in suits was standing over her now. He was tall and thin with a prominent Adam's apple. His face reminded her of Frank Sinatra.

Terri sat up. She was in a daze, as if everything she saw was swirling around her in some kind of movie that hadn't been invented yet. It's all being done with laser beams, she thought; it's not real.

"I'm Simon Stark, Meadowview police." He held up his badge. It said Detective Sergeant on it.

Terri nodded. He would tell her what had happened now. She steeled herself. Even if this was just a movie, she had to be prepared for the news.

"Do you own a gun?"

"A gun?" Why had he asked her that?

"A gun. Do you own one?"

"No." Did he think Stanley had shot himself? She had to explain, make him see. "We would never have a gun in the house. We hate them. We give money to organizations that want to control them."

"So do a lot of cops," Stark said. He studied her a moment, then said, "Tell me what happened."

She explained about coming home, looking for Stanley, finally finding him in the bathroom. "What happened to him?" she asked. "How . . . how did he get hurt?"

Stark looked at her for what seemed a long while before answering. "He was shot," the detective said finally.

"Why?" She demanded. "Why?"

"That's what we're trying to find out."

"Who . . . who shot him?"

"That's something else we're trying to find out."

She knew there was something she wanted to tell this police officer, but it floated just out of reach in some dark corner of her mind. And then she knew what it was. "He said 'Connie.' "

"What?"

"When I found him, he said 'Connie.' He said it twice."

"Did he say anything else?"

"No. Just that one word."

"Do you know anyone named Connie?"

"No."

"Did your husband?"

"Not that I know of."

A man carrying a large silver case came in. Stark and the other man in a suit conferred with him in the kitchen. Although Terri could hear their voices, the words were muffled. The man with the silver case emerged from the kitchen, headed for the stairs. Stark returned to Terri.

"Is anything missing?" he asked.

"I don't think so."

The detective nodded. "Have you washed your hands since coming home?"

"My hands? Why do you want to know that?" Next he'd be asking if she'd washed behind her ears.

"It could be important," he said cryptically.

"After I fell . . . there was dirt in the scrapes."

"May I see your hands please."

They seemed to weigh tons, but Terri managed to lift them up so the detective could examine them. He took each, turned it back and forth so he could check both sides.

"How'd you get those scrapes?" he asked.

"When . . . when I fell."

"Tell me about your fall."

"I . . . I told you. When I came home, I looked all through the house for Stanley." She had to stop for a moment. Saying his name brought tears to her eyes, and something inside seemed to twist agonizingly. This is all being done with lasers, she reminded herself. It's not real.

"I went into the backyard to see if he was there," she continued. "Then I heard the phone ring. I . . . I ran to answer it, and I slipped and fell by the fountain. I landed on my hands and knees, and I bit my lip. The phone stopped ringing. I never found out who it was."

"Can I see the injuries on your knees?" he asked.

"I . . . I guess so." It seemed to take forever to get the legs of her pants pulled up above her knees, and then she felt ridiculous sitting here like this, looking as if she were about to go wading. The policeman quickly looked over her scrapes and bruises, then told her she could cover them again.

"Can you tell me how you spent the afternoon?" he asked.

For a moment, she seemed unable to recall anything that had happened before she got home. Then it came to her. "I was at my ceramics class."

"Where is this class?"

"Across town." She gave him the address.

"Who teaches this class?"

"Richard Altman. He used to be a potter. In Greenwich Village. He was a professional, an artist."

"What time did you leave?"

"Uh . . . five, I think. Yes, five."

Stark glanced at his watch. "Did you come straight home?"

"No. I went for a drive in the country."

"Where exactly did you go?"

She told him.

"Did you stop to visit anyone or ask directions or buy anything?"

"No."

"What time did you arrive home?"

"I . . . I don't know. It was almost dark."

"Were the doors locked when you came home?"

"Yes. Why are you asking me these things?"

"We have to find out everything we can."

That made sense, Terri supposed. Still, it seemed these were the sorts of things a suspect would be asked. She tried to reason the matter out, but her brain seemed incapable of any analytical thought. She felt sedated, and yet she was unable to recall having taken anything. She was just floating along, an unwilling participant in the laser movie. Drifting down from upstairs came the sound of a vacuum. Was someone cleaning her house for her?

Stark and the other men went upstairs. Again she heard voices but not the words. A flash reflected off the wall near the landing. Were they taking pictures? Time passed. Finally the man with the silver case came downstairs, followed by Stark and the other man.

"I'd like to have that blouse you're wearing," Stark said to her. "Do you need some help getting somewhere that you can change it? I can have a policewoman help you if you like."

A part of her mind noted that he hadn't really asked her for the blouse, that it had been more like an order. Although Terri had no idea why he wanted it, she was too confused to attempt discussing the matter with him. It was easier just to comply.

"I don't need any help," she said, rising.

Though wobbly, she managed to make her way to the laundry room, which was off the kitchen. There was a basket of things there that hadn't been washed yet. She slipped off her blouse, put on a dirty one. She couldn't have faced going upstairs—even if she was up to the climb, which was questionable. Returning to the living room, Terri handed the garment to Stark.

"Thank you," he said. "We're about done here for the moment. Do you need medical attention for the injuries you got when you fell?"

"No. They're not that bad." Suddenly feeling too weak to stand, she sat down on the couch.

"Do you want us to notify anyone—you know, somebody who could stay with you?"

Terri shook her head. She didn't want people around right now. She just wanted the movie to end.

When the police left, Terri sat for a long time, staring at the living room carpet, not thinking about anything, as if she and the carpet were the only two things in the world. Finally, reality settled in, and it was stark and cold and excruciating.

She screamed. A long piercing scream that became a wail and finally deteriorated into sobs. Tears rolled down her cheeks. Her body shook.

More than two hours passed before she was able to pull herself together enough to call her daughter.

Detective Sergeant Simon P. Stark sat at his desk in the investigation division's office. The room was spacious, well lighted, carpeted. The beige metal desks at which the detectives sat were new.

In front of Stark was the *Atlanta Constitution*. The story about the murder of Stanley Ferguson was on the front page, below the fold. Murders in the suburbs weren't always accorded that much attention. But Ferguson was a prominent citizen. He owned one of the biggest furniture stores in the country. It was always being advertised on TV. Occasionally Ferguson even appeared in his own commercials. Like Victor Kiam or Lee Iacocca. The newspaper story didn't say much, because there hadn't been much for Stark to tell the reporter. Just what Terri Ferguson had told him. And she was a suspect. At the moment, the only suspect.

Most murders were committed by someone known by and usually close to the victim. A friend or lover or husband or wife or brother or sister or son or daughter or parent. Great world we live in, he thought. Best way to avoid being murdered is to never get close to anyone.

But that reminded him of his recent and rather bitter divorce, which was something he particularly wanted to avoid thinking about. Looking up he saw Pat Beauchamp walking toward him. Beauchamp was the detective who'd accompanied him to the Ferguson house last night. They were partners; they'd work the case together.

Beauchamp pulled over a chair. "Anything new on the ten-fifty-one last night?"

"I'm waiting for the lab and coroner's reports."

"Think there'll be gunpowder traces on that blouse you got from her?"

"Let's just say I wouldn't be surprised."

"Too bad she'd washed her hands."

"It's surprising how many guilty people remember to wash their hands, then forget to change their clothes. Too many things to think about, I guess."

Beauchamp fingered his moustache. He was on the plump side and had the blackest eyes Stark had ever seen, which Beauchamp attributed to being part Indian—an eighth or a sixteenth or something like that. His dark hair was thick and curly. He was one of those people whose beard was so coarse that it began to show an hour or two after he'd shaved.

"Nothing was taken, no sign of forced entry," Stark said. "Whoever killed Ferguson was only interested in killing Ferguson."

"If it was her, what do you figure she did with the gun?"

"Buried it in the garden, put it in a secret hiding place, who knows? She probably had time to throw it in the Chattahoochee."

"You believe her story about falling out in the backyard?"

"I don't know. She fell all right, but under what circumstances? Was it in the backyard, like she says, or somewhere else? She also had a cut lip. Maybe she was punched, knocked down."

"You figure her old man was beating on her? Good, respectable, high-class people like them?" Beauchamp was being facetious, of course. People in those five- and six-hundred-thousand-dollar houses were as mean to each other as people living anywhere else.

"I asked the coroner to check Ferguson's hands, see if they looked like he'd hit anybody lately." He sighed. "Well, we can either sit here and shoot the breeze while we wait to hear from the lab and the coroner, or we can go out and do some policework while we're waiting. What would you suggest?"

"You're the sergeant. I'm just a lowly detective second. I just follow orders."

"Come on," Stark said, rising.

"Where we going?"

"Let's go talk to the Ferguson's neighbors, that guy who gives Mrs. Ferguson her ceramics lessons, and the good folks at Ferguson's Furniture City. If we haven't heard from the coroner and the lab by then, we'll pay them a visit, try to look real impatient."

"Maybe we'll run into somebody named Connie," Beauchamp said. "Maybe she'll be in her twenties, a looker, somebody who likes rich middle-age guys."

"If there really is a Connie," Stark replied.

Michelle appeared in the crowd of passengers emerging from the jetway, spotted Terri at the same time Terri spotted her, and the two women rushed into each other's arms. They were both crying; neither tried to speak.

After they'd released each other and begun making their way to the baggage pickup area, Michelle said, "God, Mom, it's awful. Just awful."

Terri squeezed her daughter's arm. She was the parent; it was her job to find the strength for both of them. But she was uncertain whether she was capable of it. Terri was functioning for the moment, and that was all she could say. There was a lot of coping ahead of her, a lot of anguish.

Suddenly Terri felt guilty. All of her sorrow was directed at herself. She was absorbed with *her* loss, *her* suffering, *her* loneliness. It was Stanley who had lost the most. A tear trickled down her cheek. Terri knew she had to end this line of thought before she stopped right in the middle of Hartsfield International Airport and started bawling.

And then she realized that she had to concentrate on herself, no matter how selfish it seemed, because that was the only way she could hold herself together.

"How was the flight from Albuquerque?" she asked. Michelle was attending the University of New Mexico, majoring in journalism.

"We got stacked up over Dallas for a while, and I only had ten minutes to change planes, but as you can see I made it."

They both fell silent then. Small talk seemed so out of place in these circumstances. How could you talk about trivial things when your husband, your father, had been murdered? Again Terri's vision blurred with tears. She fought them back.

Michelle glanced at her. The younger woman's eyes were red and had bags under them. She had Terri's freckles and reddish-brown hair, which she wore short, businesslike, the way a no-nonsense reporter might. Shorter than her mother, she was slightly fuller figured and had a ready smile, intelligent, friendly eyes.

Michelle's luggage never arrived at the baggage pickup area. The airline said that when passengers had to rush to change flights, their bags often didn't make the connection. They'd be along sometime today. The airline would phone.

As they drove away from Hartsfield in Terri's station wagon, Michelle said, "Are you going to have a funeral?"

The question surprised her. "Of course, there's going to be a funeral. Why wouldn't there be?"

"I've heard that a lot of people are opting not to these days. There's a lot of resistance to the huge prices the funeral homes charge, so they'll cremate the . . . the remains and have a memorial service—or nothing at all."

Terri hadn't even thought about funeral arrangements. There were going to be all sorts of things to do, things she hadn't even considered yet. That was good, Terri supposed, for it would keep her mind occupied. All she had to do was plod along, keep functioning. Maybe time would lessen the horror of it all.

No amount of time could bring back Stanley. Terri's eyes filled with tears and she wished she hadn't thought that. She couldn't cope with thoughts like that.

"Your father was an important member of the community," Terri said. "He has to have a funeral, a full funeral. It would be expected."

Michelle looked out the window, watched the gas stations and other small businesses they were passing. After a while she said, "Have you heard anything from the police? Do they have any idea who . . ."

Terri shook her head. "I haven't heard anything."

They drove in silence for a few moments; then Terri said, "Does the name Connie mean anything to you?"

Michelle looked puzzled. "Connie?"

"Does the name mean anything, anything at all?"

"Well, there's a Connie Aragon in the room across from mine in the dorm. Why?"

Terri told her. "It was the last thing he said. He said it twice, and then . . ."

Despite her efforts to hold them back, tears rolled down Terri's cheeks. She had to pull the car into the lot of a small shopping center and let the tears come. Michelle was crying, too.

Sarah Jenkins was a plump gray-haired woman with sky blue eyes. Sitting on a couch in her surgically antiseptic living room, she gestured with her hands as she talked. Stark and Beauchamp sat in matching upholstered chairs.

"She called to ask whether I knew where Stanley was," she said. "I think she might have been calling all the neighbors, but I'm not sure."

"What exactly did she say?" Stark said.

Sarah Jenkins frowned, making a small circling gesture with her hand. "She just wanted to know if he might be over here. She said his car was there but he wasn't, so she must have figured that he had to be somewhere in the neighborhood."

"She sound worried, or was she just asking casually?"

"She wasn't frantic or anything like that, but I'd say she was . . . well, concerned."

"Was he in the habit of visiting with people in the neighborhood?" Beauchamp asked.

"Well, no, not really. We'd speak to each other if we were outside working on the flower beds or something like that, but we didn't get together for dinner or bridge or anything. I don't think many of the neighbors do, really. It's not that kind of a neighborhood. We all have our own social lives, and they don't overlap too much."

Stark asked, "Then why would Mrs. Ferguson think her husband might be here?"

"I . . . Well, there's really no way for me to know." She held her hands in front of her, turning them palms up. "Like I said before, his car was there but he wasn't. How far could he have walked?"

"Fergusons good neighbors?" Stark asked.

"They're fine. All the neighbors are fine. This simply isn't the sort of neighborhood where you'd find objectionable people."

"Did they get along, the Fergusons?"

She made the same palm-up gesture, using just one hand this time. "People here don't make a public display of their private affairs. If they had problems, they dealt with them discreetly."

Stark checked the notes he'd been scribbling into a small spiral notebook. "What time did Mrs. Ferguson call you to ask if you knew where her husband was?"

"I think it must have been—oh, dear, let me see. I guess it was between six-thirty and seven."

"Did you hear any sounds that might have been gunshots?"

"No."

"Do you know if the Fergusons owned any guns?"

"No. I'd have no idea."

"Do the Fergusons have any friends named Connie?"

She frowned, gave her right hand an irritated flip. "As I told you, we really don't know their friends."

Beauchamp said, "Do you know of anyone named Connie who's connected in any way with the Fergusons? Someone who does cleaning for the both of you maybe. Or yard work."

"No. I'm sorry."

Stark glanced at Beauchamp, who gave him a nod indicating that he had nothing further to ask. "I guess that's all we have," Stark said, closing his notebook.

"It's perfectly awful, " Sarah Jenkins said, "something like this happening in this neighborhood. Things like this just don't happen here."

"Not very nice when it happens anywhere else either," Beauchamp said.

"No, of course not," she said. "I certainly hope you catch the person who did it." She looked at them expectantly, as if she hoped they might tell her who the guilty person was.

The officers thanked her and left. As they were walking toward the house across the street, Stark said, "What do you make of her phoning to ask if her husband was there?"

"What's to think? His car was there. She figured he had to be somewhere within walking distance."

"Would you call a neighbor if you were looking for your wife and she never went over to the neighbor's house?"

Beauchamp thought about it a moment. "I might."

"You know what I see when I close my eyes and think about it? I see Mrs. Jenkins and however many other neighbors Mrs. Ferguson might have phoned sitting on the witness stand, telling how Mrs. F. called, looking for her husband, sounding all worried."

"That's what you think, or are you just tossing out ideas?"

"Let's just say it's interesting. No murder weapon, her hands washed because she fell, the phone call to the neighbor, and a little tidbit to get our interest, give us something to think about. Connie. Her husband's dying words—or word in this case. Except we've only got her word that he said it."

"We don't have a motive," Beauchamp pointed out.

"Not yet. But then we haven't started looking very hard for one, either."

They stepped onto the brick walk leading to a sprawling white home with wrought iron bars over the windows. Maybe Sarah Jenkins thought bad things didn't happen in this neighborhood, but her neighbors weren't taking any chances.

SEVEN

"This is what I use as an office these days," Ward Greenfield said. He motioned for Captain Cantrell to sit down.

The office was one of the bedrooms in a very small three-bedroom house. It contained a scarred wooden desk that reminded Cantrell of his own back in the Chickasaw County Courthouse, a telephone, and a row of file cabinets along one wall. On another wall was a calendar from the First National Bank of Gainesville. It displayed the page for March. This was April.

"I'm what you'd call semiretired, I guess," Greenfield said. "I do a little work every now and then, when I've got too many unpaid bills mainly. Anyway, that's why I keep my name in the Yellow Pages, which I imagine is what enabled you to find me." He was about seventy, tall and thin, with white hair and a red nose that most likely got its color from years of serious drinking.

"I'm surprised you still have files from twenty years ago," Cantrell said. "With the filing system in my department, you're lucky if you can find the paperwork from last month."

Greenfield chuckled. "Maybe it was just a silly notion, but I always imagined that maybe someday somebody would come all the way to Florida from someplace exotic and ask me about some case from twenty or thirty years ago. Maybe that's why, instead of throwing anything away, I just keep buying file cabinets.'' He smiled, showing teeth much too perfect to be the ones God had given him.

"I've heard Chickasaw County called a lot of things," Cantrell said, "but never exotic."

Greenfield shrugged. "After you phoned, I got to looking through the Connie Stewart file, and it started to come back to me. She was a blond girl, no raving beauty but pretty in her own way, I suppose. She was going wild—I guess that's the delicate way to put it. I had the impression that there was more to it than her acting crazy because she was young and away from home. It seemed like she had something eating at her, that she was troubled deep down inside."

"Family pressure?"

"Don't know. I'm not a shrink, just an observer."

"Can I see the file?"

"Stewart say it would be okay?"

"He didn't say it wouldn't."

Greenfield thought that over a moment, then shrugged and pushed a file folder toward Cantrell. In it were copies of the reports Greenfield had sent to Jonathan Stewart. The information in them was pretty much what Stewart had indicated. Also in the folder were Greenfield's field notes—dates, times, places, and observations recorded as the private detective checked up on Connie Stewart. She'd spent a lot of time at the apartment of a guy named David Young.

"Who's this David Young?" Cantrell asked.

"I never could quite get a handle on their relationship. It seemed like when she had no place else to go she'd stay there. That might not be right at all, but it was the way it seemed."

Cantrell spotted an entry in Greenfield's notes indicating that Young had taken Connie to the hospital emergency room one evening. The private detective had followed them. He'd written, *Left hand apparently bandaged. SA?* The last was circled.

"What's this about?" the captain asked, showing the circled letters to Greenfield.

"That's my shorthand for suicide attempt."

"Why didn't you mention it in your report to Jonathan Stewart?"

"Because it was just a guess, a hunch if you will. The hospital won't tell you anything because of the rules of confidentiality. And I couldn't ask Connie or David Young because I wasn't supposed to let her find out I was checking up on her. All I could say for a fact was that she'd gone to the emergency room, that I thought her hand was bandaged near the wrist, and that she went home a while later, so the injury couldn't have been too serious. Also, the hospital didn't notify the police, which they're supposed to do in the case of anything suspicious."

"How strict are they about reporting stuff like that?"

"I think it would be safe to say that they've been known to be a bit lax." He shrugged. "Still, it was nothing I could report to her father."

"What kind of a relationship did she have with the men she associated with? Besides spending most of the time with her clothes off."

"I don't really know."

"Were the men violent? Was she?"

"Again, I don't know. Or if I did, I don't remember after all this time. She seemed to be looking for something, and when she didn't find it, she looked even harder. It never occurred to her that she might be looking in the wrong place. But now I'm starting to sound like a shrink. And like I told you, that's an area where I'm not qualified."

"You don't by any chance know where she is now, do you?" Cantrell asked

"Nope. I filed my report, Stewart quit paying me, and that was the end of my interest in Connie Stewart."

"Is anybody still around who'd remember her?"

"David Young is."

"Here in Gainesville?"

"Yup. You can find him at St. Anthony's Church. He's a priest."

"Can I borrow your phone book?"

Greenfield handed it to him.

Father David Young lived in a frame house behind the church. He was turning over the soil in a large vegetable garden when Cantrell arrived.

"You mind if I keep working while we talk?" the priest asked. "I should have done this weeks ago, and if I don't finish it today it'll probably be days before I get around to it again. I'm going to plant tomatoes along this edge. Home-grown are so much better than store-bought tomatoes, don't you think?"

Cantrell said he agreed. The priest was about forty, balding, and had a potbelly. He was working up a pretty good sweat as he broke up the soil with his digging fork.

"I remember Connie Stewart," he said. "Even after all this time."

"Apparently she had a way of making an impression on people," Cantrell noted.

Father Young glanced at him, then returned to his gardening. "How much do you know about her?"

"I know that she was from a wealthy family in Nashville. And I know that the ROTC guys at the university referred to her as the duty punchboard."

The priest nodded. "She was probably the most promiscuous girl I've ever met—even taking into account all the exploits I've heard about in the confessional. She was a very insecure girl who desperately wanted to be loved. I think that's what she was doing, seeking love the only way she knew how."

"Wasn't her behavior a little . . . well, extreme?"

"It was, yes, because it was so misdirected. But it's not all that unusual for girls who feel unloved to become promiscuous. It happens more often than you'd think with girls who aren't pretty, girls who don't ordinarily attract boys. They discover that by being free and easy they can get the attention they want so badly. They go from being shunned to being in demand."

"I've seen a picture of Connie. She wasn't Bo Derek or Farrah Fawcett, but she wasn't going to scare anyone away either."

"Her situation was a little different than the one I described. She wasn't just seeking attention. She wanted love. She craved it."

"And she didn't find it."

"No."

"Do you have any idea what caused her to feel this way, to want love so badly?"

Father Young leaned on his digging fork. "I wasn't one of her . . . well, what I'm trying to say is that we never had sex together. I could have, of course. I wasn't studying for the priesthood then. I hadn't made any commitments to the Church yet. But we didn't have that kind of a relationship. I liked her, and I guess you'd say I wanted to help her. Maybe I had the instincts of a clergyman even before I decided to become one.

"In any case, I let her come and stay with me when she needed somewhere to go—somewhere safe, someplace where nothing was expected. We talked a little, but she didn't let too much out. She kept things to herself. What you saw was what she wanted you to see, and what was on the inside was well guarded. You didn't know things about Connie; you sensed them."

"And what did you sense about her?"

"That she was in a lot of pain. That her family had been cold and fairly rigid. That she had a real bad need burning inside her."

"She ever attempt suicide?"

The priest studied him a moment, then said, "She slit her wrists once while she was staying with me. I took her to the hospital, but the damage was minor. I wouldn't be surprised if she made other attempts, but I'd have no way of knowing. As I say, she wouldn't tell me much."

"How did you meet her?"

"I had a party at my place. You know how it is in college; everybody's always having parties. She came to the party with a guy I knew, and we talked. About a month later she showed up one evening and asked if she could stay. I guess she knew somehow that there'd be no obligations, that she could get some sleep, leave in the morning if she wanted, stay longer if she wanted. And that's how it went. She'd show up from time to time, get away from . . . from the life she was leading. My place was a sanctuary, a place she could escape to every now and then."

"Do you know where she is now?"

The priest was still leaning on the fork. Although he was looking at the soil he'd turned, his gaze seemed distant. "I transferred from the university to a seminary near Miami. I hadn't seen her for a couple of months when I left. I looked for her, but no one seemed to know where she was. I never saw her again."

"Do you know anyone who might know where she is now?"

"No. I'm sorry."

Cantrell used the priest's phone to call for a cab. Father Young continued digging in his garden while Cantrell waited for the taxi.

"Something just occurred to me," the priest said. He stopped digging. "I think Connie had been really hung up on a guy. It broke up for some reason, I think. I don't know too much about it because she wouldn't talk about it. I don't recall the guy's name, but on one of those rare occasions when she let something out, she referred to him as Mr. Heartache. If she'd used his name, I'm sure I'd never have remembered it. But Mr. Heartache was so mysterious that it stuck in my mind."

On the way to the airport, Cantrell decided that his search for Connie Stewart had just died from lack of information. He had learned a lot about her. And had no idea where she was.

* * *

On Monday afternoon Sergeant Simon P. Stark sat at his desk in the Meadowview police station, reviewing the coroner's report on Stanley Ferguson. Shot twice with a .25 caliber weapon, DOA Meadowview General. Time of death, approximately seven-thirty in the evening, but then Stark already knew when Ferguson died, since the paramedics had been there at the time. More significant was the time he was shot. The coroner speculated five-thirty—give or take twenty minutes. No indications of a struggle, nothing to suggest that he was responsible for his wife's split lip.

The time Ferguson was shot was the most important information in the report. Five-thirty. Half an hour after the ceramics teacher said Terri Ferguson left his house, which was a fifteen-minute drive from the Ferguson place. A time at which Terri Ferguson claimed she was driving in the country. But no one saw her. No one could verify that.

Stark closed the coroner's report and opened the lab report. No powder burns on Terri Ferguson's blouse. Things vacuumed from the house included a button, all sorts of fibers, a price tag, a variety of hairs, a pin. The list went on and on. A lot of it was stuff that might be useful if you had a suspect to compare it with, but by itself it was damn near worthless. There were more hairs than could have come from the Fergusons. One was blond; another was red-brown and had apparently come from a wig. The hairs could have come from someone who was in the house the day of the murder or weeks ago. And they could belong to a friend, a repairman, a lover, anyone. They hardly proved the presence of a murderer in the house.

And the absence of gunpowder on Mrs. Ferguson's blouse could be taken two ways. As an indication that she hadn't fired a gun. Or as a demonstration of how clever she was. Wouldn't someone smart enough to get rid of the gun, to wash her hands and have an excuse for having done so, to call the neighbors and ask if they'd seen her husband, wouldn't she also be smart enough to change her blouse?

The employees at Ferguson's Furniture City had said

that as far as they knew Stanley Ferguson had no enemies. They hadn't known of any problems between Ferguson and his wife. Nor had anyone been fired recently. The only Connie working there was a man. Connie was his nickname. His real name was Timothy Connors, and he drove a delivery truck. He said he'd been at his brother's house, along with his wife and two kids on Saturday afternoon. The brother's wife confirmed that Connie had spent the afternoon and part of the evening at her place. He'd left about seven-thirty.

There were a number of things Stark needed to find out. What did Terri Ferguson stand to gain from her husband's death? Did she have a lover? Did he? There were a lot of reasons for one spouse to murder the other. They did it for money, for love (of someone else), and because one party or the other got mad as hell, lost control, had a weapon handy. Every American has the right to own a gun, right? Might come in real handy if you get the urge to blow someone away.

"Hey, Stark," Hank Cosgrove said. He was a chunky guy with a crewcut, who sat in the desk behind Stark's. He was holding up the receiver of his phone. "You'd better take this. Line four."

Stark punched the appropriate button. "This is Sergeant Stark. Can I help you?"

"It's about the murder on Lyndale Avenue. I was driving in that block on Saturday, and I saw somebody with a gun." The voice belonged to a young woman. She said, "I didn't really think it was important at the time. I mean it's not against the law to carry a gun or anything." She paused. "I would have called sooner, but I didn't know there'd been a murder. I was so busy typing that I didn't see the news or read the paper or anything—oh, I'd better explain that. You see, I'm typing—"

"Before we go any further, let me get your name and address," Stark said.

"Mary Ann McCabe. I live at 1607 Danbury, in Rosemont."

"What time was this when you saw the person with the gun?"

"About a quarter of six. I was going to pick up some typing. I mean I was going to do the typing. Uh, I mean there's this woman in my church who's writing a book, and she lives on Lyndale, and I'm typing for her."

"What did the person with the gun look like?"

"Uh, well, her hair was brown. But not a real dark brown. It had some red in it. She was . . . well . . ." The woman faltered.

"A woman. How old was she?" Stark prompted.

"Oh, I guess about thirty-five or forty."

"How about her build?"

"She was slender. Very slender."

"Tall, short, what?"

"Average, I guess."

"What was she wearing?"

"A white dress with blue flowers on it. A summer dress."

"Ma'am, I think we'd better get a statement from you. Would it be more convenient for you to come down here or for us to come out to your place?"

"Well, I guess you could come here—I have a little one, so that might be easier. Right now?"

"If you wouldn't mind."

"That was the funeral home," Terri said, setting the phone down beside the chair. She and Michelle were in the den, watching television, the great mind-deadener. That was what they needed right now, something to deaden their minds, keep them from thinking.

"The . . ." Terri searched for a word other than morgue. Or coroner. Finally, she said, "The authorities have released Daddy's body. The funeral will be tomorrow morning at ten."

Michelle nodded. Her face was puffy and red. Her cheeks were wet with fresh tears. Terri shifted her gaze back to the TV set. She didn't want to cry anymore. It left her feeling empty and weak and miserable.

Earlier she and Michelle had gone by the funeral home. Never having arranged for a funeral before, Terri had simply let the man at the mortuary lead her along, telling her what she needed, what she had to do. Although Michelle urged her to shop around, compare prices, consider whether certain things were really necessary, Terri had lacked the strength to do so. And the one time she did question him—about the casket—the funeral home man had given her a scalding look that seemed to imply she really didn't care about Stanley, that she was being selfish. Terri had withered under that look. The cost, which included the cemetery plot and headstone, was enormous. But it was a one-time expense and she could afford it. She'd send Stanley off right.

The doorbell rang. Getting up to answer it, Terri tried to figure out who could be calling. Friends had been in and out all day, offering sympathy and support. Marlene had brought a ham. Richard Altman, her ceramics teacher, had brought a cake he'd made himself. Neighbors had brought still other things. The kitchen table was covered with cakes and pies; the refrigerator was overflowing. In a way it seemed like a strange custom. Everyone brought you food at a time when you were almost certain to be too miserable to eat. She opened the door and found herself looking at Sergeant Stark and another policeman. When the three of them were standing in Terri's living room, Stark handed her a paper.

"This is a warrant to search the premises for a lightweight white dress with blue flowers on it. Do you own such a dress?"

She stared at the police officer, confused. "What? I don't understand. You want a dress?"

"Do you own such a dress?" Stark asked again.

"Yes. It's upstairs. In the closet."

"Would you mind showing us?"

"No, of course not."

Terri and the two police officers went upstairs. She entered the bedroom reluctantly. Unwilling to sleep in the room in which Stanley had been murdered, she had moved into one of the guest rooms. Averting her eyes from the bathroom, she opened the big walk-in closet and began looking for the dress. She remembered seeing it a couple of weeks ago when she'd moved her warm weather things to the front of the closet. But it wasn't here now.

She went through the clothes again, then moved to the rear of the closet and checked her winter things. The dress simply wasn't there.

"I don't know what happened to it," she told the detectives. "It should be here." She was getting worried. She had no idea what this was about.

Stark moved past her and conducted his own search of the closet. "When did you last wear it?" he asked.

"Not since last summer. What's so important about this dress that you'd get a search warrant for it?"

"The warrant's routine," Stark said.

Terri doubted that. What was happening here? Did the police suspect her of. . . . No, she thought. They can't. They just can't. Not that. Stark was studying her, his expression revealing nothing.

"I saw the dress a couple of weeks ago," she said. "I don't know what happened to it. It should be here somewhere. It has to be." Her voice seemed high pitched, on the edge of panic. Had the killer taken one of her dresses? But why would he? It made no sense.

"We're going to have to look through the house," Stark said. He nodded to his companion, who left the room, presumably to search elsewhere. Stark began looking through the dresser.

"Why didn't you do that last night?" she asked.

"We did. But we weren't looking for a dress then."

Terri started to leave the room. If he was going to look, he was going to look; there was no need for her to watch.

"I'm sorry," Stark said. "But I'll have to ask you to remain within my sight."

"I . . ." She'd planned to say something indignant, but the words just weren't there. She stared at the detective.

"It's the way it's done," he said. "I can't come in with a warrant to search for a specific thing, then give somebody a chance to get rid of it."

"Get rid of it? Do you really think I'd—"

"It's the way it's done," he repeated. "It's police procedure, that's all."

She stayed with Stark as he moved through the house, looking in the laundry hamper, opening closets and cabinets, peering under some things, behind others. When he finished with the second floor and moved downstairs, Michelle hurried to her mother's side.

"Mom, what is all this?"

"They're searching for a dress."

"A dress?"

Terri revealed what little she knew.

"Mom, this is ridiculous. You're the victim. Why are they picking on you?"

Terri waved her hand in a gesture of helplessness. She didn't know. She didn't understand. How could she explain anything?

When Stark had finished searching the house, the other detective came in from outside, shook his head. Apparently he'd been snooping around the yard and hadn't found the dress out there either.

The four of them were standing in the living room when Stark said, "Mrs. Ferguson, I wonder if you'd mind coming down to the station with us."

"What for?" she asked, taken aback.

"I'd like you to appear in a lineup."

"A line . . ." The words trailed off. Terri saw herself standing under bright lights, on display, a criminal by implication. The image went away. Something icy seemed to settle in her stomach.

"Why do you want to put my mom in a lineup?" Michelle demanded.

"Someone matching her description was seen outside

this house with a gun in her hand Saturday," Stark said. "The witness has already identified this house as the one she came from."

For a moment both Terri and her daughter were dumb-struck. Then Terri said, "I don't know who this person saw, but it wasn't me. It very definitely wasn't me."

"That's what we want to find out," Stark said.

Michelle asked, "Is my mom under arrest?"

"We're asking her to come in voluntarily," Stark explained, something in his eyes warning there were other ways it could be done.

"I think you should call a lawyer," Michelle said.

Terri looked at her, looked at Stark. "I've got nothing to hide. I'll do what you ask, Sergeant."

"Mom!" Michelle protested.

"Call Bruce Gossetter," Terri said. "He's in the book. He's the attorney your father uses." She winced, knowing she should have made it past tense. "Tell him what's happening and ask him to meet us at the police station." To Stark she said, "I'll go to the station with you, but I won't appear in any lineup until I see my attorney."

"Give me the keys to your car," Michelle said. "As soon as I get you a lawyer, I'm coming down to the police station."

Getting her purse, Terri gave her daughter the keys.

EIGHT

Connie Stewart lay on the bed in her motel room, remembering. It was something she did a lot, remembering. Whenever her mind relaxed, images came to her, vivid as motion pictures, except the screen was somewhere in her head. She wondered whether it was like this for everyone, having a head full of memories constantly struggling to get out.

At the moment, she was recalling an incident that occurred when she was a teenager. She'd been secretly in love with Lee Warner, a tall good-looking boy with a nice smile and a quick mind. He'd stop her in the hall, make casual conversation, ask how her parents were, and her sister Cindy. Her hope—and it was the most important thing in her life at that particular moment—was that Lee would ask her to the prom.

In the private school she attended, which clung to some Old South traditions, a boy was expected to go to the girl's home and ask her father's permission to escort her to the dance. Connie didn't know whether it had truly worked that way in the old days, but none of the kids seemed to mind it. The formality of it all made them feel special, set them apart from the kids in other schools.

It was Saturday. Looking out the second story window

of her bedroom, she saw Lee Warner walking toward the front door of their house. She gasped, then squealed, spinning around the room with her arms out. Connie had dreamed about this happening. She'd sat in class, filling page after page in her notebook with Lee's name. Once, she'd even dared to try "Connie Jane Warner" and "Mrs. Connie Warner," along with other variations. Then, knowing how embarrassed she'd be if someone saw the page, she'd ripped it from her notebook and torn it into tiny pieces.

Now her dream had come true. Lee was downstairs, asking her father's permission to take her to the prom. Her father would have taken him into the library. Suddenly, Connie wanted desperately to hear what her father and Lee were saying.

She slipped out of her room, moved along the hallway to the stairs, started down. She heard voices, her father's, Lee's, muffled by the closed library doors. If someone saw her, she'd die of embarrassment. But she continued down the stairs.

Suddenly the library door opened, and Connie rushed back to her room, gently closing the door. A few moments later, she saw Lee walking away from the house. She didn't know how these things worked. If Lee was leaving, then presumably her father would be the one to notify her of what had transpired. She sat on her bed, picked up a book, tried to look casual. She was so excited she felt as if she were twitching all over.

Connie heard footsteps in the hall. They passed by her door. The house creaked, made other noises you usually only noticed at night. Minutes passed. Why hadn't her father come to tell her? She waited, her rapture beginning to fade, vague anxieties creeping in. Finally the door to her room burst open, but it wasn't her father who rushed in; it was her sister.

"Guess what!" Cindy exclaimed.

Connie stared at her, confused. Something somewhere

in her mind had already guessed what Cindy would say, but Connie refused to hear it. No, not that. Not true.

"Lee Warner just asked Daddy if he could take me to the prom," Cindy proclaimed excitedly. "And he's a *senior*. I didn't even know he *liked* me." And Cindy babbled on and on.

And Connie wondered whether her sister was telling her this to hurt her. But then how could she have known? Connie had told no one of her feelings about Lee Warner.

When her sister tired of telling Connie all about it, she hurried from the room, presumably to call her girlfriend Joanie and tell her the news. Connie lay on her bed, the joy jerked from her the way you'd yank a blanket off of someone who was asleep. She began to tremble, and then she cried.

And she wondered whether she could ever love anyone again. Whether she could ever trust anyone enough. Whether she could risk the hurt.

"I wish I was dead," Connie sobbed, and she wasn't just venting bitterness. She truly wished she could say some magic word, press some button, and simply stop living.

The memory faded away. Connie lay on the motel bed, her face wet with tears, uncertain whether she was crying for the miserable teenage girl of her memory or for the thirty-eight-year-old woman who had shot and killed a man yesterday.

Her teenage self had been right. To love someone was to risk too much pain, too much cruelty. But then she'd already known that. It was why she'd taken the gun and the wig and the makeup with her to the Ferguson house.

Burying her head in the pillow, she cried for the love she could never have.

Stark watched as Mary Ann McCabe peered through the one-way glass, studying the six women lined up in front of her. She was tall and thin with straw-colored hair cut short, green eyes, pale skin, and she didn't use any makeup. Stark thought she looked like a country girl, someone originally from Baxley or Calhoun or Homeville or some other rural place.

"Gee," Mary Ann said, frowning, her eyes moving from woman to woman.

Also watching her were Stark's partner Pat Beauchamp and Bruce Gossetter, Terri Ferguson's lawyer. No one spoke. It was Mary Ann McCabe's show; nobody wanted to say anything that could be construed as prompting her. The woman in the lineup included secretaries from the records division, a couple of police officers, and a computer programmer. And, of course, third from the left, Terri Ferguson, who stared vacantly at her unseen watchers.

Bruce Gossetter folded his arms, wrinkled his brow. Stark figured Gossetter wasn't the sort of attorney who was used to working on the weekends or visiting police stations. His clients were businesspeople, corporations, the upper crust. He wasn't a criminal lawyer. He wasn't used to associating with lowlifes. You could tell by the expensive pin-striped blue suit, the carefully styled brown hair, the superior look. And by the way he remained aloof from all this, as if cops and the messy stuff they had to deal with were beneath his dignity.

"Gee," Mary Ann said again.

"Take your time," Stark said.

The way he figured it, Terri Ferguson must have panicked, made a mistake. She'd been careful about everything else, kept her cool. Then maybe the shock of what she'd done had made her lose control for a moment, run into the street with the gun in her hand. He'd seen it happen before. Sometimes a person would forget all the planning and become overwhelmed with the need to get away, escape. Like the robber who'd dashed out of the bank, leaving the bag containing the money on the counter. It was a powerful thing, the need to get away.

Stark didn't like the way Mary Ann McCabe was hesitating. If she'd pick out Terri Ferguson, be positive about it, he'd have Mrs. Ferguson at the booking desk, being photographed and printed. She'd spend the night in jail,

97

then go before a judge in the morning to see whether bond would be set. For her, an upper-class woman with no record, bond would be granted, the only question being how much. No matter. She'd be charged with murder. Maybe she'd confess, make it easy on everybody.

Stark fixed his eyes on Mary Ann, willing her to make a positive identification.

"Her," Mary Ann said, pointing.

"Which number?" Stark asked.

"Three. Number three."

"That's the woman you saw yesterday on Lyndale Avenue, with a gun in her hand?"

"I . . . I think so."

Shit, Stark thought. "Can you say positively that this is the woman you saw?"

She studied Terri Ferguson. "I'm pretty sure it's her."

Gossetter was watching him closely. Stark said, "Are you saying that this is the woman you saw, or that she merely resembles that woman?"

"I think it's her."

Stark sighed. "You're not sure."

"No. Not absolutely." She looked at Terri Ferguson again. "But it might be her."

After Beauchamp had taken Mary Ann McCabe from the viewing room, Gossetter said, "I presume Mrs. Ferguson is free to go."

Stark nodded. She was free for now. But he'd be seeing Terri Ferguson again. It was one of those things you could count on.

The minister said Stanley Ferguson was a good man, a credit to his community, so successful he'd been named Georgia Businessman of the Year. Loyal husband. Loving father. Although these things were true, Terri saw the phoniness in the ceremony. The minister would have said many of the same things if Stanley had been a jerk, a wife beater, a child molester; it wouldn't have mattered.

But then she was in her bitter time now, feeling betrayed

by life. Her husband was about to be buried, and the police thought she did it. It was all so unfair. Neither she nor Stanley had harmed anyone. They'd had a good, happy life. Suddenly Stanley was dead, and she was left behind to suffer. Why? The word bounced around in her head, getting mixed up with the words being spoken by the preacher. Why, why, why, why?

Terri and Michelle sat in the first pew. Maybe fifteen feet away from them was the casket, its lid raised. Stanley lay within, looking white and pasty and lifeless. Supposedly, he looked content, at peace, life's struggle behind him. Off to a better world. One of the people from the furniture store—a blond woman—had peered into the casket and said, "He looks so natural." Terri had wanted to slug her. The natural Stanley had been full of vitality, happy, joking, hard working. The one in the casket looked pale and still and very dead.

A tear trickled down Terri's cheek, clung to her chin a moment, then dropped, making a soft plop when it landed in her lap. Another tear followed it. Terri knew she had to stop being so bitter. It was a form of self-pity, she knew that. And it was making her misery even more unbearable. She had to put the bitterness behind her if she was ever going to recover.

In addition to the blond woman, there were many others from the furniture store here. Although some of their faces were familiar, Terri couldn't recall their names. The business had been Stanley's affair; she'd stayed away from it. Bruce Gossetter, her lawyer, was here. So was Richard Altman, the ceramics teacher. And Marlene. And Sergeant Stark, although he wasn't here to pay his respects. There were many faces Terri had never seen before. Members of the business community, she supposed. Stanley had been important in Meadowview.

Missing was family, all the children and brothers and sisters and aunts and all the rest. Neither she nor Stanley had any family. She was an only child whose parents were dead. Stanley's father was dead, his mother in a nursing home, and his only sibling was a sister who was doing missionary work in Africa. Terri had attempted to notify her, but she was in an isolated area, and it could be days before she received the message.

Terri noticed that the minister's face had a blue-red color to it because the light coming through one of the big stained-glass windows was falling directly on the pulpit. The church was new and expensive and enormous.

When the minister had spoken the necessary words and the required prayers had been prayed, the scene moved to the cemetery, the hearse followed by a line of cars with their headlights burning, Terri and Michelle riding in a big black limousine. Bruce Gossetter accompanied them.

"After we're done at the cemetery, I've got some things we need to talk about," the attorney said. "Would you mind if I dropped by the house this afternoon?"

Terri told him that would be fine.

By the time they reached the cemetery, Terri had retreated into herself, the things around her once more seeming movielike, unreal. As she stood over the grave, watching the coffin slowly descend, she picked up a handful of dirt, and tossed it into the hole, listening to the pebbles clatter as they fell onto the casket. Michelle did the same. Then they were heading for the limousine again, leaving the cemetery workers to fill in the hole, covering over the three-thousand-dollar box containing the white, dead thing that the silly blond woman had said look so natural.

"Oh, Stanley," she sobbed.

People came to her house—to offer their sympathies, to keep the bereaved company, to do whatever it was you did on the day of someone's funeral. A lot of them brought food, and Terri was beginning to wonder what she was going to do with it all. Although they had good intentions, Terri supposed, she wished they'd all go away. She wanted to be with her daughter so they could talk, start to work things out, decide what they were going to do. All the people, all the confusion and discussion and offerings of sympathy, it was all too much for her to handle.

They did thin out after a while. Then Bruce Gossetter showed up, which the remaining visitors took as a sign that it was time to go. Terri showed the attorney to the den, where Michelle joined them. Sitting in an easy chair, Gossetter laid his briefcase on the floor in front of him and opened it.

"I'm sorry this has to be done now," he said, "but I'm afraid there are some things that simply can't wait."

Terri and Michelle were sitting together on the couch. Terri said, "It's all right. I'm sure there are a lot of things I'll have to do."

"You really won't have to do that much," the lawyer said. "I'll handle the details. But there are things you have to know and some things you'll have to decide." He got some papers from his briefcase, flipped through them. "I have your husband's will, but there really isn't any point in my reading it to you. It's straightforward. He leaves everything to you, and in the event that you die before him, everything goes to Michelle. There are no trick provisions, nothing that could be challenged, as far as I can see."

Putting on a pair of plastic-framed glasses, he studied his papers again, then looked up. "Among the things that become yours is Ferguson's Furniture City, Incorporated. It was jointly owned by you both, and there's a survivor's clause stating that, in the event either owner dies, the survivor becomes the sole owner of everything."

Terri thought Stanley had explained that to her once, but she wasn't sure. She said, "I know nothing about running a business. I wouldn't know where to begin. Can I put it up for sale, just take the money?"

Gossetter frowned. "I'm afraid the only way to tell you this is just to come out and say it. You can definitely sell the business. In fact, you really don't have any choice under the circumstances. But I'm afraid you won't get any money out of it."

"I don't understand. Why not?"

"The value of a business is determined by its assets and liabilities. In the case of Ferguson's Furniture City, the liabilities outweigh the assets."

"But . . ." Terri searched for the right words. She felt weak, unable to think. "I mean, the business is successful. It's growing. It's got all that furniture and the appliances and all the rest of it. It's got that huge building. How could all that not be worth anything?"

"Oh, it is worth something. Something in the millions, no doubt. But the building isn't paid for. A great deal of the merchandise isn't paid for. The delivery trucks aren't paid for. The business is running on borrowed money, and it has a huge payroll."

Terri just shook her head. She didn't understand any of this. How could something so vast, so impressive not be worth any money? It didn't make any sense.

"I know this is hard for you to understand," Gossetter said. "I don't think the business was in any immediate danger of going under, but Stanley was walking a very narrow path; he had to be very careful. Given enough time, all his borrowing probably would have paid off. Then he'd have been in a position to sell the business, if that's what he wanted to do. But now is the wrong time to sell, the worst possible time."

Michelle said, "Couldn't Mom hire somebody to run things for her?"

The attorney considered that. "Maybe, but I doubt it. You see, Stanley was a whiz at this sort of thing. He was stretched wire thin, but he was brilliant, so the lenders went along. Without him, I think they'll force you to sell."

Terri recalled how Stanley had seemed worried the past few months. Now she knew why. He was balancing so much, risking so much. "How much money will there be?"

"From the sale of the company? I doubt you'll see any. I'm sorry."

"We'll be okay," Michelle said. "The house is paid for. We can sell one of the cars. I'm sure you have some money in the bank."

Terri just looked blankly at her. She had no idea how much money they had in the bank except for the household account. It was the only money she ever dealt with. Stanley handled everything else.

Gossetter stared at his papers. "I'm sorry, but the BMW Stanley drove isn't paid for. The payments are about five hundred a month. He took out a new mortgage on the house so he could put the money in the business. But then you already knew about that," he said, looking at Terri, "since you had to sign the papers."

"I . . . I didn't know," Terri said, stunned. "Whenever Stanley asked me to sign something, I just did it. I didn't question him about it. I just left all that sort of thing to him."

"The payments on the mortgage are three thousand a month," the lawyer said.

Michelle said, "Jesus."

"As for money in the bank," the attorney continued, "all Stanley's bank accounts added together—including your joint account—contain about five thousand."

"Five thousand?" Terri couldn't believe it. They'd lived as though they were wealthy. They had everything they wanted. She didn't understand any of this.

"Stanley didn't have any stocks or bonds or any other investments that you could liquidate," Gossetter said. "He put all his money into the business."

"What about life insurance?" Michelle asked. "Daddy always had insurance on everything. He was an insurance fanatic."

"He had a hundred-thousand-dollar policy," the lawyer said. "But he'd borrowed against it. Heavily. There's about eight thousand left in it for you."

"The funeral expenses are almost ten," Terri said weakly.

"What about the station wagon?" Michelle asked, and there was helplessness in her voice, as if she were asking, don't we own *anything*?

Gossetter consulted his papers. "That's paid for," he said.

For a few moments, they were silent; then Terri said, "All of a sudden, I'm not sure I can afford your fee, Mr. Gossetter."

"That's taken care of. The company's paying my fee."

"If you're representing the company," Michelle said slowly, "shouldn't my mom have her own lawyer?"

He shrugged. "Your mom owns the company."

"For all the good it's doing me," Terri said.

Gossetter sighed. "There is one area where we've got a problem, I think. Because I work for the company and did most of your husband's personal legal work as well, I think it could be construed as a conflict of interest for me to represent you in the criminal matter you're involved in. Actually, I'm not really a criminal lawyer anyway. You'd be much better off being represented by someone who specializes in that sort of thing."

"I see," Terri said, because it was the only thing she could think of to say.

"I can give you the name of some good criminal lawyers. And, uh, I strongly suggest you get in touch with one of them. That police officer, Sergeant Stark, considers you his prime suspect. If that woman's identification of you hadn't been iffy, I think he'd have booked you on the spot."

"It wasn't me," Terri said softly. "I don't know who that woman saw, but it wasn't me. I've never fired a gun in my life. I hate them. I'd never even touch one." She stared into the attorney's eyes, willing him to believe her.

Getting up from the easy chair, Gossetter handed Terri a yellow sheet of paper from a legal pad. "These are all good criminal lawyers," he said.

Terri held the paper without looking at it. "How am I supposed to pay them?"

"You'll have to work that out with the attorney you select."

"You can get a public defender, Mom," Michelle said. "It'll be okay."

Terri thought, a public defender? Three days ago the idea would have seemed ludicrous.

"I'm not sure you could qualify for a public defender," Gossetter said. "Not as long as you own two cars and this house and Ferguson's Furniture City."

"But you just told us we can't get any money from those things," Michelle said, hostility creeping into her voice.

"There's a little in the house," the lawyer said. "Enough to cover your legal fees."

"Sell the house?" Terri said. It hadn't occurred to her that she might not be able to live here anymore. Her whole world had been smashed into little pieces. Smithereens. Her life had been smashed to smithereens.

"Can you afford three-thousand-dollar-a-month payments?"

The question hung there. It was ridiculous. It was like asking whether she'd like to buy the Pentagon.

Despite her surroundings—the expensive furniture, the top-quality carpet, the stereo TV, the bar—for the first time in her life Terri had an inkling of what it was like to be poor. She felt like a guest here, a visitor who'd come to admire all the pretty things rich people had, things she'd never be able to afford.

Michelle gripped her hand. Terri was uncertain whether the girl was offering strength or seeking it.

NINE

Connie Stewart sat on the wobbly chair in her motel room. She held her hand out in front of her, watched it shake. No matter how hard she tried, she was unable to hold it steady. Nerves, Connie decided. Nerves. She had awakened a number of times last night, trembling and afraid because of unrecalled nightmares.

Now, sitting here in this cheap motel room, Connie felt confused, uncertain whether she should have killed Stanley, wishing she could take it back, like rewriting a scene in a play. She'd come here with hope—unrealistic hope maybe—but at least hope had been possible then. Now it was not. She pushed her palm against her forehead, as if she were trying to steady all the doubts and confusion tumbling through her brain.

Getting up from the chair, she lay down on the bed, closing her eyes, remembering the day she killed Stanley Ferguson.

Stepping through the unlocked back door, Connie found herself in a big kitchen with a floor of shiny brownish-red quarry tiles. An island separated the cooking and eating areas, each spacious enough to be a good size room all by itself. Connie listened, hearing nothing. She moved on.

It was a big house, not as large or luxurious as the one

she grew up in, but not bad. It should have been her house, hers and Stanley's. Connie checked all the rooms on the ground floor, finding no one. She started upstairs, clutching the box that contained the wig.

Connie should find Stanley at any moment now. She didn't know what would happen. A part of her was telling her to turn around, run down the stairs, out of the house. Get away before it was too late. But she couldn't do that. Her future was somewhere on the second floor of this house. She was committed to it. She'd never go back to the life she'd been leading. Never.

At the top of the stairs, she stopped, listened. And she heard a sound, a thump, maybe a drawer being pushed closed. It had come from a room to her left. When she reached the open door, Connie stopped. A man was in the room, standing with his back to her, taking off his shirt.

"Hello, Stanley," she said, stepping into the room, and the man spun around to face her.

"Who are you? And what are you doing in my bedroom?"

That he might not recognize her hadn't occurred to Connie. She was stung. How could someone who'd been so important in her life not even remember her?

"Don't you know me?" she asked, hearing the shakiness of her voice.

He studied her, frowning. "Should I?"

"I'm . . . I'm Connie."

He looked bewildered.

"Connie Stewart."

"I don't know who you are, Connie Stewart, but I do know that you're not supposed to go around walking into people's houses uninvited."

"You loved me once. You made love to me. You were my first."

Stanley sat down on the bed, staring at her, the first signs of recognition appearing on his face. "You mean . . . at the University of Florida?"

"Yes." She wanted to say something more, to explain, but she was uncertain how.

"But . . . that was twenty years ago."

Connie nodded.

"But why are you here? What are you doing in my house?"

Connie found herself at a loss for words. She knew why she'd come, inside she knew, but how to explain it?

"Because . . ." She faltered, afraid to say it, afraid of being rebuffed.

"Because why?"

"Because you're the only man I've ever truly loved," she blurted. "Because you truly loved me once. Because we belong together."

"Connie . . ." He was staring at her, stunned.

"If you think about it, you'll know it's true." Connie's words came in a rush. "It was a mistake to lose what we had, but . . . but we can still get it back. It's not too late. We're young yet. We could have years together."

Stanley shook his head. "I don't believe this."

She rushed to the bed, sitting down beside him. "Let it happen, Stanley. It's right. Don't fight it. Let it happen."

"Look, Connie, I'm married, happily married."

"You said you loved me; then you made love to me. For me, it was the first time for both. I gave you everything I had, Stanley. My love, my devotion. It was all for you. I'd have been loyal to you, and faithful to you like no one else could have. You threw away so much, Stanley. Too much. But you get a second chance. You can get it back."

He was eyeing her curiously now. "Connie, we broke up, that's all. People do that, especially in college."

"No, it wasn't like that. I didn't break up with you. Only you wanted to break up. And it was wrong. It shouldn't have happened." Her eyes were moist, but she didn't want to cry. She had to make him understand.

"We only went together for a few weeks, as I recall."

"It was long enough."

"Connie, I didn't love you."

"Don't say that!" she snapped. "Don't lie."

"But I didn't. I didn't love you."

"You said you did." Despite her efforts to hold back her tears, she was crying now. "You weren't lying. I would have known if you were."

"I remember what happened. We were in bed . . . making love. And you said you loved me. I said the same thing back to you, but it just came out. It was just . . . just words. I was just repeating what you'd said."

"This is going all wrong," she said. "I didn't come here to argue. It's going to work out the wrong way."

"Look, Connie, I'm sorry if this has been some kind of a thing with you all these years. Maybe I did love you when I said it, but it was only for that particular moment, for that instant while we were making love. Since then we've gone off to make our own separate lives. There hasn't been anything between us for twenty years."

"I never got over you," she said.

"There shouldn't have been that much there to get over."

"There was. Oh, believe me, there was."

He searched her face. "Connie, do you think that maybe you should get some help?"

"Help? You mean like a shrink? You think love is a sickness?"

"I think you might need some . . . some counseling or something."

"You left me in a big ruined heap," she said. "I tried to commit suicide."

"Don't lay that on me. Look—"

"You ruined me," she said. "You can't take that much from a person, hurt them that much, without ruining them."

He sighed. "There's nothing I can do to help you, Connie. You've built a relationship that lasted a few weeks into something it wasn't, something it could never be. Don't you see that? I mean, my God, I didn't even recognize you. I didn't even recognize your name."

Connie had been holding the box containing the wig on

her lap. Putting it to the side, she tried to sort out the jumble of conflicting emotions she was experiencing. She'd known it might be like this, which was why she'd brought the gun in her purse, along with the wig and the makeup. She'd known, but she'd also hoped. Hoped too much. Now she was paying the price. She felt miserable, empty, rejected.

Connie's hand slipped into her purse, felt the gun, hesitated, then came out of the bag without the automatic.

She threw her arms around Stanley, hugging him tightly, crying. Although she couldn't see the expression on his face, she felt his arms slip around her, hold her gently. And the hope was back. It was going to be all right.

"Just hold me," she half sobbed, half whispered. "Just hold me." And Stanley abruptly withdrew his arms.

"Connie, listen to me."

She hugged him even tighter, clinging to the hope, not wanting to let it slip away. Stanley pushed her away.

"Please," she said, trying to get her arms around him again.

"You have to go," he said. "Is there someone I can call, someone who can come for you?"

"You son of a bitch!" she screamed, slapping him. She started to slap him again, and he grabbed her hand.

"I've got other things to do," Stanley said firmly. "If you won't leave, I'll call the police."

She struggled to free her hand, but he held it tightly.

"It's your choice," he said. "Do you want to leave calmly, or do you want me to call the police?"

Connie stopped struggling, tried to look calm, tried to conceal the rush of hatred she was feeling. For she loathed this man now, despised him for rejecting her, for causing everything that had happened to her.

Stanley stood up, moved away from her. He was watching, waiting to see what she would do. Reaching into her purse, Connie pulled out a tissue, blotted her eyes. She put the tissue back in her purse, and when she withdrew her hand this time, it held the gun, which she aimed at Stanley.

"You son of a bitch," she hissed, hating him as she had never hated anyone before.

Stanley's eyes had widened at the sight of the automatic. "Wait a minute," he said, clearly uncertain how to handle this turn of events. "Let's not have—"

"Shut up!" she screamed. "Just shut up!" Tears were running from her cheeks. She tried to hold them back, so she could see clearly, think clearly.

"Connie," he said gently.

"Bastard," she sobbed. "Bastard."

For a long moment, he stared at her; then he began moving slowly toward the door.

"Take one more step and I'll blow your goddamn head off."

He stopped. "Connie, put that thing down. Please."

She shook her head. "We're going to talk."

"Okay," he said. "Sure. What do you want to talk about?"

Connie didn't know what she wanted to talk about. She only knew that if they didn't talk, she would have to shoot, and even though she hated this man, killing him would not be easy. How did you kill the only person who ever loved you—even if he hadn't loved you very long or very well? Once he was dead, in all the world there would not be a single man who had ever loved her.

"You're the only man I ever loved," she said, immediately wondering why she said it. He didn't care. He'd refused her love. "I hate you," she whispered.

Stanley started to say something, then changed his mind.

"Talk to me," she said.

"I don't know what to say."

"Tell me why."

"Why . . . what?"

"You know." She put tension on the trigger, thinking maybe she should just do it and get it over with. But she didn't. She eased off on the trigger. "Tell me why. Am I ugly, stupid, what?"

"I never thought of you as ugly or stupid."

"Than why?"

"It just didn't mesh. It wasn't a good fit. We weren't right together."

"Sit down on the floor," she said. Stanley complied.

They talked, saying the same things over and over in different words. An hour passed, then another, and before long the afternoon was nearly gone. Soon she would have to do something because she had no idea when his wife was due home. And Connie wanted to be gone before she arrived.

"I have to go to the bathroom," Stanley said, inclining his head toward the door a few feet away. He was still sitting on the floor.

"All right," she said.

As he got up, she followed him with the gun. While they talked, she'd rested it in her lap, keeping her hand on the grip, ready to do what she had to if Stanley moved. Stepping into the bathroom, he started to close the door.

"Leave it open," she said.

Stanley shrugged.

Connie watched as he turned to face the toilet, unzipped. He was turned sideways to her, but because of the shower stall she could only see his back half. She heard his stream hitting the water in the toilet. When he was done, he zipped before turning. Then he stood in the doorway to the bathroom, looking at her, rebuttoning the shirt he'd been about to take off when she surprised him.

"This is over now," he said. "I'm going to call the police."

"Your wife Terri is going to pay, too," she said.

"Leave Terri out of this. She's not involved."

Aren't we macho and brave? she thought. Going to protect the little woman. With me all you did was get into my pants a couple of times, and then you were through with me. You didn't care how much it hurt. You didn't care what happened to me.

She was going to shoot him now. It was time.

"It's over," he said and took another step toward her.

And Connie shot him. He took a wobbly step backward into the bathroom, his eyes confused, not believing.

"I hate you!" she screamed, and then she shot him again. Stanley took another step backward and collapsed on the blue tiles of the bathroom floor.

For a long moment, Connie sat on the bed and stared at the man who lay bleeding on the bathroom floor. And then she had her first doubt. What she had just done was irreversible. Had it been a mistake? She shook her head, trying to chase the confusion away. She'd done what she had to; there had been no other way. Going to the bathroom door, she used the barrel of the gun to pull it closer so she wouldn't be able to see Stanley.

Why couldn't it have worked the other way? she wondered miserably. Just once why couldn't something have worked out the way it would have been best for me?

Good fortune smiling on Connie Stewart? she thought bitterly. Fat chance.

But she had no time for self-pity. There was still one thing to be done. Terri Ferguson was partially responsible for what had happened here today. And for that she would pay. Connie knew that what she had in mind might not work. She had no idea where Terri was right now, whether she had an alibi. Still, it was worth the attempt, for what better punishment could there be than having her accused of killing her own husband?

Going to the closet, she looked through Terri's clothes, selecting a white dress with blue flowers. Connie had thought she and Terri were about the same size, and she was right; the dress fit perfectly. Not wanting to look at Stanley, she used the main upstairs bathroom to add temporary coloring to her eyebrows, put on the wig, apply makeup. When she was finished she washed out the sink and picked up the facial tissues she'd used, putting them in her purse. She put her clothes and the box the wig had come in next to the back door. Then, taking the gun, she slipped out the back door and along the side of the house.

Connie hid behind a tall lilac bush until she saw the car coming.

After dashing out in front of the car, gun in hand, Connie rushed back into the house through the rear door, quickly changed back into her own clothes, then left, taking the wig and Terri's dress with her. Keeping the dress had been an impulsive act. Maybe the police would ask to see it, and if Terri was unable to produce it, the cops might be even more suspicious of her.

And as she left the house, Connie wondered whether Terri Ferguson was with someone or whether just maybe she was alone, doing something that could not be substantiated. Would it work out the way she wanted, just this once?

The memory faded away. Connie lay on the bed, staring at the ceiling. There was a big water stain right over her head. At one time the motel roof must have leaked badly. She had no idea whether her attempt to make the police suspect Terri Ferguson had worked. The newspaper stories she'd read made no mention of any suspects in the case.

Why was she still here? She'd done what she'd come here to do. Why didn't she go home? Home? Where was home? Was that where she'd lived with Jack Martin? Or was it the big Southern mansion in Nashville where she'd grown up? She had no home. She had nowhere to go.

Of course, she could do as she had done so many times before. She could go to a bar, make herself available, leave with a man.

As she considered the possibilities, Connie became more and more dejected. She couldn't go to a bar and let herself get picked up, because she didn't think she could face that. Would she live her whole life that way, going to bars, getting picked up by men like Jack Martin, sometimes living with them for a while, moving on after she tired of the abuse?

A tear slid toward her ear. What was she going to do? Where was she going to go?

The trip here, seeing Stanley again, it had all been a

waste of time, for she was even more miserable now than she'd been with Jack Martin. And she wondered why she'd been born, what purpose it had served. Perhaps she was one of God's experiments, to see how much suffering one person could endure.

Another tear slipped from her eye; it ran past her ear and was absorbed by her hair. Connie stared at the stain on the ceiling, waiting for more tears. But none came. She had sunk to a level of misery in which nothing mattered anymore. Even crying was simply too much trouble. She seemed withdrawn from the world, as if she'd slipped out of it and become invisible, her only company the grinding misery that was trying to consume her.

She sat up, raised her hand in front of her face, seeing nothing. She was invisible, she really was. It was symbolic of her worth in the world. Unseen, unimportant, unable to control her fate. And were she dead, she'd be unmissed. And unloved, she thought bitterly. Accompanied by her crushing pain, Connie moved slowly to the chair beside which her purse sat. Sitting down, she reached into the bag, took out the gun.

Holding it in her lap, she studied it, noted the shape of it, like an L; the dark gun metal, black as death. Who would cry for me? she wondered. She made a sound that was a cross between a chuckle and a snort. No one would care. No one would even notice, except whoever had to remove her body from the motel room. The world would go on, and her absence would make absolutely no difference.

All I wanted was someone to love me, she thought. That was all. She slipped the end of the barrel into her mouth.

Pulling the trigger would mean no more misery, no more pain. She was already invisible; dying would be just one more step in the direction in which she was already headed. Despite her fundamentalist upbringing, she didn't believe in life after death, so firing the gun would mean the end, blackness, nothingness, nonexistence. And the misery would be over. She'd be rid of it. Forever.

I know how to take care of you, you son of a bitch, she mentally told the pain. I can fix you right now.

Connie was holding the gun with both hands, her thumbs on the trigger. She pressed them against it. The trigger began to move.

And then she stopped, eased off on the trigger, took the gun from her mouth. She still had something to do, something important. Terri Ferguson was getting off too easily. Her life would go on. In time she'd put her husband's death behind her, steal someone else's lover. What happened had been Terri's fault. And she would do it again, to someone else, unless Connie prevented it.

Kill her, Connie thought, looking at the gun.

No, not that. For dying merely put an end to the pain. And then a plan began to form in Connie's mind, a way to punish Terri Ferguson. Suddenly Connie realized she was visible again. She could see her hands, her arms and legs. And her misery, though still in the background, wasn't the dominant thing in her head anymore. She had a purpose, something to do.

Putting the gun in her purse, Connie left the motel room. The borrowed pickup was parked a couple of blocks away, in a neighborhood with numerous apartment complexes. It was an area where many people parked on the street, where the stolen truck would blend right in. And even if the police did spot it, there was no way to connect the pickup with anyone staying at the Dixie Darling Motel. The only risk was that the police would stake it out, but that seemed unlikely. It was a lot of trouble to go to over a stolen truck that wasn't worth that much to begin with. If the police had discovered it, the pickup simply wouldn't be there anymore.

The truck was where she'd left it. Connie quickly hot-wired it and headed for the airport. It was time to swap the pickup for something else. With every day that passed, the risk grew greater that the truck would be reported stolen—if it hadn't been already. She would leave it at the airport and look for another car old enough not to have a steering wheel lock.

Of course, it was impossible to be certain she was always driving a car that wasn't on the police hot sheet yet, but at least using the cars of people who were out of town, and only keeping them for a couple of days, minimized the risk.

And she couldn't afford to take any risks right now. Because she had something important to do. She had a purpose.

TEN

"I'm selling the house," Terri said. "I called a real estate agent today."

She was sitting in the living room with Marlene Williamson. Marlene was her best friend. In addition to playing tennis together and being on the board of the same charity, they were confidants, each the one with whom the other could share things, even intimate, personal things.

Marlene gently squeezed Terri's shoulder. "I'm so sorry about all this, Terri. After the funeral, I went home and cried all night."

Terri nodded. She knew about crying all night.

Five days had passed since Stanley's death. The crippling weight of her grief had lifted a little, enough for her to realize that she had things to do. Things like selling the house and the BMW. The furniture store, too, would soon be for sale, although the prospects for finding a purchaser seemed poor. For one thing, it was closed. It had shut down on the day of Stanley's funeral as a tribute to Stanley and so the employees could attend the service. It had never reopened. One of the major creditors had sent in accountants. Bruce Gossetter said he really didn't know what was going on, except that it seemed the financial condition of the store was worse than he had figured. He also warned

118

her that the business might have to go into receivership. Terri didn't know what that meant.

So far, Terri had told no one about her critical financial situation, not even Marlene.

"It can take a long time to sell a house in this price range," Marlene said. Although she was about Terri's age and had the same trim figure, she was more attractive than Terri. Her thick black hair had a lovely sheen; it complemented her skin, which was very white and flawless.

"How long's a long time?" Terri asked. The real estate agent had hedged, saying sometimes a house sold quickly, sometimes it didn't.

"It can take years," Marlene said.

"Years?"

"You don't have to stay here," Marlene said. "Go stay somewhere else and leave the house in the hands of the real estate people. I'm surprised you stayed here this long. I mean, well, you know, with what happened here and the reminders and all." She searched Terri's face, apparently worried that she might have gone too far.

Terri thought of the bedroom in which she refused to sleep, the dim stain by the bathroom door that wouldn't come completely out no matter what she did. But she wasn't selling her home because of what had happened here. Although it was the place where Stanley had been murdered, it was also the home in which they had shared so much. Being here made her miserable. But so did the thought of leaving.

Marlene was looking at her sympathetically, obviously concerned, wanting to help, and Terri felt herself slipping back into that state of grief that rendered her unable to do anything except suffer. She didn't want to go back to that state; it was you and your misery, alone together, as if nothing else existed in the universe. Terri heard a distant voice, and it took her a moment to realize it was hers.

"I can't go anywhere," she said. "And I can't even stay here. I . . . I don't have anywhere to live." She began to cry.

Sliding over beside her, Marlene guided Terri's head to her shoulder, held her. "Want to tell me about it?"

For a while, Terri let her tears flow into the material of Marlene's blouse, her body shaking. When her tears had subsided, she told Marlene everything.

"My God, Terri," Marlene said, stunned. "I had no idea. What are you going to do?"

In answer Terri slowly shook her head; she didn't know. "The funeral costs will take all of the life insurance, plus some. This morning I paid three thousand on the house and five hundred on the BMW. In four weeks I'll have to do it again, and I can't."

"Maybe everything will sell right away," Marlene said, trying to sound encouraging.

"The car maybe. You just told me the house could take years."

Looking as though she wished she could take back the words, Marlene said, "Can't you get the mortgage company to give you some time?"

"Bruce Gossetter—he's my lawyer—he says they may give me a few months, but eventually they'll repossess, and I'll lose whatever chance I had to get any money out of the house. If I price it low enough to ensure a quick sale, I could wind up owing money after I pay the real estate commission and my share of the closing costs." She shook her head. "At least that's what Gossetter tells me. I don't really understand any of this. Like how a multimillion-dollar business could be worth nothing. How could something so big not be worth anything?"

Marlene looked at her helplessly. After a moment, she said, "If there's anything I can do to help . . . if you need money or anything . . ."

"You couldn't give me enough to help very much, Marlene, and if you were silly enough to offer me that much money, I couldn't accept it."

Marlene frowned. "Maybe Milt can do something. He could make you a loan or extend you a line of credit or something like that." Marlene's husband, Milton Williamson, was the president of Meadowview's largest bank.

"I don't think so. I'm like the furniture store. I already owe more than I'm worth."

"But . . . there's got to be something I can do to help, Terri."

Terri made herself swim upward, out of her overwhelming misery. It was like drowning in quicksand. She had to get out of it. She had to function. She had to deal with things.

"There might be one thing," she said.

"What?"

"Do you know any place I might be able to get a job?"

"A job?"

"I have to go to work, Marlene. It's either that or welfare—and I doubt that the owner of Ferguson's Furniture City could get welfare, even if the place isn't worth anything."

"Maybe Milt can find you something. He says he always has openings at the bank."

"Marlene, I can't type or take shorthand or use a computer. I can barely use a pocket calculator.

"Maybe you should learn how to do some of those things, take a course or something."

"I'd be living on the street by the time I graduated. I have to have something now."

"I still think Milt might be able to help. Let me talk to him."

Terri felt more tears welling up, but she held them back. She'd never held a real job in her life; she was unqualified to be anything other than a volunteer charity worker or a housewife. What kind of work could she get? Laundress? Sweatshop worker? Maid?

Inwardly she laughed bitterly when she thought of being a maid, because she'd had to let her own cleaning lady go. Rosalee had come in three times a week to get the laundry done, keep the house scrubbed and vacuumed and shiny. In the short time Terri had been doing her own cleaning the ceramic tiles on the kitchen floor had lost the sheen Rosalee always gave them; now they were dull and streaked. The vacuum cleaner bag had exploded because she'd forgotten she was supposed to change it. Figuring out *how* to change it had taken her twenty minutes. And then she'd spilled the dusty contents all over the living room carpet.

"There's another reason I don't think Milton would want to hire me," Terri said. And then she hesitated, uncertain whether she really wanted to tell Marlene this.

"What reason?" Marlene asked.

"The police think I'm the murderer."

"Terri, what on earth are you—" And then shocked realization spread across Marlene's face. "Oh, my God, Terri, they don't think you . . ." Her words trailed off, and she completed the sentence with a wave of her arm.

"I'm their prime suspect."

"But why?"

Terri told her about the woman seen running from the house with a gun in her hand, about her missing dress, about the lineup. "It hasn't been mentioned in any of the news reports I've seen," Terri said. "I guess the police are keeping it to themselves for some reason."

"Jesus," Marlene said. "I can't believe all this. On top of everything else that's happened to you." She shook her head.

"I think the woman was Connie."

"Connie?" And then she realized what Terri was talking about. "Of course! Terri, that should prove to the police that you're not involved. Stanley's last"—she paused, as if maybe she shouldn't mention that, then plunged ahead— "his last words were a woman's name."

"But they've only got my word that he actually said it."

Marlene stared at her a moment, then sighed. "I see your point. Does the name Connie mean anything to you, anything at all?"

"I've thought about it and thought about it, Marlene. I

don't know any Connies. I don't recall ever knowing any Connies."

They were silent for a moment; then Marlene said, "Listen, Terri, now don't you worry about this policeman, whatever his name is."

"Stark."

"Yeah, Stark. There are a lot of people—prominent people—around here who know you and like you and will be willing to speak up for you. I know that Milt will, for one. And I'll bet he can find you a job, too."

"I think I'm going to need all the help I can get in that department," Terri said.

"Now, listen," Marlene said, looking at her sternly, "when things are going bad, don't keep them to yourself. You don't have to prove how strong and independent you are by handling everything all by your lonesome. You can't do it, Terri. You've been through too much. I don't think anybody could handle it all by themselves." She squeezed Terri's arm. "You've got friends who can help, but you've got to let us know what's happening."

Terri nodded, blinking back her tears.

"What were you going to do, wait till you were living on a park bench before you let anybody know you had money problems?"

Terri shrugged.

"Well, I can help you, if you'll just let me."

"I won't take money from you, Marlene. It wouldn't be right."

"It wouldn't be right of me *not* to offer it and then make darn good and sure you accept it."

"I appreciate what you're saying, Marlene. I appreciate it a lot. But I can't take money from you. I just can't."

"You're letting pride get in the way, Terri. Accepting a little help from a close friend's nothing to be ashamed of."

"It's not pride. It's . . . well, it's just a matter of what's right."

"Principles?"

"Yes, I suppose so. And whatever you're about to say about principles, don't say it. The subject is closed."

"Terri!" Marlene said, looking exasperated.

"No."

"Okay, you win. For now." Rising, Marlene said, "I've got to run, Ter. I'll check with you tomorrow."

Terri accompanied her to the front door.

"Oh," Marlene said, reaching into her purse. "I brought that book I promised to pass along to you. It's here somewhere. Ah, here it is." She handed Terri a paperback novel. It was by an author of romantic suspense whose books she occasionally read, an author Marlene was much more fond of than Terri was. It looked pristine, as if it had never been opened.

"I don't remember asking you for this," Terri said.

"I could have sworn you did. Anyway, I'm through with it, so you might as well read it. It's the best she's done. Steamiest, too. Read it, you'll like it." And with those words, Marlene hurried out the door and was gone.

For a moment, Terri simply stared at the book. Then, as she turned away from the door, something fell from between the pages. Picking it up, Terri found herself looking at a fifty-dollar bill. Marlene had given her the book as a way of giving her the money. As she stared at the bill, Terri felt grateful that she had a friend who would go to all this trouble to give her money, but she also felt belittled, as if she'd been reduced to living off the kindheartedness of others, living off handouts.

And the sad part was that the fifty dollars wasn't going to do her any good. Fifty-thousand dollars might help, but not fifty. It was too small an amount to make any difference. And it made her feel low and ashamed and terrible.

Suddenly, she hurried out the door, hoping to catch Marlene, make her take back the money. But Marlene's car was already halfway down the block. I shouldn't have told her, Terri thought. But she hadn't brought her financial plight up because she wanted a handout. She'd just needed to talk with a friend about her troubles. A sympathetic ear, that was all.

Terri watched as Marlene's car stopped at the end of the block, then turned left. Abruptly a blue car pulled away from the curb, moved to the end of the block, turned left. For a long moment, Terri stood on her sidewalk, watching the spot where both Marlene's car and the blue car had disappeared. The blue car looked like the one that had been behind her yesterday when she'd gone to the grocery store.

I'm imagining things, she decided.

While driving Michelle to the airport the day before yesterday, she'd thought she'd seen a green car following her. There were always people going the same way you were; it hardly meant you were being followed.

And yet someone had been following her before Stanley was killed, someone in a beat-up old car.

She'd told Stark about the battered car. Although he said he'd look into it, his words had lacked sincerity. Clearly, he thought he already knew who killed Stanley.

Suddenly she shivered, her skin crawling into gooseflesh. Could Stanley's killer still be hanging around, watching her, watching her friends?

Paranoia, she told herself. Nonsense.

Like the little noises that kept her awake at night. She heard every thump and creak and squeak. Rationally she knew these were the sounds of the house adjusting to the cooler nighttime temperatures, dogs and cats on their nocturnal prowls, a raccoon or some other wild creature digging in a garbage can.

And yet there was a part of her that didn't believe what she knew rationally. That part was convinced that the sounds of the night were made by the killer, that Connie was in the house. That she'd come back. For her.

Nonsense, she told herself again.

The reason she lay awake was because whenever she closed her eyes she'd see Stanley lying on the floor, hear him say the last word he would ever speak, watch as the paramedics struggled and that fragile force that was life left him. It was like a loop of film, both ends spliced together, running through a projector. The horror repeated itself. Again and again. Endlessly.

If only she hadn't gone on that drive. If she'd been here, maybe it wouldn't have happened. Maybe she could have done something. Maybe the killer would have had second thoughts if there had been two people in the house.

She shook her head. It wasn't her fault. She would have done anything to prevent what happened. And yet the guilt hung in the back of her mind, refusing to go away. If she'd been here, maybe things would have been different. Of course, Terri realized that, had she been here, she could have died that day, too. And a part of her wondered whether that might have been better.

She turned and started back inside, but suddenly she was afraid to enter the house. The nightmare was in there, the constantly running film loop she could see just by closing her eyes. No, she told herself, it wasn't in the house; it was in her head. It would follow wherever she went.

Taking a moment to steel herself, she walked back into her house and immediately sought the mind-deadening escape of the television set.

Two days later, Terri sold the BMW. She drove it to the nearest BMW dealer to see whether he'd sell it for her on commission. To her surprise, he looked the car over, then made what seemed like a reasonable offer for it. Terri accepted.

After paying off the loan and absorbing the depreciation, Terri had ended up with $761.23. But then it was $761.23 she hadn't had before, and she was free of the five hundred a month car payments. Now all she had to contend with was the three-thousand-dollar house payment.

The next day, Marlene called to say, "Can you meet me at the tennis club?"

"Marlene, I really don't feel much like playing tennis."

"We don't have to play. Let's just have lunch."

Sitting at the kitchen table, she held the phone to her

ear, trying to think of an excuse not to go. She was functioning, doing the things she had to, but she wasn't at all sure she was ready for a social setting like the tennis club. Besides, she had phoned the club yesterday to say she was canceling her membership. In her new economic status, she could be a waitress or a dishwasher at the club, but no longer a member.

"I . . . I'm not sure I want to go there," Terri said.

"It'll do you good. You have to get out, Terri. You have to get back into the world."

"But . . well . . ." Terri was still trying to think of a good excuse not to go.

"Besides, I have some news for you."

"What news?"

"I'll tell you when you get there."

Terri hesitated, then said okay.

"See you in about an hour," Marlene said.

Marlene was waiting in the lounge when Terri arrived at the tennis club. She walked over to Marlene's table and stopped, making no move to take a seat.

"Sit already," Marlene said. "Why are you standing there?"

"I won't sit down until you take this," Terri replied, holding a fifty-dollar bill in front of her friend.

"Why would I want that?"

"No games, Marlene. You slipped this into that book you gave to me, and you have to take it back. I'll stand here until the janitors start dusting me if I have to."

Reluctantly, Marlene took the money.

"I appreciate what you did, Marlene," Terri said, sitting down, "but I just can't take money from you. Besides, I don't need it. I just sold the BMW."

"Great," Marlene said. She hesitated, then put the fifty into her purse. "I'm taking this back only on condition that you let me buy you lunch."

"All right," Terri said. She picked up her menu. She would eat something inexpensive, and the matter of the fifty dollars would be resolved.

There were only a few people in the lounge, middle-aged women in tennis outfits. Wives of the well-to-do. Although they were familiar, Terri was relieved to see no one here she knew well.

"Oh," Marlene said, "I forgot to tell you the news. I think I've found you a job—if you want it, that is."

"If I want it? Tell Milton I'll do anything. I'm a very willing worker."

"This doesn't have anything to do with Milt," Marlene said, a trace of annoyance creeping into her voice. Is she put out with him? Terri wondered. Because of me?

Terri said, "Don't tell me, let me guess. The stockholders of some big corporation stopped you to ask whether you knew of anyone who'd like the president's job at two mil a year, and you naturally thought of me."

Marlene laughed. "It's not quite that good," she said. "I have a friend who's helped me out a few times with the Cancer Society fund drive. She owns a small gourmet kitchen shop on Azalea Avenue. It's called the Cook's Nook; you may be familiar with it."

Terri said she wasn't.

"Anyway, the woman who was working for her just quit, and she needs to hire someone to replace her. Her name is Ellen Farley, she's very nice, and I think the two of you would hit it off very well. Of course, I should warn you that she probably couldn't pay you much above the minimum wage."

Terri had no idea how much that was. She said, "Marlene, that would be great. I mean, I'd pictured myself shoveling out septic tanks or something like that. A gourmet shop sounds wonderful."

Marlene frowned. "Does anyone really have to go down into septic tanks and shovel them out?"

"I don't know. I hope not."

"Ugh. What a horrible topic for lunch."

The waiter came over and took their order. Marlene said, "I told Ellen Farley you'd stop by and talk with her if you're interested."

Terri said she'd stop on her way home. When their food arrived—a club sandwich for Terri, chef's salad for Marlene—the women ate in silence. Letting her eyes wander to the women in tennis outfits, Terri thought about how she had been one of them only a few days ago, and how they seemed like strangers now, people from a different world.

Terri tried to shift her thoughts to the job she might get at the gourmet shop, but instead she found herself wondering what had happened when Marlene had asked Milton about a job for her. Had he said merely that she had no experience? Or that he had no intention of hiring someone suspected of being a murderer?

And then she found herself thinking about Stanley, remembering how excited she'd been because the hunk whom all the girls in her dorm drooled over had asked her for a date, remembering how he'd proposed the night before their graduation from the University of Florida, remembering how he'd turned and run into the closed bedroom door the night he'd rushed her to the hospital because she was about to give birth to Michelle. She had to force the memories from her mind. Not because she didn't treasure them, but because they were just too painful to deal with. Terri had to work hard to keep herself from crying.

"I really appreciate your helping me out, Marlene," Terri said with as much cheer as she could put in her voice. "I phoned some private employment agencies, and they told me that with my total lack of qualifications it would be a waste of time even to come in and fill out an application. Except the place that charged the seventy-five-dollar registration fee. They said they'd be real happy to have me come in and fill out the forms."

"Listen," Marlene said, "if there's anything I can do to help, just let me know. I mean it. I really do."

Reaching across the table, Terri squeezed her arm. "Thanks," she said.

Suddenly Terri had the feeling that someone was watching her, but when she looked around the room, she saw the same tennis-outfit-clad women who'd been here all along. None of them was paying any attention to her. Through the entrance to the lounge, she caught a glimpse of someone walking away, a woman with blond hair who was dressed in jeans—clearly not a member.

She might have imagined the feeling. Or maybe someone in the room had pointed her out, saying, "She's the one whose husband was—"

Terri refused to complete the thought.

ELEVEN

After slipping into the tennis club to see what the woman was up to, Connie had returned to her "borrowed" car. She was pleased to have found Marlene Williamson with Terri Ferguson. She was glad now that she had decided to follow the Williamson woman instead of Stanley's wife.

Learning the woman's identity had been no problem. Connie had followed her home from the Ferguson house. The name Williamson was on the mailbox. Both husband and wife were listed in the phone book.

The tennis club—the interior portion of it anyway—was housed in a one-story brick building. Located in a wooded area on the edge of town, the facility was a short drive from two wealthy neighborhoods. Connie was parked away from any other cars, in a corner of the lot. Her stolen car this time was a '62 Mustang that someone had restored to fresh-from-the-assembly-line condition. It had a V-8, four on the floor, shiny blue paint, and matching upholstery that was spotless. Connie was so fond of the car that she had been using it four days, even though she knew that keeping it so long was unwise.

Connie stretched her legs, yawned. And suddenly she was remembering again. It had been happening even more than usual since she'd started watching Terri Ferguson and Marlene Williamson. Surveillance was extremely boring. It involved a lot of sitting in the car, waiting, getting tired and stiff and cramped. So her mind wandered, remembered. And her memories were becoming more and more vivid, as if she wasn't just recalling past occurences, but as if she'd been yanked back in time to experience things again exactly as she'd experienced them before.

Connie was eight years old. It was raining, so she and Norma Jean Oldfield, a red-haired, freckle-faced girl who lived down the street, had been forced to give up their game of jacks and come inside. They were playing dolls in Connie's bedroom. Annie, the plump black woman whose job was to take care of Connie and her younger sister, had the day off.

"Do these dolls have names?" Norma Jean asked, holding up two miniature people. The man was dark-haired and handsome, the woman blond and beautiful.

"I call them Mr. and Mrs. Teater," Connie answered, "because they like to have tea together." The girls were sitting on the bed. Getting up, Connie went over to the table on which a number of toys were scattered, located a plastic table and chairs, and took them back to the bed. Within a few seconds, she had both dolls seated at the table.

"See? They fit perfectly. They have dinner plates, cups, everything they need."

"Can they wet?" Norma Jean asked.

"Wet? Of course they can't wet. Only baby dolls can wet. These are grown-ups. Don't you know anything, Norma Jean?"

"I've got a doll that cries, and she's a grown-up," Norma Jean said defiantly.

Connie sighed. "Well, sometimes grown-ups cry, but they don't wet." And then she recalled hearing something about how her grandmother had to wear something like a diaper because she sometimes wet her pants. And her grandmother was for sure a grown-up. But then she had no intention of admitting this to Norma Jean. Besides, who would *want* a grandma doll that wet its pants?

"I've seen grown-up dolls that wet," Norma Jean said, but not convincingly.

Not wanting to continue this conversation, Connie shrugged. Although Norma Jean was a pretty good friend, she lied a lot. She was always making up stories about the things she'd done or seen or knew. It seemed to Connie that if you asked Norma Jean if she liked ice cream, she'd say no just to avoid telling the truth.

"You like ice cream?"

Norma Jean stared at her, surprised. "*Everybody* likes ice cream."

Well, she only lied most of the time. not all the time.

Connie glanced quickly around the room to make sure all her possessions were here. Her sister, Cindy, sometimes sneaked into her room and took things. Dolls and stuffed animals of all sizes lay on the bed, stood along the walls, sat on the dresser. In one corner a wooden toy box stood beside a big dollhouse. As far as Connie could tell, nothing important was missing.

The room was done in pink and white. The carpet and the French provincial furniture were white. The curtains and the spread on the child-size canopied bed were pink. Pink flowers decorated the white wallpaper. Cindy's room was similar, except that it was lavender and white.

"How come Cindy's not around today?" Norma Jean asked.

"She's over at Shirley Atherton's, playing Monopoly."

"Oh. Wanna play doctor?"

"Okay. Who gets to be the doctor?"

"We'll take turns," Norma Jean said. "I'll go first."

Connie ran over to the toy box, rummaged through it a moment, then returned with a toy stethoscope, which she handed to Norma Jean. Then Connie picked up the large doll that had been lying on the pillow.

"I think Mary's very sick, Doctor."

"Let me see," Norma Jean said, taking the doll from

her and laying it on the bed. She pressed the stethoscope to the doll's chest, listened intently.

"What's wrong with her, Doctor?"

"I'm afraid she's got old-monia."

"What's that?"

"It's what they had before new-monia, and I'm afraid it's much worse."

"Will Mary be all right?"

"I hope so." Turning from the doll, Norma Jean pressed the stethoscope to Connie's chest. "I've got to make sure you don't have old-monia, too. It's very easy to catch."

"I'm more worried about my little girl than about myself," Connie stated bravely, just as someone in a movie might have said it.

Norma Jean giggled. "You should take your clothes off."

"How come?" Connie asked, not altogether sure she liked that idea.

"That's what the doctor made me do the last time I was there."

"I don't know."

"Why not? That's what real doctors do."

"Not unless you take off yours, too."

"The doctor doesn't take off his clothes. Just the patient."

"The doctor would if he wanted the patient to feel comfortable," Connie insisted.

"Okay," Norma Jean said after thinking it over a moment. "The doctor will get undressed, too."

Connie could see her mother barging into the room and finding them both naked. "Maybe we should do it in the examining room," she said, looking at the closet.

Norma Jean said okay, and they both moved into the closet, turned on the light, and closed the door. Giggling, they pulled off their shoes, dresses, and panties. Norma Jean had forgotten the stethoscope, so she had to run out and get it. Then she pressed it against Connie's bare tummy and pretended to hear things.

"I'm afraid this might be serious," Norma Jean said. "Worse than old-monia."

"What's worse than that?"

"Old-gonia."

Connie giggled. "There's no such thing. I don't believe in old-monia *or* old-gonia. There's only *new*-monia."

"How do you know? You're not the doctor."

Norma Jean moved the stethoscope, finding a ticklish spot near Connie's ribs. Connie yelped, tickled the other girl in retaliation, and then they were both giggling, rolling around under Connie's hanging clothes, trying to tickle each other. The first clue Connie had that something was wrong was the sudden breeze she felt. It took her a moment to realize that it had been caused by the closet door opening. Connie stopped playing and looked up; then so did Norma Jean. They were staring into the furious eyes of Connie's father.

"I'm going to leave this room," he said, the anger showing through despite the monotone in which he was speaking. "And when I return in one minute, I want to see both of you dressed and waiting, like little ladies." He turned and stalked from the room, closing the door.

Nervously, without saying a word, Connie and Norma Jean put on their clothes, then stood by the bed and waited for what would happen next. The door opened; Connie's father stepped into the room.

"Norma Jean, I think you should go home," he said, his voice flat, lifeless. Norma Jean hurried from the room, leaving Connie alone with her father. She felt terribly afraid and vulnerable.

"We were just playing," she said weakly.

"Shut up!" he snapped.

And then he slapped her, the force of the blow carrying her backward. Losing her balance, she sat down hard on the white rug. She stared up at him with tear-filled eyes, stunned. He had never hit her like that before.

"Christian young ladies do not romp around naked with other children," he said. "Only sluts do things like that, and I'll be damned if I'll have any daughter of mine acting like a slut or a—or something worse. Do you understand?"

Afraid that if she tried to speak no words would come out, Connie nodded. Tears ran down her cheeks.

"A Christian young lady only undresses in the privacy of her bedroom—and only when she's alone. No one but her husband may see her naked body. Is that clear?"

"We were only—" The look in her father's eyes made her stop.

"I'm ashamed of you," he said. "You've shamed yourself and this family."

Abruptly he turned and left the room. Connie's cheek felt hot where he had struck her. She heard voices in the hallway, and then her mother entered the room. Connie started to get up, to run to her for love and forgiveness, but the expression on Rebecca Stewart's face stopped her.

"Your father told me what you were doing in here," she said.

"Mommy, I'm sorry. We were just—"

"You're to stay in your room for the rest of the day. You're not to come out for any reason, not even for supper."

Confused and miserable, Connie stared at her mother, trying to figure out what she could do to earn this woman's forgiveness.

"I want you to spend the rest of the day reading your Bible. Understood?"

"Y-yes, ma'am."

Her mother hesitated then, as if about to say something else. A second passed during which Connie silently pleaded with her mother to forgive her, to hug her and love her, but then Rebecca Stewart turned and left the room, closing the door behind her. It occurred to Connie then that her parents almost never hugged or loved her, even when they weren't angry with her.

Tears were dripping onto the white carpet. Lying on the floor, Connie cried for a long time. When her tears finally stopped, she got her Bible from the bedside table, sat down on the bed, and began to read.

The memory vanished as quickly as it had come, and Connie was again sitting in a stolen blue Mustang that was parked at a tennis club in Meadowview, Georgia. Her cheeks were wet. The memories were becoming too real. Connie was beginning to fear that she'd get trapped in one of them, find herself unable to get back to the present.

"That's silly," a man's voice said. "You can't get trapped in a memory."

Startled, Connie looked around, seeing no one.

"It's me, Connie. Don't be afraid."

Connie looked in the back seat, finding nothing. Her eyes darted in various directions, looking for the source of the voice. It was familiar. And it seemed able to read her thoughts. Which was ridiculous. No one could read another's thoughts.

"You're the only one for me, Connie. I know that now. I only wish I'd known it sooner."

"Stanley?" Her heart was pounding. How could this be?

"I'm with you now. I'll always be with you."

"I . . ." She didn't know what to say. And then she did. "It's been lonely without you, Stanley."

"I know. For me, too."

Terri Ferguson and Marlene Williamson emerged from the tennis club, each heading for her own car.

"She's the one who took me away from you," Stanley said. "She should be punished for that."

"What should I do, Stanley?"

"Your plan's a good one, my love. It's the best way."

Terri Ferguson's station wagon pulled out of the tennis club parking area, followed by Marlene Williamson's white Cadillac. Connie followed the Cadillac.

"You have to get rid of this car," Stanley said.

"Yes," she said. "I've had it too long."

At that moment, Connie felt more content than she'd ever been in her life.

Arnie Jordan—he pronounced it the Southern way, *Jer-den*—stood behind the stained and gouged wooden counter in the office of his junkyard, wishing he had some customers. Lifting off his grimy cap, he laid it on the counter, then ran a greasy hand through his thin hair.

There was a time when people bought a lot of used parts. Hell, used to be people couldn't *afford* to keep their cars running without going to the junkyard for cheap parts. But now there were discount auto parts places everywhere. Sold new parts for less than you could get rebuilt. Made in Korea, most of them, or Taiwan. Places where they didn't have to pay the workers anything.

Used to be everything worth anything was made in the U. S. of A. Now nothing was made in America.

Jordan heard the rear door open, and a moment later his nineteen-year-old son walked around a small pile of rusty brake drums and joined him. Emmett was a lanky young man with light brown hair. Like his father, he wore permanently stained jeans and an equally ratty plaid shirt.

"You want me to put that old Chever-lay in the crusher?" Emmett asked.

"What old Chever-lay?"

"The one with Alabama plates that you got from that woman."

"Oh, that one. Can't see crushing it if it runs, even if it isn't any good for parts."

"What you want me to do with it? Battery's gone dead, and it's just sitting there."

Arnie Jordan thought for a moment. "Got another battery you could put in it?"

"There's a Pontiac's got a battery ought to fit."

"Put it in the Chever-lay. We'll let Bobby use it to run

errands." Bobby was Emmett's younger brother. He was still in high school and helped out at the wrecking yard on weekends.

Emmett said, "He'll probably wreck it first time he uses it, way he drives."

"He does, I'll leave him in it when we put it in the crusher."

Emmett snorted. "Serve the little turd right, you ask me."

"That's no way to talk about your brother, Emmett."

Ellen Farley turned out to be a plump woman with gray hair who had a winning smile and eyes that were a dark, dark blue. The Cook's Nook was part of a small commercial complex that also contained a video rental place, a florist, and an auto parts store.

"I don't want to say anything that would discourage you from hiring me," Terri said. "But to be completely honest, you have things here that I've never seen before. If someone were to ask me what they were, I wouldn't know what to say." She and Ellen Farley were sitting in the Cook's Nook's tiny office. Like the rest of the shop, it was uncluttered and spotless. Clearly, Ellen Farley was a stickler for neatness.

"Don't worry about the things you don't know," Ellen said. "You can learn what's necessary in no time. I select my helpers because of the kind of people they are. People pay a little more for things in a small shop like this, and for that extra money they expect a relaxed atmosphere and personal service from someone . . . well, someone intelligent, gracious, reliable. My customers are mainly middle-aged women with husbands who earn enough so that their wives don't have to work. They need someone they can feel comfortable with."

Terri had already told Ellen Farley about her situation, including her sudden downward economic mobility. She would fit right in with the women the shop owner had described; until a few weeks ago, she had been one of them. Besides, she was a fellow retailer. She owned Ferguson's Furniture City.

Reaching across her desk, Ellen Farley put her hand on Terri's. "Look," she said, "I'm a widow myself, so I know just how hard it can be. If you'd like to work here, I think I can help."

Although Terri didn't think she had let any of the pain inside her show, it must have been obvious to Ellen Farley. Unexpectedly, Terri's vision clouded with tears, and then they were trickling down her face. The shopkeeper continued to hold her hand.

"How . . . how long ago did you lose your husband?" Terri asked.

"About seven years ago." Her eyes found Terri's. "You may not believe it now, but the hurt goes away after a while. You still have the good memories, but none of the pain."

"How long does it take?" Terri asked, holding back her tears now. This was the first time she'd talked to anyone about this. She could discuss some things with Marlene, but not the pain of losing Stanley. It was something only another widow could understand.

"I don't remember exactly," Ellen Farley said. "The hurt starts to lessen after a few days. That makes some people feel guilty, I think. But it's natural. You have systems inside that pick you up, get you going again. Sure, you grieve for a long time, but the grief that just about incapacitates you goes away. I think you're at that point now. You'll learn to smile and laugh again, feel good again."

"Sometimes it's okay," Terri said. "I mean, I can talk and laugh and everything, but afterward I feel funny, like—"

"Like you're being unfaithful somehow?"

Terri nodded.

"Well, you're not. Clinging to your grief doesn't do you any good. And if you think about it, what would your husband have wanted you to do?"

"I . . . I don't know."

"Okay. What would you have wanted your husband to do if the situation were reversed?"

Terri considered that. "I'd want him to get on with his life. I'd want him to stop grieving."

Ellen Farley raised an eyebrow.

"I guess that's what he'd want for me, too."

"I know it is." She removed her hand from Terri's. "Gillian—she's the woman who just quit—was a widow, too. She lost her husband about five years ago. The reason she left is that she got married again."

The notion hit Terri all wrong. Sure, maybe she could learn to enjoy life again, but remarry? She'd be betraying Stanley if she did that—at least that's how she'd feel, which was all that really mattered. Besides, the whole idea of meeting men, dating, it all sounded so . . . so alien. It was a thing done in one's youth, a thing done by people who went to school dances or college parties or singles bars.

"I, uh, I hope you don't think I'm being too forward, talking to you like this. I used to be a volunteer counselor with a widowed persons organization, and I can recognize the look of someone who needs to talk about things."

"I don't mind," Terri said quickly. "I'm glad you did. I did need to talk to someone who . . . who's been there."

The shopkeeper nodded. "Anyway, the reason I need help here is because I'm into so many things. I'm not in the widowed persons group anymore, but I think I'm involved in just about everything else. I'm even starting to give gourmet cooking lessons at my home." She smiled. "As you can see, I need help. Gillian left yesterday, so you could say I need someone desperately. Do you want to work for me?"

"I'm not exactly sure how to go about these things, but I think I'm supposed to ask you what the salary is."

"Good point. I'll pay you the minimum wage to start,

forty hours a week. If you're working out okay, I'll give you a raise of fifty cents an hour every six months forever—or until I can't afford it anymore. What do you say?''

"When do I start?"

"How about tomorrow morning at nine?"

"I'll be here."

They shook hands.

TWELVE

Marlene Williamson drove along the quiet street, enjoying the pretty spring afternoon. This time of year, she could still drive with the car windows open, savoring the fresh scents of trees and flowers and all the other things that were just starting a new season. Soon, it would be so hot that she'd dread the short trips between her air-conditioned Cadillac and an air-conditioned building. Marlene pitied the people who'd lived in the South before air-conditioning.

On each side of her were big brick houses with well-tended yards. As were many of Meadowview's streets, this one was lined with young trees that were still years away from providing any significant shade. Dwarfed by the large homes, the trees looked like miniatures, plastic replicas on an architect's model of the neighborhood. Marlene's own house was in the next block.

Terri had been working at the Cook's Nook for about a week now. She seemed to like the job, and Ellen Farley seemed happy to have her. Though pleased about that, Marlene worried about Terri. Not only had she lost her husband, but she'd abruptly been deprived of a whole way of life. She'd gone from riches to rags. There had to be a lot of shock in something like that. The whole thing—the sudden poverty, the loss of status, the drastic change of lifestyle—had to be catastrophic. Marlene was surprised that Terri had the strength to cope. She wasn't sure she would.

Glancing at the dashboard clock, Marlene saw that it was five-thirty. Terri would get home from work in about an hour, and Marlene wanted to call her, see how things were going. As she pulled into her wide cement driveway, she pressed the button on the transmitter, and the middle one of the three garage doors opened automatically. Marlene drove the Cadillac into the empty garage, pressed the transmitter again, and the door lowered itself. To her left was the space where Milton parked his Mercedes. To her right was the large boat with twin outboards that they usually took to a nearby lake for a week or two each summer, to get away from the heat and grime that went along with urban life even in places like Meadowview.

Marlene poured a glass of white wine at the bar in the den, then lowered herself onto a blue satin chair and sipped her drink. She would be meeting Milton for dinner at eight. She had plenty of time to get ready, and her thoughts turned to which dress she should wear.

Two hours later, wearing a green dress with matching accessories, Marlene stepped into the garage, pressing the button that controlled the middle door. She had tried to call Terri, getting no answer. No matter. She'd call her tomorrow—or maybe go by the Cook's Nook and buy something minor, just as an excuse to chat for a few moments. Marlene started to open the door of her white Cadillac, and suddenly she was knocked to the side with such force that she bounced off the car's fender, lost her balance, and fell, hearing her dress rip as it caught on the bumper. The garage door closed itself again.

For a moment, Marlene simply lay on the cement floor, dazed. And then she realized that someone had knocked her down. Someone was in the garage. I'm going to be robbed, she thought, and maybe raped and . . .

Refusing to complete the thought, Marlene slowly sat

up, making her eyes focus. For a moment, she thought she was alone in the garage, that whoever had been here had knocked her down to give himself the chance to slip out of the garage and escape unseen, that she might have foiled a burglary. But then she heard a noise by the boat. A blond woman was standing there, smiling at her.

"I didn't think you were coming out again," the woman said. "I was just about ready to come in and get you."

"What . . . what do you want with me?" Marlene asked.

"Your name's Marlene Williamson, that right?"

It was disquieting that this woman knew her name. "What do you want with me?" Marlene asked again.

"You a good friend of Terri Ferguson's?" the woman asked. She had a Southern accent, but not Georgia. It had a peculiar mix of upper and lower-class intonations.

"What does Terri Ferguson have to do with anything?"

"You her friend?" the woman asked casually, as if they were just talking over old times.

Remaining silent, Marlene studied the woman. She was about forty and had a face that was plain but not unattractive. The way she applied what little makeup she wore seemed to say that this was a working-class person, someone unacquainted with fashion. She wore jeans and a blue shirt.

As she studied the woman, Marlene began to realize that they were about the same size. And Marlene was in good shape. She exercised daily, played tennis, swam, jogged. There was no reason for her to be afraid of this intruder. Marlene slowly stood up.

"Get out of my garage," she said. "Right now. Or I'll call the police."

The woman just smiled at her. She was holding her hands at her sides. She had no weapon.

"If you don't leave, I'm going to call the police," Marlene threatened again. Although she wanted to go back into the house and make the call, first she wanted to see this woman leave, know she was out of her garage, out of her home.

"Tell me about Terri Ferguson," the intruder said.

"No!" Marlene snapped. "Get out of here. I'm not telling you anything."

The smile faded from the blond woman's face. "Fucking rich bitch," she sneered. "You're all alike. All you give a shit about is your image, about what's proper for you and your little rich-bitch brats."

Uncertain how to interpret this change in the woman's behavior, Marlene watched her, said nothing.

"Terri Ferguson used to be a rich bitch," the intruder said, and the smile momentarily returned, only to be replaced by a distant, introspective look.

Marlene's instincts told her to run back into the house and lock the door, then call the police. Which was what she decided to do, except she wasn't going to run. She was going to walk, dignified, in control, unafraid.

"I hope you're still here when the police arrive," Marlene said. She started toward the door.

"Stop!"

And something in the woman's voice made her do it. When she turned, Marlene discovered that the woman was aiming a gun at her.

"Is this a robbery?" Marlene asked, her voice weak, tremulous. And she was surprised to realize that she *hoped* it was a robbery, for all the alternatives she could think of were worse.

"You get Terri Ferguson that job at the gourmet place?"

"Yes," Marlene replied, her voice barely audible. She wanted to run, to be defiant, to do something to show that she had some control over the situation. But she didn't have any control. The gun said so. It said she would do whatever she was told, that she would try her best not to provoke the person holding it. "What do you want?" she asked. "I'll do whatever you want."

"Terri Ferguson shouldn't have interfered," the intruder said.

"No," Marlene said. "She shouldn't have done that."

"You should have left her alone. If you hadn't been such a good friend to her, I wouldn't be here right now."

Marlene shivered, because she just realized what this woman's name might be. She didn't look right; she didn't resemble Terri. Yet appearance could be altered. "Who are you?" she asked.

"My name's Connie."

Marlene stared at her, trembling.

"It's a terrible thing to be all alone," Connie said. "If I let Terri have friends, she'll never learn what it's like."

Marlene studied the distance between herself and the woman. They were about fifteen feet apart, too far for Marlene to have any chance of rushing the woman. And that was the last thought she had of resistance. Suddenly she was consumed with the need to ingratiate herself to this woman, to be so humble and cooperative and meek that this woman wouldn't want to shoot her. Marlene slid to the floor beside her car, tears streaming down her cheeks.

"Please don't hurt me," she pleaded. "Please don't."

Connie studied her in silence.

"I haven't done anything to you," Marlene sobbed. "Please don't hurt me."

Doubt or maybe it was just sympathy appeared in Connie's eyes, and then it vanished as quickly as it had appeared. She raised the gun.

"Noooo!" Marie shrieked. "God, please don't!"

And then something snapped into her body. Pain and confusion erupted in Marlene's mind. She couldn't have been shot; it just couldn't happen. She wasn't dead because she was thinking these things. She . . . she . . . she . . .

Her thoughts swirled away as a flash of light exploded in front of Marlene's eyes. And then it began to dim, move away. The pain and confusion were going, too, and yet Marlene found herself fighting to hold onto the light. It hung there, like the moon about to drop below the horizon, and then it was gone.

"I'm sorry," Connie said and shot her again.

* * *

Terri pushed her grocery cart past the supermarket deli section. Once, she had bought a lot of things there, things like fresh jumbo shrimp, hard salami for Stanley to nibble on, imported Parmesan cheese. Now she couldn't afford such things. At the meat counter, she wheeled her cart past the steaks and roasts, stopping in front of the ground beef. She put a package of it in the cart, then continued on.

Her grocery buying habits had changed in other ways, too. Instead of prepared foods, she now bought less expensive things like tuna and cottage cheese, and she made her meals from scratch. Now she planned a menu and made a list instead of buying whatever looked good. Now she ate at home instead of dining out regularly. And when she did eat out, it was McDonald's or Burger King. She added a loaf of none-too-fresh bread, the store's own brand, to her cart, thinking, The checker's going to expect me to pay with food stamps.

Inwardly, she shuddered. She didn't think she could bear to pay with food stamps. She had always supported the program, but there was a stigma to standing there at the checkout, peeling the damned things out of the book with everybody watching you, thinking you were freeloading off the system. If she was ever forced to use them, she'd go to another town, somewhere no one knew her.

But then, she wasn't likely to qualify for food stamps. When she got to the part about listening her assets, she'd have to put down a half-million-dollar house and a multi-million-dollar business. No matter that neither was worth anything to her. The food stamp people would shake their heads, show her to the door.

Of course, that she could even *imagine* herself using the stamps showed just how drastically her situation had changed. Terri had no idea what to expect. Events had swept her along, and she tried to cope, but she had little control. She had become a store clerk who was cautious with her grocery money, as were store clerks the world over, she supposed. But this was only part of what was going to happen to her. She would find somewhere else to live, the kind of place people of her economic means resided in. She would make new friends. Her whole life would be different, and she could only imagine part of it.

Still, coping as best she could and seeing what came next kept her going. As long as she was busy, she didn't have time to feel sorry for herself. She didn't have time to cry.

It was about six-thirty. Before Stanley's death, Terri had grocery shopped in the mornings, and the evening shoppers here now were entirely different from those she usually encountered in the supermarket. In the mornings, the shoppers were mainly women, middle-aged and well dressed even if their clothes were casual. But at this time of day, the people were younger, their clothes less expensive. Men and women shopped together, sometimes with young children. Unlike the women who bought their groceries in the mornings, these were working people. Like me, Terri thought, and yet she didn't feel as though she belonged.

And then she saw someone she recognized. A middle-aged woman with short dark hair who was wearing a red dress. Her name was Bonnie Gramley, and she lived down the block from Terri.

"Hi," Terri said as their carts approached. They were in an aisle that contained a jillion kinds of cold cereal.

Keeping her eyes straight ahead, Bonnie Gramley wheeled her cart past Terri's. At the end of the aisle, she turned the corner without looking back.

Terri was confused. The woman must have seen her. They weren't close friends or anything like that, but they knew each other by sight and usually spoke when they met. Had the woman not heard her? It seemed unlikely. And then Terri wondered whether Bonnie Gramley had simply chosen not to notice her, whether she was no longer the sort of person the Bonnie Gramleys of the world associated with.

Terri pushed her cart into the aisle containing paper products and selected a roll of store-brand paper towels. Suddenly, she realized that Bonnie Gramley was at the end of the aisle, talking to another woman. They were both looking in her direction. The instant they realized she'd spotted them, they looked away. What were they thinking? There's the woman whose husband was murdered? There's the woman the police suspect of murdering her husband? Or maybe just, there's the store clerk, the outcast? A hot tear trickled down Terri's face. She wiped it away. She wasn't going to let the stares of Bonnie Gramley and her unknown companion get to her.

Terri pushed her cart to the checkout, paid for her purchases, and left. When she pulled into her driveway, she tried not to notice the for-sale sign on the front lawn. Although at first she had wanted to get away from the house as fast as possible, now she had conflicting feelings. The place was all that remained of the life she had led with Stanley; yet at the same time it was a constant reminder of what had happened to him. She didn't want to go. But she was desperate to leave.

As she carried her groceries inside, Terri experienced the fear that had started greeting her whenever she entered the house. The certainty that Connie was waiting inside. That she'd come back for her.

Terri put the groceries on the table, then sat down and stared at them, trembling. After a few moments, she got up, walked through the house, finding that no one else was here. Then she put the groceries away and assembled the macaroni casserole that would be her dinner the next couple of nights.

Detective Sergeant Simon P. Stark said, "I still think she could have killed him to inherit the business."

He and Beauchamp were sitting at a table in the employee's lounge in the Meadowview police station. They had the room to themselves. Around them were tables with imitation wood tops, on which were piled the debris of the day. It included crumpled napkins, wrappers from the various food items that were dispensed by the vending machines, and empty soft drink cans that were used as ashtrays despite the "No Smoking" sign on the wall. The bullet-shaped trash container was full, its spring-closed door held open by wadded-up wrappers and paper cups.

"But the business is worthless," Beauchamp said. "She had to sell her husband's car, the house is up for sale, and she's working as a clerk in a little shop that sells banana peelers or some shit like that. She was a hell of a lot better off with her husband alive."

"Yeah, but she could have *thought* she was going to inherit the business and become both rich and independent instead of just rich."

"Ferguson's friends and the neighbors say she and her old man got along just fine. Why whack him?"

"The friends and neighbors don't always know."

Beauchamp shrugged. "Well, considering the way it worked out, you might have a pretty tough time convincing a jury that getting control of the business was her motive."

"If that McCabe woman had only got a better look at her, I'd have her."

"The flip side of that is that if McCabe had got a better look, she might have said it definitely wasn't Mrs. Ferguson. You don't seem to want to allow for that, Sarge."

Stark snorted. "If the wife didn't off him, who did?"

"How about Connie?"

"Come on, Pat. We've checked, and as far as we can tell Ferguson's never known any woman named Connie. If this Connie had a relationship with him that was important enough for her to kill him, we'd have turned something up."

"Not necessarily. She could be a whacko, and whackos do things for strange reasons. Maybe she was his nursemaid when he was a kid, and thirty-five years later she decides he's a child of the devil and has to be destroyed or something like that."

Stark stared at him. "You've been watching too many of those late-night horror movies on TV."

"Come on, Sarge. It happens, you know that. There's a lot of crazies out there, and they do stuff that doesn't make any sense."

"Sure seems funny that this nursemaid looked a lot like Terri Ferguson when she ran into the street."

"I'm not saying Mrs. Ferguson's not our best suspect. I'm only pointing out that there are other possibilities."

"Like the person who'd been following Mrs. Ferguson? Someone no one but her saw—except her husband, of course. But then he can't exactly back up her story."

Beauchamp said nothing.

Stark sighed. "Hell, the trouble is that we've been working on this thing for a couple of weeks now, and we don't have enough to move on anyone, not even Mrs. Ferguson. If something doesn't come up quick, this is going down as an unsolved. I've thought about bringing Mrs. Ferguson in, booking her on a murder charge, and letting her see the inside of a cell overnight. See how she holds up, see if she might like to get a few things off her chest after spending the night locked up with the undesirable elements. What do you think?"

"I think that with what you've got, she'll be out as soon as she gets before a judge on token bail, maybe even her own recognizance. I think the judge will be pissed at you for wasting his time, and the DA will laugh. Otherwise, it's a great idea."

"That wasn't what I wanted you to say."

"I'm just telling you what you already know. I'm not going to encourage you to make a bad move."

The two men were silent for a moment. Then Stark said, "Why the hell are we sitting here at eight-thirty at night? Why don't we go home?"

"I've been spending so much time here, I thought it was my home. My wife would agree."

At least you've still got a wife, Stark thought. But then maybe he was better off single. Although divorce had left him with no one to go home to, there was no one to bitch at him about things either: *You care more about your job than about your family.* But when he was home: *All you ever do is watch football games.* Or: *You drink too much beer.*

152

Okay, so it was her way of coping with the stress of being married to a cop. It still didn't make her any easier to live with.

As the two detectives stood up to leave the room, Stark grabbed up the paper cups and other debris that had been on the table next to them and carried it to the trash bin. It was too full to hold any more and most of the trash the detective was trying to force into it fell on the floor, where he left it.

"Ought to get a bigger trash can," he muttered.

"Sergeant," a young uniformed officer said, stepping into the room, "Detective Menton just called in. He's on a ten fifty-one, and he says the victim is somebody you interviewed in connection with the Ferguson case."

"Did he give you the victim's name?"

"Yeah." He consulted the piece of paper in his hand. "Williamson. Marlene Williamson." He gave the address.

"Come on," Stark said to Beauchamp. "You didn't really want to go home anyway."

"I'd better call my wife," Beauchamp said, following him out of the room.

THIRTEEN

After eating her macaroni casserole and washing the dishes, Terri switched on the big console TV in the den and sat down on the couch. The recliner would be more comfortable, but it had been Stanley's, and she couldn't bring herself to sit in it.

Using the remote control, Terri switched channels, finally stopping on Showtime, which was showing a movie, a Chevy Chase comedy. That's all she watched now, comedies. She'd paid the cable TV bill just before Stanley died. Meadowview Cablevision would want to be paid again in a couple of weeks; Terri would have to cancel the service.

When the house sold, the console TV would have to go too, along with most of the furniture. She could keep the small television set in the kitchen, cookware, clothes. Almost everything else would have to go. Although she had no idea where she'd be going, she was sure her new place wouldn't be large enough to hold many of the things in this house. Besides, she was going to need the money she could get from selling them.

As with the house itself, she was uncertain whether she wanted to get rid of these things because of the bad memories or keep them because of the good ones. Not wanting to think about these matters, Terri forced herself to concentrate on the movie. Midway through it, she fell asleep. She was awakened by the phone, which sat on a small table by the couch.

"Hello," she said, trying to clear the sleep from her head.

"Hi, Mom. It's me." Michelle called every few days, and they ran up a phone bill they couldn't afford, but neither of them wanted to give up the conversations.

"How's everything at school?" Terri asked.

"Oh, okay," Michelle responded without enthusiasm. "How's your job going?"

"I'm kind of enjoying it. I'm not making much money, but for the first time in my life I'm earning what I do get. It's a whole new experience. I'm learning things, too. I know what a tortilla press is now, although I'm not sure I could use one. I even know the difference between chef's knives and slicing knives and filleting knives. Did you know that some of them cost as much as eighty dollars a knife?"

"For one knife? Wow." But this, too, was said without enthusiasm.

"Honey, is something wrong?"

"Oh, nothing much, I guess. I flunked a test today. I can't seem to concentrate on my classes anymore. I just can't seem to keep my mind off . . . you know. It's hard not to think about it."

"Michelle, listen. We've both got to pull ourselves together and go on with our lives. Things are going to be different from now on. We've been through something terrible, but even as awful as it is, we have to live with it. We have to be strong because . . . well, we have to. We just have to do it."

Terri wished she could accomplish half the things she was urging her daughter to do. Still, what she was saying was true. And the words had to be said.

"I know all that, Mom. It's just not easy." She sounded on the verge of tears.

"I know it's not easy. I know it's not." Terri was about

to cry herself, and she paused, making sure her voice wouldn't crack when she spoke. She and Michelle had had too many crying sessions over the phone. It was time to stop. "Are all your classes going badly?"

"Almost all of them. Finals are coming up, and I don't know what's going to happen. No, that's not true. I'm afraid I do know what's going to happen. I'm going to flunk the whom damn semester. Maybe I should give the whole thing up and come home."

"No, honey, don't do that. Please. This semester's paid for. There may not be any more college after it's over, unless you can earn the money yourself somehow."

"I know that, Mom, but what good's it doing me to stay here if all I accomplish is flunking and feeling miserable. At least, if I was there, we could be together. I could help."

"I'd feel better with you here, too, Michelle. But I really think you should stick it out if you can. And try to study. Try to save the semester."

There was a long silence before Michelle said, "I'll try, Mom. But I don't promise what the results will be." She changed the subject. "Sell the house yet?"

"Yesterday, when I got home from work, I found a real estate agent's card, which means the house was shown to someone, but I haven't heard anything, so I guess they weren't interested. I've just about given up on getting any money out of it. All I want is to get out from under the payments." Although she'd thought about simply letting the mortgage holder repossess the place, Terri didn't mention that to her daughter.

"Are you going to make it okay, Mom? I mean, you know, are you going to be all right?"

"I'll get by, hon. We both will. Honest."

"When I get home this summer, I'll get a job. Maybe with both of us working, things will be easier."

"Let's not worry about that until summer. For right now, I just want you to concentrate on your studies. Okay?"

"Okay, Mom." They talked for another few minutes

and then ended the conversation. The phone call had depressed Terri. She was worried that Michelle would flunk out and that the failure in school, added to her father's death, would just make things worse for the girl—assuming it was possible for things to get worse for either of them than they already were.

She watched the rest of the movie, then switched to HBO and started watching another one. Midway through it, she found her attention wandering and switched over to the eleven o'clock news, which was in the middle of a story about the Atlanta school board. That was followed by a story on food prices, which in turn was followed by a commercial. Terri was just drifting off to sleep when she heard the anchorman say something about Meadowview.

". . . is at the scene with a live report."

A young blond woman appeared on the screen. Behind her were police cars and a brick house, most of which was obscured by shadows. The house looked familiar. The reporter said, "The woman's body was discovered by her husband. Apparently, they had been planning to meet for dinner, and when his wife didn't show up, the man phoned, got no answer, then finally decided to come home. He found the body of his wife in the garage. So far, police haven't released the name of the victim."

Terri stared at the TV screen. Although she could only see a portion of the house, it still seemed familiar. If she could see more of it, she was sure she could recognize the place.

"Detective Jim Menton of the Meadowview police is here with me now," the reporter said. Standing beside her was a tall man with curly brown hair and a crooked nose. "How was the woman killed?" the reporter asked.

"She was shot twice with a small caliber weapon."

"Is anyone in custody yet?"

"No. Uh, we're still investigating. We, uh, have no suspects at this time." Apparently, being on TV was making him nervous.

"When will you be able to tell us the victim's name?"

"Just a moment," he said, leaning away from her and talking to someone who wasn't in the picture. Turning back to the reporter, he said, "I, uh, I can give you that information now. The dead woman is Marlene Williamson, age thirty-nine. Her body was found by her husband, Milton Williamson, who—"

Terri didn't hear the rest of what the reporter said. Shaking, she stared at the television set, horrified. Marlene! she thought. Who would want to hurt Marlene? The anchorman was back on the screen again, speaking words Terri didn't hear. She realized she was crying.

"I just don't understand what's happening," she sobbed. "I just don't understand."

She sat there, staring blankly at the television set until a sound intruded on her confused thoughts. It took her a moment to realize that someone was ringing the front door chimes. Slowly, mechanically, Terri went to the door and opened it. She found herself staring at Sergeant Stark and his partner. She simply looked at them, said nothing.

"I'm going to have to ask you to come with us," Stark said.

When Terri didn't move, he took her elbow and guided her back into the house. "Get your keys and turn off whatever needs turning off," he said.

Terri turned off the TV set, locked the house, and found herself in the back of a police car, a heavy wire screen separating her from the two police officers in the front seat.

"What time did you leave work?" Stark asked.

"I already told you that three times," Terri said. She was in a cream-colored room at the Meadowview police station, facing Stark across a small wooden table. The other officer, Beauchamp, was leaning against the wall behind her.

"Tell me again," Stark said.

Hot, bitter tears welled up in Terri's eyes, but she held them back. Despite everything that had happened, she wasn't going to let this son of a bitch reduce her to a

158

sniveling wreck—at least not in front of him. She clung to that thought; it gave her strength.

"I left work at six," she said. "It's when I always leave work. You can check it with Ellen Farley."

"Where'd you go?"

"The grocery store."

"Which one?"

"Bagley's."

"Which Bagley's."

"The one on Fairmont Boulevard."

"See anyone you know there?"

"I told you. The only person there I knew was Bonnie Gramley. She looked right at me. She must have seen me."

Terri had considered calling a lawyer. The problem was that the only attorney she knew was Bruce Gossetter, who didn't want to represent her in any criminal matters. He'd given her a list of attorneys, but she doubted she could afford any of them. And, at least according to Gossetter, her owning the house and business would make her ineligible for a public defender. There weren't many benefits to being poor, but those few that existed were denied her.

"What time did you leave the grocery store?" Stark asked.

"About six forty-five."

"Where'd you go?"

"Home."

"Anyone see you at your house?"

"I don't know. I don't think so."

"What time did you get home?"

"A few minutes before eight."

"Eight?"

'No, I mean seven. It's ten minutes from the grocery store."

"Why'd you say eight?"

Terri had been answering his questions mechanically, trying not to think about what had happened to Marlene. She didn't understand what was happening to her. Stark, for some ludicrous reason, already thought she'd killed

Stanley. Did he now think she'd killed Marlene, too? How could this be happening? It was insane. Madness. Suddenly she was angry, angry for everything that had happened, angry at this asshole who had the nerve to think she'd killed her husband and her best friend.

"I said eight because of the stupid questions you keep asking over and over again!" she shouted. "I said eight because I'm confused. And I'm confused because I've been through hell the last couple of weeks, and because I just learned that my best friend has been murdered. Wouldn't you be confused? Wouldn't you get your times mixed up after a while?"

Stark just looked at her, a hint of a smirk on his face. It seemed to say, *Got to ya, didn't I?*

"Why am I here?" she demanded. "What the hell do you think I've done?"

"You're here because you're involved in the investigation of two murders."

"What the hell does that mean?"

"Just what it says. How did you know Marlene was dead?"

"I saw it on the eleven o'clock news."

"What time did you say you got home?" Stark asked. That infuriating suggestion of a smirk was on his face again.

Ignoring his question, she said, "What makes you think I had anything to do with what happened to Marlene? She was my best friend. I'd never hurt her."

"What time did you arrive at Marlene's house?"

"I haven't been there in days."

She thought of Marlene then, and her vision blurred with tears. For a moment Terri was sure she'd break down and cry. She fought to maintain her composure. If she let herself go, she'd weep uncontrollably. And if she was going to do that, she wanted to do it alone, in the privacy of her home, not in front of this son of a bitch who thought she was a murderer.

"You're a bastard," she said to Stark, and then she had

160

to close her eyes and squeeze her hands into fists to keep from crying. Her shoulders heaved once and a short sob escaped, but then she was in control again.

"For trying to catch a murderer?"

Terri ignored that. Mustering what strength she had left, she asked, "What do you plan to do with me?"

"We're just talking, you and me. That's all."

"Then am I free to go, or do I need to call a lawyer?"

"You're free to go. For now." The last he added ominously.

"Good." Terri stood, surprised at how shaky she felt.

"There's one thing you should know," Stark said. "Ballistics says the bullets that killed Marlene Williamson came from the same gun that was used to murder your husband."

Stunned, Terri sat down again. "You mean the same person . . . But why? They had nothing in common. They hardly knew each other.

"There must be a connection, don't you think? Someone who knew both of them."

Terri simply stared at him, dazed. Clearly, he thought that someone was her, and she was too confused to say anything that might convince him otherwise. Why would anyone kill both Stanley and Marlene? It just didn't make any sense.

"It was Connie," she said softly.

The policeman eyed her skeptically, said nothing. She might as well have suggested that the Easter Bunny did it, for all the credibility Stark gave to Connie.

Terri rode home in a cab. Sitting in the back seat, she tried to make sense out of everything and found she couldn't, so she emptied her mind. stared blankly at the passing scenery. She paid the cabbie, thinking bitterly that she should be able to bill Stark for it. Then she hurried to the door, and the usual fear came over her. Whoever killed Stanley has come back for me. Except this time it was whoever killed Stanley *and* Marlene.

Terri stood at the front door, key in hand, afraid to go

inside. Until now the fear had been a subtly nagging thing, something she could eliminate by looking through the house and satisfying herself that it contained no killers waiting to pounce on her. But this time the fear was much more intense. Someone was in the house, waiting for her.

She stood there, holding the house key, uncertain what to do. She could call the police, but what would she say, that she *thought* someone was inside even though she'd seen no one, found no signs of forced entry? They'd think she was some sort of fruitcake. Besides, she'd had enough to do with cops for one night.

Terri hesitated, then shoved the key into the lock and opened the door. Stepping into the living room, she stood perfectly still, listening intently, hearing only the emptiness of the big house. Then, gathering her resolve, she moved through the house, turning on the lights as she went. When Terri finished with the ground floor, finding nothing even remotely suspicious, she felt better.

Moving upstairs, she checked the spare bedrooms, including the one she'd moved into. Then she stopped at the door to the master bedroom. And the fear came over her again.

The door was closed. She kept it that way so she wouldn't see into the room as she passed through the hall. She hadn't entered it since moving all her things out. If the killer was here, this was where he'd be. Taking a moment to steady her nerves, Terri pushed the door open. The darkness in the room seemed to float into the hallway, surround her. She snapped on the light. Although the room itself was empty, someone could be hiding in the closet or the bathroom.

Terri didn't want to go in. The images of what had happened were just too strong here. And yet, if she wanted to feel secure in the house, she had to check out this room. She stepped into the doorway, moved quickly to the closet, opened the door.

For just an instant, her mind saw a hand reaching out,

closing on her throat. But there was nothing inside the closet except Stanley's suits.

Backing quickly away, Terri closed the door. She didn't want to see Stanley's belongings. Although she'd eventually have to do something with them, at the moment disposing of Stanley's things was still too painful for her to deal with. She headed for the bathroom.

Keeping her eyes averted from the unremovable stain by the door, she stepped into the room, and another image rushed into her head: She sees a blurred shape behind the glass door of the shower stall. As she starts to run, the door opens, two shots ring out, and she's lying on the floor in the same spot where Stanley had lain, her own blood adding to the stain.

No one was in the bathroom.

Terri went downstairs and collapsed on the den couch. Although she managed to keep her mind blank for a while, eventually she found herself thinking about how huge and empty the house was with only her in it. And then what had happened finally hit her. Marlene was dead, murdered by the same person who'd killed Stanley. She hadn't been able to deal with her friend's death yet, because Stark hadn't given her the chance. A feeling of utter helplessness and loneliness rushed over her, and she began to cry, letting out all the feelings she'd made herself keep under control at the police station.

FOURTEEN

Like many teenage boys who'd had their driver's licenses only a few months, Bobby Jordan thought that operating a motor vehicle was better than all the things he used to *think* were fun. It gave you power, speed. You could tool around, acting grown up, go just about anywhere you wanted to.

That he was driving an old beat-up car his dad had nearly put in the crusher didn't matter. It was a *car*. It ran. He had his window rolled down, his elbow hanging out. Casual, like it was no big deal. He kept hoping some of his buddies from Cresthaven High might spot him, so he could wheel up to them, say hi, maybe burn a little rubber when he took off.

Business had got so bad that his dad had begun delivering parts to people who couldn't come to the wrecking yard. It was mainly on the weekends, shadetree mechanics who had their cars all torn up and had no way to get out to the junkyard. Bobby was the official delivery boy. At first he'd used his dad's pickup, but ne'd gotten into a drag race with Ted Crenshaw, who was driving his father's Dodge, and in the process Bobby had smashed the front fender. He hadn't been allowed to use the pickup since.

It hadn't been his fault. Some old woman in a Toyota had pulled out in front of him, forcing him to swerve. He'd hit a tree. He'd actually been slowing down from the drag race at the time. Ted Crenshaw had already beat him.

The part he was delivering lay on the floor in back. A distributor for a Buick. It was going to some guy in West Cresthaven.

The street along which Bobby was driving cut through a neighborhood of old wood houses with weed-choked yards. On some of the houses the paint was cracked and peeling; on others it was entirely gone, leaving the houses a sort of gray-brown and weatherbeaten. Two black kids were playing catch in the street. They moved to one side so he could pass. Bobby had seen white neighborhoods in Cresthaven that were nearly this bad. It was hard to believe that the next town over was Meadowview, where everybody was rich.

Bobby stopped at a red light. When it turned green, he crossed a four-lane street, and the neighborhood changed dramatically. Here there were small but well-maintained homes with nice lawns. Several had paved driveways with basketball hoops fastened above the garage doors. Most had decorative shutters painted to match the trim. It occurred to Bobby suddenly that Carol Denton lived not too far from here.

Carol went to his school. Carol was stacked. She looked damned fine in tight-fitting pants, and she had the second best set of tits at Cresthaven High. Darlene Murphy had the best set, but then in all the world, there was probably only one Darlene Murphy. Feeling a tightening in his crotch, Bobby realized that thinking about Carol Denton was giving him a hard-on.

Bobby wondered whether he had the nerve to go by her house. He and some of his friends had been standing in the hall at school, and Carol and a couple of other girls had come up to them and started a conversation. Carol had smiled at him real big, told him where she lived, said he could stop by her place sometime if he wanted to. But did she really mean it? Girls were hard to figure out sometimes. And then he thought of how she looked in a tight sweater, and the ache in his crotch intensified. At the end of the block he turned right, toward Carol's house.

He'd just drive by, and maybe she'd be out front or something. He could act surprised to see her, say he was on his way to deliver a part for his dad, just passing through the neighborhood. Fancy running into you and all that.

Forty-three-oh-three Pittman Avenue, Carol had said, and Bobby had memorized it. Absently, he wondered why, if he was so good at memorizing things, he always did so poorly on examinations. He dismissed the matter from his thoughts. He could remember what was *worth* remembering, which definitely didn't include the stuff they were telling him at school.

Like making him read Shakespeare. Man didn't know how people really talk, and Miz Holmes, his English teacher, said Shakespeare was such a great writer. What a bunch of crap. "Friends, Romans, and countrymen, lend me your ears." Now who the hell would say something like that? A real person might have said, "Listen up, men." Or maybe, "Pay attention, y'all." He shook his head at the silliness of it. And then he was turning left, onto Pittman Avenue. His attention shifted from the ache in his crotch to the tingly nervousness spreading through his gut.

Leaning to the side so he could see himself in the mirror, he decided his unruly curly hair wouldn't benefit much from being combed. The dark line on his upper lip—he'd been trying for months to grow a moustache—looked sort of silly, but there was nothing he could do about it now. Forty-three-oh-three was a small white house with green trim and shutters. There was a boy's bicycle out front, a Japanese car with faded paint in the driveway. Carol was nowhere to be seen. At that moment, Bobby's courage failed him, and he stepped on the gas, leaving a cloud of burned oil in front of the Denton house.

Should have gone to the door, he concluded when he was in the next block. What was he, chicken? She'd told him he could stop by. What was he afraid of? Bobby sighed, then pulled into a driveway and turned the car around. But as he approached the Denton house, his resolve once more began to slip away, and he knew he would never be able to walk up to the Dentons' front door.

"Hey, Bobby!"

For a moment, he wasn't sure who was calling, but then he saw her running across the lawn toward him. She was wearing jeans and a shirt. The tails of the shirt were tied together in front of her, revealing the flesh above her pants. He stopped the car. The ache in his crotch had become a throb.

"I thought it was you," she said, bending forward to see into the car and showing her cleavage. She had shoulder-length light brown hair and blue eyes. She had a few zits on her chin, but Bobby didn't care one way or the other about her complexion.

"Hi, Carol. What're you up to?"

"Didn't I see you go by once before, going in the other direction?"

"Yeah. I'm delivering some parts for my dad."

"To somebody around here?"

He shook his head. "Over on the west side of town."

"I hate to tell you this, Bobby, but you're going the wrong direction."

"I got turned around."

She smiled knowingly. "Your car?"

"My dad let's me use it to deliver parts. But I think he's going to give it to me," Bobby lied. "It's kinda beat up, but I guess it's better than no car at all."

"Nothing wrong with that. Car like this is a fun car. You can have a good time in it without worrying about denting it up." She cocked her head, gave him a wicked little grin.

"Yeah," he said slowly, "you can have a pretty good time in it all right."

"Take me with you while you deliver that part," Carol said. She'd already begun moving around the car before she finished speaking—not that there was any chance Bobby would have said no.

"Don't you have to tell somebody where you're going?" Bobby asked as she slipped into the car and closed the door.

"Naw, they don't care," Carol replied, and Bobby took off. He had no intention of arguing the point.

When they reached the end of the block, Carol asked, "What's it got in it?"

"V-8."

"Burn rubber?"

"Sure. It's a V-8, ain't it?"

"Let's see."

At the end of the next block was a stop sign. Bobby made sure he stopped with the rear tires on the patch of sand in the street; then, hoping the transmission wouldn't fall out, he stomped on the accelerator. The engine sputtered, damn near died, then caught, and the rear wheels spun in the sand, hit the asphalt, and squealed. The car shuddered.

"Needs a tune-up," Carol said.

"Need to jack up the radiator cap and drive a whole new car underneath."

Carol smiled.

Bobby turned onto a four-lane street, then picked up speed. "It doesn't do too bad once it's rolling," he said.

Glancing at Carol, he floored the accelerator pedal, and this time the old car shot forward in a burst of power. Behind him an oily cloud hung in the air.

"Got glass-packs on her?" Carol asked, referring to the loud rumble coming from the engine.

"Don't know," Bobby said. "I haven't looked." Actually he had looked. What it had was a big hole in the rusty muffler.

Ronnie O'Dell claimed he had made it with Carol once, and Bobby wondered whether it was true. The thought that she might put out, that he was here alone in the car with her and might get some—if he was really, really lucky—was almost more than he could take. What did you do, just drive somewhere and park and start kissing her? Did you hint at it first or just drive to a good spot? He didn't know any good spots.

And then a terrifying realization settled over him, much worse than not knowing any good spots. If he was lucky enough to get anywhere with her, he wouldn't know what to do. He'd mess it all up, embarrass himself. She'd know he was a virgin. She'd laugh. Worse, she'd tell Beverly and Janice and all her friends, and *everyone* would know.

"You can take him," Carol said excitedly.

Sam Tucker was beside them in a green pickup, grinning at them, gunning the engine. Bobby didn't know where he got the pickup. It was nearly as old as the car Bobby was driving, although it was in better condition. It sounded as though it had a V-8, but a small one. A truck engine at that.

"If he beats me, he's not going to beat me bad," Bobby said, pushing the gas pedal all the way down.

The old Chevy shot forward. So did the pickup. Both engines screamed. For a moment, they remained side by side, and then Bobby's car was inching ahead.

"You got him!" Carol squealed.

Abruptly, the pickup dropped back, defeated.

"If I was him," Bobby said, "I'd hide my face, getting beat by an old heap like this."

Ahead was a traffic signal that had just turned orange. Realizing that he was going too fast to stop in time, Bobby sped into the intersection, reaching it just as the light turned red.

"Made it," he said. And then he heard the siren. Hoping it was an ambulance or a fire truck, and knowing it wasn't, he raised his eyes to the mirror, seeing a blue-and-white Cresthaven police cruiser. "Oh, shit."

"You going to try to outrun him?" Carol asked, sliding over next to him on the bench seat.

If he could get away, he wouldn't get a ticket, wouldn't have to face his father. And it might impress the hell out of Carol, might ensure that this was the day he stopped being a virgin. But it was a stupid idea. He couldn't outrun a police car in this old thing. And if he tried, he'd be in trouble the like of which he'd never even imagined.

Fuck it. He stomped on the accelerator. Carol squealed.

Officer Chuck Enders of the Cresthaven police looked through his windshield at the cloud of smoke coming from the old Chevy that had just taken off on him. His own engine revved as he started in pursuit, and he grabbed the microphone from its holder on the dash.

"Twenty-two to Cresthaven."

"Go ahead, twenty-two," the woman dispatcher replied.

"I'm in pursuit of a green Chever-lay, westbound on Graceland."

"The air is ten-three," the dispatcher said at once, indicating that all other units should stay off the radio. "Twenty-two is in pursuit, westbound on Graceland. Any further description, twenty-two?"

"It's an old model, green, real beat up, Alabama plates. First three digits are 669. Can't make out the rest. We're still westbound on Graceland."

"All units, be advised that the pursuit is still westbound on Graceland. The car is green, old, and beat up, Alabama license plates 669, rest unknown."

A brown van pulled out of the police car's way. Very few people ever succeeded in outrunning the police. Not because police cars were extremely powerful—not in Cresthaven anyway—but because of the radios, whose signal traveled at about the speed of light. You had to be real lucky to get away. This was the second chase for Chuck Enders in his four years as a cop. The driver involved in the first one had wrecked his car, gone to the hospital, then to jail.

He was gaining on the old car, which was less than half a block ahead of him now. Suddenly the driver cut to the left, sliding through the intersection.

"South on Shelton," Enders shouted into the mike.

"South on Shelton," the dispatcher repeated. "Any unit that can intercept?"

"Fourteen's at Norton and McGregor," came the response. "I'm headed that way."

"Twenty-seven's coming from Anderson and Tenth," another officer said.

"Fourteen and twenty-seven move to intercept," said the dispatcher. "All other units disregard."

"Shelton and Lake, still heading south," Enders said. He was still gaining on the old Chevy. Only a few car lengths separated them now. Smoke and the odor of burned oil filled the air.

"You'd better turn again, Bobby," Carol yelled, looking behind them. "He's catching us."

Bobby could see that for himself. If he could do it over again, he would have just stopped, accepted his ticket. But it was too late for that now. He had to see it through to the end.

"Here!" Carol shouted. "Take a right!"

Bobby wasn't so sure that was a good idea. It was a small street that led into a newer part of town, a section he didn't know very well.

"Turn!" the girl hollered. "He's almost on top of us!"

Bobby slid the car to the right, nearly knocking down a stop sign, and then he was speeding down a narrow street lined with new houses, some still under construction. Bobby felt hemmed in by the workers' cars and pickup trucks that were parked on both sides of the street.

"You did it, Bobby! You did it! He's almost a block behind us now."

And for just a moment, he foolishly allowed himself to feel good about having impressed Carol, feel as though he might just get away, might just lose his virginity. Then he saw what was ahead of him.

"Shit!" he screamed. "It's a goddamned cul . . . a goddamned turn-around, a dead end."

He swung the car around the cul de sac, and when he was headed back the way he had come, he saw that the road was blocked by three police cars, their red lights flashing.''

"Oh, shit," Carol said in a loud whisper.

"GET OUT OF THE CAR," a cop's voice boomed over a loud speaker. "PUT YOUR HANDS ON YOUR HEADS AND MOVE AWAY FROM THE VEHICLE."

As Enders was driving toward the police station, the boy handcuffed and in the back seat, the girl in another patrol car, the dispatcher said, "Cresthaven to twenty-two."

"Twenty-two," he responded.

"Your Alabama plate is a NCIC hit. Stand by, I'm still getting the information from the computer."

He had routinely run a computer check on the license plate. A hit meant that the number had been entered in the nationwide crime information system.

"You wanted in Alabama, Robert?" he asked the boy.

"No, sir," the boy said, his voice barely audible.

"Well, we'll see about that, won't we?"

The boy said nothing.

Then the dispatcher said, "Twenty-two, the hit is out of Chickasaw County, Alabama. The car is registered to a woman wanted for questioning in connection with a homicide investigation. It's authority Chickasaw County Sheriff's Office."

"My, my, my," Enders said.

The boy remained silent.

Captain Eugene Cantrell was sitting in his office, talking to Detective Sam Johnson, when the blond secretary brought him the message. Scanning the sheet of paper, he said, "Well, well. Connie Stewart's car has turned up in Georgia."

"How about Connie Stewart?" Johnson asked. "She show up, too?"

"No."

"Where in Georgia did it turn up?"

"Place called Cresthaven."

"Where's that?"

"Don't know. But I'd better find out since I'm going there."

"Comptroller had a conniption fit and a double hissy after your plane rides to Tennessee and Florida. Another trip this soon might kill him."

"He's got to learn to stop taking it personally," Cantrell replied. "It's not really his money. He just thinks it is."

"Man would part with his kids before he'd part with a dollar," Johnson added.

But the captain wasn't listening. He was wondering why Connie Stewart had gone to Georgia. Had she just fled, picking a direction at random? Or had she gone there for some reason?

"Maybe I'll get lucky," he said. "Maybe I'll find Connie Stewart, and she'll have the murder weapon in her purse."

"And she'll hand it over and confess, right? Shoot, when's the last time you been that lucky?"

"When I won a dollar with my bingo card at the Wynn-Dixie?"

Johnson just raised an eyebrow.

"Get me an atlas," Cantrell said, "so I can find out where Cresthaven, Georgia, is."

FIFTEEN

Marlene's memorial service was conducted on a pretty spring afternoon, at the same church at which Stanley's funeral had been held. Although neither the Williamsons nor the Fergusons had gone to church very often, when they did go this was the one they attended. Terri sat beside Ellen Farley, who had closed the shop for the rest of the afternoon.

The minister said all the usual things, talking about Marlene's selfless involvement in community affairs, how she went out of her way to help others. Terri recalled how Marlene had tried to give her money, then had arranged for her to get the job at the Cook's Nook. Marlene had been a good friend who'd stuck by her, and Terri was going to miss her very much.

The loss of her friend on top of Stanley's murder had devastated her. She had slept very little in the last few days. And the fear that the killer was waiting for her in the house had grown progressively worse. Terri worried that she might eventually become too terrified to enter the place.

Why would anyone want to kill Stanley and Marlene? Terri had asked herself that question again and again, but she had no answer for it. Except that Connie had done it. But she had no idea who Connie was. Maybe there was no such person. Maybe Stanley had said something else, something that sounded like Connie. Terri was beginning to doubt her recollection of the word he had spoken.

A lot of people had turned out for the service. Terri suspected that many of them were here because Marlene had been the wife of the president of the largest bank in town, not because they'd known Marlene all that well. Terri could see the back of a head with thick brown hair. That was Milton Williamson. She hadn't spoken to him yet. She'd have to express her sympathies after the service. Terri recalled Marlene's telling her that Milton wore a toupee. In these circumstances, the thought seemed friviolous, disrespectful.

When the service ended, Terri and Ellen waited outside the church for Milton Williamson. Terri saw some people she knew, but apparently none of them saw her. At least none stopped to speak to her. The dark stone and stained glass of the church towered over the massive wooden doors through which people were leaving. Terri had always considered it one of the most impressive structures in Meadowview.

"Marlene was my best friend," Terri said sadly. "I loved her a lot."

Ellen said she felt the same way, and then Milton Williamson emerged from the church, accompanied by some people Terri didn't recognize, presumably members of the family. Terri and Ellen stepped forward.

"Milton," Terri said, "I just wanted to tell you—" The look he was giving her made her falter.

"Was it you?" he asked in a hoarse whisper. His eyes were reaching into her, turning her insides to ice.

Terri just stared at him, afraid she knew what he was talking about, but hoping—praying—she was wrong.

Suddenly his arms reached for her, found her shoulders, and began shaking her hard. Deep, racking sobs erupted from his throat. One of the men with him tried to break him away, but his grasp on Terri wouldn't loosen. He stared madly into her eyes.

"Did you kill Marlene?" he asked. Everyone was staring. No one was standing up for Terri, telling Milton she wasn't capable of such a thing.

"I . . . oh, my God, Milton. How could you . . ." Trying desperately to think of words that would convince him, she stared at him with her mouth open.

Abruptly the people with Milton Williamson whisked him away. Terri was left standing there, feeling on display. Suddenly, burning anger and embarrassment rushed over her, and she turned and ran from the church. Tears streaming down her cheeks, she looked for Ellen's car, and for a moment she was unable to recall what it looked like or where they'd parked. Just as she spotted the blue Ford, a hand took her gently by the elbow and began guiding her toward it.

"Everything will be all right," Ellen said. "Let's just get you out of here."

When they were in the car, driving away from the church, Ellen said, "You want to tell me what that was all about?"

Terri hadn't told her that Sergeant Stark considered her a suspect in Stanley's death, and now in Marlene's as well. It was something she wouldn't reveal to anyone, unless she absolutely had to. You didn't go around announcing to the world that you were a murder suspect. Now it seemed she had no choice but to tell Ellen.

Terri wondered how Milton had known she was a suspect, but then she realized the answer was obvious. Stark. He'd been investigating her, talking to people who knew her. When she finished explaining the whole thing, Ellen was pulling into a parking space in front of the store. Terri was crying.

"I'm so sick of crying," she said. "It seems that's all I do anymore."

"Here," Ellen said gently, handing her a tissue.

Terri blotted her eyes. "I keep thinking there are no more tears left." She shook her head. "I guess there are always tears left."

"If anyone's got a right to shed them, it's you," Ellen said. "I'm not sure I'd have held up as well as you have."

"Do you still want me to work for you?"

"Why wouldn't I?" Ellen asked, surprised.

"I'm a murder suspect."

"You're also innocent until proven guilty, as I recall."

"But if people think I did it, and they see me working in your store . . ."

"I'm not going to worry about what people think. *I* think the idea that you'd kill anyone is ridiculous. And in my store, it's what I think that matters." She smiled, looking determined.

"Thank you," Terri said, holding back more tears. The two women embraced, unaware that across the street in a yellow car someone was watching them intently.

Captain Cantrell rented a car at the Atlanta airport—something else to send the comptroller into hysterics. Following the directions given him by the young woman at the car rental counter, he headed for the suburb of Cresthaven.

Located between a bowling alley and a burger place on a four-lane thoroughfare, the Cresthaven police station was a one-story white building with a big gravel parking lot. Cantrell was directed to the office of a Lieutenant Robertson, the watch commander for the patrol division. A lanky man with thin blond hair, he sat behind a metal desk in an office with cinder-block walls and worn vinyl floor tiles. He rose to shake hands with the Alabama officer; then both men sat down. Cantrell had phoned to let the Cresthaven authorities know he was coming, so Robertson already knew the purpose of his visit.

"The boy was released to the custody of his father," the lieutenant said. "It was the first time he'd been in any serious trouble, so the judge didn't see any reason to make him post bond. The girl riding with him wasn't charged."

The policeman handed Cantrell a copy of the arrest report. The two teenagers were Robert Arnold Jordan and Carol Lee Denton, both of Cresthaven. Cantrell scanned the details of what had happened that day, then looked up at Robertson as the lieutenant said:

"The boy said the car was sold to his daddy's junkyard for scrap. Apparently his daddy let him use it to deliver things on the weekends. I think the person you want to talk to is Arnold Jordan, the father. If someone turned the car in for scrap, he's the one who'd have made the arrangements. Actually, that sounds a little peculiar to me, someone scrapping a car that still runs. Some kid wanting a first car might give a few hundred for it. Junk man would pay less than fifty, I'd imagine."

"She must have known we'd be looking for her car, so she took it to the junkyard, figuring it would be crushed. There'd be nothing for us to find, no way to trace her here."

"You want me to put the name through the computer at the motor vehicle department, see if she bought another car? From what you say, she'd probably have enough sense not to use her own name, but you never know. Sometimes they'll surprise you."

"I'd appreciate it."

"Check back with me tomorrow morning. I should have heard from the motor vehicle department by then. You plan to extradite this Connie Stewart if you find her?"

"It might develop into that. Right now all I can say is that I want to talk to her. Actually you could put it a little stronger than that. You might say I'm real anxious to talk to her."

Robertson nodded. "Okay, well, if you need any help like computer checks or things like that, just let me know. Also, if you need to make an arrest in this jurisdiction, we'll have an officer accompany you."

The lieutenant's words contained a polite reminder that Cantrell had no real authority here, and they let him know that computer checks were about the extent of the assistance he could expect. It was what he'd anticipated. The authorities in Cresthaven, Georgia, had their own crimes to solve. And their salaries were paid by people who weren't worried about what happened in Chickasaw County, Alabama. Cantrell would have extended about the same amount of professional courtesy, had the situation been reversed.

"Where's the car that the Jordan boy was driving?" Cantrell asked.

"It's still impounded."

"Mind if I take a look at it?"

"Don't see why not. The impound area's behind the station. I'll have someone unlock it for you."

A young uniformed officer took him into the fenced compound, then waited while he examined the car. It contained nothing that would help him with the Jack Martin murder case. After getting directions from the officer, Cantrell drove his rented compact to the junkyard owned by Arnold Jordan.

"They told me someone from Alabama might be coming to talk to me," Jordan said. A chubby man wearing jeans and a faded red shirt, he stood behind a grease-stained wooden counter. He needed a shave.

"I let Bobby use that old car to run errands," Jordan said. "I knew he was kinda wild when it came to driving, but most kids his age are. Usually they manage not to get into too much trouble." He shook his head. "I sure as hell never would have figured that he'd try to run from the cops."

"Maybe he's learned his lesson."

"He damn well better have." For a moment, he seemed on the verge of saying more on the subject, but then he just sighed, readjusted the grungy cap he was wearing. "He's not here right now. He's in school. If you need to talk to him, I guess he'll get home around four."

"I think you can tell me what I need to know. Where'd you get the car?"

"The old Chever-lay? Woman brought it in, said I could have it for scrap, it wasn't worth fixing anymore. Gave her twenty-five dollars for it. Would have put it in the crusher, but it was still running, even if it wasn't worth much. So I hung on to it, decided to let Bobby use it to deliver parts. See, if a guy's got his car all tore up, he can't go to get parts, so I deliver. Figured it was a good way to get some more business." He shrugged. "Helped a little, but not as much as I'd hoped. Maybe I should advertise. I've been sorta relying on word of mouth. What do you think? Would advertising help?"

"Sounds like a good idea to me. Can you describe the woman sold you the car?"

"Let's see." He wrinkled his brow, thinking. "Blond and kinda ordinary looking. Mighta been cute when she was younger, might not. Hard to say."

"How old was she?"

"If she wasn't forty, she was right up next to it."

"Anything special about her, anything unusual?"

"Not that I can recall."

"How much did she weigh?"

"Oh, gosh, I'm not very good with numbers when it comes to things like that. She was in the middle. I mean, she wasn't fat so you'd notice or skinny so you'd notice."

"She give her name?"

"Sure. I mean, well, it was on the title to the car. I got it over here."

Moving to an old wooden file cabinet that was nearly as greasy as the counter, he opened a drawer and removed some papers, which he placed in front of Cantrell. They were the Alabama title and registration for a twelve-year-old Chevrolet registered to Connie Jane Stewart. Her address was familiar. It was the house in which Jack Martin's body had been discovered.

"She mention where she's living now?"

Jordan shook his head. "If she did, I don't remember it."

"This her?" Cantrell handed him a copy of the photo he'd gotten from the Stewarts. "It's an old picture."

The junkyard man studied it, frowning. "You know, I

believe it is. Like you say, it's an old picture, but it sure could be the woman."

"She say anything at all that might help me locate her?"

Jordan handed the picture back, shook his head. "Sorry."

"If you think of something, call the Cresthaven police. They'll know how to get in touch with me."

Although he'd known it was likely to work out this way, Cantrell was still disappointed. He'd risked the wrath of the comptroller only to reach an abrupt dead end.

"I just thought of something," Jordan said. "Young guy came in looking for a carburetor. She got a ride with him, the woman who sold me the Chever-lay."

"Do you know his name?"

"No, but Emmett might. He's my other boy, Bobby's older brother. Hang on and I'll ask him."

Jordan hurried into the back of the building, and Cantrell heard a door slam. About five minutes passed before he reappeared.

"Emmett doesn't know his name," Jordan said. "But he knows who I'm talking about. The guy's a buddy of Nick Kirby's. You should check with Nick." He pulled a soiled phone book out from under the counter, found the K's. "This is it. Kirby on Hannett Street." He turned the book around, showing the listing to Cantrell, who copied down the address in his notebook.

"How do I get there?" the Alabama policeman asked.

Jordan gave him directions.

Nicky Kirby's mother said her son was working at a supermarket. Cantrell tracked him down there. Although at first reluctant to talk to a police officer, Kirby finally said the person Cantrell was looking for was Greg Scott, who'd been looking for a carburetor manifold for an old Dodge V-8 he was fixing up. Scott could be found at a gas station on Dellman Avenue, where he worked as a mechanic. Cantrell got directions.

* * *

"Yeah, I remember her," Greg Scott said. Dressed in green coveralls, he was leaning against the car he'd been working on. He was about eighteen and had sandy hair, a mild case of acne.

"Where'd you take her?"

"Motel over in Meadowview."

"Meadowview? Where's that?"

"Next town over. Meadowview and Cresthaven touch each other. Probably makes the people in Meadowview real unhappy."

"Why?"

"They all got lots of money over there. Girls from Meadowview won't even look at guys from Cresthaven. Too bad, too. They got all the pretty ones."

"What's the name of the motel where you let the woman off?"

Scott considered that. "I don't remember. All I can recall about it is that it seemed like a pretty shabby place for being in Meadowview."

"Could you find it again if you looked for it?"

Scott looked toward the door that led from the service bay to the gas station's office. "Hey, Frank," he yelled. "I gotta take off for a while. This cop wants me to show him something."

"You still got two cars to get out today," came the deep-voiced reply.

"No problem. This one's almost done, and the other's just a minor tune-up."

The man in the office muttered something.

"Let's go," Scott said.

"Connie Stewart?" the man behind the counter said. "Don't have anybody here by that name."

He glanced pointedly at Scott, clearly curious as to why the boy was accompanying the police officer. Cantrell hadn't introduced the boy and saw no reason to do so now. The desk clerk was about sixty, a frail-looking guy with thin white hair and prominent veins in his arms. His name was Oldman. He owned the Dixie Darling Motel.

The Alabama policeman said, "She's a blond woman, average-looking, thirty-eight years old. She probably would have been by herself."

Oldman considered that a moment. "Sounds like Linda Barnes. She checked in about a month ago."

"This her?" Cantrell showed him the photo.

"Yeah," he said immediately. "She's a lot older now, but it's her."

"What room's she in?"

"She was in seven."

"Was?"

"She checked out."

"When?"

"About two days ago."

"You have any idea where she went?"

"Nope."

Inwardly, Cantrell shrugged the disappointment off. Things usually worked this way. You got used to it. "What room was she in?"

"Seven."

"Has it been cleaned since she left?"

"Course it's been cleaned," Oldman said indignantly. "I mean, it's not the goddamned Waldorf, but we clean the rooms. Been cleaned twice, as a matter of fact. Someone stayed in seven last night."

There was no point in looking over the room. "Who cleans the rooms?"

"Me and my wife. But I always do seven. We split it up. I do one through eight. She does nine through sixteen."

"You ever find anything unusual in room seven?"

"Like what?"

"Anything at all."

Oldman shook his head. "About all she had was a suitcase. I think she used it instead of using the dresser. She was paying the weekly rate, so I only cleaned up in there once a week."

"What can you tell me about her?"

"Nothing. She paid up on time, didn't act wild, and didn't damage anything. That's about all we care about when it comes to guests."

"She have any visitors?"

"Not that I know of."

"Did she ever say anything about why she was here or where she went when she left her room?"

"I hardly ever saw her. And when I did she never said much. You know how some people are. They'll say good morning and maybe something about the weather, and that's about it. That's how she was."

"What kind of a car did she have?"

"Well, when she first got here, she was driving an old beat-up thing, but then she must have got rid of it, or it quit on her or something, because she didn't have it anymore. Far as I could tell, she didn't have a car at all. There was never one outside her room, and whenever I saw her leaving, she was walking."

"No one picked her up?"

"Not that I saw."

"Can I see the registration card she filled out?"

Oldman rummaged around under the counter for a moment, then handed Cantrell the card. Although she'd used the name Linda Barnes, Connie Stewart had put down her car's correct make and license number—probably because the correct information was too obvious to lie about. And she'd given what was most likely a fake address in Mobile. He copied it into his notebook.

"Your wife around?" the captain asked, handing back the card.

"Sure is. You want to talk to her?"

"Please."

Mrs. Young was a chubby woman with curly hair and brown eyes that seemed lifeless somehow, as if there were no intelligence behind them. Cantrell asked her the same questions he'd asked her husband. She gave the same answers. Cantrell asked them to contact the Cresthaven police if they thought of anything.

He drove Scott back to Cresthaven, then checked into a motel there. The place was a little nicer than the Dixie Darling but, in deference to the comptroller, not much nicer. Cantrell sat down on the bed to think.

Why had Connie Stewart come to suburban Atlanta? Did she know someone here? If so, why did she stay in a motel instead of with the person she came to see? She could have just been running, ended up here by chance. But Cantrell didn't think so. If she was just running, she'd have headed for the city, for Atlanta itself, not for suburbs no one ever heard of. One came to places like Cresthaven and Meadowview only if one had business here.

Had she finished her business and moved on? Or was she still here? Tomorrow he would start looking for the answer. Lying back on the bed, he rubbed his eyes, debated whether he should check in with the Meadowview police, since the motel at which she'd been staying was in their jurisdiction. He decided against it. He'd already checked in with the Cresthaven police, and for now that was enough.

He lay on the bed another few moments, then sat up and picked up the phone. He hesitated, uncertain whom to call first, his office or his wife. Then he phoned home.

SIXTEEN

"It's good that you got another motel room," Stanley told her. "You shouldn't stay in one place too long."

Connie was lying on the bed with her eyes closed. She was glad Stanley was here. She always felt warm and secure when he was with her. "You're right, darling," she said softly. "You're always right."

Several minutes passed during which neither of them spoke; then Connie said, "Stanley, I've got a problem."

"What's wrong?"

"This room is more expensive than the other one, and I'm almost out of money. I've only got twenty dollars left."

"Do you have any ideas as to how you might get some money quickly?"

"Well, I have one, but I'm not sure how much you're going to like it." She told him what she had in mind.

"That's a good idea," Stanley said enthusiastically.

"Are you sure you don't mind? Wouldn't you be at least a little bit jealous?"

Stanley laughed. "Of course I'll be jealous, but nothing will happen, not really."

"No, I'd never do anything like that. Now that I've got you, darling, I'll be faithful to you always. I've given up my old way of life forever."

"Don't worry," Stanley said. "I love you, and I trust you."

"Oh, Stanley," she said, tears coming to her eyes, "I'm so glad we're finally together. This is how it should always have been."

"Oh, yes, my darling. Oh, yes."

When Connie opened her eyes and sat up a few moments later, Stanley was gone. But Connie wasn't worried. He'd be back.

The room really was nicer than the one she had at the Dixie Darling. It wasn't luxurious or anything like that, but it had carpeting that looked fairly new, a color TV set, furniture that wasn't ready for the junk pile. The motel was in Atlanta. Connie had decided it was safer to hide in the anonymity of the city. Meadowview was only a twenty-minute drive, as long as she avoided the rush hours.

Stretching, Connie stood up. She would have to shower and get something to eat before doing what she had in mind. It was early yet. She had plenty of time. Her eyes traveled to the box containing the wig. She had worn it when she checked into the motel, just as a precaution. And now she was glad she had. She would have to wear it every time she left or returned to her room. Because very soon now, the Atlanta police would be looking for a blond woman.

Doug Glockner sat in a corner of the bar, nursing his beer. Two tables away from him two guys were sitting with a couple of women. One of the guys told a joke. The women laughed. On the walls were illuminated signs advertising Bud and Jax and Falstaff. Country music was coming from the jukebox. This was a workingman's bar, a place to drink beer by the pitcher and hope you could score with a woman.

That was why Glockner was here. He wanted to get laid. And going to a bar and trying to pick up a woman was the only way he knew to go about it.

Glockner was a carpet installer. Kenny, the guy he

worked with, liked to tease him, tell him, "Shoot, Doug, I bet it's been so long since you had any pussy, you probably don't remember what to do with it." Kenny wasn't far from being right. Since his divorce three years ago, Glockner hadn't had many women. Two to be exact. And one of them had been so drunk she probably didn't remember it.

It wasn't just physical. It was a matter of self-esteem. You had to get some every now and then just to prove that you could, to prove that you were capable of attracting a woman. Scoring with a woman made you feel good about yourself.

And, being completely honest with himself, he had to admit that he'd been lonely since Denise divorced him, took the house and the kids, and left him with nothing but monthly child support payments. To this day, he didn't understand why she had wanted to end their marriage. He was a reliable provider, faithful, even-tempered. Denise had simply said that he was dull, so dull she couldn't take it anymore.

So every now and then he went to a bar, tried his luck. He didn't do it too often though. He was usually unsuccessful, and the rejection was hard on the self-esteem he was trying so hard to bolster by scoring.

Glockner sipped his beer and sighed. Women went for looks, style, charm. Things that weren't exactly his strong points. He had a prominent potbelly, a bulbous nose, and a round face that always looked flushed—as if he were constantly embarrassed or out of breath. Though only thirty-six, he was bald. Not sexy bald like Yul Brynner had been, but just plain old homely bald.

Naturally quiet and shy—especially around women—he wasn't real big in the style and charm departments either. He also had a ninth-grade education, although that was a handicap that could probably be overcome. Tad Newcombe, a guy he used to install carpets with, only had a sixth-grade education, but he sure had a way with women. He knew just what to say to make them laugh, to make them like him. Tad never went home alone unless he wanted to, which didn't seem to be very often.

As Doug Glockner was thinking this, two women came into the bar. At first he thought they were together, but then one moved to a table, the other to the bar. He waited to see whether any other guys would try to put a move on them. Glockner had learned long ago that competing with other guys never worked well for him. But no other guys seemed interested. Most of them were already with women or too drunk to care.

He sized them up. The one at the bar was sort of lanky, with long dark hair that seemed to shimmer when she moved her head. She was in her twenties and had a pretty face, nicely shaped boobs. The woman at a table was blond, about forty, small breasted, and just sort of ordinary looking. The dark-haired woman was too pretty to be interested in him, so he got up and moved toward the blond. Had there been a third choice, a fat woman with a bad complexion, he'd have tried her first. The less attractive they were, the less his chances of being rejected.

Reaching the blond's table, he did as he almost always did and ran out of nerve. He stood there, looking at her, trying to force his mouth to say something.

"Hi," she said, looking up at him.

"Hi," he replied. "Uh, can I buy you a drink?" He braced himself for the rejection.

"Thank you," she said, smiling. "Sit down. Please."

Glockner sat, surprised he'd gotten this far.

"What's your name?" she asked.

"Oh, uh, Doug."

"Hi, Doug. I'm Lora. Lora Atkins." She reached across the table and shook his hand. Her small hand seemed fragile surrounded by his chubby mitt, and he was careful to squeeze it gently. "What's your last name?" she asked.

"Glockner."

"German?"

"Name is. I just think of myself as being an American.

189

My great-grandparents were the ones came over from Germany.''

"You from Atlanta originally?"

"I was born and raised in a little town south of here. Seems like Atlanta's grown so much lately that not many people were actually born here."

"I guess you're right," she said. "I'm from South Carolina myself."

"You like it here?"

"It's nice. More to do in a big city, if you know what I mean."

Glockner agreed. The barmaid came and took their orders, beer for both of them. Beneath the table, her leg touched his, lingered a moment, then withdrew. She smiled. Glockner was allowing himself to hope.

"What do you do for a living, Doug?"

"Install carpets."

"Like it?"

"It's okay. At least, with all the new houses they're building around here, there's lots of work. What do you do?"

"I'm just an ordinary old secretary, trying to keep the boss's hands off my body and get my work done." She laughed. "Oh, hell, shouldn't complain, I guess. It's an honest living."

"Where do you work—I mean, if you don't mind my asking."

"Small company downtown called Barnes and Lindley. They import stuff from . . . well, from just about everywhere. It's specialized. They mainly handle scientific stuff."

"You mean like microscopes?"

She nodded. They had more beer. They talked some more.

After about an hour, Lora said, "Well, I guess it's about time to call it an evening."

This was the moment Glockner had been both waiting for and dreading. He knew he had to handle it carefully if he wanted to sleep with her tonight. And again he found himself at a loss for words. Then Lora reached across the table, putting her hand on his, looking into his eyes.

"Doug," she said gently, "would you like to go home with me?"

Knowing that he might not find the right words, he simply nodded.

She smiled. "Come on," she said, rising. "You mind taking my car? I'll give you a ride back here to get yours in the morning."

"Fine by me," Glockner said.

"My car's in back."

They left the bar. Although it was at the intersection of two major streets, the parking area behind it was so dark it was nearly impossible to see where you were going. It was a little brighter when they reached an area where the light from the street seeped in between two buildings. Glockner could make out the rear entrances to businesses, dumpsters, a few parked cars. Lora had been holding his hand. Suddenly she released it.

"Doug," she said, "I hate to do this to you."

For a moment, he thought she meant that she'd changed her mind about sleeping with him, but then he saw the gun in her hand.

"Give me your wallet, Doug."

He simply stared at her, stunned.

"Doug, you don't give it to me, I'm going to have to shoot you."

He'd never been robbed before, and when he'd imagined it happening to him, this was certainly not what he'd pictured. And yet he could tell the woman meant business. Reaching into his back pocket, he pulled out his wallet.

"Hand it over, Doug. All I want's the money. You can keep the rest of it."

He started to comply, then stopped himself. Suddenly he was getting angry. He was used to being rejected by women, sometimes quite cruelly, but being robbed at the same time was the final indignity.

"Piss on you," he said, then added, "bitch." He wished he could see her face.

"Doug, there's men I wouldn't mind hurting, but you're not one of them. Don't be stupid, okay?"

He put the wallet back into his pocket, turned. "All I got's about twenty-five dollars," he said and began walking away from her. "You want to shoot me over that, go ahead."

"Doug . . ."

He could hear the strain in her voice. He didn't care. He wasn't giving her his money. "Go find some other sucker," he said.

And then something slapped his back so hard it pushed him forward, and he heard the bang, and he knew he'd been shot. Confused, he stumbled, hit the ground, pain erupting in the area where he'd been hit. Pain and, strangely, numbness that seemed to spread throughout his body.

"Sorry, Doug," she said, and he felt her hand removing his wallet.

He thought he heard her walking away. Then he heard other noises, cars passing, a horn honking. The noises became one, grew fainter, and then there was only silence.

He was unaware of the young man and woman standing over him, the man saying, "Hey, buddy, you okay? Hey, man, you all right?"

The next day, Terri sold her house. She was at work when the call came from Fay Laughton, her real estate agent.

"I won't give you all the details now," Fay said, "but the bottom line is that when you pay all the expenses you've got to pay, you should still have about twenty-five hundred dollars left. I've got a thousand dollars earnest money, so it's a serious offer. When can we get together?"

"This evening?"

"Okay, fine. I'll go over everything then. See you at the house at, say, seven?"

"Fine. Uh, is this it? I mean is it sold?"

"Well, not yet. First, you have to accept the offer; then the buyer's financing has to be approved—although they said they might pay cash. They haven't decided yet. Even if they do, there's a lot of little details that can go wrong before you close. But, like I said, it's a serious offer, and I think it looks good. Frankly, it's a little more than I thought we'd get. I'd certainly have no qualms about accepting it. Anyway, we'll talk about that tonight, and I'll go over all the figures, okay?"

"Okay."

Terri was in Ellen's small office. When she hung up, she hurried into the store, spotting Ellen rearranging a display of Cuisinart food processors.

"I've sold the house!" she exclaimed.

Ellen came over and hugged her. "I'm so glad you're going to be out from under that huge payment. Have you given any thought to where you'll live now?"

Terri shook her head. "I'll have to find a place. And I've got to sell the furniture. There's going to be so much to do."

"I'll help you with it. Listen, I know someone who's got a small pickup I can borrow when you move."

"Ellen, I can't ask you—"

"Hey, I'm your friend, right? I want to help."

Terri squeezed her arm. "Thank you."

Mixed with Terri's relief was a feeling of loss. Gone would be the financial burden, the fear that the killer had come back for her, the horror of being in the place where Stanley was murdered. But gone, too, would be the place of so many good memories, not to mention the last vestige of the life she had once had—and might never have again. A tear slipped from her eye.

"You okay?" Ellen asked.

Terri nodded.

"Want to talk about it?"

Terri told Ellen about her mixed emotions concerning the sale of the house. "I don't know what's going to happen to me," she said. "It's all so new, so strange. It's a whole new life. And I feel so . . . so powerless." She wiped away another tear. "I'm sorry, Ellen. I shouldn't lay all this on you. You've already done so much."

"Now listen," Ellen said, "at a time like this you have to lean on someone, or you're not going to make it. I said I wanted to help, and I meant it."

Terri rested her head on Ellen's shoulder. "I don't know what I'd do without you."

The blurry white thing moved to the right, then to the left. It was a blob, a curious blotch of whiteness. It wasn't real. Then all of a sudden it came into focus. It was a nurse. And Doug Glockner realized he was alive.

"Well, I see you're awake," the nurse said. "How are you feeling?" She was young, dark-haired, pretty. She reminded Doug of the woman in the bar, the one he hadn't tried to pick up.

"I guess I feel okay," he said in a scratchy voice. His throat was dry, and there was a plastic tube taped to his arm. He tried to think of the proper way to put the question he wanted to ask, but his brain didn't seem to want to function, so he said simply, "Am I going to live?"

"The bullet missed all the vital organs," she said. "It chipped a rib, but that shouldn't cause you any serious problems." She smiled. "There will be a doctor along to see you shortly. You'd better save your other questions for him."

The doctor showed up about half an hour later, a young guy with a foreign accent who repeated what the nurse had said and assured him that he'd be good as new in no time. Shortly after that a plainclothes police officer arrived.

"Hi," the woman said. "I'm Detective Francine McMurtry of the Atlanta police. Feel up to talking to me for a few moments?"

Glockner said sure. She was in her early thirties and had light brown hair that was almost blond, cut short. Her face was lightly freckled. She took out a notebook.

"Wanna tell me what happened?"

Glockner gave her the essentials.

"Did she say where in South Carolina she was from?"

Glockner shook his head, which made it hurt. He decided to answer verbally from now on.

"Did she say anything else that might help us identify her?"

Glockner thought for a moment. "Yes, she said she worked for an outfit that imported medical stuff, microscopes and things like that."

"Here in Atlanta?"

He started to nod and caught himself. "Yes," he said.

"Did she mention its name?"

"Yes . . . uh, let me think. It was two names. Barnes and something. I don't remember the other name."

"Anything else that might help us identify her?"

"No."

"Did you see her car?"

"No."

Glockner answered no to another four or five questions; then the police officer said, "Describe her as carefully as you can. Try not to leave anything out."

Glockner described her. The cop pressed for more detail, color of eyes, length of hair, complexion, jewelry, nail polish, watch, clothes. Glockner told her what he could.

"Your description matches exactly with what the people in the bar said. If I send by an artist, you think you can come up with a picture of her?"

"I'll sure try. You think you can catch her?"

"I'll sure try," she said and smiled. It was a dazzling smile.

Glockner wanted to chuckle, but he thought he might damage something if he did. "You think she gave her right name and told me the truth about where she worked and all that?"

"I doubt it. Her purpose seemed to be robbery, and she'd have to be crazy to tell you her real name and where she works. But we'll check it out to be sure. Sometimes crooks are amazingly stupid.''

''I hope you get her,'' Glockner said bitterly. ''She had no right to do that to me, to lead me on like that and then shoot me.''

''No,'' McMurtry said somberly. ''She had no right to do that.''

SEVENTEEN

"You just take your time," the woman said. "If you decide you want the place, it'll be two-eighty-five a month, with a two-hundred-dollar damage deposit. If you need me, just knock on my door."

The woman left. She was about sixty with graying brown hair. She shuffled when she walked, the way patients in mental hospitals did sometimes.

Terri looked at the apartment. The carpet was worn and dull looking, with a cigarette burn near the entrance to the kitchen, a stain in one corner. The paint on the walls was discolored with age. There were clearly discernible rectangles where pictures had hung.

In the kitchen was a small gas range. Terri opened the oven door, and the odor of old burned grease wafted out. Years of charred spills and spatters had accumulated inside. Like the stove, the refrigerator had been made in the 1950s. It had a small freezer inside the main compartment, the kind you had to defrost, knocking off big chunks of white ice. The refrigerator was turned off, and it smelled vaguely sour. The floor was covered with scarred pink linoleum. Dead wax had built up in the corners of the room.

The place had two bedrooms, a requirement because Michelle would be coming home soon and need a place to stay. Both were small, just big enough to hold a double bed and a couple of small pieces of furniture. She realized suddenly that her oversize bed wouldn't even fit in the room. A lot of the furniture she planned to keep would be just too big for a place like this. And it would look horribly out of place.

God, she thought, why am I even considering this place? But the reason was obvious. It was the best deal she'd seen. The nice places were priced out of reach for a person of her income. Some of them rented for more than she made in a month. Even affording this place would be difficult.

The bathroom had a damp and vaguely fetid odor. The linoleum at the base of the toilet was beginning to rot away. The sink was one of the old varieties that was mounted directly to the wall. It had a brown stain where the water had been dripping from the tap. Terri hadn't known there were places like this in Meadowview. She'd thought it was all shiny and new, expensive houses with pretty lawns, backyard tennis courts, private pools. But then the people who cleaned the pools and scrubbed the floors and did other such jobs had to live somewhere.

For a long moment, Terri stood in the bathroom and stared at the bathtub, which still bore the ring of someone's last use of it. Then, desperately wanting to get out of this place, she ran out the door, past the manager's apartment, out of the two-story brick building. When she reached her station wagon, she leaned against it, trembling.

She thought of the person who killed her husband, the person responsible for everything that was happening to her. "I hate you," she said, fighting to hold back the tears. "Whoever you are, I hate you."

And at that moment, a part of her wished that Stanley's murderer was here right now so she could attack him, claw him, smash him. It was someone named Connie. Terri couldn't recall ever having felt this way about another human being. But if Connie were here right now—whoever Connie was—Terri would probably try to kill her.

And then her rage dissolved into confusion, which faded,

leaving only the pain. Feeling drained and numb, Terri climbed into her car.

Connie lay on the bed beside Stanley. She was naked. They had just made love.

"I'm going to have to do it again," she said. "He only had twenty-four dollars in his wallet. It's not nearly enough."

"That's just the chance you take," Stanley said. "There's really no way to tell how much money someone is carrying."

"I wish I hadn't had to shoot him."

"You only did what you had to do."

"I know, but he seemed like a pretty nice guy. You know, he wasn't like Jack Martin or any of those other assholes."

"You didn't want to shoot him. He forced you to do it."

"I wonder if I killed him."

"You can buy a newspaper later, see what it says."

"I think I will. I hope I didn't kill him."

"Maybe you didn't. You shouldn't worry about it, darling."

"I guess you're right. He can identify me, but so can everybody in the bar, so it doesn't matter."

"When are you going to try it again?"

"Tonight. I have to get some money."

"I have complete confidence in you, darling. This time it will go just as you want it to."

She dozed for a while, and when she awakened, she lay perfectly still, keeping her eyes closed but feeling Stanley's presence beside her. Slowly her hand slid down to her thigh, began stroking it; then her finger teased the lips of her vagina, entered it, slid out, rubbing over her clitoris. And suddenly Stanley was making love to her again.

"Darling," he whispered.

"Yes, Stanley," she said, moaning. "Yes, yes."

* * *

Captain Eugene Cantrell sat at a desk in the detective squad room at the Cresthaven police station. Because the motel would have charged him for each call, he'd asked permission to use a phone here, and this was where they'd put him.

The room was like detectives' work areas everywhere, a space with too many desks crowded into it. Some of the desks, like the one he was using, were old and made of wood; others were gray metal, new but cheap.

Cantrell had gone through the phone book, calling all the motels in metropolitan Atlanta. He hadn't counted them, but as his grandfather was fond of saying, there were more of them than Carter had little pills. And Carter, he was sure, had a *lot* of little pills. None of the motels had registered anyone named Connie Stewart or Linda Barnes, not that he expected her to use her real name or the alias she'd used at the Dixie Darling. Nor did any of the motel clerks and managers he talked to recall registering a lone blond woman who fit the description of Connie Stewart.

He'd checked in with Sam Johnson back in Chickasaw County, and Sam told him that the address in Mobile that Connie had used to register at the Dixie Darling Motel was a phony. He'd also checked out the name Linda Barnes, coming up with nothing.

Cantrell phoned Connie Stewart's parents in Nashville. Mrs. Stewart told him she'd never heard of Linda Barnes, and she had no idea why Connie might have gone to Georgia. He phoned David Young, the priest who'd known Connie in Florida; he, too, was unable to help. Cantrell charged all the calls to Chickasaw County.

As promised, Lieutenant Robertson had run Connie Stewart's name through the motor vehicle department's computer. One person by that name had bought a car recently in Georgia. She was fifty-seven and lived in Savannah. She was also a Constance officially, not a Connie.

He decided to ask the lieutenant to do the same with the name Linda Barnes. Leaning back in the chair, Cantrell rubbed his eyes, wondering what he was going to do next.

He could stay here only so long, even if he started getting close to Connie Stewart. And right now he wasn't close. Modern transportation being what it was, Connie Stewart could be hobnobbing with the folks in Karachi right now.

Cantrell decided to check with the airlines and other transportation companies, see whether anyone named Connie Stewart or Linda Barnes had bought a ticket. Pulling over the phone book, he opened it to airlines. Cantrell wondered how much money Connie had with her when she left Alabama. Not that much, he imagined. And if she'd used it up, how was she supporting herself?

"Careful, honey," Connie said as the man nearly tripped. They were leaving the Brickyard Bar, which got its name from having been built on a site once occupied by a brick manufacturing company. There was a picture of it on the wall. The man with Connie was named Henry. He was about six and a half feet tall and nearly as thin as a piece of spaghetti. He was also so drunk he could barely walk.

"I think I'd better drive," Connie said. "If you don't get us killed, you'll get busted for DWI. I think that would sort of spoil the mood, don't you?"

"Shit, Judy, I can drive." He laughed drunkenly. "I may get so shitfaced I can't walk, but I can still drive. Ask anybody knows me. They'll tell you."

"Where's your car?"

"That's it over there, the blue pickup across the street." It was right under a streetlight.

Connie stopped him, pressed her body against his. "Please," she said seductively. "Let's go to my car."

"Where you parked?"

She pointed across a residential side street where an abandoned gas station was obscured by shadows. "It's just right over there," she said, pressing her pelvis into his leg.

"You ever do it in a car?" Henry asked teasingly.

"No, but I'm willing to try."

"Come on," he said, pulling her along now. "We'll use your car, like you want."

The bar was on a minor commercial street, squeezed between a laundry and a used clothing store. Although the lounge was pretty much white, the neighborhood was mixed. Anxious to get to the car, Henry pulled her across the intersecting street and into the abandoned gas station.

"Where you parked?" he asked.

"In back."

"Why'd you park there?"

"There's somebody I don't want to see my car, find out where I am."

"Oh. You got boyfriend troubles, huh?"

"You could say that."

They moved around the building, avoiding a stack of old tires that had apparently been left behind when the service station closed. There was enough light to see here, but Connie and her companion couldn't be seen from the street.

Reaching into her purse, Connie said, "Let me get the keys."

"Hurry, baby," he said, letting his hand slide over her ass.

She stepped back from him, pulling the gun from her purse. "Give me your wallet, Henry."

He stared at her, wide-eyed.

"Give it here, Henry."

He was trembling.

"Henry, if you don't give me the damn thing, I'm going to have to shoot you."

Slowly his hand went behind him, came back with the wallet.

"Throw it to me, Henry. Careful, so I can catch it real easy."

Henry tossed it to her. Still holding the gun on him, she used her free hand to thumb open the money compartment. It contained about thirty dollars. Connie took the money, tossed the billfold back to him. It landed at his feet, and

202

for the first time Connie noticed the dark area around Henry's crotch.

"Hell, Henry, you pissed yourself."

Connie turned and hurried away, slipping the gun and money into her purse. Only thirty dollars. Didn't anybody carry cash with them anymore? So far two nights of armed robbery had netted her a little over fifty dollars.

Ahead, parked in the shadows of a residential street was her latest car—a blue Pontiac. She would have to drive to another part of town, find another bar, try again.

Lloyd Porter was feeling aggravated with the world when he pulled into the trailer park where he lived. Ignoring the CHILDREN PLAYING/5 MPH sign, he stepped down hard on the gas, throwing up gravel with the rear tires of his yellow Ford pickup. Old Mrs. Gilmer, who was standing beside her double-wide, watering her flowers, gave him a dirty look. Lloyd ignored her.

When he got off work at the building supplies company, he found both rear tires of his pickup flat, the valve stems cut off with a knife. Kids had done it, he was sure. People didn't control their kids anymore, just let them run loose, do as they pleased. If Lloyd Junior ever behaved like that, he'd kick his ass around the trailer park a few times until the boy got the idea.

Lloyd had to remove the flat tires and, because there was no one around to give him a ride, he had to roll them to a gas station that must have been half a mile away. Then it had taken the damn nigger working there an hour to get around to fixing his tires. As he pulled up in front of his own trailer—a twelve wide he'd bought used—he was two hours late.

Glancing at himself in the rearview mirror, he saw that his blond hair was mussed and that he had a smear of dirt on his cheek. Reaching into his shirt pocket, he discovered his comb was missing, presumably lost while he was fooling with the truck tires. He got out of the truck, slamming the door.

Carrie Sue met him as he stepped into the mobile home. She was a bony woman with dark hair, big eyes, a nose that was a little too big for her thin face. Like Lloyd, she was twenty-six.

"Where have you been?" she demanded.

Ignoring her, he went into the kitchen, got a beer, then switched on the TV set, and sat down on the couch. Popping open the beer, he took a big gulp.

"Dinner's ruined," Carrie Sue said. "You can only keep food warm for so long; then it dries out, and it's not worth eating anymore."

He drank some more beer, watched the comedy on TV. It didn't seem very funny. His wife stared at him, angry. Chugging the rest of the beer, Lloyd crumpled the can, carried it into the kitchen, and threw it into the trash. He returned with another beer, sat down again.

"Lloyd, don't you at least want to go out and get us some hamburgers or something?"

He drank some more beer.

"Aren't you even going to speak to me? I'd like to know where you were."

"Where's Lloyd Junior?" he asked.

"He already had his dinner, and he's over playing with Teddy Morrison. Are you going to tell me where you were?"

"Somebody gave me two flat tires on the truck. I had to get them fixed."

Carrie Sue folded her arms, looked exasperated. "Well, shit, Lloyd, why didn't you call me, so I'd have known? I could have held up on dinner and everything would have been okay."

"I didn't get a chance to call you."

"All you had to do was walk in the door and pick up a phone. That place you work at is full of phones."

Lloyd hurled his half-drunk beer across the room. It bounced off the wall and landed on the carpet, spewing white foam.

"Jesus, Lloyd! What good do you think—"

Carrie Sue stopped talking because she saw it coming. She backed away, but she was too late. Lloyd backhanded her so hard he knocked her backward into the wall. He grabbed her, spun her around, and hit her again, with his fist this time. She landed on the couch, sitting there as if she were watching TV.

"Lloyd!" she screamed. "Stop it!"

Lloyd straddled her, smacking her face with one slap after another. Her head moved back and forth with the blows, as if she were watching a tennis match. Her eyes seemed to have lost their focus. Her face was red and puffy. A trickle of blood ran from the corner of her mouth. Lloyd stopped hitting her.

"Next time, you keep your goddamned mouth shut," he said.

He didn't know whether she heard him. He really didn't care. He'd beat her up twice before when she'd mouthed off. Wasn't his fault if she didn't learn. He went into the kitchen to get another beer, but then he realized that he didn't want to sit home and drink beer. The energy generated by his anger was still burning in him; he needed some excitement. Without even giving a glance in Carrie Sue's direction, Lloyd walked out of the door.

He threw up gravel again as he drove out of the mobile home park. A brown dog standing in the park's entrance quickly moved out of his way. It was that damned mutt the Morrisons had. Always barking at night and getting into people's garbage cans. Oughta go back and run it over, Lloyd thought. But he kept on going.

The two-lane street he was following ran through a residential area; then became commercial. The golden arches appeared ahead, and he considered getting something to eat. He passed the McDonald's. He didn't want food; he wanted action. He wanted to find a woman wouldn't run off at the mouth all the time, one that would treat him right.

Connie sat at the bar, drinking a draught beer. This place was a little classier than the others she'd tried, and she hoped its customers might have a little more money. She'd been here ten minutes. So far no one had approached her.

The lounge was L-shaped. The longer leg of the L stretched out behind her. The tables were there. Some were occupied by couples; others had been pulled together to accommodate larger groups of men and women. The only unattached males were two guys to her left, in the other leg of the L, where there was a pool table. They were shooting eight-ball. She'd smiled at one of them once, but he'd been too involved in the game to notice.

When the blond guy with a smudge on his face came in, Connie thought he was a friend of the pool shooters, because he walked right toward them. But he abruptly turned and went into the men's room. When he came out, the smudge was gone from his face. He was in his mid-twenties and had thick, slightly mussed hair. He wasn't bad looking. Connie watched in the mirror behind the bar as he sat down at an empty table. The barmaid took his order.

About five minutes passed before he sat down on the stool beside hers, smiled real big, and said, "Would you be interested in letting a fellow buy you a beer?"

"And give up this marvelous conversation I'm having with this beer glass?"

It took him a moment to figure out where she was coming from; then he grinned real big again. "I think I might be a little bit more fun to talk to than that glass. Anyway, my name's Lloyd, and my table's over here if you'd like to join me."

She smiled, then nodded. When they were sitting at his table, she said, "What do you do, Lloyd?"

"Sell building supplies." He smiled again, real self-confident. "I saw you watching me in the mirror."

"And here I thought I was being sneaky."

He laughed. "I like you. You got a good sense of humor."

She smiled, said nothing.

"You know, you haven't even told me your name."

"Candy."

206

"Candy what?"

She sighed. "It's spelled B-a-h-r. It was my daddy's idea. Thought he was being real clever, I guess."

"Oh, I don't know," he said, grinning again. "You look good enough to eat to me."

Again Connie smiled, remained silent. Beneath the table, he pressed his leg against hers. She let him do it. Twenty minutes later, they were leaving the bar together.

"My truck's over here, sugar," Lloyd said, guiding her by the elbow. This was a busy street. In addition to the bar, there were gas stations, fast food places, convenience stores. Places that were open at night.

"I need to get something from my car first, okay?"

"What?"

"Just something," she said mysteriously. She giggled, pulling him by the arm.

"Where's your car?"

"Around the corner there."

"I got a rubber if that's all you're worried about." He was standing still now, not letting her move him.

"It's not that, honey. It's . . . it's just something I've got to have."

Clamping his hand on hers, he led her in the opposite direction. "Whatever it is, you don't need it. Come on."

"I do need it. Honest."

But he wasn't paying attention.

When they reached his yellow pickup, he opened the door for her, helped her inside. A moment later, they were driving away from the bar.

"Can we go to your place?" he asked. "Or should we go to a motel?"

Connie had been desperately trying to think of a good way to handle this unexpected situation. She said, "Let's go to my place."

"Where is it?"

"I'll show you. Go straight."

Connie watched him as he drove. Although he was fairly attractive, there was a hardness to his face, a hint of cruelty. Glancing at her, he gave her his good-old-country-boy grin.

"Slide over here beside me," he said, patting the seat.

Connie complied, and he put his hand on her leg. Connie's fingers found the zipper of her purse, rested there. Ahead was a dark street.

"Turn left," she said.

He did, and they were driving into a neighborhood of large two-story houses that weren't being maintained too well. A lot of cars were parked on the street; the houses here had apparently been divided into upstairs and downstairs apartments and rented out, the original owners moving on as the neighborhood began to deteriorate.

"How much farther?" Lloyd asked.

"Just a little farther. I'll show you."

She knew Lloyd, knew him real well, even though she'd just met him tonight. Lloyd was Jack Martin, and he was a million other guys just like Jack Martin. And Connie knew she would have to be careful. The Lloyds of this world would not like getting robbed by a woman. Women washed the dishes and cleaned the house and provided sex. Never complaining when their own sexual needs went unfulfilled. Always encouraging their men, flattering them. And never, never giving them any shit.

Well, here comes some shit, Lloyd.

"Pull in where that space is," Connie said.

It was the darkest part of the block, a few hundred feet from the nearest streetlight. The truck headlights picked out a rusty child's wagon on the sidewalk. One of its wheels was missing. She slid over to her side of the seat as Lloyd maneuvered into the parking space. She waited until he'd killed the engine; then she pulled out the gun.

"Give me the keys, Lloyd. Toss them real gently, okay?"

He stared at her, apparently trying to decide how to play it. Then his face reddened slightly. "You bitch. All you wanted was to get me alone somewhere so you could rob me."

"That's all I wanted, Lloyd. Give me the keys."

"What you going to do if I don't, little girl?"

"I'm not a little girl, Lloyd. And if—"

"Yeah, you do look sort of shopworn, don't you?"

"—if you don't give me the keys, I'm going to shoot you."

He hesitated, apparently uncertain; then he said, "Shoot me? You? I don't believe you got it in you, woman."

He used the term as if it were an insult. He was getting bolder. She would have to do something quickly, or she would lose control of the situation.

"Lloyd, it would make me real happy to shoot you, and if you don't start cooperating, that's exactly what I'm going to do. You can count on it."

Connie didn't understand why she didn't just shoot him. The world would be better off without him. And then she realized that she wanted to put him in his place, belittle him, make him—even if only for a moment—fear a woman. If she killed him, he'd simply be dead. Like Jack Martin. But this way he'd remember what happened this night forever. Connie lowered the gun, aiming it at his crotch.

"You don't want to lose all that male equipment between your legs, give me the keys."

Lloyd paled. "Okay," he said. "Okay."

He tossed the keys at her, but it was a bad throw. They hit the dash, dropped to the floor by her feet.

"That's okay, Lloyd. Don't be nervous. All you got to do now is hand over your wallet, and you can get out of the truck."

He removed it from his back pocket, hesitated, then tossed it. The billfold landed next to her on the seat.

"There's a hundred and fifty in there," he said unhappily.

"Appreciate it, Lloyd. You just hop on out now, and you'll be fine."

"What about my truck?"

"I'll take real good care of it, Lloyd. Don't you worry."

He sat there, studying her from the corner of his eyes, apparently trying to decide whether to make a move.

"Don't be stupid, Lloyd." Using both hands to steady the gun, she applied a slight amount of pressure against the trigger.

Lloyd got out of the truck. Connie picked up the keys, then quickly slid over to lock the driver's side door. Her fingers were inches from the locking button when the door was yanked open, and Lloyd was throwing himself into the cab, grabbing the hand in which she held the gun. She tried to pull it away from him, and it fired, the bullet going through the roof of the truck.

As they struggled, the gun was knocked from her grasp. Connie heard it land on the floor. Lloyd was on top of her now, pressing her down on the seat. His face was inches from hers. She could smell the beer on his breath.

"Think you're smart, do you, bitch?"

He raised up, pulling back his hand, but there was no room for him to swing in the truck, and most of the blow went into the seat back.

"Goddamn whore," he said, and this time he lifted himself farther off her. Connie turned her head; the blow caught her on the cheek. Although he still wasn't able to get his weight into it, the punch had hurt. He raised himself up again. Suddenly Connie's legs were no longer pinned, and she pulled them up, trying to get her knees between herself and Lloyd. With her right hand, Connie grabbed the door handle on the passenger side, trying to pull herself out from under him. And then she had her knees against his chest.

He took a swing at her, and she pushed against him as hard as she could, pulling on the door handle. Suddenly the door opened and she tumbled out, Lloyd coming after her. She heard a clunk and realized that she must have kicked the gun out with her.

Connie groped in the darkness for it, but before she could find the automatic, Lloyd had her, pulling her to her feet, his fist slamming into her face. She stumbled backward, trying to maintain her balance. Then Lloyd was in front of her again. He threw her to the ground.

Looking down at her, he said, "So you were going to rob me, huh? So you were going to steal my truck, huh?"

She couldn't see his face in the dark, but his voice seemed to carry a mixture of anger and disgust. He kicked her in the side, and she tried to roll away from him, but she was stopped by an object. It was metal, the wagon she'd seen as they pulled up. Connie expected him to kick her again, but he didn't. She managed to get to her knees. She was dizzy. If she tried to stand she'd probably collapse.

"I could just kick the shit out of you," Lloyd said. "But first I think I'll take what you were promising me before. You can either give it to me nice, or we can do it the hard way. All the same to me."

Connie watched him, said nothing. The dizziness was starting to go away.

"Come on," he said, reaching down for her with his hand. "We can't do it here."

Ignoring his hand, Connie started to stand up. As she did so, she gripped the handle of the wagon. Then, abruptly straightening, she swung the wagon at Lloyd as hard as she could. It hit him in the side of the head, knocking him off his feet. Connie scrambled to the truck, feeling in the shadows for the gun. Behind her Lloyd moaned. Connie's search become more frantic. Run, something inside was screaming at her, run while you still can. And then she found the gun.

Picking it up and turning around, she saw that Lloyd was standing but dazed. He took a wobbly step toward her, apparently unaware of the gun.

"You should have just given me the money," she said and shot him. He took a staggering step backward. She shot him again. He fell. Connie walked up to him, aimed between his legs, and shot him again. Lloyd twitched but made no sound.

Connie glanced around her. No one was in sight. Suddenly the lights went out in the house they were in front of. Its occupants didn't want to be involved in whatever was happening out by the street. Atlanta was getting to be just like New York. Or maybe it always had been. Connie neither knew nor cared.

She found the keys where they had fallen on the driver's seat, started the truck, and drove off, wanting to be several blocks away before the police arrived. She would abandon the truck back at the bar, where her latest "borrowed" car was parked.

EIGHTEEN

Terri stood in the middle of her now empty living room. Indentations in the carpeting marked the spots where the furniture had stood. Empty like this, the house was cold, lifeless, no longer a home in which people had loved and laughed and lived.

Her gaze settled on the corner in which they always put the Christmas tree, and she wondered whether the new owners would put it there. She recalled the year they'd given Michelle, who was only five or six then, an enormous stuffed bear nearly as big as she was. The girl had saved the enormous box until last, and then her eyes had widened in delight when she'd seen what was inside.

What are you going to feed it? Stanley had asked. And for a moment, Michelle had looked at him as though he were crazy; then she'd caught on to the game, replying, *It eats daddies that say silly things.* She named it Mr. Toggy. Nobody knew why.

The portion of Terry's brain that defended her against things that were too painful started to push the memory away, but she clung to it a moment longer, then let it go reluctantly. It was something to be cherished. Memories were all she had now, and if she forced herself to abandon them, she would have nothing at all.

And then she amended that. She had her life. She had Michelle, Stanley's daughter. She had whatever the future held.

A doctor was buying the house. The deal would be formally closed in a couple of hours. Only a few days had passed since he'd made the offer. He was paying cash, which eliminated the usual long wait while the mortgage company processed the paperwork.

Terri moved into the kitchen. Suddenly feeling weak, she leaned against the counter. This room looked a little less empty because it contained things that were permanent, like the cabinets, the built-in oven and range. The big side-by-side refrigerator-freezer was still here, too. It had been sold with the house.

All the furniture and appliances in the house had come from Ferguson's Furniture City. Everything was the best, top of the line. Terri wondered whether she would ever again own anything that was top of the line.

An auction house had taken everything away, which had seemed easier than trying to sell it all through newspaper ads. Besides, she had no idea what the things in the house were worth. That was ironic, she supposed, considering that she owned an enormous furniture store. The auction would be held tomorrow. Terri had no intention of being present.

Studying the kitchen, Terri noted the huge size of it, the abundance of oak cabinets, the brownish-red quarry tiles. She and Stanley had the house built to their specifications. Hers had included a big kitchen with lots of storage space. As of midnight tonight, Terri wouldn't live here anymore. A doctor would live here. Terri would live in a two-eighty-five-a-month apartment in which the linoleum was rotting around the commode.

Although she hated the place, it had turned out to be the best deal she could find. She'd gone back, paid the shuffling woman manager the damage deposit and her first month's rent. Ellen and two teenage boys who were cousins of hers had helped Terri move in yesterday. She'd found a dead cockroach under the sink, mouse droppings in the clothes closet.

The furniture she'd taken with her had mainly come from the den and guest rooms. Everything else had been too big or expensive looking for the cheap apartment. And, of course, there had been the question of money. The bigger, nicer things would bring more at the auction, and she was going to need every penny she could get.

Terri had gathered up Stanley's things, taken them to the Salvation Army. She'd simply put everything in cardboard boxes, not letting herself recall anything special about this garment or that pair of shoes, forcing herself to view the task the way one viewed cleaning out an attic. It was the only way she could have gotten through it. Items with value—like golf clubs and power tools—had gone with the auctioneer.

Slowly, she left the kitchen, headed for the front door. She'd told herself she was coming back for a final look, to make sure she hadn't forgotten anything. But she knew now that wasn't true. She'd come to say good-bye.

Remembering that she'd promised to leave any duplicate keys in the house, she hurried back into the kitchen and put her key on the counter. Then she walked to the front door, made sure it was set to lock automatically, and closed it behind her.

At the Cresthaven police station, Captain Eugene Cantrell stepped into Lieutenant Robertson's office, lowered himself into a chair.

"Came by to thank you for your help," Cantrell said.

"I'm afraid we weren't able to offer you very much. You on your way back to Alabama?"

Cantrell nodded. "I've done about all I can do here, and I think the taxpayers of Chickasaw County would rather have me back home, dealing with criminals that are stealing the tape decks from their cars, instead of worrying about the ones that have run off to places like Georgia and aren't bothering them anymore."

"You get any leads on the Stewart woman?"

"All I know is she was here. It was her took the car to the junkyard, and she was staying at a motel in the next town over, Meadowview. I don't know why she came to Georgia. I don't know if she's still here."

"Well, if anything comes up we'll get in touch with you."

"I'd appreciate it." He handed the lieutenant an envelope. "My phone number's in there along with a picture of Connie Stewart that's about twenty years old. It's the most recent picture of her we've been able to come up with."

Robertson slipped the photo from the envelope and studied it, frowning. "Damn if she doesn't look familiar." He tapped it with his finger. "Where have I seen her?"

Cantrell remained silent. Nothing he could say would help the lieutenant remember.

Suddenly Peterson snapped his fingers. "Sure. There was a circular came over from Atlanta PD yesterday." He rummaged through the stuff on his desk. "Here it is," he said, handing a sheet of paper to Cantrell.

The Alabama policeman found himself looking at an artist's drawing of a woman who strongly resembled the girl in the photo. She also fit the description of Connie Stewart as she looked now. The Atlanta police wanted her for murder, aggravated battery with a firearm, and robbery. She'd been picking up men in Atlanta bars, then robbing them at gunpoint. One of her victims was wounded when he resisted. Another was killed. She'd used a variety of names with her victims, all thought to be aliases. Contact Detective Francine McMurtry, Atlanta PD.

"Can I have this?" Cantrell asked.

"Sure. Think it's her?"

"Sure looks like her."

"I take it you're not flying back to Alabama today."

"Not today," Cantrell said.

* * *

"Her name's Connie Stewart," Cantrell said. "I think she killed the guy she was living with back in Alabama."

Detective Francine McMurtry sat across from him in the booth. When she'd called, she suggested meeting for lunch—his treat—so they could talk away from the confusion of the squad room. The restaurant was a small place not far from downtown Atlanta that specialized in basic Southern cooking. The menu included catfish and chicken with dumplings, along with such vital accompaniments as black-eyed peas, fried okra, and slaw. The quantities were large, the prices reasonable, the decor humble.

Detective McMurtry looked like Doris Day, back in the days when she was making movies with Rock Hudson. Squeaky clean, freckle-faced, and cute. She seemed to be constantly burning up energy, even just sitting there. Cantrell thought it was a trait common to big city women. He told her what he knew about Connie Stewart.

"I showed your artist's sketch to the guy at the junkyard and the kid who gave her a ride to the motel. They both say it's her, no question."

"You got prints?" she asked, the piece of catfish on her fork poised midway between her plate and mouth.

"We found a lot of prints around Jack Martin's house that we assume are hers. You got anything to compare them with?"

"Lloyd Porter's pickup was full of prints. We're hoping some of them belong to the woman who killed him."

Cantrell nodded. "I'll get them run over to the highway patrol, so they can be wired to you."

"If she was staying at a motel in the suburbs, then there's a good chance she's still staying at one. We're going to check them all out."

"I already did that by phone," Cantrell said. "Of course, that's not a real reliable way to go about it. And I could have missed the clerk who checked her in."

"We'll have to make the rounds with the sketch, give everybody a copy."

"It'll take a while. It took me a while just to phone them all."

She shrugged. "It's got to be done. We don't have lead number one in this case. The bars where she hits on the men are all over town. We don't even know what section of the city she might be staying in. Until you came along, we didn't even know her name. She uses a different one each time she robs a guy. And a different life story."

"How many has she hit so far?"

"Seven. Sometimes she'll hit two in one night."

"How many times has she shot one of her victims?"

"Just twice. She wounded one guy, killed the other. Apparently she doesn't shoot unless the victim resists."

"Why you figure she's doing it?" Cantrell asked.

"What do you mean?"

"Well, as far as I can tell, she's never done anything like it before. She hasn't been what you'd call a good church-going Christian, but she hasn't committed any violent crimes either. Suddenly she whacks the dude she's living with, runs off to Georgia, and starts a brand new career as an armed robber. Why?"

"She couldn't take it anymore, living with this Jack Martin guy, so one day she just snaps, blows him away. It's a big line to step over, killing somebody, but once she's done it, hell, armed robbery's nothing."

Cantrell shook his head. "One's a crime of passion; the other's the sort of thing a crazy kid does, or an addict looking for a fix. Most criminals are under thirty-five. She's thirty-eight. I never ran into anyone before took up armed robbery at thirty-eight."

"She's running, she's scared, she doesn't know what she's doing."

"Maybe. But why'd she run in the first place? First offense. A good lawyer claims the guy was about to kill her and she shot him in self-defense. She's seen enough murder trials on the news to know that someone like her isn't going to do much in the way of hard time."

"Hey, people get scared and they run. They don't always think it out."

Cantrell rubbed his brow. "That's true enough. But I think she came here for a purpose. For one thing, I can't figure her going to the suburbs. To Atlanta, sure. You run for the big city. Nobody runs to Cresthaven or Meadowview unless they've got something in mind. There's nothing to draw them there. Most people have probably never heard of those places."

"She's in Atlanta now."

"Maybe it's because she needs money."

The Atlanta detective frowned. "You mean it's a better place to rob guys in bars?"

"Well, isn't it?"

"Sure. In the suburbs, what she's doing would be a crime wave. Here it's not so unusual."

"As far as I know," Cantrell said, "she's not an addict. That means she's stealing just to survive. It would be a lot safer just to get a job or move in with a guy, let him take care of her. She's lived with guys most of her life, and she's always worked—at least since her rich daddy cut her off, which was a long time ago."

"So what are you saying?" McMurtry asked.

"I don't know what I'm saying. I'm just thinking out loud."

She was quiet for a moment, thinking, too. Then she said, "You're right that she should be able to move in with a guy if she wanted to. From what her victims say, she's not extremely pretty or anything, but she knows how to come on to a guy. She's real good at it."

"As many guys as she's been with, I'm not surprised."

"And most of them were jerks, right? The sort who'd slap her around a lot."

"Seems that way."

"Think she's a man-hater?"

"Better ask a shrink about that. I'm just a country cop."

She ate a forkful of slaw, then said, "Witnesses to the time she killed the guy say there was a struggle. Apparently he was beating on her pretty good. Somehow she came up with a gun and blew him away. She shot him twice before he fell. Then she walked up to him and shot him again.''

"He'd made her angry."

"Real angry. the bullet hit his thigh, right where it meets the pelvis." She looked up, her eyes meeting his.

"You mean she tried to . . ." He hesitated, searching for the right words. His Southern upbringing made it difficult for him to say "shoot his balls off" in front of a woman, even if she was a cop.

"She wanted to emasculate him," McMurtry said, apparently amused at his discomfort.

Taking a bite of his chicken and dumplings, Cantrell considered that a moment, then said, "You dig any bullets out of the guys she shot?"

"We got slugs from both of them. She used the same gun, twenty-five caliber."

"That's what she used on Martin."

She nodded. "You going to stick around? She's wanted for murder here, too, so even if we get her you're not going to get a crack at her until she's spent some years with the Georgia Department of Corrections."

"I'll stick around until we confirm that your murderer and my murderer are the same person. After that I guess I better head home, make sure the dog doesn't bite me, thinking I'm a stranger."

Ellen Farley was standing at the cash register, counting receipts.

"Good night," Terri Ferguson called, waving as she stepped through the front door of the shop.

Ellen waved back. She liked Terri a lot and wished she could pay her more. Although the shop made a profit, it was a very small profit, and if Ellen paid Terri as much as she'd like to, Terri would probably be making more money than she did.

The Cook's Nook provided Ellen with everything she needed. Because her husband had left her with a house that was paid for, her expenses were minimal. She drove a four-year-old Ford and had no interest in owning anything newer or fancier. Although her social life was hectic, it was also inexpensive. She helped out with charities, volunteered at the hospital, played bridge, gave cooking lessons. The profits from the store provided her with everything she wanted, except the ability to pay Terri a decent salary.

She wished Terri would find a nice man, get married. It would get her out of that terrible apartment, and it would end her loneliness. But Terri was a long way from being able to do anything like that. In a year maybe, or two. Hang on, Terri, she thought. Things will work out in time.

She realized suddenly that she'd lost count of checks she'd been adding up. She canceled the figures in the pocket calculator she was using, put the checks back into a single pile, and started again. Then a customer came in. Ellen started to say she was closed, then decided she shouldn't turn away business. She put the checks and calculator under the counter.

"Can I help you find something?" she asked.

"Do you sell happiness?" the blond woman asked.

"I beg your pardon."

"Never mind," the woman said, shaking her head. Wearing jeans and a wrinkled shirt, she was untypical of Ellen's customers, most of whom were middle-aged and fairly well off.

"Are you looking for anything in particular?" Ellen asked, feeling vaguely uneasy about the woman.

"I'm looking for you."

"For me?" When the woman failed to respond, Ellen said, "What can I do for you?"

Standing with her back to Ellen, the woman was examining an electric coffee mill. When she put it down and turned to face Ellen, she was holding a gun.

"You got paper bags there?" she asked.

Too terrified to speak, Ellen just nodded. She'd operated the store for nearly five years, and this was the first time she'd been robbed.

"Take the money from the cash register and put it into a bag."

Ellen did as she'd been told, taking the bills from each compartment of the cash drawer, dropping them into a bag.

"Now the big bills you hide under the cash tray," the woman said, moving to the counter. She kept the gun pointed at Ellen.

Ellen lifted it out, revealing two fifties, which she put into the bag.

"Got a money bag under the counter or a safe? Tell me the truth because I'm going to check."

"I . . . I don't have a safe," Ellen said, her voice barely more than a nervous whisper.

"And a money bag?"

Ellen got it from under the counter, held it up. "It's mostly change," she said. "I . . . I don't keep much cash here. Most of my customers use charge cards."

"Drop it in the paper bag."

Ellen complied.

"I didn't come here to rob you," the woman said. "But I need the money."

Ellen just stared at her. What was she supposed to say: It's okay, I don't mind?

"I'm sorry," the woman said. "I wish it didn't have to be this way."

"Just . . . just take the money and go."

"I told you," the woman said. "I didn't come here to rob you."

The gun in her hand fired. And then it fired again.

NINETEEN

As she usually did, Terri parked on a side street, leaving the spaces in front of the store for customers. It was one minute before nine, as close to being late as she'd come since starting work at the Cook's Nook. When the alarm had gone off this morning, she'd turned it off, rolled over for what she thought was just a moment. It was forty-five minutes.

She'd rushed out of the apartment, barely having had time to comb her hair and brush her teeth. Her stomach was churning disagreeably, partly due to the mad rush to get here and partly because there had been no time for breakfast.

Locking her car, Terri hurried to the small complex that housed the Cook's Nook and three other shops. She walked quickly past Meadowview Movies, a video rental place that didn't open until noon. Glancing into the next shop, she saw Mr. Weisberg, the florist, standing at the cash register. She waved, but apparently he didn't see her. Terri didn't spot the sign until she was reaching for the door of the Cook's Nook. It said:

CRIME SCENE
DO NOT ENTER
MEADOWVIEW POLICE DEPT.

Terri stared at it, confused. Looking through the glass front door, she thought the shop looked as it always had. What crime had been committed here? Where was Ellen? Hesitantly, she gave a gentle pull on the door. It was locked.

Terri tried to think of a reasonable explanation. Maybe the shop had been broken into last night. If that had happened, Ellen would be down at the police station, signing forms or whatever the victim did in such circumstances. Although there were no signs of a break-in at the front of the shop, there could be around the back. Terri ran past the florist's and the video rental place, around the side of the building, and into the alley that ran behind it. The rear entrance to the Cook's Nook's looked undisturbed. She tried the metal door. It was locked.

She knocked on the door, thinking that maybe Ellen had been in her office or the bathroom, out of sight when Terri had looked through the front door. Maybe it was okay for her to be inside as long as the store remained closed so no customers could mess up the crime scene.

But Terri knew she was desperately grasping for explanations because she didn't want to face the possibility that something really terrible had happened. She stared at the gray metal of the door, waiting for it to open, waiting for Ellen to say, Oh, hi, we got burglarized last night, but it's okay because the insurance will cover it.

"It's awful, isn't it? Simply awful."

Startled, Terri spun around to find herself looking at Kenneth Weisberg, the florist.

"Such a terrible thing," he said, shaking his head. He was a small man in his sixties with a bald head and a curly gray beard.

"What is?" Terri asked, afraid of what she'd hear.

"You mean you don't know?" he asked, surprised. "It was on the news this morning and everything."

"I don't know what happened," she said weakly. "Please tell me. Please."

"The store was robbed last night. Mrs. Farley was . . . was killed."

"Killed?" Terri had to lean against the wall. She heard noises in her ears, like waves smashing into rocks. The world seemed to be swirling around her.

"Are you all right?" Weisberg asked.

"Yes," she replied, but she thought she might collapse at any moment.

"I don't know exactly when it happened. The police found her body last night some time. The patrolman noticed that all the lights were on, not just the lights that are usually on at night. He found the door unlocked, and when he went inside he found Mrs. Farley lying behind the counter. The cash drawer was open."

"I'm surrounded by death." It took her a moment to realize she'd spoken the words as well as thought them.

"What did you say?"

"Nothing."

"I think you should come inside with me and sit down."

Terri let him lead her through the rear door of the flower shop. Potted plants were lined up on wooden shelves, growing under fluorescent lights mounted a few inches above them. The damp smell of earth was mixed with the perfume of flowers. The humidity was like a slap in the face.

"I buy everything wholesale," Weisberg said. "These potted plants, cut flowers, everything. People always seem to think I grow everything here, but it would be impossible. There's not even a greenhouse."

And then Terri was in the front of the shop. Weisberg showed her to a chair behind the counter.

"Can I get you anything?" he asked.

She shook her head.

Terri sat there, staring at the back side of the counter, trying not to think about what it must have been like for

Ellen, trying not to wonder why everyone she came into contact with died violently. A big blond woman came in to order flowers for a funeral. Then a man who spoke with a New York accent came in to order a spray for the same funeral. Suddenly Terri didn't want to be where people were discussing funerals, so she thanked the florist and left.

She had driven halfway home before realizing that she was headed for her old residence, the place now owned by a doctor. She turned at the next through street and headed for her new home—not that she accepted it as that. It was the place where she stayed. Nothing more.

Although her vision clouded a number of times as she drove, no tears came. Had tragedy become so much a part of her life that it had become unworthy of tears, too commonplace to cry over? But she didn't want to think about that. She didn't want to think at all.

Reaching her apartment, she sat down on the living room couch, tried to empty her mind. But after a few moments, she found she was unable to stop herself from thinking about Ellen. And lingering in the background was a persistent question she simply wasn't ready to deal with yet: What am I going to do now? Not only did she have no answer for that, but thinking about her own problems when a good person like Ellen had just been murdered made her feel selfish.

At least Ellen's death was just a robbery, unrelated to the murders of Stanley and Marlene. Even so, she felt vaguely guilty about it, as if Ellen's murder were somehow her fault.

To give her mind something else to focus on, Terri got up, intending to turn on the TV. But before she reached the set, someone knocked on the door. Opening it, she found a red-haired woman looking at her sheepishly.

"Hi," the woman said. "I know this is going to sound corny, but I just moved in across the hall and I need to borrow a cup of sugar." She held up an empty coffee cup.

"Sure," Terri said, pulling herself together. "Come in. I'll get you some."

"Oooo," the woman said as she followed Terri into the kitchen. "You've got nice furniture. I rented my place furnished, and you should see the dilapidated old junk in it."

"It's furniture I had when . . . when I was married."

"Divorced, huh? Me, too."

"No, uh, I'm a widow."

"Oh, hey, I'm sorry if I . . . well, you know."

"It's okay," Terri said. "You had no way of knowing." She took the cup from the woman and began filling it from a canister.

"I'll replace that as soon as I get to the store," the woman said. "This is my first morning here, and I put on some coffee to brew, poured myself a cup, and found out I didn't have any sugar. I know some people like coffee that way, but to me it's just so bitter that I can't drink it."

Terri handed her the cup of sugar.

"Thank you." With her free hand she slapped the side of her head. "What's the matter with me? Here I come into your place, take your sugar, and don't even introduce myself." She stuck out her hand. "My name's Nettie Cownars. I'm from Louisiana, little town you never heard of."

"Terri Ferguson." She shook the woman's hand.

"Short for Theresa?"

"No, it's just Terri."

"Oh. Nettie's another name for Janet. That's my real name, Janet. But nobody's ever called me that. If anyone did, I don't think I'd know who they were talking to."

"Nettie's a nice name," Terri said. "Sort of old-fashioned sounding." She started to put the lid back on the canister, and she realized her hand was shaking. She put the lid down.

"You okay?"

"Yes. I think so." But she didn't feel okay. She felt as though she was about to collapse.

"I noticed when I came in that you looked kind of pale and shaky. You sure everything's all right?"

"I've just had quite a shock. That's all."

Nettie studied her a moment. There was concern in her eyes. "Would you like to talk to somebody about it? Mostly I'm a talker, but when I put my mind to it, I'm a pretty fair listener, too."

"I'm sure you've got enough troubles of your own," Terri said. "You don't need mine." And in the next instant she heard a voice that almost seemed to come from someone else telling this stranger from across the hall what had happened this morning. When she finished, she was shaking.

"Come on," Nettie said, taking Terri by the arm. "Let's go into the living room and sit. I definitely think you could use somebody to talk to."

When they were both seated on the couch, Terri said, "Your coffee's going to be stale."

"Don't you go worrying yourself over that. I can always brew up another pot." She smiled.

For the first time, Terri looked closely at Nettie Cownars. Her red hair was shoulder-length and fairly straight. She had gray eyes and the sort of pale skin that usually sunburned easily. Her mouth seemed a little too big, but she had a nice smile, pretty teeth.

"It's terrible, the crime these days," Nettie said. "Aren't but about five hundred people in the town I'm from, and there was a guy killed there right before I left. Same as what happened to your boss. He was a clerk in one of those 7-Eleven stores. Some guy robbed him and then shot him."

Suddenly Terri was telling Nettie about Stanley, about Marlene, about the abrupt change in her life that accompanied her husband's murder. Twice she stopped on the edge of tears when she was talking about Stanley, but the tears never came. And she wondered whether she really

228

had become accustomed to tragedy or whether something inside prevented her from crying because it knew that if she ever started she might never stop.

"Sweet Jesus," Nettie whispered when Terri had told it all. "It's not very often I'm at a loss for words, but I don't know what to say. I never heard of so much happening to one person before."

Terri told her story in more detail then, omitting only the part about Stark and his suspicions, and after she'd told it, the conversation began to change. Terri wasn't sure at what point the change came, but all of a sudden Nettie was talking about growing up in Louisiana, telling her about shrimpers and fishermen, and gators and swamps. Though slowly at first, Terri began easing into her own anecdotes from her childhood in south Florida. How she lived next to a vacant lot full of grapefruit trees because the subdivision in which she lived had once been an orchard. How the boys had BB gun fights in the lot, using the trees for cover, and how she had always been afraid they'd hurt each other or start shooting at her cat, Beanie. Nettie told her how the girls she grew up with had French names like Antoinette, Dominique, and Marguerite. And how many of the children spoke Cajun, which she had never learned.

"I remember a few words, from hearing them so often. Like *lagniappe*. If you say that's *lagniappe*, it's like saying that's gravy, a little something extra." She shrugged. "People say it a lot in southern Louisiana."

It was nearly noon when Nettie went back to her own apartment. She told Terri to come over as soon as everything was put away and straightened up, and the place wasn't such a mess. Terri said she would.

When she sat down on the couch again, she let her eyes travel around the room and found she was getting used to seeing her good furniture in this shabby room. If nothing else, the place looked a lot better than it had when it was bare.

Nettie Cownars had been a big help; the woman had

shown up just when Terri desperately needed someone to talk to. But the warm feeling that comes with companionship was cooling. Terri was alone again, with only her thoughts for company.

"Murder follows me," she said after a moment. The notion hung there, demanding her attention, but she didn't know how to deal with it.

Connie.

And the name, too, seemed suspended in the room, like a presence. And yet Terri wasn't sure she still believed in Connie. The name could have been some unrelated memory—from childhood maybe—a thing that swirled through the mind of a dying man. Maybe the woman running from the house had been a burglar surprised in the act.

Terri reminded herself again that even if Connie did exist, she hadn't killed Ellen. A robber had done that. It happened all the time. Stores were held up, innocent people hurt.

Suddenly, Terri clasped the sides of her head with her hands, as if doing so would stop the thoughts churning within. Getting up, she switched on the portable color TV that had been the kitchen set in her previous house and now was the only television set she owned.

"I think Terri Ferguson's the killer," Sergeant Stark said. "I think she murdered all three of them."

He and Beauchamp were sitting in the office of Dr. Grace Smythe, the psychiatrist who advised the Meadowview police department. The doctor, who sat behind a massive and expensive-looking wooden desk, was a tall, slender woman with dark hair and the most penetrating eyes Stark had ever seen. He had already told her what he knew about the murders of Stanley Ferguson, Marlene Williamson, and Ellen Farley.

"Trouble is," he said, "I don't have a motive. By killing her husband, she wound up losing the good life she'd been leading. Killing Marlene Williamson cost her her closest friend. Killing Ellen Farley cost her job. So, on the surface anyway, she'd have every reason not to kill these people.''

"Murder is often a crime of passion," the psychiatrist said.

"If there's any passion in these murders, I can't find it," Stark said. "There's no indication that she argued with any of the victims, not even her husband. She had no reason to be angry with Williamson or Farley. Hell, she'd only worked for Farley a couple of weeks. Are you suggesting she's so explosive that the smallest thing can make her kill someone?''

"I'm not suggesting anything, Sergeant. I merely pointed out that murder isn't always done for nice logical reasons like what the murderer may gain through the act.''

No kidding, Stark thought. The psychiatrist studied him and the sergeant felt as if she could look right into him and know all there was to know. It wasn't a feeling he liked. He said:

"What I need to know is whether such behavior could be accounted for psychologically.'' This was the third time Stark had dealt with the psychiatrist, and she usually annoyed him. He sensed that she didn't like him very much.

Dr. Smythe thought for a moment; then she said, "If this Terri Ferguson is truly the one murdering these people, then I think you should look at what they had in common.''

"Except for being killed by Terri Ferguson, they had almost nothing in common," Stark said.

"If that were true, Sergeant, I don't think she would have killed them—unless she's just killing for the thrill it gives her, and from what you've told me about Terri Ferguson that doesn't seem too likely.

"What do the victims have in common?" Beauchamp asked.

"They were all people Terri Ferguson was close to. In

fact, at the times they died, each one was the person she was closest to at that particular moment.''

"Doesn't seem like much of a reason for murder," Beauchamp said.

"You're not threatened by it," Dr. Smythe replied, shifting her gaze to Beauchamp. "Sometimes getting close to someone can be quite threatening. It means giving of yourself. It can mean giving more of yourself than you're willing to part with. But the relationship keeps demanding that you part with it.''

"Why not just pull out?" Beauchamp asked. "Why kill the person?''

"We're talking about someone who's disturbed, a person whose unconscious mind is terrified by the prospect of giving too much of the self to another person. It's your core, your essence. It's a sacred thing, to be treasured, guarded, kept secret. Letting it out is like losing everything that's you. What could be more threatening than losing yourself?''

She shifted her eyes back to Stark, and some inner part of himself wanted to shrink away from them. "But like Pat said, why not just end the relationship?" he asked.

"I'm getting to that. It's what's known as approach-avoidance conflict. She wants to be with people. She wants to be loved. She wants to have friends. Who doesn't? Let's take this Ellen Farley. She's the goal, all right? In approach-avoidance conflict the goal has both positive and negative valences. The positive valence is friendship. The negative one is the fear of a close relationship, which can lead to loss of self. Terri Ferguson doesn't know what to do. She's drawn to Ellen and frightened of approaching her at the same time. Usually the conflict is resolved by making a choice. You opt for the positive things the goal offers, or you decide the negative things outweigh the positive ones and you move on. But if you can't make that choice, you're stuck. And that can be a terrifying situation. It can render you helpless, unable to do anything.

"Or . . ." She paused, apparently considering her

words. "There is one other way to get out of the conflict situation. You can destroy the goal altogether."

Stark said, "You mean this . . . this conflict situation could be strong enough to make Terri Ferguson kill people?"

"In Terri Ferguson's case, I can't say. I've never met her. But such a situation could definitely cause someone to take extreme measures."

"Even kill?" Stark asked.

"Oh, yes," the psychiatrist replied. "As I said, you can become stuck in an approach-avoidance conflict situation. It's intolerable, and yet you can do nothing. You can't approach because of the negative valence, and you can't retreat because of the positive valence. You have to do something, anything. But you can't."

"Except kill off the person putting you in the situation," Stark said.

"You can decide the goal itself is the problem," Dr. Smythe said. "You destroy it for causing you so much pain, which ends your problem."

"What about her husband?" Beauchamp asked. "She lived with him for twenty years."

"The conflict could have been there the whole time," the psychiatrist responded. "After twenty years of it, she snapped."

"And then once she'd found the way to take care of her problem," Stark said, "she just kept on doing it."

"Yes, but this is only a generalized discussion. I can say nothing specific about anyone I've never seen professionally. I've given you an explanation that's possible. I don't know how probable it is."

"Under the circumstances, I'd say it's very probable," Stark said.

Beauchamp leaned forward in his chair as if he was about to ask another question, but he didn't say anything. Stark thanked the psychiatrist for her help, and the two detectives left. As they walked away from the one-story brick building in which Dr. Smythe's office was located, Stark said: "Now I've got a motive."

"What are you going to do?"

"I'm going to bust her."

TWENTY

Although Terri wasn't surprised to open her door and find Stark and his partner, she was totally unprepared for what happened next.

"You're under arrest," Stark said.

And then he was saying words she'd heard many times before on TV cop shows, words she had never dreamed a police officer would actually say to her. She had the right to remain silent. She had the right to have an attorney present during questioning.

She had all the rights except the one that mattered: the right to refuse to go, to throw Stark out of her apartment, and tell him never to come back again.

And when Stark was through advising her of her constitutionally guaranteed protections under the law, he nodded at the other police officer, who stepped forward, producing a pair of handcuffs. She stared at them in disbelief. Some part of her mind had clung desperately to the notion that all this could simply not be happening, but the handcuffs made it clear that this was very real indeed. The officer cuffed her hands behind her back, the metal hard and cold against her flesh. She felt helpless.

"Regulations," the officer said. "Anyone taken into custody has to be cuffed while being transported." Despite the official-sounding words, there seemed to be a note of apology in his voice.

As she was being led out of her apartment, the door across the hall opened, and Nettie Cownars stepped out, her eyes widening when she saw the handcuffs. "Terri, what's happening?"

Not knowing what to say, Terri just shook her head.

Nettie followed them down the hallway. "Terri, is there anything I can do?"

"Call Bruce Gossetter," she said suddenly. "He's a lawyer. He's in the book. Tell him I've been arrested. Tell him I need help."

"Okay," Nettie said. "Whatever I can do to help." She ran back into her apartment.

Outside, the detective who'd cuffed her opened the rear door of a plain brown sedan, then guided her into the backseat, placing his hand on her head to make sure she didn't bump it against the top of the car. And then the car was moving. Through the wire grill that separated the cops from the bad guys, she stared at the two men in the front seat.

"What exactly are you charging me with?" she asked.

Stark's partner looked at him, apparently leaving it up to the sergeant to answer her questions. Stark said, "Murder."

"Of whom?" she asked, although she was fairly sure what he would say. It just seemed like a good idea to have it stated formally, so she could be sure exactly where she stood.

"Of Stanley Ferguson, Marlene Williamson, and Ellen Farley."

"Ellen . . . ?"

Terri was stunned. She'd thought Ellen had been killed by a robber, that Ellen's death was unrelated to the murders of Stanley and Marlene. Or maybe she'd just made herself think that, because she didn't want to think that Ellen's murder could somehow be connected to her.

And then she wondered whether the police even had any evidence that Ellen had been killed by the same murderer,

236

or whether Stark just assumed that no matter who was killed it had to be the work of that murderous fiend Terri Ferguson.

She shook her head, bewildered. And then for the first time, it occurred to her that she might really go to trial, might really go to prison. She forced the idea from her consciousness. It was unthinkable. She couldn't deal with it.

Terri stared out the window, watching the scenery go by. Though familiar, the streets and buildings of Meadowview seemed different somehow, as if something had affected the entire community, made it alien.

At the police station, she was taken in through a side entrance, into a part of the building most people never saw. Here the floor was plain cement, and the smell of disinfectant hung in the air. The police officer at the counter was protected by a wire mesh.

He said, "Take everything out of your purse, then empty your pockets."

Terri did as instructed.

The cop was a burly man with thick curly hair on his arms, an expressionless pudgy face. He checked to make sure her purse was empty, then slipped it into a large paper bag, saying, "One brown purse." He noted it on a form. "One brown leather wallet," he said and again wrote on the form.

He continued on, counting out Terri's cash, listing her credit cards, noting her comb, her lipstick, her keys. When he'd written everything down on the form, he told her to sign it. Then she was led to a room in which a camera waited on a tripod. The same burly copy told her to back up against a wall. A sign with her name and a number and some other things on it was hung around her neck. Lights came on. She was photographed in full face and profile views.

The burly cop led her to another room, where he inked her fingers and pressed them onto the empty white squares printed on the special fingerprint cards. Giving her a paper towel, he told her to wipe off the ink. Through it all, Terri was in a daze. She allowed herself to be led here, pushed there, turned this way or that. Finally a woman in a khaki uniform took her to a private room and frisked her thoroughly to make sure she wasn't hiding anything. Taking Terri back to the burly cop, who was again safely behind his protective cage, the woman said: "She's clean. Make a note that no body cavity search was requested."

Inwardly Terri winced at the thought. That would have been the ultimate indignity. And it was unnecessary. She already felt powerless, completely at the mercy of her captors. And yet a part of her was screaming, I don't belong here! This is a place for robbers and rapists and killers! I'm not a criminal. I'm not, I'm not, I'm not!

The burly cop took her to an interrogation room. It looked like the same cream-colored room she'd been in the last time, but she couldn't be sure. Accompanied by his partner, Stark came in, put a tape recorder on the table, turned it on, said into it the date, time, that this was an interrogation of Terri Ferguson, age forty, who resided at 1218 Atley Street in Meadowview and who was charged with the murders of Stanley Ferguson, Marlene Williamson, and Ellen Farley. Officers Stark and Beauchamp were present.

"Do you acknowledge that you've been advised of your Miranda rights?" Stark asked. "If you don't so acknowledge, I'll read them to you again so it will be on tape."

"You read them to me," Terri said, her voice sounding hollow, as if it were coming over a child's string-and-tin-can telephone.

"Do you understand the charges against you?" Stark asked.

"The charges are absurd," Terri said.

"Just so there's no doubt, you are charged with the murders of—"

"I want a lawyer. I'm not saying anything until I get one."

"You can call one just as soon as I explain the charges."

"I'm not listening to anything either." She clapped her hands over her ears.

Stark switched off the tape recorder, and the two officers took her back to the room in which the burly cop waited within his cage. They led her to a table with a telephone on it, then went over to the counter and talked in low tones with the burly cop. There was a tattered phone directory on the table. Terri looked up the number of Bruce Gossetter. The pages on which lawyers were listed were the most ragged ones in the book.

"Noble, Gossetter, and Page," the cheerful woman's voice said.

"Bruce Gossetter please."

"Who shall I say is calling."

"Terri Ferguson."

"Just a moment."

Terri waited.

"Mr. Gossetter is with a client. Can I have him call you back?"

"No, please, I have to speak to him now. It's urgent."

"Just a moment, please."

Again Terri waited. Finally Gossetter's voice came over the phone. "Mrs. Ferguson?"

"Yes. I'm in jail. I need your help."

"A Nettie Cownars called me a little while ago and said you'd been arrested. I'm afraid all I could do was wait until I heard from you."

"Well, you're hearing from me now. I've been charged with . . . with murder."

"Are they charging you with killing your husband?"

"Yes, and two other people. Marlene and the woman I was working for."

"Marlene Williamson?"

"Yes. I need your help. Please."

Gossetter was silent a moment; then he said, "I've told you that I really can't represent you in criminal matters. I even gave you a list of good criminal lawyers."

"I didn't call any of them. I couldn't afford it. But now

I don't have any choice. If you won't help me, can you send me someone? Please."

"You want me to pick your attorney for you?"

"If you can't help me, send me someone who can. Please. I'm confused and afraid, and I don't know what to do."

"I'll see what I can do," Gossetter said, not sounding too happy about it.

"Please, I don't even know if I get another phone call. I've never been in a place like this. I don't know what to do. Please don't leave me here." Terri heard her voice rising, heard the desperation in it.

"I'll get you someone," Gossetter said.

Stark and the other policeman were there as soon as she hung up. They took her to a door, waited a moment, and then the door opened and the woman who'd searched her appeared.

"This way," she said.

The woman in khaki took Terri down a hallway with bars at the end. As they neared the bars, the woman raised a portable radio to her mouth.

"Oh-one-nine to control."

"Go ahead."

"Open Baker main."

As the bars slid to the side, Terri noticed the TV camera above her head. The guard led her into a passageway with two more doors of bars leading from it, each to a different corridor. Again the guard spoke into the radio, and the door on the right opened. The woman in khaki took Terri into a corridor lined with cells. Most had two or three women in them, who stared at her silently.

Back before all this began, she had passed this building many times. It was only a couple of years old, a structure of concrete and glass. A sign indicated that it was the city-county law enforcement center and the county jail. Terri had always been so unconcerned with the county jail that she didn't even have a preconceived notion of what it might look like.

Had there been a time before Stanley's murder? Had there been a nice house with a huge kitchen and a fountain in the backyard? It all seemed like a dream, like the wishful thinking of someone who led a life of misery and craved something better. Her thoughts were such a dazed muddle that she was uncertain what was real and what wasn't.

Terri studied the guard escorting her down the hallway lined with jail cells. The woman appeared to be in her mid-thirties. Although not especially tall, she was big-boned, with sandy hair, a plain face, no makeup. She walked briskly, looking straight ahead, and Terri found she was unable to picture the guard smiling. They stepped in front of an empty cell.

"Oh-one-nine to control."

"Go ahead."

"Open William twenty-two."

The door slid open, and the guard steered Terri inside.

"I've asked for a lawyer," Terri blurted. "He should be here any time now."

"You'll be called," the guard replied. Then into her hand-held radio, she said, "Close William twenty-two."

The bars slid shut, closing with the same resounding clang that so often ended the don't-drink-and-drive or don't-use-drugs spots on television. Don't drive drunk or this could happen to you. *Clang!*

Don't get accused of killing three people, even if you're innocent.

Then, as she stood there staring at the stained cement floor with a drain in the middle, she wondered whether she really was innocent. Could Stark be right? Had she killed three people, pushed the memory from her consciousness? She shook her head. Though in a daze, she wasn't crazy. She wasn't a killer.

I'm a victim, she thought. A victim of the killer. A victim of the police.

But standing in the cell, she felt ashamed. To the guards, the cops, the other inmates, she was simply another resident of this place, another criminal. Scum.

The cell contained four bunk-type beds with skimpy, filthy-looking mattresses. There was a toilet, a sink, three walls of cement, one door of bars. Terri sat down on one of the bunks. The place smelled dimly of urine and vomit and sweat.

She didn't know it was coming until the shriek escaped her lips, a long piercing cry of desperation and misery and fear. The sound echoed off the cement walls. From down the corridor came the voices of the other jailed women.

"What's the matter, honey? You see a nasty old cockroach?"

"You better call Orkin, baby."

"Sheeeit! Orkin man gets in here, I'll keep him too busy to kill roaches."

"Hell, Dora, you probably making it with the cockroaches. You'd make it with anything moves."

There was laughter then. More insults were traded. The women had lost interest in Terri. She hadn't known there were people like that in Meadowview. But then she recalled that this was the county jail, located here because Meadowview was the county seat. The prisoners could be from Rosemont, Cresthaven, anywhere in the county.

Suddenly feeling weak, she lay down on one of the dirty, smelly bunks, and then she was crying. She did it quietly, so the other prisoners wouldn't hear.

An hour and a half later, the same guard who'd escorted her to her cell returned. She took Terri to a small room where a woman was waiting for her.

"I'm Kathleen Nystrom. Bruce Gossetter tells me you need an attorney."

A blond with thick shoulder-length hair and large, intelligent blue eyes, she was absolutely stunning. And she was tall, five-ten or so, one of those women who could cause heads to turn merely by entering a room.

"I certainly am glad to see you," Terri said.

The lawyer sat down at the small wooden table, motioning for Terri to do the same. "I've talked to the police, so

I already have an idea of what's going on. What I need to do now is get your side of things.''

Beginning with Stanley's murder, Terri told the attorney everything that had happened. The lawyer made notes on a yellow legal pad.

''Do you have an alibi for any of the murders?''

''No. I was always home alone or driving or something like that.''

''Think carefully. It's very important.''

''I have,'' Terri said. ''Believe me, I have.''

''Okay, here are some things you may not know. The police say the same gun that killed your husband and Marlene Williamson was also used on Ellen Farley.''

Terri nodded. She'd figured as much. Stark wouldn't have charged her with the third murder without something to tie it to the other two.

''I don't know why *anybody* would want to hurt them,'' Terri said. ''They were all good people. And I should be the least likely suspect there is. I've lost the husband I loved dearly. I've lost my house, my lifestyle, everything I had. I lost my best friend. I've lost my job. This is what I've gained from the three murders.''

The attorney studied her a moment, then said, ''Stark thinks you're a psycho who kills anyone who gets close to you. He's got some psychological bullshit to back it up, but how good it would be in court . . .'' She shrugged.

Terri shook her head, bewildered. Nothing really surprised her anymore. She was like a cork bobbing along in a rapid stream. She swirled around, at the mercy of the current, forever moving but without a destination.

''What's going to happen to me?'' she asked.

''Right now, I don't know. They have enough to go to trial, but their case against you is pretty weak. I imagine they'd like to get some more on you before going to trial. It's possible there won't even be a trial. Stark could have done this mainly to get you into a cell, give you a little taste of jail, see what happens.''

The lawyer glanced at her notes. ''Anyway, I don't see

any benefit in your talking to them, so let's exercise your right to remain silent. I'll tell them you state flatly that you're innocent of all the charges against you and that you have nothing further to say."

"However you want to handle it is fine with me," Terri said, beginning to feel a little more confident about things. She was in the hands of a competent professional who would see her through this thing.

"Now, about bail. I don't think we'll have too much trouble convincing a judge that you've been a solid citizen for years and that you're not likely to skip town before the trial. I think there's a pretty good chance you can get out on your own recognizance. We'll see."

"When will that happen? I don't want to spend a moment longer in this place than I have to."

"You should be out of here tomorrow morning."

"Tomorrow . . ." The lawyer's words had come like a blow. "Can't we do it this afternoon?"

"We can't just run over to the courthouse and have your bail set. Arraignments are in the morning."

"You mean . . . I'll have to spend the night here?" The voice Terri heard sounded like a little girl pleading with her mother.

"I'll make sure it's just one night," the beautiful blond woman said reassuringly.

Terri shuddered.

TWENTY-ONE

When she got back to her cell, there was a young black woman stretched out in one of the lower bunks. She opened one eye, taking Terri in, then closed it.

Terri sat down on the other bunk. "Hi," she said nervously.

Opening one eye again, the woman said, "Hi."

Terri had no idea how to respond. There was an etiquette, she supposed, a correct way of behaving. But never having been in jail before, Terri had no idea what it was. Was it permissible to ask what someone was in for? Were you supposed to talk?

"You don't look like you spent too much time in places like this," the black woman said. Her mouth was large and turned up a little in the corners, her nose wide, and if her hair hadn't been cut short she might have looked something like Whoopi Goldberg.

"No," Terri replied. "I've never been in jail before."

"And here I thought you were a hardened criminal."

"Is it okay if I ask . . ." Still uncertain whether it was appropriate to say such things, Terri let her words trail off.

"You want to know what I was arrested for, is that it?"

"If it's okay to ask."

The woman laughed. "Hell, girl, you can ask anything

you want. Let me tell you about being in jail. There's two kinds of rules. There's the rules of the guards and the administrators and all them dudes. Forget them rules. They don't mean nothin'. The rules that matter are the rules of the people in the jail. You'll learn 'em, you around here long enough.

"The first rule for beginners like you is don't go out of your way to piss anybody off. The second rule is don't take any shit from anybody, because if you do, you won't do anything but take shit for the whole time you're here. Rule number three is learn to size people up. There's always a couple of people you do gotta take shit from. Learn who they are and stay out of their way. Course, you hang around, go to the pen, then you got to learn even more rules. But these'll get you started."

"Thank you," Terri said.

"Hell, girl, talk is free. And it passes the time. That's what you do in here. You pass time."

They were silent for a few moments; then Terri said, "My name's Terri."

"We're trading names now, are we? Okay, mine's Tyleen, with a y."

"Glad to meet you, Tyleen."

"Yeah."

"It's an unusual name: Tyleen."

The black woman laughed, amused by Terri's statement. "My mamma made it up. I think she wanted a boy so she could name him Tyrone." She stretched. "Shoplifting."

"Shoplifting?"

"You asked what I got busted for. That's it. And before you ask, this is my fourth time here. Twice for shoplifting. Once for using a credit card I happened to find. Once for aggravated assault."

"Aggravated assault?"

"I tried to cut my old man's throat with a kitchen knife."

"Your father?"

"No, not that kind of old man. My husband, if you want to call him that. Son of a bitch never worked, drank up whatever money I brought in, and to show his gratitude he used to beat me up. One night I decided to put a stop to it." She waved her arm dismissively. "He ran off right after that. Last I heard he was in California. Hope it falls off and takes him with it."

Tyleen sat up, fixing Terri with both eyes. "You?"

"I . . ." Suddenly she was afraid to say it. "I'm here because I'm charged with murder."

To Terri's surprise, the woman showed almost no reaction. "Figures," she said. "Your kind's almost always in for murder. Either you go crazy and blow away your old man, or you do it for money or power. Which reason you do it for?"

"Someone killed my husband." Uncertain why she put it that way, Terri stopped. She didn't know how much to tell.

"That's a good one, girl. Next time someone asks you why you're here, you just tell 'em somebody killed your husband."

"I mean . . . the police think I did it. But I didn't. Someone else did."

Tyleen eyed her skeptically.

"I didn't," Terri insisted. And then she blurted out the whole story. When she was finished, Tyleen studied her neutrally, saying nothing to indicate whether she believed Terri to be innocent or guilty. The black woman had undoubtedly heard many protestations of innocence from guilty people.

Terri found herself wondering how Tyleen felt about being locked up with an accused serial murderer, someone thought to be a psycho. The black woman, after all, was only a shoplifter.

A khaki-uniformed guard brought them dinner. Butter beans with a few tiny specks of ham in them, cornbread, unidentifiable greens. Tyleen ate hungrily. Terri picked at hers.

After they'd eaten, Terri had no choice but to use the filthy, not-at-all private toilet. Using a public rest room had always embarrassed her, but this, she was sure, would be a thousand times worse. Although she could control her bowels until tomorrow, when she'd get out of this place, her bladder had no intention of waiting that long. Reluctantly, feeling exposed and ashamed, she moved to the toilet, raised her skirt, pulled down her panties, and did what she had to do. Tyleen ignored her. A guard passed before she was finished, but the woman in khaki paid her no mind. When she was finished, Terri felt as if she'd demeaned herself. She felt dirty.

Later, a guard brought Tyleen some paperback books that had been delivered to the jail by a friend. Two romances and a horror story. Tyleen chose one of the romances, gave Terri her choice of the other two. In no mood for more horror, she chose the romance. They read until about ten o'clock, when Tyleen put down her book and announced it was her bedtime.

"Never gets dark in jail," Tyleen said. "You got to get used to sleeping with the lights on."

Terri stretched out on the bunk. It had a mattress and a blanket, no pillow. The bed was narrow and uncomfortable, and it smelled of sweat and human misery. Like the toilet, it made her feel unclean. But Terri was too exhausted to care for long about the bed. She slipped into sleep almost immediately.

She was awakened by the sound of the cell door opening. Focusing her eyes, Terri saw a guard and a disheveled blond woman. The prisoner was swaying back and forth. The guard gave her a push, and she stumbled into the cell.

"Close William twenty-two," the guard said into her radio, and the cell door slid shut. The guard left.

The woman who stood swaying in the center of the cell was about Terri's age, heavy-set, and reeked of alcohol. Suddenly she gagged, vomit spewing from her mouth, spattering on the floor in front of her. The odor of it washed over Terri, causing her stomach to constrict.

"Rotten liquor they serve at Casper's," she said, her

words slurred. "Screw Casper's. Screw the whole damned city of Cresthaven."

She glanced around the cell, abruptly fixing her eyes on Terri. "Move," she said. "I don't use no top bunk."

Terri just stared at her. The woman took a step toward her, and Terri shrank back against the wall.

"Hey," Tyleen said. "Remember what I said about not taking any shit from anybody you didn't have to. Well, you sure don't have to do crap for this old alcoholic tub of shit."

The woman turned to look at Tyleen. "Why don't you just shut the fuck up, nigger? I sure as hell ain't gonna pay no attention to anything some nigger says."

"Right," Tyleen said, "you being the mistress of the plantation and all."

The woman looked puzzled, as if trying to figure out whether she'd been put down. Then, losing interest in Tyleen, she turned toward Terri again. "Move," she said. "Or I'll throw you out of the damned bed."

She moved toward the bunk, reaching for Terri. Repulsed by the thought that this woman might touch her, Terri squirmed out of the way. The woman instantly claimed the bed, lay back, closed her eyes, and within moments she was snoring drunkenly. Terri climbed into the bunk above Tyleen's.

She wondered whether she should have done as Tyleen urged and stood up for her rights. It had seemed to her that avoiding a physical confrontation was more important than worrying about the jailhouse pecking order. She would be out of here tomorrow, and the pecking order would no longer matter. It was comforting, the thought of getting out of this place, and Terri was still contemplating it when she drifted off to sleep.

She awakened some time later, thinking she was at home, tangled in the covers and trying to free herself. Then she heard a voice yell something. It was Tyleen. And Terri realized she wasn't at home; she was in jail. And someone was attacking her. Suddenly two beefy hands had her throat, and they were squeezing. Terri was unable to breathe.

"Gonna kill you, Eunice. Gonna kill you for what you done to me."

It was the woman who'd vomited on the floor earlier. Tyleen was there, trying to pry the woman's hands off of Terri's neck. Terri added her strength to Tyleen's, but the woman's was stronger than both of them. Terri's lungs struggled to find air. The woman had a distant look in her eyes, as if she were unaware of anything except for the need to strangle Eunice, whoever Eunice was.

"Help!" Tyleen yelled. "Someone's being murdered here!"

Finally the woman's grip loosened slightly. A little desperately needed air got into Terri's lungs. Tyleen jumped on the woman's back, grabbing her around the head. Suddenly the woman let go of Terri, managed to knock Tyleen off, and turned to grab her. Tyleen gave her an uppercut that hit with a resounding smack, then followed it with two quick blows to the gut. The woman grunted, but she wasn't stopped.

"Help us!" Terri yelled, her voice raspy from the choking she'd received. "Help us! Please!"

When the woman advanced on Tyleen, the black woman lithely stepped out of the way. "Come on," Tyleen said. "Let's see if you can catch me."

The woman hesitated, then lunged at Tyleen. Again Tyleen moved quickly, but not quickly enough this time, because the woman managed to grab her shirt and fling Tyleen against the bars. Tyleen looked dazed. The woman reached for her.

Instantly Terri was off the bunk, throwing herself at the woman. They collided, and the woman fell, grabbing Terri as she did so, pulling her down. Terri struggled to free herself, and for a moment she thought she would get away, but then the woman was on top of her, choking her again. Tyleen, still looking dazed, grabbed the woman's hair, pulling on it with all her strength, but the woman didn't seem to notice. Terri caught a whiff of the woman's unbelievably foul breath before the pressure on her throat cut off her supply of air.

Suddenly a guard was there, saying something into her portable radio. Another guard appeared, and the cell door slid open. The guards grabbed the woman, who flung them back with her arms, giving Terri an instant of air, but then she was being strangled again. One of the khaki-uniformed woman smacked the attacker in the head with a billy club. When the blow had no effect, she hit her again, harder. Blood trickled down the woman's forehead, but she continued strangling Terri. Terri's vision was getting fuzzy. Her lungs were in agony.

She heard rather than saw the *crack! crack! crack!* as the guard swung the baton. Something wet spattered on Terri's face, although she was barely aware of it. She was still unable to breathe, but she wasn't struggling as hard to find air anymore. She seemed to be floating in a dark cozy place where there was no pain, only a lazy, engulfing comfort.

And then the pressure was gone from Terri's throat, and she was back in the real world, taking in huge, delicious breaths of air. The scene around her came into focus. There were three guards here now. The blond woman lay on the cement floor, blood on her face and oozing into her hair.

"What the hell happened here?" one of the guards demanded. She was a heavy-set woman with very dark red hair and black eyes.

"She's crazy," Tyleen said. "She attacked us in the middle of the night. If I hadn't jumped her, she'd have strangled Terri."

The guard eyed Tyleen skeptically, as if to say she knew Tyleen was lying because the scum in this place always lied. The guard and her two companions managed to get the blond woman on her feet. They moved her out of the cell and into the hallway out of sight, the cell door closing behind them. On the floor, blood was now mixed with the vomit.

"You okay?" Tyleen asked.

"I think so," Terri said.

Tyleen helped her get up. Terri sat down on the bunk that had been hers before the blond woman evicted her. Tyleen sat down on her own bunk. The guard with dark red hair appeared at the cell door.

"Anyone here need medical attention?" she asked.

"No," Terri said.

"Me neither," Tyleen said, and the guard disappeared.

Terri touched her throat. It was tender. Although there was blood on her blouse, it was the blond woman's, not hers. Then, remembering the blood that had spattered in her face, Terri got up and rinsed it off in the sink.

Returning to her bunk, she said, "How badly do you think that woman was hurt?"

Tyleen shrugged. "Don't know. Can't say I care very much either."

"What was the matter with her? Why did she act like that?"

"She's crazy. Lot of people in jail should be at the funny farm, but a court's got to do that, so they just run around loose until they get into trouble. Then they put 'em in here with honest folks like you and me who just happen to have been wrongly accused of breaking the law."

Terri looked at her wrist to see what time it was, but her watch was in the custody of the authorities, along with the rest of her belongings. Her eyes returning to Tyleen, she said, "Thank you for rescuing me."

"You rescued me, too. We're even."

A part of Terri was gratified by Tyleen's words. Although thrust into this strange situation, she'd managed to earn the respect of another; she had done what she had to do. But the feeling abruptly evaporated, and Terri began to shake uncontrollably. A vile, filthy woman had just tried to kill her—would have killed her if it hadn't been for Tyleen. And then the woman had been beaten bloody and senseless by the guards.

Terri lay back on the bed. She felt a scream building

somewhere deep within herself, but she clamped her mouth closed, refusing to let it out. She didn't want to embarrass herself in front of Tyleen. She didn't want to bring the guards.

Terri's mind replayed the incident, reliving the desperate struggle of her lungs for air, the *crack! crack! crack!* of the guard's truncheon, the blond woman's bloody face. She was unable to stop shaking.

TWENTY-TWO

Terri's arraignment the next morning was almost an anti-climax. Accompanied by Kathleen Nystrom, she appeared before Judge Helene Copeland, a stern-looking woman with straight black hair. Terri nearly panicked when the district attorney asked for bond to be set at a million dollars. But Terri's lawyer pointed out that her client was a solid citizen who'd never even received a traffic citation, that she had no history of violent behavior, that she was hardly the type to skip town. The DA countered that someone accused of three murders might not be safe to have on the streets, but he said it almost matter-of-factly, as if it were merely a thing he was obliged to say, and in the end Terri was released on her own recognizance. The whole thing took about five minutes.

Earlier Sergeant Stark had showed up outside her cell, smiled, asked how she was feeling. Terri had looked at him, said nothing.

"Hear you had a little trouble last night," Stark said.

Again Terri said nothing. Tyleen grinned at him. Both women were sitting on their bunks.

"Is there anything you'd like to talk to me about?" Stark asked.

"I thought my lawyer told you I had nothing to say."

254

Stark shrugged. "That was yesterday. You might have changed your mind."

"I haven't," Terri said, and Stark went away.

"Man's a pig," Tyleen said.

Although Tyleen was also arraigned that morning, Terri had no idea what happened to her. In a way, Terri wished she'd said good-bye, said something, but she wasn't sure people who met in jail were supposed to do things like that. Her lawyer gave her a ride home, said she'd be in touch. As Terri unlocked the door of her apartment, the phone began ringing. She hurried inside, forgetting for a moment where the phone was. It had a long cord and could go anywhere in the small living room. She spotted it on the floor by the couch.

"Hello."

"Mom, thank goodness you're all right!"

Terri sat down on the couch. Had Michelle already heard what happened? How could she have? "I . . . I'm okay, honey."

"I called you last night and got no answer. I kept calling and calling. With you living in that apartment and with what happened and everything, I was getting frantic."

Terri hesitated, uncertain what to say. Michelle had received so much bad news already. Now was she supposed to hear that her mother had been arrested and charged with three murders, including the murder of her father? And yet how could Terri withhold that information? She didn't want to lie to Michelle. Besides, the girl had a right to know.

"I was in jail last night," Terri said.

"In jail! How . . . how did you get in jail?"

Terri explained, not mentioning the woman who'd attacked her, and when she was finished Michelle spoke in a stunned whisper. "Mom . . . my God, how can all this be happening? It's like a horror novel. I keep waiting for it to end so I can put down the book, get back into the real world. But—" Michelle's voice cracked, and Terri could picture her struggling to fight back tears. "But it never ends, Mom. It just keeps going on and on and on."

"I know," Terri said softly and then fell silent because she could think of nothing else to say.

"Can this policeman get anywhere with this charge? I mean . . . could anything happen, anything bad?"

"Kathleen Nystrom says their case is weak. The woman who saw someone running from the house made a pretty iffy identification. There's no physical evidence, and the supposed motive is some sort of psychological mumbo jumbo. Still, it's enough to go to trial, and you never know what a jury will do. Kathleen says they may be trying to work on me right now, get me scared, get me to confess, or, more likely, go for a plea bargain."

"But you're innocent," Michelle said.

Terri sighed. "I wish I could convince the authorities of that."

"This is so unfair. It's just so unfair."

"Michelle, there's something I have to say. Just to . . . well, just to say it. I am innocent. I've never shot anybody."

"No, Mom, you didn't have to say it," Michelle said gently. "There's no way anyone could make me believe that you'd do anything like that."

Terri found she was out of words at that point, and several silent moments passed, that low long-distance hum the only thing being transmitted over the connection between Georgia and New Mexico. Finally Michelle said:

"What are you going to do now?"

Terri's first reaction to the question was simply that she didn't know. But in the next instant she realized there was only one thing she could do. "I'm going to look for another job."

"Do you have enough money? I mean, how are you going to pay your lawyer?"

"I've got the money from the sale of the house and the furniture. It'll be enough for a while." At least she hoped it would. She didn't even know yet how much Kathleen Nystrom was going to charge—although the attorney had mentioned something about sitting down to "iron out the details."

"Mom, I—hang on."

For a moment, Terri heard Michelle's subdued sobs; then the sound became muffled, as if the girl had put her hand over the mouthpiece. More silence was transmitted between Meadowview and Albuquerque.

"Hi," Michelle said shakily. "I'm back."

"I love you," Terri said suddenly, and then she had to hold back her own tears.

"I love you, too, Mom. I think that's about all we've got left, isn't it?"

"Yeah," Terri said, and they both fell silent again.

This time the silence was broken by someone knocking at the door. Terri told Michelle someone was here. The girl said she'd call back this evening. When Terri opened the door, Nettie Cownars rushed into the room.

"What happened?" she asked breathlessly. "I called that lawyer you asked me to, and then I called the police, but they wouldn't tell me anything."

Terri was uncertain what to say. She didn't want everyone in the apartment building to know that she'd been charged with three murders. And yet she didn't want to lie to Nettie, who seemed so genuinely concerned about her welfare. Besides, the woman already knew she'd been arrested for something.

"If I tell you something, will you promise not to let anyone else find out?" Terri asked. It sounded silly, as if she were about to reveal some hot gossip. Betty's been sleeping around. Sarah's getting a divorce. But then she *was* going to tell some hot gossip. Terri's been charged with three murders.

"You don't have to worry about that," Nettie said. "Nobody'll learn a thing from me."

It was the statement Nettie would have been expected to make, and yet there was something trustworthy about this woman from Louisiana. Terri told her why she had been arrested.

257

Nettie looked shocked. "Sweet Jesus! What's wrong with that cop anyway? Any judge of character at all could tell that you wouldn't hurt a fly."

"I'm afraid Sergeant Stark doesn't think much of my character. He thinks I'm a psycho."

"Pooh," Nettie said. "Shows you what Sergeant Stark knows."

"Would you like to sit down?" Terri asked.

"Depends on you. Would you like to be alone right now, or could you use someone to talk to?"

"I think I'd like someone to talk to."

Terri told her about her night in jail, about the woman who'd attacked her, about the DA asking for a million dollars bond.

"Sweet Jesus," Nettie said again.

After a while, after Terri had said all there was to say about her troubles, the conversation began to change. They started talking about things like the weather and TV shows, avoiding subjects like cops, jail, murder charges.

"Why did you come to Meadowview?" Terri asked.

"It's a compromise. I got divorced a couple of years ago, and ever since then I've been working as a secretary in a place sells plumbing supplies, making barely enough money to live on. Basically, I decided to get out to make my fortune, I guess you could say. There wasn't squat in that little town in Louisiana, so I decided to head for the city. The trouble is I don't really like big cities very much, so I decided to try the suburbs, thinking maybe I could find the opportunities of the city without actually having to live in one."

"How's it been working out?"

"Don't know yet. Check with me in a few weeks."

When Nettie left, saying she had a job interview to go to, Terri felt much better about things. Although her problems were far from over, having someone to talk to helped. At least she wasn't totally alone in the world. Terri was looking into the refrigerator, trying to decide whether she wanted to eat lunch when the phone rang. She sat down on the couch as she answered it.

"I'm coming home, Mom."

"Michelle?"

"I'm coming home. Can you meet me at the airport at three-forty-seven tomorrow afternoon?"

"Michelle, what are you talking about? The school year's almost over."

"I've got to go home, Mom. You need me."

"No, Michelle. It's only a few more—"

"If I take finals now, I'll flunk every last one of them. I've talked to my advisor. He says I can take incompletes for now and work out what to do about them later on."

"Oh, Michelle, I wish you'd think about this. You may never get back there to get it straightened out. You could be throwing away a whole semester."

"No, Mom, you're wrong. I'm not throwing it away. I'm doing the only thing I can to save it. If I stay, I'll flunk everything. I can't concentrate. I can't study. All I do is cry all the time. One night I even went out and got drunk, but that just made me feel even worse. At least if I take incompletes I've got a shot at straightening it all out someday." She choked back a sob.

"Michelle, I didn't know you were having so much trouble coping. I thought—"

"You had enough to worry about without hearing about me," Terri's daughter said weakly. Then she added, "I'm coming home, Mom. I've got to. I've just got to."

"Okay, honey," Terri said softly. "You know your situation, and you know what you have to do."

Michelle sniffed. Terri could picture the tears running down her daughter's cheeks. She began crying herself, softly so Michelle wouldn't know. A sob came over the phone all the way from New Mexico.

After several moments, Michelle said: "We can't afford this. Let's wait until tomorrow afternoon, and we can cry together all we want without having to pay the phone company for the privilege."

Terri agreed that was a good idea. She got Michelle's flight number. After hanging up, she stared at the floor for a long time, just staring, not thinking. And then, all at once, she found herself pondering the unthinkable. A few months from now, she could go to trial. The jury foreman would rise, say: *Your Honor, we find the defendant guilty.*

Khaki-uniformed guards would handcuff her, lead her back to the cell in which the crazy blond woman had tried to strangle her. She'd be there with people who puked on the floor and fought over the bunks, not leaving until the judge was ready to sentence her.

You are to be incarcerated at the women's correctional facility at . . .

Terri realized she had no idea where women prisoners were sent. What was it like? Was it an old dungeon of a place, damp and musty, surrounded by high walls of brick and cement? Or was it new, like a campus that just happened to be surrounded by a tall fence? And what kind of people would she find in prison? There would be robbers and burglars, murderers—real murderers, not mistakenly convicted ones like her. How many of them would be like Tyleen? And how many like the blond woman?

The rules that matter are the rules of the people in the jail, Tyleen had said. What would their rules be? Would they murder each other, beat up on the weaker ones, force the new inmates to submit sexually? An image of herself being forced to commit an unnatural act with the blond woman who'd attacked her in the county jail started to form in Terri's mind, and she forced it from her consciousness.

How many years would she get? Ten? Twenty? Life? But then there was an even worse possibility, one even more terrifying than being in prison with the blond woman. Georgia had the death penalty.

I sentence you to die in the—

Terri refused to complete the thought. She was trembling. It seemed she trembled a lot lately. She went through stages in which she was unable to cry and stages in which

260

she could cry at the least provocation. Maybe this was her trembling stage.

"Oh, God," she said aloud. "I just can't sit here like this. I have to do something."

Grabbing her purse, Terri hurried from the apartment. There was a small convenience store at the corner. She'd buy a newspaper, read the help wanted ads. Terri walked down the hall, stepped into the midday sunshine.

One- and two-story brick apartment buildings lined the side of the street on which she was walking. Small white frame houses occupied the other side. It wasn't a slum, it wasn't even close, but it looked shabby compared to the rest of Meadowview, an enclave of the working class in a community of affluence.

Terri bought a newspaper, walked back to her apartment building. As she started down the hallway, a chubby little girl emerged from apartment 104. Her head was a mass of blond curls, and she smiled up at Terri, displaying two missing front teeth and dimples. She reminded Terri of Shirley Temple.

"Hi," the girl said. "Do you live here?"

"I sure do," Terri replied. "I live in apartment 108. My name's Terri. What's yours?"

"Crystal," the child answered shyly.

"I'm glad to meet you, Crystal."

The door to apartment 104 opened again, and a thin young woman with dishwater hair stepped into the hallway. Her pale blue eyes casually focused on Terri, then opened wide in shock. The woman yanked Crystal back into the apartment and slammed the door, as if she'd been afraid Terri would give the child some horrible disease. Terri stared at the closed door, confused.

A part of her wanted to knock on the door, ask the thin young woman what that was all about. But the urge quickly passed. Maybe the child had been breaking some rule by being in the hall. Maybe she'd broken her mother's favorite sugar bowl. Maybe. But that wasn't how it had looked. It had seemed as though the woman was getting the girl away from something vile, threatening.

Inside her own apartment, Terri sat down on the couch and opened the paper, looking for the classified ads. The story was on the front page of the metropolitan section, and she nearly missed it. Terri stared at the headline, transfixed, almost afraid to read on.

WIDOW CHARGED WITH SLAYING FERGUSON, TWO OTHERS

The story recounted details of the deaths of Stanley, Marlene, and Ellen Farley, stated that she had been charged with all three. And it gave her address—her new address. Now Terri knew why the woman had yanked the little girl who looked like Shirley Temple away from her. The woman thought Terri was a crazed killer, thought she might harm the child.

And then Terri put herself in the woman's place. How would she feel living two doors down the hall from a murderer? She'd feel threatened, afraid for her family, just as Crystal's mother did. The person accused of murder could be innocent, of course, but Terri wouldn't know that. She'd only know what it said in the paper. *Arrested. Charged. Murder.*

Terri dropped the newspaper on the floor. Looking at the employment ads would be pointless. Who would hire her? She was trembling again.

Sitting on the edge of the bed, Connie penciled in the answer to the anagram she'd been working. She had a whole book of them. Although they supposedly grew more difficult as you went along, Connie was three-quarters of the way through the book, and it hadn't taken her more than a few moments to work any of them. But then she'd always been a whiz at anagrams. It was like a lot of things. Some people had natural talent, got real good at doing something, but there was no money in it. Not a marketable skill, as her father would say.

Connie hated her father.

It was true; she did. But she still hadn't reconciled herself to it. Every time she stated the obvious fact that she hated him, a wave of guilt would rush over her. You weren't supposed to hate your father. It was a no-no, forbidden.

And yet she had spent her life doing things that were forbidden. For most of them she felt no guilt. The world didn't like what she did, the world could shove it. Her father could shove it—especially her father.

When I'm through with Terri Ferguson, maybe I'll shoot him, she thought. But the thought didn't charge her with any emotion; it left her with an empty feeling. Connie dropped the book of anagrams on the floor, lay back on the bed, closed her eyes.

"I saw the story in the newspaper," Stanley said. "You managed to get Terri Ferguson charged with all three murders."

"It was just luck. Except for the first one, I just did them at times Terri was unlikely to have an alibi."

"No, darling, it was much more than just luck. You pulled it off beautifully. I'm impressed."

"I'm sorry I killed you, Stanley."

"It doesn't matter. I'm back now."

"I love you, Stanley. Never leave me, all right?"

"Never, my love. Never."

They lay on the bed not speaking for a few moments; then Connie said, "Stanley, let's go away together and forget about Terri."

"I think she should suffer some more. Look at what she did to us."

"Why don't I just kill her?"

"The suffering would end too soon."

"How much longer should she suffer?"

"Not long. Another week or two should do it."

"And then?"

"And then you should kill her."

"Yes," she said. "Yes. I think that's how we should do it."

"We can go away together."

"And be together forever."

"Yes, darling. Forever."

Connie felt Stanley's hand unbuttoning her blouse, caressing her breasts. He unfastened her pants, pulled them down, then her panties. With one hand he stroked her bare thigh; with the other he teased her erect nipples.

And then he was making love to her.

TWENTY-THREE

Terri and her daughter stood by the gate at which Michelle's plane had arrived, hugging each other, saying nothing. Terri was uncertain whether they were trying to draw strength from each other or give it, but just this physical contact between them seemed to be all the communication that was needed.

After a few moments, Michelle said, "Has anything else happened, with the police and everything?"

"No. Not yet anyway."

"Mom . . . I just don't know what to say. It's all so unbelievable."

They hugged each other for another moment or two, then walked silently to the baggage area. Michelle was no longer the exuberant girl Terri had always known. Now she seemed silent, morose, and Terri wondered whether her daughter would ever be happy again. A part of her said, it's my fault. I've done this to her. But it was just a mother's guilt, the compulsion to assume blame for all the bad things that happen to your children no matter how foolish doing so might be. Terri was every bit as much a victim as Michelle. She had brought none of this on her daughter.

And yet the guilt hung there, refusing to be reasoned away by mere facts.

As they were driving home, Michelle said, "Do you have a newspaper at home?"

"No." She'd thrown away the one she got yesterday. She'd carried it out of the building, put it in the dumpster.

"I want to check out the want ads," Michelle said. "I'm going to look for a job."

Terri just nodded.

"I don't know what kind of a job to look for. I need to find out what's available."

From college in New Mexico to being a waitress or maybe a counter girl at a fast food place, Terri thought glumly. What's going to happen to you, Michelle? What's going to happen to us?

"We've got a nice neighbor," Terri said. "Her name's Nettie Cownars. I told her you were arriving today, and she's real anxious to meet you. She's looking for a job, too. Maybe the two of you can go together."

Michelle shrugged.

Terri was driving along a two-lane throughfare, passing side streets that led into the gently rolling hills, big houses, and immaculate lawns that were the splendor of Meadowview. She had taken living here for granted most of the years she'd been a Meadowview resident, never considering even for a moment what it must be like to be an economic outsider surrounded by so much affluence, a have-not in the world of the haves. Suddenly she felt as though she'd been unfeeling and greedy most of her life, and now she was paying the price.

But Meadowview was full of people who would never pay the price, people who would never know anything but the comforts of being well off. Why me? she wondered, and then she pushed the thought away, for it had no answer.

"Why don't you stop at that drugstore," Michelle said. "I'll run in and get a newspaper."

It was on the other side of the street, a small brick building with a sign identifying it as Draper Pharmacy. Because there were no unoccupied spaces in the drugstore's small parking area, Terri pulled to the curb on her side of the street.

"Want anything?" Michelle asked, getting out of the car.

"No," Terri answered, wondering absently whether it was possible to take enough aspirins to make Sergeant Simon P. Stark go away. She sighed. It was a stupid thought.

Michelle waited for a car to pass, then hurried across the street and disappeared into Draper Pharmacy, leaving Terri to think about things like lawyers, prison, the death penalty. And Connie. Had Stanley had a lover? Was he having an affair with someone named Connie? Did he die as a result of a lover's quarrel? Terri shook her head. Stanley's mistress had been Ferguson's Furniture City. There had been no other women in his life. She would have known.

Suddenly a screech of tires and the roar of an engine snapped Terri out of her thoughts. Looking in the direction from which the sound came, Terri saw nothing. Holding a newspaper, Michelle had emerged from the drugstore and started across the street. And then Terri saw the white car, speeding down the street, swerving toward Michelle.

"Michelle!" Terri screamed. "Look out!" And then she was out of the car, running into the street. It was a spontaneous act, a mother's instinct to save her child, and it was done without any thought to just what she intended to do.

Michelle's head turned in the direction from which the car was bearing down on her. And then she began to move out of the way, and the car was there, a white blur that cut off Terri's view of her daughter. Suddenly newspaper pages flew into the air. Terri tried to scream, but her dry throat seemed incapable of making a sound.

The white car sideswiped a parked van, making a tremendous crash, and then it was speeding down the block. Newspaper pages fluttered to the ground. Suddenly Terri spotted Michelle lying on the grass strip that separated the sidewalk from the street. Terri ran to her, telling herself that Michelle had tripped over the curb, that she was okay, refusing to let that other possibility into her thoughts.

And then she was dropping to the ground beside her daughter, desperately saying, "Michelle, Michelle. Are you okay? Speak to me. Please speak to me."

Suddenly a white-jacketed man was there, bending over Michelle, looking into her eyes, feeling her pulse.

"Doctor, thank God you're here," Terri said.

"I'm not a doctor. I'm a pharmacist. I own the drugstore."

"I've got to call an ambulance," Terri said, rising.

"The car didn't hit her," the pharmacist said. "She fell getting out of the way. I think she hit her head."

"Does she need an ambulance?"

But before the pharmacist could answer, Michelle's eyes blinked open, and she looked up at Terri and the pharmacist with a puzzled expression on her face. Then Terri had her in her arms, hugging her, crying, Michelle protesting that she was okay.

"I got the license number," the pharmacist said. "It looked deliberate to me, like the driver wanted to hit her."

Still holding Michelle, Terri nodded.

"It was a woman," the pharmacist said.

"A woman? What did she look like?"

"Well, I only got a glimpse of her, but I'd say she was about forty. And she had dark hair."

"Connie."

"You think you know who it was?"

"Oh, God, it was Connie. Trying to . . . to kill Michelle."

"I'm going to call the police," the pharmacist said.

"It's Connie," Terri whispered.

"Ma'am, are you going to be all right?"

Terri didn't answer.

"Ma'am, do you need an ambulance for the girl?"

"I'm okay," Michelle answered. "I don't think I need an ambulance."

"I'm going in and call the police," the pharmacist said

268

again. "Also, I want to write down the license number before I forget it."

Terri said, "Tell the police my name is Terri Ferguson. Tell them to notify Sergeant Stark—he's a detective."

"Yes, ma'am. Terri Ferguson. Sergeant Stark. I'll tell them." The pharmacist hurried away.

Terri was shaking again.

"It was Connie," Terri said flatly. She was standing outside the pharmacy with Sergeant Stark, his partner, two uniformed officers, and the pharmacist.

Stark said, "All we know is that your daughter was nearly hit by a speeding car."

"It looked deliberate to me," the pharmacist said. "The car swerved right for her." His name was Nathan Draper. He was slim, with dark thinning hair.

"Now do you believe me?" Terri demanded.

"I believe that someone may have tried to run down your daughter."

"It was Connie."

Stark said nothing.

The cruiser in which the two uniformed officers had arrived and Stark's unmarked car were parked at the curb, their two-way radios constantly crackling. Stark's partner, Beauchamp, apparently heard something significant, because he hurried over to the unmarked car and began talking over the radio. When he returned, he had a notebook in his hand.

"Car's registered to a C.R. Grigoryev, 1429 Deaton Heights Circle, Atlanta. Atlanta PD's checking on him."

"I don't care who it was registered to," Terri said. "It was Connie driving it. I know it was."

Ignoring her, Stark turned to the pharmacist. "Would you recognize the driver if you saw her again?"

Draper shook his head. "A middle-aged woman with dark hair. That's all I can say. I was more interested in getting the license number than looking at the driver."

"You got a good memory."

"Always have had. When I was in college I could read complicated stuff like a chemistry text; then I could take an exam and I'd remember all the symbols and formulas. It was a pretty handy talent for a pharmacy major."

Beauchamp returned to the car to talk on the radio some more. To Michelle, the pharmacist said, "You should go to the emergency room and have your head checked out. You're probably all right, but when you hit your head hard enough to lose consciousness, it's nothing to take any chances with."

Michelle said she would, as soon as she was through here.

"What did you see?" Stark asked her.

"Nothing. I heard a car, heard my mother yelling, and then I saw this white car, and I moved as fast as I could. The next thing I knew my mom and Mr. Draper were bending over me."

"Did you see the driver?"

"No."

Stark turned the matter over to the two uniformed officers, who took a routine report on the incident and promptly left.

Beauchamp returned from talking on his two-way radio. He said: "Atlanta PD got hold of Grigoryev's wife. She says he's in Minnesota on business. He's a salesman for some Atlanta firm that makes high-powered computer equipment. His car's supposed to be at the airport. Also, patrol division found Grigoryev's car. It's about fifteen blocks from here, in a shopping center parking lot. They wouldn't have found it so quick, except that it's in the handicapped parking space, and some handicapped guy called to complain."

Stark and Beauchamp left to take a look at the white car. Terri drove Michelle to the hospital, where they checked her over, proclaimed her fit except for a nasty bump on the head. The young doctor who'd examined her suggested that she might want to stay overnight, just to be safe, but

Michelle was having none of that. She bought another newspaper at the hospital.

When they were in the car again, Terri said, "Michelle, you can't stay here. You have to go somewhere else, somewhere safe."

"Mom, I've got nowhere else to go."

"Don't you understand? Someone's trying to kill everyone who's close to me. First your dad, then Marlene, then Ellen Farley because she befriended me and gave me a job. You're next. If you stay, she'll kill you."

"Mom, I'm staying here with you. You need me."

"Please, Michelle, you're young and intelligent. You could get a job somewhere. You could save yourself."

"You wouldn't abandon me if the circumstances were reversed, and I'm not abandoning you."

Terri was shaking again. She tried to control it so Michelle wouldn't notice. A car pulled out in front of her, and Terri jammed on the brakes, causing the tires to squeal. Then she realized that the car had been a safe distance in front of her, that merely easing off on the accelerator would have been enough.

"Mom . . . do you want me to drive?"

Terri hesitated, then nodded. She wanted to demonstrate to Michelle that she was in control, that she could handle the situation, but not at the cost of getting them both killed in a traffic accident. She pulled over and they changed places. Terri directed her to the apartment building.

Terri watched her daughter's reaction as they carried the girl's two suitcases into the apartment. But Michelle remained poker-faced, making a couple of noncommittal comments. They put the suitcases in Michelle's bedroom.

"It's all I could afford," Terri said when they were back in the living room.

"You ought to see what some of the places students at UNM live in. By comparison, this is the presidential suite."

"I'm not a student," Terri said sullenly.

"Mom, the place is fine. I've seen a lot worse, believe me."

Terri started to ask her what kind of people she was associating with at school; then she recalled her own college days, remembered the ramshackle, cluttered places some of her friends had rented. Some had come complete with roaches and rodents. As long as the landlords hadn't minded wild parties, the tenants hadn't complained very much.

"I guess we might as well sit down," Terri said, lowering herself onto the couch. Michelle sat beside her.

Looking at the apartment that always seemed to smell vaguely musty and that seemed such an unlikely setting for her nice furniture, Terri decided she should be glad that, although she'd found mouse droppings, at least she hadn't found any live mice. And that so far the only cockroaches she'd seen had been dead ones. Maybe she hadn't yet reached the level of squalor in which her college student friends had lived. Count your blessings, she thought. Count your blessings.

What blessings? Terri wondered. In her circumstances, the absence or presence of a few household pests was unimportant. Her husband was dead, her friends were dead, and someone had just tried to kill her daughter. Who cared about a rat or a roach? They were the concern of people who'd run out of other things to be concerned about. People who had homes and jobs, people who were comfortable and secure.

And then she realized she did have something to be grateful for, a very major blessing to count. Connie's attempt to kill Michelle had failed.

Absently Terri picked up Michelle's newspaper. Unfolding it, she revealed the banner headline, which proclaimed:

STATE SUPREME COURT UPHOLDS DEATH SENTENCE

Death sentence. The words bounced around inside her head like a ricocheting bullet. Terri closed her eyes, only to see an image of herself being led down a long corridor by uniformed guards, a minister at her side mumbling a prayer. A sign at the end of the corridor became visible: DEATH ROOM.

They began buckling her into the electric chair.

The image vanished, but the words from the headlines were still tumbling through her head. Death sentence . . . death room . . . death death death death. . . .

"Mom, are you okay? You're . . . shaking."

"I'm okay," Terri answered, forcing herself to be outwardly calm.

But the word *death* was still reverberating in her head. And she was seeing the white blur as the car swerved toward Michelle.

TWENTY-FOUR

"I just barely missed her," Connie said. She was lying beside Stanley on the bed.

"If you'd hit her, you would have wrecked the car. You might have been hurt. You did the best you could."

"You're not upset, are you, that I tried to kill your daughter?"

"You know better than that. She's Terri's daughter. I should have had a child with you. The one I had with her doesn't count."

"Stanley," she said, feeling her love for him rush over her.

They dozed for a little while, and when they awakened Connie said, "I finished my book of anagrams. Even the hardest ones only took me a few minutes."

"You're a whiz at those things."

"I'm almost out of money. I'm going to go back to the bars again."

"No," Stanley said. "I don't want you to do that."

"How will I get some money?"

"I think it's a sign. You finished your book of anagrams just as your money ran out. I think it's time to end it."

"But you just told me we should wait another week or two."

"I was wrong. Terri deserves to suffer a while longer—after all, look how long you suffered—but we've got our own lives to lead. It's time to get away, to have time just to enjoy being with each other."

"Oh, yes, Stanley. I'd love that."

"I think we should kill them both. First the girl, then Terri."

"Do you have a plan?"

"Yes." He told her about it.

"I'm going to start looking for a job today," Michelle said.

She and Terri were sitting at the breakfast table. Michelle had made their breakfast. Poached eggs on toast. Although Michelle's plate was empty, Terri had only eaten part of hers. She wasn't hungry. Constantly tormented by thoughts of death and speeding white cars, she had slept very little.

"Do you want to come with me, do some job hunting?"

"I can't get a job. Who's going to hire an accused murderer?"

"You have to try, Mom."

"Not today. I don't think I could face it today."

For a long moment, Michelle studied her mother, the concern apparent in her eyes. "Mom, are you going to be . . . okay?"

"I've survived this far. I can see it through." But she wasn't sure she meant it. She was on the edge, but she wasn't sure on the edge of what. Madness maybe. Escape into insanity.

"I won't take too long," Michelle said. "I just want to get the first few applications in. We need the money."

"Where are you going to apply?" Terri asked, forcing herself to ask a coherent question.

"There are some ads in the paper. A couple of fast food places have openings, things like that. They're not good jobs, but they're the easiest jobs to get. I'll have some money coming in while I look for something better."

"Michelle, don't go."

"Why?"

"There's someone out there who wants to kill you. Connie's out there."

"I'm not going to let her run my life. I'm not going to hide here because I'm afraid of Connie. I won't live like that."

"She kills, Michelle. She's killed three people. She killed your father."

"None of them knew it was coming. I know to be careful."

"But you won't know where she might strike—or when or how. Michelle, if—"

"No, Mom, I won't stay here and hide. I have a job to find. I have things I have to do."

Forty-five minutes later, wearing a blue skirt and jacket that made her look like a young woman on the way up, Michelle asked for the keys to the station wagon.

"Be careful," Terri said, and her daughter went out the door. After the door had closed, she added, "You're all I've got."

Standing in the living room, staring at the closed door, Terri was suddenly overwhelmed with the certainty that something awful was going to happen. Opening the door, she stepped into the hallway, seeing no sign of Michelle. She rushed to the door at the end of the hall, hoping she was in time to catch her daughter. If she couldn't change Michelle's mind, then she'd go with her, protect her. But as Terri dashed from the building, she saw the station wagon at the end of the block. Michelle signaled for a left turn; then she was out of sight.

For a long moment, Terri stared at the spot where she'd last seen the station wagon. Then she walked back to her apartment, still deeply troubled by her feelings of foreboding.

Michelle drove away from a McDonald's. The opening there had been filled, but the other burger place at which she'd applied still needed someone. The manager there had made her assure him that she wouldn't quit in two weeks, as the last girl had, then said he'd let her know in a couple of days.

Although there were other places she could apply for a job, Michelle was heading for the apartment. She was worried about her mother. Her mom had been through a lot, and it was starting to take its toll. She seemed close enough to a breakdown as it was, without having to worry about her daughter. Michelle was convinced she had made the right decision when she left college and came home. Her mom had withstood all she could by herself; now she needed some help.

The whole thing confused Michelle. A lunatic named Connie who killed her father, two of her mom's friends, and tried to run down Michelle herself in a car. To Michelle it still seemed like being trapped in a horror novel. Her mother had said it was more like a movie, one of those terrifying films in which a bloodthirsty lunatic kills and kills—except in this movie there was no Dirty Harry to show up at the last moment and blow the killer away. There was only Sergeant Stark, and he suspected her mother.

Was there actually a murderous psycho named Connie? Michelle's mom thought so. But she was the only one who had heard Michelle's father say those words. Maybe her dad had meant something else. Or maybe her mom had misunderstood.

"Do you really exist, Connie?" Michelle wondered aloud.

"Oh, yes," a voice behind her said. "I definitely exist."

Michelle had been gone nearly five hours.

Terri paced the length of the small living room. Michelle hadn't said how many places she was going. Nor had she said how long she'd be gone. Job seeking was time-consuming and frustrating. Still, Terri worried. Michelle hadn't come home for lunch, hadn't called.

Stanley had been murdered, then Marlene and Ellen. Anyone she was close to died. Michelle was all she had left. I should have gone with her, Terri thought. I could have protected her.

But the idea was ridiculous. The girl couldn't drag her mother around while she was looking for a job. Oh, by the way, this is my mother, who goes everywhere with me. Who'd hire someone like that? Michelle had to go places on her own. There was no other way.

I should force her to go away, Terri thought. Maybe she knows someone in Albuquerque she can stay with. But that thought brought on a numbing feeling of loneliness. Terri didn't want to be alone. She was falling apart and she knew it. She needed someone. Still, if she thought there was a chance she could talk Michelle into leaving, she would do so.

Terri was so startled when the phone rang that she gasped. Then she realized that it had to be Michelle, since no one else would phone. Terri hurried to the telephone, which still rested on the floor by the couch, and answered it.

"Terri Ferguson?" a whispery voice asked.

"Yes."

"The people in this building think you should move somewhere else," the male voice said. "They're good, hard-working, honest people. They don't want to live with a murderer." And then the line clicked dead.

Terri replaced the receiver with a trembling hand. She had nowhere else to live; she had to stay here with the people who didn't want her, people who snatched their children away if she came near. A tear trickled down her cheek. Her husband and friends had been murdered, and everyone blamed her.

And for the second time, she wondered whether she really had killed Stanley and the others. Could she have done it but not remembered it? Could she be a split personality, the other half of herself some kind of demented butcher?

278

"Noooo!" Terri screamed into the empty room. "I've never killed anyone! Never! Don't you understand?"

And then she collapsed on the couch, crying. For several minutes, she simply sat there, crying, shaking, wondering whether she was going to throw up. The phone rang again, and this time she let out a small scream of terror. She stared at it, hating it, afraid that if she answered it, she'd hear the whispery voice again. But it continued ringing, tirelessly, insistently. Finally Terri lifted the receiver, put it to her ear.

"Mom?"

"Michelle," Terri said, relieved and trying to sound normal. "Where are you?"

"Mom . . ."

Terri thought she heard a tremor in her daughter's voice. "Michelle, is everything all right?"

"Mom . . . listen carefully. Connie's with me. She's—"

"Michelle, what—"

"Mom, just listen. We're in a phone booth. She's got a gun. Now I'm going to say what she's told me to say. Do you know where Dalton Road is?"

"Michelle, are . . . are you all right?"

"I'm okay. Do you know where Dalton Road is?"

"Yes."

"Drive out Dalton Road until you get to a dirt road on the right. It'll be about seven miles from the city limits, and there'll be a sign there that says Night Crawlers. The sign's old and faded. Take the dirt road and follow it. When you get to the end of the road, you'll find an old cabin. Go inside and wait."

While Michelle had been speaking, Terri heard a voice in the background, telling her what to say. Terri said, "Michelle, I don't have a car. You took the station wagon. I—"

"You'll find a car around the corner." Again the voice in the background gave instructions. Connie's voice. "It's on McGuire Street, a red Buick, an old one. The door's unlocked, and the key's under the seat on the passenger side.''

Michelle fell silent, but Terri didn't speak. Her brain seemed stunned, unable to function. And then a new voice came on the line, a woman's voice. Connie's voice.

"Don't call the police," she said. "If you do, the girl's dead. That's a promise.'' Then there was a click, and Terri was listening to the phone company's electronic silence.

Michelle! she thought, a part of her trying frantically to reestablish the connection through sheer force of will. But it couldn't be done that way. The phone on which Michelle had been speaking had been hung up. Michelle was gone. She was in the hands of a lunatic, at the mercy of a crazed killer.

"Oh, God," Terri said, her voice a fluttery squeak. She was still holding the phone. For several moments, she simply stared at it, and then she put the receiver back on its cradle. Her insides felt brittle, as if they might shatter.

She'd seen things like this on TV, situations in which someone is warned not to call the police, and she'd always known that she would be smart enough to contact the authorities immediately. But now that it was really happening, the choice didn't seem so clear-cut anymore, not when Michelle's life could be the cost of making the wrong decision.

If she followed Connie's instructions, what would happen? Why did Connie want her to go to an isolated cabin? And then Terri realized that she'd have almost no chance against an armed killer. Instead of saving Michelle, she'd probably get them both killed if she tried to rescue her. This was more than she could handle alone. She had to call the police.

If you do, Connie had warned, *the girl's dead. That's a promise*.

Suddenly Terri seemed unable to think. She stared at the phone, afraid to touch it. Finally she extended her hand toward it. The phone was help. The phone was her link to people who would know what to do, know how to help her.

That's a promise.

Terri yanked her hand away from the phone as if it had burned her. She was trembling so violently her teeth were chattering. She didn't know what Connie wanted. Maybe Michelle was just a tool to get her to the cabin. Once Terri showed up, Connie might release her. No, Terri thought, no. Connie could kill us both. You have to call the police.

But the police meant Sergeant Stark, who didn't believe in Connie, who thought Terri was the killer. Did she really want to put Michelle's fate in the hands of Stark?

That's a promise.

Although she hadn't met her face-to-face yet, Terri had heard Connie's voice. Connie was real. She existed. Her words had been somewhat muffled, as if she'd held something over the mouthpiece. Still, her threat had been quite clear. She would kill Michelle. And Terri believed her.

A part of Terri's brain latched onto the notion that Connie might have been attempting to disguise her voice, realized that there was only one reason for her to have done that: so Terri wouldn't recognize her voice. But Terri was unable to hang onto the thought. She had too many other things to worry about.

Terri wasn't sure at what point she'd made up her mind, but a few moments later she was leaving the apartment building, walking toward McGuire Street. Maybe if she could have been sure that she wouldn't have ended up dealing with Stark, she'd have called the police. She doubted it though. She took Connie's promise seriously.

Terri rounded the corner. The houses in this block of McGuire Street were small but neat; in the next block they were bigger, increasing in value the farther they got from Terri's apartment building. She saw the red Buick. Parked under a tree, it was one of those monster cars Detroit used to turn out twenty years ago. Tons of steel and chrome. It was shiny and well cared for. Someone had restored it, or maybe just loved it for a long, long time. As promised, the door was unlocked, the key under the seat. The engine roared to life instantly, a big gas-guzzling V-8.

"I'm going to try, Michelle," Terri said, as she slipped the shift lever to drive. "I'm going to do my best to get you out of this."

And even though she was heading into an unknown and dangerous situation, Terri wasn't shaking anymore. She had heard Connie's voice; she knew her adversary existed. She was no longer dealing with a name on the lips of her dying husband. Now she was up against a real person.

TWENTY-FIVE

Dalton Road became a county highway as soon as it left Meadowview. It cut through a pretty area of woods, country houses, and small farms. Later in the year, people would come here to buy fruit and vegetables from roadside stands.

Terri paid no attention to the scenery. She was watching the odometer. The dirt road she wanted was seven miles from the city limits. She had driven two. Terri wondered whether Connie was following her. So far there had been nothing to indicate that he was. Glancing in the rearview mirror, Terri saw a blue pickup behind her. It closed the gap, lingered a moment, then pulled out and passed her. The driver was a man wearing a western hat.

Was she doing the right thing? She could stop somewhere, call the police. Once she reached the cabin, there would be no turning back. The logical thing to do would be to call the police, get help. But then she imagined a small log cabin surrounded by the police. As they rushed the place with their guns drawn, Terri heard Michelle cry out, and then a single shot from inside. Terri forced the image from her mind. She was gripping the wheel so tightly her knuckles had turned white.

She wasn't going to call the police. She couldn't take the chance.

The countryside changed, becoming progressively more forested, with fewer homes and farms. The odometer informed her that she'd gone six point eight miles. She started looking for a dirt road to the right. At seven point two miles from the city limits, there was still no sign of the road, and Terri was starting to get nervous. What if she'd misunderstood? What would happen to Michelle? And then she saw the road. A badly faded sign said Night Crawlers with an arrow pointing to the right.

It was a private road, little used, not maintained. The big car wallowed, scraped against the encroaching trees and bushes. The road climbed a low hill. It took her five minutes to reach the fork. To this point the road had been narrow, but still recognizable as a road. Now it branched off into two tracks that were nothing more than ruts with grass growing between them. Terri took the one to the left. It made an abrupt dip, and the car scraped bottom.

I should have taken a weapon with me, Terri thought. And she began looking for something, a stick, a big rock, anything. Then she realized that she couldn't carry something so obvious into the cabin.

Maybe if she had a gun . . .

Suddenly, she wished that she'd stopped and bought one. They were available everywhere, guns for the multitudes. Use them to rob and kill and maim. It's the American way. But then she realized that such a notion was stupid. She'd never owned a gun. She had no idea how to fire one. Abruptly the road ended in a clearing.

Unlike the log cabin she'd pictured, the structure in front of her was a dilapidated one-room building with white clapboard siding. The windows had been smashed by vandals. The door stood partway open. As far as Terri could tell, no one was around.

Getting out of the car, she walked toward the cabin. There was nothing to think about, no reason to hesitate. Michelle could be inside, and Terri was going to do what she had to do. It was as simple as that. She stepped onto the small stoop, the rotten wood sagging under her weight, and she pushed the door open. The cabin was empty. Terri went inside.

The only furniture was an old wooden table that stood crookedly on legs that seemed ready to fall off. Three empty beer cans lay in a corner. Spiders had made webs in the corners, where the walls met the ceiling, where they met the floor, where they met each other. Then Terri saw the message. Written in the dust on the tabletop was a single word:

WAIT

Terri waited. She circled the table, the warped floorboards creaking as she stepped on them. The place smelled of dust and rot. Someday it would fall down, and the termites and other things in the soil would eat away what was left, and nature would prevail.

Where was Michelle? What had Connie done to her?

Although she was still determined to save her daughter, Terri felt a growing panicky feeling. Not knowing what would happen was part of it. Another part was the fear that she would be unable to help Michelle. Stanley was gone, and the thought of losing his daughter, too, was unbearable.

Although praying wasn't something she did often, Terri bowed her head and begged for Michelle's protection. Let her be all right, Terri pleaded. No matter what happens to me.

Hearing the sound of an engine, Terri rushed to the door. She was unable to see the car through the trees. Connie must have been watching to make sure Terri was alone, that she hadn't brought the police. And she was glad now that she hadn't. Michelle would be dead.

In the next instant, Terri wondered whether Connie was really coming. Maybe it was just someone who liked to drive in the woods. You saw those high-centered four-wheel drives everywhere. There had to be lots of people who liked to drive in the woods.

A blue pickup appeared at the edge of the clearing, pulled to a stop beside the Buick. Although the sun was reflecting off the windshield, Terri could tell there were two people in the truck.

"Michelle!" Terri yelled, starting toward the pickup.

"Stay there!" a woman's voice commanded, and Terri froze just outside the doorway.

The driver got out of the truck, and Terri was shocked when she saw her. This was not a dark-haired woman who resembled Terri enough to confuse the witness who'd seen someone running from the house after Stanley's murder. The woman looked absolutely nothing like her.

It was Nettie Cownars.

For a moment, Terri thought there must be some mistake. Nettie was here by sheer coincidence. Or maybe she knew Terri was in trouble and had followed her so she could help. But then Nettie walked around the truck and opened the passenger side door. Michelle got out.

Terri's daughter walked toward the cabin with her hands behind her back, as if they were tied. Nettie had a gun now. She walked behind Michelle.

"Oh, honey," Terri said as Michelle approached her, and then she was hugging her, Michelle unable to hug back because her hands weren't free.

"I'm okay, Mom," Michelle said gently.

"Get inside," Nettie said.

As they moved into the cabin, Terri saw that Michelle's hands were bound with a white cord that looked like the stuff used to open and close curtains.

"Over there," Nettie said, indicating a corner in the back of the cabin.

Terri and Michelle did as they'd been told, and Nettie positioned herself between them and the door. She kept the gun trained on them.

"Why?" Terri asked, staring at Nettie. "Why have you done all this?"

"Because you had to suffer as I have suffered."

"I don't know what you're talking about."

Nettie shrugged. "It doesn't matter."

"Who . . . who are you?"

"Connie Stewart. Or if you prefer, Nettie Cownars. It's the same name with the letters switched around. It's an anagram."

"I've never hurt you," Terri said. "I never even met you before. Why do you want to hurt me?"

"You took Stanley away from me. I lived in hell for twenty years."

"Twenty years? When I was in college? You held a grudge that long?"

Connie didn't respond to that. She was studying the gun in her hand. "This gun has killed a lot of people," she said softly. She seemed to be talking to herself. "First, there was Jack Martin. And then Marlene Williamson, Ellen Farley, a guy in Atlanta named Lloyd Porter."

"You forgot Stanley," Terri said bitterly. "You killed him, too."

"Stanley?" Connie said, looking confused. "I wouldn't hurt Stanley."

"You shot him."

Connie shook her head. "That's impossible. Stanley's here with me."

Terri and Michelle exchanged looks. Connie started rambling then, talking about how much she'd loved Stanley when they'd been at the University of Florida, how much it had hurt when he'd dropped her. She told of two marriages and many men, all of them basically the same guy, all of them just like a jerk named Jack Martin. Every now and then she made vague references to incidents that occurred when she was a child.

"The closet door opened, and my father was there, and we were naked . . ." she said. Terri had no idea what the woman was talking about.

And then she was talking about a time when she tried to commit suicide. Abruptly she shifted to seeing Stanley's picture in a business magazine, saying that's why she came to Georgia. She switched topics again, mumbling about how she wore a dark wig to make herself look like Terri and how she dyed her hair red because the Atlanta police were looking for a blond woman.

"Now you know loneliness," Connie said, looking at Terri. "Not twenty years of it, but you know."

"Connie," Michelle said, "we can help you, if you'll let us."

"Sure," Connie replied. "I untie you, give you the gun, and then you'll help me, right?"

"No, really, we . . ." Michelle's words trailed off. Apparently she'd realized the attempt was pointless. Connie just grinned at her.

And then, her grin fading, Connie aimed the gun at Michelle. She said, "Now you'll know what it's like to be all alone, Terri. To have nobody."

Both Terri and Michelle stared at her, dumbstruck, afraid, uncertain what to do. Terri considered rushing Connie, but the space between them was too great; she'd never even get close before Connie shot her. She felt frozen to the spot where she stood, unable to move, unable even to breathe.

Terri knew she and Michelle were going to die here. Connie was going to shoot Michelle, then her; she had no doubts about that. And all she could do was stand here and let it happen. Her mind frantically searched for something she could do—anything. And then she recalled something Connie had said earlier.

"No," Terri blurted, "you can't shoot Stanley's daughter. He'll . . . he'll leave you again if you do."

Suddenly Connie beamed. "The daughter he had with you doesn't count. Tell her, Stanley." She fell silent, apparently listening to some inner voice. Finally, she said, "See? I told you so."

"You told me what?" Terri said, uncertain just what was happening.

"Not me," Connie snapped, annoyed. "Stanley told you."

"I . . . I didn't hear Stanley."

Connie frowned, considering this. Then she said, "I guess he's not speaking to you anymore. You really can't blame him. You did ruin his life, you know, making him spend twenty years without me."

Connie's eyes lost their focus then, and she was again hearing that inner voice, that part of her brain that spoke to her as Stanley, told her what she wanted to hear.

"Yes, darling," Connie said softly. "Oh, yes." A peaceful smile appeared on her face.

And Terri hurled herself at her.

Knowing that this was probably the only chance she'd get to stop Connie from killing them both, she rushed at her, hoping the inner voice would distract Connie long enough for her to reach her. In the blur of her mad dash, Terri saw the blissful look on Connie's face vanish, saw the gun move in her direction, and then she collided with Connie, grabbing for the gun, and both women were on the floor.

The automatic flew out of Connie's hand, skidding across the floorboards. Although Terri was on top, Connie was strong. She rammed her fist into Terri's face, stunning her, and then Terri found herself rolled over so that Connie was on top. Connie hit her again. Terri struggled, but she wasn't strong enough to free herself. From the corner of her eye she saw Michelle trying to pick up the gun. The girl was sitting down, with her back to the weapon, feeling for it with her bound hands.

Terri got her hands on Connie's face, tried to push her away. When that didn't work, she tried to gouge Connie's eyes. Connie slapped her hand away, smashed her in the mouth. Terri tried to hit her back, but Connie simply moved her head out of the way. Terri was no match for her.

"Connie!" Michelle screamed. "Leave her alone or I'll shoot you!"

Michelle had the gun. Standing sideways and aiming it from behind her back with her bound hands, she was more or less pointing the gun at Connie. Suddenly, Connie lunged at her. Terri tried to grab her, but she was too late.

The gun fired, and then Connie knocked Michelle backward with the weight of her body. Michelle was thrown against the wall, the gun squirting from her hands, sliding under the old wooden table.

Scrambling to her feet, Terri dove for it at the same moment that Connie did. They hit the table, overturning it, and then Connie was kicking at her, reaching for the gun, her fingers inches from it, and Terri knew there was nothing she could do to prevent Connie from retrieving it.

"Run!" she screamed at Michelle, who had just gotten to her feet.

Mother and daughter dashed for the door. Michelle got there first, and Terri shoved her through it just as Connie fired, the bullet ripping splinters from the door frame. Then they were outside, running toward the cars.

"The Buick," Terri yelled. She had left the key in it. If they could just make it to the car, get it started.

Suddenly a hole was punched through the Buick's windshield. Terri grabbed Michelle, swinging her toward the trees. As they ran into the woods, another shot rang out. Terri had no idea where the bullet went. She only knew that it hadn't hit either of them. They were deep enough into the woods now so that there were trees between them and Connie. For the moment at least they were safe from a bullet in the back. They kept running, Michelle going as fast as she could with her hands tied.

Finally Terri grabbed Michelle's shirt, and they stopped, listening for any sound of pursuit. For a while Terri was unable to hear anything but their own labored breathing. Then she heard the silence of the woods.

"Maybe she's not coming after us," Michelle said breathlessly.

Terri held her finger to her lips. Connie, too, could be listening; there was no point in giving their position away. Michelle turned around, holding her bound hands where Terri could see them, and Terri began working on the knots. It took her a couple of minutes to untie Michelle's hands, and when she'd finished, she heard the sound of someone moving in the woods. Connie was coming after them.

Terri and Michelle exchanged glances. The sound had come from Terri's left. They headed away from it, moving as quietly as they could, trying not to crunch any old leaves or snap any twigs. They moved cautiously like this for three or four minutes, Terri having no idea where they were going, hoping they weren't simply moving in a circle. And then, as they started down a steep, grassy slope, Michelle's foot slipped in the moist earth. She let out a small cry, and she was sliding downward, Terri hurrying after her as fast as the footing would allow. She found her daughter sprawled in the tall grass at the edge of a small stream.

"I'm sorry," Michelle whispered, getting to her feet. "I didn't mean to cry out."

Terri dismissed the matter with a wave of her hand. "We're in the open here. We've got to keep going."

She was surprised with the way her mind had come to grips with the situation. Although having an armed maniac chase her through the woods was the most dangerous, the most terrifying thing that had happened so far, it was real. She understood what was happening, knew the face of her enemy. Having her husband murdered, her life ruined, her friends killed—all at the hands of an unidentified someone who might have been named Connie—had left her confused, numb, miserable, barely able to cope. It had seemed impossible, too awful to be real. But what was happening now was very real indeed. And for the first time, Terri had some control over the situation. She could fight back.

As they moved to the edge of the stream to look for a place to cross, something splashed into the water. It took her a second to realize that Connie had fired a shot at them. Apparently Michelle realized it at the same moment, because they simultaneously plunged into the stream. The water came to their knees. The bottom was rocky, and although they both slipped a couple of times on the slick surfaces of the stones, neither of them fell. They scrambled up the bank on the other side and plunged into the safety of the forest.

Glancing behind her, Terri was surprised to see how close Connie was. She stood on the other side of the stream, aiming the gun with both hands, and suddenly Terri realized that she and Michelle were still targets, that they hadn't gone far enough into the woods to be safe. A shot rang out. Michelle gasped, tripped, and fell.

"Michelle," Terri cried, dropping to her side.

"My shoulder," the girl said. "It . . . it hurts."

Terri saw the blood seeping into the material of her daughter's shirt. She carefully unbuttoned it, looked at the wound. It wasn't her shoulder. The small bloody hole was in the inside portion of Michelle's upper arm. For a long moment, Terri just stared at it, her ability to fight back evaporating the longer she stared at the wound in her baby's arm.

My little girl's been shot. She's hurt. She could have been . . .

Suddenly Terri remembered Connie. Looking back across the stream, she saw no sign of her. But she had to be close. She had to be coming to finish it.

"This is going to hurt," Terri said.

She grabbed Michelle under the arms, began dragging her into the woods. The hand that gripped Michelle's wounded left arm was bloody. She was making the wound worse, she knew that, but she had to get Michelle away from Connie. She dragged the girl through the woods until she was completely out of strength. Sinking down beside her, she noticed that Michelle's face was white. Terri touched the girl's forehead. It was cool, clammy. Michelle was in shock.

Terri needed something to cover her with, keep her warm. She had nothing. She began looking around, searching for she didn't know what, something to keep her daughter warm—anything. And then she saw the twin furrows in the soil. Grooves left as Michelle's heels cut through the layer of last fall's leaves and into the black

292

moist earth beneath. To find them, Connie would only have to follow the trail.

Listening intently, Terri heard the mad pounding of her heart, the chirp of a bird, a flutter of wings, something small hitting the earth—maybe one of last season's nuts. Then she heard the rattle of a branch swinging back after something had pushed it aside. The sound came from the direction of the stream. It had to be Connie.

Terri looked down at her daughter's pale face, then looked back along the twin tracks in the forest floor, and suddenly what she had to do was completely clear. She hurried back toward the stream, her eyes scanning the area for something she could use as a weapon. She didn't question what she was doing. If she did nothing or if she tried to drag Michelle farther into the woods, Connie would just walk up and shoot them both. She had a chance this way. That was all that mattered.

Terri saw what she was looking for, a chunk of tree limb about three feet long. Picking it up, she moved as quietly as she could toward the stream, studying the trees, trying to find one the right size. Finally she spotted a tree with a trunk about two feet thick. It wasn't exactly what she had hoped for, but there wasn't time to find anything bigger. Holding the piece of wood at her side, she hid behind the tree. The trail left by Michelle's heels was about five feet away. Terri waited.

Except for the occasional chirp or tweet of a bird, the forest was quiet. Terri began to worry that Connie had figured out what was happening, had circled around her. Or maybe she'd given up, made her escape. But that notion was ridiculous. Connie was driven by her madness. She wasn't about to give up.

Minutes passed during which Terri had visions of Connie slipping past her unseen, finding Michelle in shock, helpless, unprotected. I should have stayed where I could see her, Terri thought. But there'd been no weapon there, no tree to hide behind. Terri waited, listened.

She was thinking seriously about going back to Michelle

when a gentle footfall came from the other side of the tree, out of her sight. Slowly, carefully, Terri raised her club. And then Connie stepped into view.

Keeping the gun aimed in front of her, she was following the twin furrows, moving cautiously, quietly. Terri waited until Connie moved a few feet farther away, exposing her back; then she rushed at her. Connie heard her coming and turned, bringing the gun to bear, but she was too late, and Terri swung the club with all her strength. It smashed into the side of Connie's face, knocking her off her feet. Instantly Terri swung the club again, then again, thinking this was the person who murdered Stanley, this is the person who tried to kill Michelle, this is the person who ruined my life. And then she had to stop because Connie's face was bloody. Terri stared at her, breathing heavily.

Dropping the club, she began looking for the gun, but she couldn't find it. Then, remembering that Michelle was in shock and needed her help, Terri ran back to her daughter. Michelle lay on the ground, looking pale and cold. Terri knew she had to find help and quickly. She stood, trying to figure out which way to go, and then she heard something that gave her the direction. In the distance was the sound of a big truck, its diesel engine winding, straining. Terri began to run.

Branches slapped her face, tore at her clothing. She didn't care. She had to find the road, had to get help for Michelle. She tripped over a tree root and fell, landing in a bush with yellowish leaves. Scrambling up, she started running again, hoping she hadn't lost track of the direction. Finally, when it seemed she couldn't possibly run any farther, she broke from the woods and there was the highway. She rushed into the center of the two-lane strip of asphalt, looking in both directions. No one was coming.

Then in the distance she heard a car. It came over a low hill, bore down on her. Terri stood in its path, frantically waving her arms. It was gray, a pickup truck. The driver honked. He wasn't going to stop. Terri waved her arms. Suddenly there was a squeal of tires, the horn again, and the truck came to a stop a few feet from her. A man wearing a red cap leaned out the window.

"Goddamn, lady! What the hell's the matter with—"

"Please," Terri screamed, running up to him. "I need help. My daughter's been shot. I need an ambulance. I need the police."

TWENTY-SIX

The first police officer to arrive was a sheriff's deputy, who pulled up beside her in his cruiser, its red lights flashing. The driver of the pickup had promised to rush to the nearest place with a phone and call the authorities. Terri had waited by the highway.

"Hurry," she said to the gray-uniformed deputy. "My daughter's been shot. We have to go on foot. Please hurry."

"How'd she get shot?" the deputy asked, climbing out of his car. He was a young guy, blond, muscular. He could have been the captain of his college football team.

"I'll explain everything later. Please, we have to hurry."

Opening the trunk of his car, the officer got some blankets and a first aid kit. Then, reaching through the window of his patrol car, he picked up the microphone of his two-way radio and explained where he was, what he was going to do. Clipping a hand-held radio to his belt, he followed Terri into the woods.

When they found Michelle, the deputy promptly covered her with a blanket, rolled the other one up and used it to elevate her feet, then checked her wound. Getting a bandage from his first aid kit, he applied it to the bloody hole in Michelle's upper arm.

"We'll need a ten fifty-five here," he said into his portable radio. "Code three. The victim has a bullet wound in her left arm. It doesn't look real serious, but she does appear to be in shock."

"Ten-four," came the reply. "The ten fifty-five is on the way. Also, be advised state police are en route to assist you."

"Ten-four." He gave directions for reaching them from the highway. Then, turning to Terri, he said, "Ambulance is on its way. Now why don't you tell me what happened here."

Ignoring his question, Terri said, "Will she be okay?"

"As I told the dispatcher, the wound's not that bad. The bandage I put on should slow the bleeding. The main problem seems to be shock. I'm not a doctor, but I'd imagine that she'll be okay once they get her to the hospital. Now, what happened?"

She gave him an abbreviated version of the events leading up to the chase through the woods, the wounding of Michelle.

"She's still here," the deputy asked, "this Connie?"

"Over there," Terri said, pointing. "I . . . I hit her until she was unconscious."

"Where's the gun?"

"I couldn't find it. It's there somewhere."

"Show me," the officer said.

Terri's eyes dropped to Michelle. She lay there under the gray blanket, looking white, lifeless. She'd left Michelle to go for help. She didn't want to leave her again. "My daughter . . ." she said.

"I've given her all the first aid I can. There's nothing more we can do until the ambulance gets here."

Reluctantly, Terri led the officer toward the spot where she'd surprised Connie, clubbed her into unconsciousness. Glancing back toward Michelle, Terri found that her daughter was out of sight. She wanted to make the deputy assure her that Michelle's wound would be okay, but he wasn't a doctor, and he'd already revealed everything he knew when he used his radio to report Michelle's condition.

"We should have come to her by now," Terri said. "I didn't think it was this far from where Michelle is."

Abruptly the twin ruts made by Michelle's heels stopped. There was blood on the leaves. This was where Michelle had been shot.

"I . . . I don't understand," Terri said. "We must have walked right past her."

The deputy frowned. And suddenly Terri realized that Connie wasn't there anymore, that she had regained consciousness, that she was somewhere in the woods. And Michelle was just lying there, unaware, completely vulnerable.

"Oh, God," Terri said, and began running back toward her daughter.

"Wait," the deputy said, but Terri was only interested in getting back to Michelle.

Suddenly there was a loud pop, and something snapped into a tree no more than a foot to Terri's left. Before she could figure out what was happening, the deputy yanked her to the ground, pulling out his service revolver. Into his hand-held radio, he said, "Twelve to control, we're under fire. Advise any responding units to use ten forty-eight."

"Ten-four, twelve. State police should be just about to that ten-twenty now. Do you need any further assistance?"

"Stand by, control." To Terri he said. "This Connie, what was she armed with?"

"A handgun. I don't know what kind. I don't know anything about guns."

"What does she look like?"

Terri told him.

"Control, be advised that the subject doing the shooting is a white female, red hair, about forty, wearing jeans and a tan shirt. She's apparently armed with a handgun."

"Ten-four, twelve. Do you need more units?"

"Ten-four. Send at least one more unit, and I'll advise if I need anyone else."

"Ten-four."

In the distance came the wail of a siren. Then a new voice sounded over the portable radio. "SP one-five-seven to sheriff's unit twelve."

"Go ahead one-five-seven," the deputy said.

"Be advised the ambulance is right behind me. What's your situation there?"

The deputy explained what was happening.

"I'll be coming in from the highway," the state police officer said. "What about the people from the ambulance company? Is it safe for them to enter?"

Oh, God, Terri thought. They have to get Michelle. They have to.

"You'll have to explain it to them and leave it up to them," the sheriff's officer said. "The victim's in shock. We need to get her out of here as quickly as we can."

"Ten-four. I'll tell them."

Terri and the deputy were lying behind a fallen tree that was old and rotten, no doubt riddled with termites. A shot rang out, and dirt and bits of wood flew up from the log about a yard from the deputy's face.

"I'm a police officer!" he shouted. "Other officers are on the way here right now. Throw down that gun and walk toward me with your hands in the air."

There was no response from Connie.

"You're in a no-win situation," the officer called. "The only thing for you to do is to come out and give yourself up."

"All right," Connie yelled. "Don't shoot me. Please don't shoot me, okay?"

And then Connie appeared from behind some trees. She was walking toward them with her hands held out in front of her. Her face was bruised and battered where Terri had hit her. Something was telling Terri that this was too easy, that Connie wouldn't just give up like this, but it was just a vague feeling that got lost in the jumble of emotions tumbling through her brain.

The deputy rose, holding his gun in both hands, keeping it trained on Connie. "Lie down," he ordered. "On your face. Then put your hands behind your back."

Connie was on a small rise, about fifty feet away. Following his commands in the reverse order, she put her hands behind her and started to drop to the ground. She was on her knees when her hand suddenly swung out from behind her, and Terri saw the gun in her hand. The deputy fired. Connie cried out, falling backward and out of sight behind the rise.

"Stay here," the deputy ordered, and then he was rushing toward the spot where Connie had fallen. Reaching it, he looked quickly around, then disappeared over the rise. Several minutes passed before he returned.

"She's gone," he said. "I found blood, so I know I hit her." He held up a clear plastic bag with a gun in it. "She left this behind."

He talked on the radio some more; then a state policeman and two white-jacketed ambulance attendants arrived. The attendants quickly checked Michelle, then put her on a gurney and began taking her out of the woods.

"I'm going with them," Michelle said.

"We're going to have to get a lot of information from you," the deputy said.

"Not now," Terri said. "Please."

"Go with your daughter," the officer said. "We'll talk later."

The ambulance rushed Michelle to Meadowview General Hospital. The girl was whisked into the emergency room, and Terri was left to wait. Eventually a young doctor came out and said, "You related to Michelle Ferguson?"

"Yes," Terri replied, and suddenly she was afraid. He'd asked for a relative, someone to whom he could impart the sad news. "I'm her mother."

"Your daughter's going to be fine," he said. "The bullet wound isn't serious and blood loss was minimal for that kind of wound. We're treating her for shock, and she appears to be responding just fine. You can see her in half an hour or so.''

Terri nodded, and the doctor went about his business. She collapsed into one of the waiting room's orange vinyl chairs. A tear ran down her cheek, clung to her chin, dropped. And then she was sobbing.

An elderly woman with white hair and old-age spots on her hands entered the waiting room and sat down across from Terri. She picked up a magazine, opened it, flipped a few pages, then put it down and moved over beside Terri.

"Did you get bad news?" she asked in a kindly voice.

Terri shook her head. "I'm crying because I'm relieved," she said. "Because my daughter's okay. Because it's over.''

Thinking she understood, the woman nodded, smiled sympathetically. Terri continued crying.

Sergeant Stark showed up at the hospital the next day. Terri was sitting beside Michelle's bed when he stepped into the room.

"Good morning,'' he said pleasantly.

Terri and her daughter simply stared at him. Michelle's color had returned. Except for the pain in her bandaged arm, she was feeling fine, anxious to get out of the hospital.

Stark said, "It looks like I owe you an apology, Mrs. Ferguson. The gun Connie Stewart had was the one used to kill your husband, Marlene Williamson, and Ellen Farley. The things she told you check out. She apparently killed a man in Atlanta, where she was picking up men in bars and robbing them. There's also an apparent murder in Alabama. We found a brown wig in her apartment, along with the dress she took when she killed your husband.''

"Then the charges against me are dropped?" Terri asked.

"Yes."

"Then I don't think we have any further business," Terri said.

"When we catch her, you'll be called to testify."

The sheriff's deputy had taken a complete statement from Terri at the hospital last night. He'd told her that Connie had apparently gotten away.

"Are they still searching for her?" she asked.

"Yes, but . . ."

"But what?"

"But they think she's probably out of the area by now."

"But she's wounded, isn't she?"

"Not that badly apparently. We didn't find much blood. She'll probably have to seek medical attention eventually, but it looks like she's got time." He made a circular gesture with his hand. It didn't seem to mean anything. "We'll get her eventually. When we do, we'll need you to testify. You, too," he added, looking at Michelle.

Fixing him with a baleful glare, Michelle said, "I'll never forgive you for what you did to my mother."

Looking uncomfortable, Stark said, "I can understand that you'd be upset, but I had three murders to solve, and the evidence pointed to your mother. I was just doing my job."

"That's roughly what the Nazis said at Nuremberg," Michelle replied.

Stark opened his mouth as if to reply, then closed it again, apparently having decided to exercise his right to remain silent. Saying he'd let them know when Connie was apprehended, he made as graceful an exit as he could under the circumstances.

Michelle muttered something profane.

But Terri's thoughts had shifted away from Stark. She was thinking about Connie now. Connie who could still be out there, who could still come after her, try to kill Michelle, try to kill anyone who got close to her. And then Terri found herself remembering the *Friday the 13th* movies. She had hated those movies, but Stanley had insisted on watching them when they came on the cable. We pay for it, he always said; we should watch it. The movies centered around a murderous character named Jason who concealed his face behind a hockey mask. He was destroyed at the end of each film. And yet he always returned. And killed and killed and killed. Again and again and again. Suddenly the names seemed to go together. Connie/Jason. Jason/Connie.

Terri shuddered.

"Are you okay?" Michelle asked.

"Yes, I'm fine, honey. It was just a chill, I think." But inwardly she was praying, *Let her get caught. Please let her get caught.*

Captain Eugene Cantrell hung up the phone. He sat at his desk in the Chickasaw County Courthouse. Sitting on the other side of the desk, Sam Johnson was watching him expectantly.

"That was a detective with Atlanta PD named Francine McMurtry," Cantrell said. He told Johnson what he'd just learned about Connie Stewart.

"You mean she went bug fuck and started killing people because she had the hots for this dude twenty years ago?" Johnson asked.

"That's how it looks."

The black detective shook his head. "It's one of the beauties of this job, all the interesting people you get to meet."

"McMurtry says you might get to meet Connie Stewart."

"She figure Connie headed back here?"

"She says it's as good a guess as any."

"That how you figure it?"

"I don't think so."

When Johnson left Cantrell's office a few moments later, the captain leaned back in his chair, considering the possibilities. After a while he picked up the phone and placed a long distance call.

Johnson was in Cantrell's office again the next day when the captain's hunch paid off. Cantrell spent five minutes talking to the person who'd phoned him long distance, then concluded by saying, "I'll get there as quickly as I can."

"You going to fly on more airplanes?" Johnson asked. Cantrell nodded.

"Comptroller's gonna shit little green bricks."

Cantrell knocked on the door of the small frame house. It had been nearly dusk when his plane had landed. In the time it had taken to rent a car and drive here, it had turned dark. The last time Cantrell had been here, the occupant of the small house had been working in the garden. The seeds would have sprouted and grown by now, but it was too dark for Cantrell to see the garden.

Beaten, wounded, and hunted, Connie would have fled the Atlanta suburbs. There was only one place she would have been drawn to, a place she'd gone before when she needed to escape, at least for a while, from the life she was leading. Cantrell corrected that thought. It wasn't the place Connie had sought out. It was the person.

The door opened, and Father David Young let Cantrell into the house. "She's in the kitchen," the priest said.

"How badly's she hurt?"

"The bullet hit her in the fleshy part of the leg. Went right through. It hurts, but I don't think it's life threatening or anything like that."

"Well, we might as well get it over with."

The priest took his arm. "What will happen to her?"

"She's killed five people, Father."

"I know that."

"Ultimately she'll have to go to Georgia or Alabama to stand trial. She can force extradition if she wants to, but it will only delay things. I'll take her back with me if she'll go with me willingly. If she won't, well, we'll see."

The priest nodded. "This way, Captain."

He led the Alabama lawman into the small kitchen. Sitting at a Formica-topped table was a middle-aged woman whose face was badly bruised and cut. She looked at him as if she was only half aware of his presence, her expression a mixture of confusion and utter defeat.

"Hello, Connie," Cantrell said.

EPILOGUE

"Will it knead bread dough?" the woman asked, looking at a Cuisinart food processor. She was about sixty, well dressed, and had the sort of wrinkle-free face that was most likely acquired with the aid of a surgeon's scalpel.

"Oh, yes," Terri said. "You can use the standard blade for small amounts, and there's a special dough blade for larger amounts. I think the bread has a nicer texture when the machine kneads it. And, of course, it's much, much faster than kneading by hand."

The woman nodded. "I'm looking for a wedding present. Daughter of a friend."

"I think the food processor would make a good gift. A couple starting out can't always afford one, and today it's just about become a kitchen essential."

"Okay," the woman said. "I'll take it."

Terri picked up a processor that was still in its box and carried it to the cash register. The woman used her American Express card to pay for it.

Terri watched the customer leave, then surveyed the Cook's Nook. She'd rearranged the store since buying it from Ellen Farley's estate, putting things that were bright and cheerful—like colored napkins—near the front and electric things—like food processors—along one wall. Terri thought it looked better this way, and so far those customers who'd chosen to comment agreed.

She had used the money from the sale of Ferguson's Furniture City to buy the store. Despite Bruce Gossetter's dire predictions, a group of investors had paid a very good price for the business. Good enough for Terri to pay off all the company's debts, buy the Cook's Nook, and have some left over.

The furniture store would be known simply as Furniture City from now on, but Terri didn't think Stanley would have objected to that. The enterprise he conceived and nurtured and poured his heart into would continue. Stanley would have wanted that. It would have been important to him.

Terri suspected that Ellen Farley would have felt the same way about the Cook's Nook. The decision to buy the store hadn't been difficult. With her lack of skills or experience, she had no chance of getting a decent job, and if she used the money from the sale of the furniture store to live on, she would eventually use it up and have nothing to show for it. This way she had created her own employment.

And Michelle's, too. Her daughter had worked full time in the store over the summer. Now that fall was here, she'd begun working part time because she was taking courses at Georgia State in Atlanta. The way they worked it, Terri provided room and board, and Michelle used her wages to pay for tuition and books.

A few weeks ago, Michelle had flown to Albuquerque to take the exams that would eliminate the incompletes she'd received as grades last semester. Two days ago, she received her grades: two A's, two B's, and a C. Not bad, especially under the circumstances.

Michelle's bullet wound had healed rapidly, a scar the only permanent damage, and that really didn't show because it was on the inside of her arm. Although the things that had happened would always be with them, deep down inside, both mother and daughter were recovering, getting on with their lives. Their husband/father was dead. Instead of living in the big house they'd once owned, now they rented a small house in a much less expensive neighborhood. They no longer belonged to the tennis club, no longer bought whatever they wanted. This was the way things were. They accepted them, made the best of them.

And more and more often there were moments of happiness, which a few months ago would have seemed impossible.

Terri and Michelle had spent weeks trying to make sense of what had happened, as if by understanding it they could somehow make it more easy to live with. But what had happened defied understanding. A person goes on a killing spree because of a twenty-year-old one-sided romance. You called it insanity, madness, but labeling didn't help you comprehend it.

Connie's fate was still undecided. She'd turned up in Florida; an Alabama sheriff's captain had talked her into waiving extradition and accompanying him to Alabama, where she was also wanted for murder. The Georgia and Alabama authorities had decided that Georgia had a better case. In the meantime, Connie had got a lawyer—a public defender—who was fighting extradition to Georgia.

As Terri understood it, Connie would eventually be extradited, stand trial, and end up in a mental hospital or prison. When the time came, Terri and Michelle would have to testify. They weren't looking forward to reliving what had happened, but it had to be done.

Terri had tried hard to hate Connie, but in the end, she'd concluded there was no point in hating her. Throughout the ordeal, Terri had felt herself out of control. And now she realized that Connie, too, had been out of control, impelled by the driving force of her madness.

The bell Terri had installed over the door tinkled, and Michelle burst into the shop with an enormous smile on her face.

"How was school today?" Terri asked as her daughter put her books on the counter.

"Fine." She was still smiling.

"You're grinning like you just aced your history final or something."

"Come on, Mom, finals are at the end of the semester. This is the beginning."

"Then how come you look so tickled with yourself?"

"Shows, huh?"

"You could say that."

"Well, I got a date tonight."

"Oh."

"Not just any date. A date with Tom Andrews."

"Who's Tom Andrews?"

"Guy I have some classes with. We talk a lot. We have a lot of the same feelings about things. We both like the same writers, the same philosophers, even the same movies. He's also a journalism major, like me."

"I'm glad to see you use those standards for chosing men instead of just worrying about what they look like. When I was in college, all girls cared about was what the guy looked like—and how much money he might make."

"Maybe I shouldn't tell you this, but he's also a fox—maybe the biggest fox in school."

"Oh."

"And his father owns a chain of newspapers."

Terri considered this a moment, then said, "Good. The girls of my era weren't all wrong, you know."

They both laughed. And they hugged.

ABOUT THE AUTHOR

B. W. Battin is also the author of ANGEL OF THE NIGHT, THE BOOGEYMAN, PROGRAMMED FOR TERROR, THE ATTRACTION, and THE CREEP, all published by Fawcett. A former TV writer and news director, he now lives in New Mexico.

By the year 2000, 2 out of 3 Americans could be illiterate.

It's true.

Today, 75 million adults...about one American in three, can't read adequately. And by the year 2000, U.S. News & World Report envisions an America with a literacy rate of only 30%.

Before that America comes to be, you can stop it...by joining the fight against illiteracy today.

Call the Coalition for Literacy at toll-free **1-800-228-8813** and volunteer.

Volunteer Against Illiteracy. The only degree you need is a degree of caring.

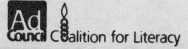

Ad Council   Coalition for Literacy

LV-2